T0002346

PRAISE FOR LORETH ANNE WHITE

"A masterfully written, gritty, suspenseful thriller with a tough, resourceful protagonist that hooked me and kept me guessing until the very end. Think CJ Box and Craig Johnson. Loreth Anne White's *The Dark Bones* is that good."
—Robert Dugoni, *New York Times* bestselling author of *The Eighth Sister*

"Secrets, lies, and betrayal converge in this heart-pounding thriller that features a love story as fascinating as the mystery itself."
—Iris Johansen, *New York Times* bestselling author of *Smokescreen*

"A riveting, atmospheric suspense novel about the cost of betrayal and the power of redemption, *The Dark Bones* grips the reader from the first page to the pulse-pounding conclusion."
—Kylie Brant, Amazon bestselling author of *Pretty Girls Dancing*

"Loreth Anne White has set the gold standard for the genre."
—Debra Webb, *USA Today* bestselling author

"Loreth Anne White has a talent for setting and mood. *The Dark Bones* hooked me from the start. A chilling and emotional read."
—T.R. Ragan, author of *Her Last Day*

"A must read, *A Dark Lure* is gritty, dark romantic suspense at its best. A damaged yet resilient heroine, a deeply conflicted cop, and a truly terrifying villain collide in a stunning conclusion that will leave you breathless."
—Melinda Leigh, *Wall Street Journal* and Amazon bestselling author

BENEATH
DEVIL'S
BRIDGE

OTHER MONTLAKE TITLES BY LORETH ANNE WHITE

In the Deep
In the Dark
The Dark Bones
A Dark Lure
In the Barren Ground
In the Waning Light
The Slow Burn of Silence

Angie Pallorino Novels

The Drowned Girls
The Lullaby Girl
The Girl in the Moss

LORETH ANNE
WHITE

BENEATH
DEVIL'S
BRIDGE

A NOVEL

Published by Montlake, Seattle

www.apub.com

Amazon, the Amazon logo, and Montlake are trademarks of Amazon.com, Inc., or its affiliates.

ISBN-13: 9781542021296
ISBN-10: 1542021294

Cover design by Caroline Teagle Johnson

Printed in the United States of America

For those who pursue truth.

AUTHOR'S NOTE

While *Beneath Devil's Bridge* is inspired by a true crime that occurred in my part of the world twenty-four years ago—one that shocked a community and garnered both national and international media attention—this story is a work of imagination, and all characters are entirely fictional. Locales have also been used in a fictional manner.

ON DEVIL'S BRIDGE

We spend most of our lives afraid of our own Shadow. He told me that. He said a Shadow lives deep inside every one of us. So deep we don't even know it's there. Sometimes, with a quick sideways glance, we catch a glimpse of it. But it frightens us, and we quickly look away. This is what fuels the Shadow—our inability to look. Our inability to examine this thing that is in fact our raw selves. This is what gives the Shadow its power. It makes us lie. About what we want, about who we are. It fires our passions, our darkest desires. And the more powerful it gets, the greater we fear it, and the deeper we struggle to hide this Beast that is us . . .

I don't know why He tells me these things. Maybe it's a way of obliquely bringing out and addressing his own Shadow. But I do think our Shadows are bad—his and mine. Big and dark and very dangerous. I don't think our Shadows should ever be allowed out.

—From the diary of Leena Rai

2:04 a.m. Saturday, November 15, 1997.

Leena Rai stumbles onto the old trestle bridge near the log sorting yard. The night is crystalline. Cold. Eerily quiet. She can hear the wind high in the tips of nearby conifers, the soft lapping of water against rocks under the bridge, the distant, omniscient thundering of the twin waterfalls that plunge down the granite cliffs of Chief Mountain from over a thousand feet up.

She shivers and draws her scarf higher around her neck. The movement makes her sway. She catches hold of the railing and laughs. Her emotion stems from a toxic mix of anxiety and a thrilling, daring sort of anticipation. Mostly she's comfortingly, numbingly, deliciously drunk on vodka from the almost-empty Smirnoff bottle in the pocket of the oversize military surplus jacket she is wearing. It isn't her jacket. It's his. Smells like him. Woodsy. Some pine resin. A residual scent of aftershave. And just the particular aroma that is him. All blended with a loamy whiff of moss and dirt from the forest floor where she was pressed on her back a short while ago. Leena shakes that unwanted memory, the pain. She waits for the heavens, the full moon, the Milky Way, the tops of the trees to stop their spinning, and when the motion slows, she sucks in a deep, steadying breath. The air tastes like autumn.

She continues her way across Devil's Bridge. She can see the black water of the sound in the distance, and a few lights from the pulp mill twinkling across the water. Her breath comes out in ghostly puffs. As she nears the south end of the bridge, nerves bite harder. She stops, reaches into her pocket, unscrews the cap on the vodka bottle, tilts back her head, and swigs. She wobbles and the drink spills out the side of her mouth and dribbles down her chin. She laughs again, wipes her mouth, and slides the bottle back into the big pocket. As she does, she sees something. A shadow. A noise. She squints into the darkness as she studies the shadows on the bridge ahead. A car approaches. She blinks into the sudden flare of headlights, then it's gone. A truck barrels past, throwing a blast of hot, exhaust-laden fumes her way. She feels turned around all of a sudden. Which way is the right way?

Focus.

She can't screw this up, this special invitation to meet beneath the bridge at the south end, a place where teens often gather to smoke, drink, make out. She wobbles onward. Another car passes, blinding her.

Leena stumbles off the sidewalk into the road. The car swerves. A horn blares. Her heart beats faster.

She squints into the darkness, her gaze fixed on the end of the bridge.

Don't screw this up. This is what you've been waiting for . . .

Leena pulls the jacket tighter around her body as though it will offer her fortitude. It's too large for even her frame. Which is why she likes it. It makes her feel petite, and that's a gift. And warm. Like a hug. Leena doesn't get hugs often. She can't actually recall when someone last hugged her. Her little brother gets hugs. Lots. He's cute. It's easy to love Ganesh. She, on the other hand, gets scowls. Warnings. People say she is stupid. Or never good enough, or right enough—just an ungainly, oversize, lumbering, inept spare part. A nuisance inside her own home. At school. She wishes sometimes she could get out of her own body. And she sure as hell can't wait to get out of Twin Falls.

But right now she's trapped. In this stupid town. Inside this physical body that people can't see past. They can't see who Leena is inside. How deeply she feels things. How she loves to write—poetry, prose. He knows, though. He says her words are beautiful. He *sees* her. When she's with him, she sometimes believes her whole world might change if she can just hold on and push through for another year or two. And then she *will* get out of this place. She will go far away. Overseas. Africa maybe. She'll work in exotic places doing things where people need her. She will write about those adventures. For a newspaper perhaps. She'll become someone different. When she's away from him too long, those dreams blur, fade. Everything goes black again. And Leena sort of just wants to do everyone a favor and die. But then she goes to him, and he says something nice about her poetry, and she feels a fluttering of her heart, a shuddering of primal wings beating through the hot darkness in her soul. *El duende.* That's what he says Federico García Lorca called it. It's the spirit of creativity, and he says Leena has it buried deep inside.

She reaches the end of the bridge and starts down the steep gravel trail that twists around and leads beneath the Devil's Bridge overpass.

A car rumbles above. Headlights silhouette trees. Then all is black. Dead quiet. Leena feels disoriented. Fear whispers. She moves carefully, feeling her way with her feet down the dark trail. A distant part of her brain sends a warning. It's too quiet. Too dark. Something is off.

But the vodka keeps her moving down the trail. To the rocks. To the water. A dot of orange suddenly flares bright in the blackness under the bridge. She sees a partial silhouette, then it fades. She smells the cigarette smoke.

"Hello?" she calls into the darkness.

"Leena—over here."

The voice sounds behind her. She turns.

The blow comes fast. It smacks her on the side of the face. She staggers sideways, stumbles, and falls hard onto her hands and knees. Gravel bites into her palms. The world spins. She's confused. She tastes blood. She tries to take a breath, but the next blow strikes her in the back of her neck. She flails face-first into the ground. Stones cut into her cheek. Dirt goes into her mouth. Another hard wallop, as if from a mallet, smacks between her shoulder blades.

Leena can't breathe. Panic swirls. She raises her hand to make it stop. But the next kick is to her head.

TRINITY

NOW

I don't even know when it started . . . long before that
cold November night when the Russian satellite hit the
earth's atmosphere. By the time it happened, there was
nothing any of us could do to stop it. Like a train set on
its rails miles away, it all just came trundling inexorably
down the track.

—From the true crime podcast *It's Criminal,*
"The Killing of Leena Rai—Beneath Devil's Bridge"

Wednesday, November 17. Present day.

I watch the green tractor move along a line of poplars in the distance.
The trees are leafless, and a ghostly mist sifts across the valley. Three
seagulls swoop and cry in the tractor's wake, diving to snatch whatever
is being exposed by the teeth of the plow. Heavy clouds hide the surrounding peaks. A soft drizzle is beginning to fall.

"I thought seagulls were supposed to stay by the sea," says Gio
Rossi. My assistant producer has his hands sunk deep into the pockets
of his black trench coat. The hem whips in the wind. It's cold. Wet

cold. The kind of cold that seeps deep into one's bones and lingers for hours after.

"Gulls have moved inland everywhere," I say absently. Because my attention is riveted on the woman driving the tractor. A black-and-white border collie sits at her side. Rachel Walczak. Organic farmer. Retired detective. A recluse by all accounts. The earth churning in her wake is black and wet. "Scavengers," I say quietly. "Survivors. The gulls adapt to humans. See them as a food source. Like the bears around here. Like raccoons in urban environments. Besides"—I glance at Gio—"we're still pretty close to the ocean."

Rachel's farm, Green Acres, nestles deep in a valley between plunging mountains carved by glaciers and scored by avalanche chutes and raging rivers. It feels remote. Hostile almost. But it's only a forty-minute drive from the town of Twin Falls, which lies at the northern tip of the sound. Twin Falls itself is about an hour or two north of the bustling Pacific Northwest city of Vancouver, yet it feels many more miles away, lost in time.

"Maybe as the crow flies," Gio mutters, hunkering deeper into his coat. "You probably need a snowmobile and snowshoes to get around here in winter. Can't imagine a snowplow coming along that shitty, twisting dirt road that leads out here."

I smile to myself. Gio in his designer shoes that are now caked with mud. Gio who is better suited to the streets and bars and coffee shops of downtown Toronto. Or Manhattan perhaps. Gio who parks a bright-yellow Tesla in his high-end condo garage back home, and who's not terribly impressed with the utility van I've rented for our West Coast podcast project. The van, however, is ideal for our sound and recording equipment and can serve as a makeshift studio. I parked it up on the shoulder of the road, behind a line of bushes, when I spied the tractor approaching the farm gate. Gio and I navigated on foot down a steep bank and through the mud, going around the side of the barn that lists alongside the old farmhouse. This time, I wanted to avoid Rachel's partner, Granger Forbes. Last week, when we drove all the way out to Green Acres in an effort to meet with Rachel, Granger told us in no uncertain terms that Rachel would never agree to speak with us.

Rachel Walczak never returned my countless phone messages, either. And I really need to interview the lead detective who worked the twenty-four-year-old Leena Rai murder case. She's key. Without Rachel, our podcast on the brutal sexual assault and killing of the fourteen-year-old Twin Falls resident will fall short of maximum punch.

Wind gusts. A cloud of drizzle kisses my face, and I shiver in the fresh bite of cold. It was a day just like this—same month—that Leena's battered body was found by Rachel's team in the dark water beneath Devil's Bridge. The tractor starts a wide turn.

"She's heading for the barn. Come!" I say. "Let's head her off there." I begin to pick my way quickly across the wet field. Mud sucks at my Blundstones. Gio curses as he follows in my tracks.

"She obviously doesn't want to talk to us!" he calls out behind me. "Or she'd have returned your messages."

"Obviously," I echo. But Rachel's avoidance has only sharpened my determination. People who don't want to talk have the best things to say. Interview subjects who eschew social media and society in general usually have something good to hide, which is why getting Rachel Walczak to open up on the record will be a freaking coup. I can almost taste it. Success. This project has the early markers of a breakout. Ratings and reviews skyrocketed after the first episode went live a week ago. The second episode, which aired yesterday, brought even better stats. Media interest is swelling. Every true crime aficionado awaiting the next episodes is *expecting* to hear from Detective Rachel Walczak. How she hunted the killer down. How she interrogated him, got him to confess. Put him behind bars.

"Don't look now, but I can see her husband up in the attic window," Gio says, coming up behind me. "He's watching us. Probably loading his shotgun. We're trespassing, you do know that?"

I keep going, excitement building as the tractor nears the barn. I move faster. The rain intensifies, wetting my hair. Mist thickens, swirls as it fingers around the barn.

Gio stumbles and curses. "Have you seen these?" he yells. "Freaking Franken-potatoes. Buried just under the surface of this mud. Big as my head."

I see the giant potatoes. Left behind at harvest—too big for market. But my attention remains locked on the green tractor. It comes to a stop outside the barn doors. The dark-haired woman climbs down. She's wearing a ball cap, rain pants, a rain jacket, and muddy gum boots. The dog jumps down behind her and starts barking as it runs toward us, hackles raised. We both stop dead in our tracks. It's obvious she's seen us, but she continues to ignore us as she removes a bucket of rutabagas from the tractor and proceeds into the barn. The dog keeps yapping, holding us at bay.

"Rachel?" I call over the barking dog. "Rachel Walczak? Can we *please* talk to you?"

For a moment Rachel hesitates just inside the doors, but then she enters the old structure and whistles. The border collie gives one more yap and runs into the barn behind the ex-detective.

I take the opportunity and quickly enter after them, wiping rain off my face.

"Rachel Walczak, I'm Trinity Scott, cocreator and host of the true crime podcast *It's Criminal*, and this is Gio Rossi, my ass—"

"I know who you are." Her voice is rich. Husky. Authoritative. She sets down her bucket and faces us. Her eyes are an icy gray, her lashes long and dark. Lines bracket her strong, wide mouth. Silver strands streak through the thick, damp braid that hangs over her shoulder. She's tall. Lithe and strong-looking despite the fact that she's almost old enough, technically, to be my grandmother. She makes me feel short even though I'm not. Rachel is everything I hoped she would be.

"I'm not interested in talking to you," Rachel says. "I'd like you to get off my land."

Hesitation sparks through me. I shoot a quick glance at Gio. His dark eyes meet mine. The expression in his gaze mirrors my thoughts: *This is our one last shot. Lose it, and we won't get another window.*

"It's been almost a quarter of a century," I say calmly, my heart thudding inside my chest. I think of Granger and the possibility of a shotgun, and the fact that we are trespassing. "It was the same time of year when your dive team found Leena's body in that brackish water. Cold. Misty. Rain hovering on the verge of sleet. Wind driving off the sea." I pause. Rachel's sharp eyes narrow. There's a subtle shift in her posture.

"Same scents in the air," I say. "Smell of woodsmoke. Rotting leaves. The dead fish. Winter coming."

Rachel's gaze remains locked on mine. I take a tentative step closer. I see that the lines that fan out from Rachel's eyes are deep. Not laugh lines—tired lines. A sudden empathy washes through me. This cop has seen things. Done things. She just wants to be left alone now.

The dog growls softly. Gio stays back.

"Your husband—"

"I'm not married."

"Your partner, Granger, told us when we drove out last week that you wouldn't want to speak to me, and I can understand your resistance."

"Can you?" Sarcasm cuts through her words.

"I've done my research. I know how the media hounded you all, and how you ended up leaving the force. But I only want to talk to you about the actual nuts and bolts of the Leena Rai investigation. The strategy behind it. How you guys brought on Detective Luke O'Leary. How you got Leena's killer to confess, which put him behind bars. That's the scope."

Rachel opens her mouth, but I shoot my hand up, stopping her. "Just the basics of the investigation, Ms. Walczak. The impact of the

9

teen's horrendous death on the small and tightly knit community—on her teachers, friends, classmates—"

"It's Hart. Rachel Hart. I no longer go by Walczak." She reaches for her bucket. "And the answer is no. I'm sorry. And like you said, I was not the only detective on the case. Try Luke O'Leary. Or Bart Tucker."

"Bart Tucker referred me to a PD press liaison officer. Detective O'Leary is in hospice care. He's lucid only some of the time."

Rachel goes dead still. Her face pales. Quietly she says, "I . . . I didn't know. Where . . . which hospice?"

"On the North Shore. Near the Lions Gate Hospital."

She stares. Time elongates. Water drips inside the barn. Then she gathers herself, and her features turn hard. "I want you to get off my farm. Now."

Gio starts to back out of the barn. But I hold my ground, my heart beating faster as I feel it all slipping away through my fingers.

"Please, Ms. Hart. I can do this without you. And I will. But having your side of the story will make it so much richer. My podcast does not aim to sensationalize, but rather to understand why. Why does a seemingly normal person suddenly cross the line into very violent crime? What are the gray areas in between? Could someone have seen the signs earlier? How does a normal schoolgirl in a normal little resource town in the Pacific Northwest suddenly become the victim of such a terrible event?" I fish a business card out of my pocket and hold it out to the retired detective. "Please take it. Please consider calling me. Gio and I will be commuting between Twin Falls and the Greater Vancouver area while we continue to interview people."

Rachel's mouth tightens. Before she can turn us away, I say in my best calm voice, nice and soft, "When Clayton Jay Pelley pleaded guilty, he denied everyone their proper day in court. He denied you all the *why*." Rain starts to drum loudly on the tin roof of the barn. I can smell the soil. The dankness of wet straw. "Clayton Pelley robbed Leena's parents. He took not only their daughter's life, but he robbed Jaswinder and Pratima Rai of the reasons. Yes, he told you *how* he did it, but according to the transcripts, he never explained why he chose Leena. Why the violence. Aren't you interested, Ms. Hart, in *why* Clayton Jay Pelley—a seemingly mild-mannered teacher, a husband, a father, a school guidance counselor, and a basketball coach—would do something so horrific out of the blue?"

"Some people are just born sick. And you're not going to get the 'why' from him now, not after all this time—"

"He spoke to me."

Rachel freezes. Time stretches.

"He what?"

"Pelley. He spoke to me. At the prison. He's agreed to a series of interviews. On the record." I pause, pacing my delivery. "He's promised to tell us why."

Blood drains from the old detective's face. "Clay *spoke*?"

"Yes."

"He hasn't said a word in twenty-four years. Not to anyone. So why now? Why to you? Why after all this time?" She stares at us. "It's because he's finally up for parole—is that it?"

I hold my silence. I have baited the hook, and I am now reeling my subject in.

"That's it, isn't it?" says Rachel, her voice louder, her eyes flashing. "He's currying favors in anticipation of a parole board hearing. He's going to play you. Use you to some end. And you're falling for it. And you're going to drag Leena's family back through hell with it all."

I remain silent. I watch Rachel's eyes. I can feel Gio getting tense.

"What did he say to you?" Rachel asks finally, her voice catching.

I proffer my business card again. This time the ex-cop accepts it.

"Our first episode went live last week. The second went on air yesterday. My website address is on there." I pause. "Please, listen to the first episodes. Then call me."

RACHEL

I watch the dive unit from the bank. I'm huddled in my waterproof down coat, my hair tied tightly back in a ponytail. Loose tendrils whip about my face in an icy wind that drives off the sea. It's almost noon, but the day is dark and hangs heavy with pregnant clouds. Somewhere up behind the clouds the sound of a chopper begins to fade. The air search has been aborted because of the foul weather. Twin Falls is my town. I was born here, grew up here. And I'm now a detective here, walking in my recently deceased police chief father's footsteps. I'm a wife and a mother, and I understand the pain of Leena Rai's parents. Their fourteen-year-old daughter has not been seen for eight days now. The missing teen is the same age as my own daughter, Maddy. She's a classmate. On the same basketball team. And I'm spearheading the search. The weight of it feels enormous. I *need* to find Leena. Safe. Alive.

Initially there was a sense Leena might have been acting out—as she had before—and that she'd show up by herself. But two days ago a rumor surfaced among the students at Twin Falls Secondary School—the only high school in town. Kids were saying Leena Rai had been drowned and her body was "probably" floating somewhere in the Wuyakan River. The Wuyakan rushes down from the high mountains, slows and widens as it nears town, then spills brackish water into the sound near a log sorting yard.

I called in a K9 team as soon as I learned of the rumor. The Twin Falls PD also tasked the local search and rescue team to search along the Wuyakan banks, starting at a swamp higher up the river and working back toward the sea.

Then yesterday morning a student—Amy Chan—was brought into the Twin Falls station by her mother. Amy claimed she had seen Leena stumbling drunkenly along the Devil's Bridge sidewalk at around 2:00 a.m. on Saturday, November 15. I immediately redeployed the SAR team to the bridge area. Late yesterday, just before full dark, the team located a backpack that had fallen between large boulders beneath the bridge on the south side of the river. It's an area where teens occasionally gather to smoke, drink, or make out. There is graffiti on the bridge trestles, an old mattress, pieces of cardboard, tins, old bottles, and other urban detritus. Inside the backpack we found a wallet. It contained Leena's ID card, $4.75, and a dog-eared photo of a ship with the words AFRICA MERCY emblazoned across the hull. Also inside the pack was a key on a fob. Near the backpack, nestled between the rocks, we found a lip gloss in "cherry pop pink," a soggy packet of Export "A" cigarettes, a lighter, an empty Smirnoff bottle, a knit scarf with blood on it, and a wet book of poems entitled *Whispers of the Trees* penned by a well-known poet of the Pacific Northwest. Written on the title page were the words *With love from A. C., UBC, 1995.*

Early this morning, when the search resumed, the K9 team discovered a Nike sneaker containing a bloodied sock. The shoe and sock were found on the north bank beneath the bridge. Leena's parents confirmed the Nike shoe was their daughter's, as were the backpack and scarf. The scarf had been knit by her grandmother. The key was for the front door of the Rai home.

Fearing the worst, I called in a police dive team. Two hours ago, after a briefing, the team began the grim search below water.

Rain begins to fall. I shiver inside my coat. I can smell the dead salmon rotting along the banks. Bald eagles watch us from high on leafless branches, waiting for the police to leave so they can resume plucking at the fish carcasses. It's an annual ritual that typifies this time of year, when the salmon swim into the Wuyakan to spawn, then die. Later, under cover of darkness, the bears and maybe wolves will come for their share.

My thoughts go to Leena's mother and father and her little brother, waiting in their modest home for news. Their only daughter and sister did not return home after attending a "secret" bonfire festival in the mountains north of town. The kids had gathered up in the forest, in a place known as "the grove," to burn old skis and snowboards in sacrifice to Ullr, the Norse god of snow. The Ullr bonfire used to be an annual celebration held in town, complete with Viking regalia, but the Twin Falls mayor and council banned it last year because of safety concerns. The raucous ritual had begun to draw a negative element from the city, and wild partying had resulted in drunken fire jumping and a few serious burn incidents. Everyone was worried there'd be a death on their watch.

Now it appears there was one anyway.

Leena was seen at the bonfire by at least twenty kids. All claimed she'd been drinking heavily. Some saw Leena with a male, but couldn't say who he was. There was a big full moon that night, the sky clear as glass, and at 9:12 p.m. an old Russian rocket reentered the earth's atmosphere and exploded into flaring comets with long, burning tails that streaked across the sky.

Everyone looked up. They all remembered that precise moment. Everyone could recall exactly where they were, their memories anchored by the bright-orange streaks flaming through the cold November night sky.

The rocket debris fell safely into the Pacific Ocean off the coast of Washington State. This much was on record.

But after that moment, no one recalled seeing Leena again.

"Party had gotten kinda wild."

"Smoking weed . . ."

"Lots of drinking."

"Maybe . . . I think I saw her go into the forest with a guy . . . He was tall. Dark jacket. Jeans. Hat on."

"No, I didn't see his face."

"She was with some guy, I think."

"Big guy. Dark coat. Hat."

"She was sitting on a log near the fire with a guy in a hat and big coat . . . No, I don't know who he was."

Their comments spiral through my mind as I watch the two dive tenders in the Zodiac inflatable. The officers hold firmly on to lines attached to two divers underwater, constables Tom Tanaka and Bob Gordon. Below the surface the constables, in dry suits, grope blindly forward in water that is murky, visibility near zero. The water below the bridge is filled with hazardous detritus—shopping carts, rusted metal, broken glass, old nails, and worse.

I check my watch. They're almost due for another break. Frustration bites into me.

"Hey, Rache?"

I spin around at the sound of the voice. It's Bart Tucker, a uniformed Twin Falls PD constable. He navigates carefully down over the slick gray boulders to where I stand near the edge of the water.

He holds a cup of coffee toward me. "Black, one sugar."

Tucker's broad, earnest, and ordinarily pale-complexioned face is ruddy in the cold. His eyes water in the salt wind, and his nose is pink. I think of Leena's mother's red eyes, and behind Tucker I catch sight of a group of people gathering up on the old trestle bridge. Anger sparks through me.

"What in the hell? Get them off, Tucker, get them the hell off that bridge!" Anger is easier than all the other emotions that threaten to overwhelm me.

Tucker stumbles back over the boulders, up to the road, taking the coffees with him.

"Tucker, wait!" I yell after him. "Get eyes on them first—video the group." I want to know who's there, who has come down to see firsthand what the police find. I should've asked for video at the outset. I'm a small-town cop, never worked a homicide—if that's what this is. What I still want is to find Leena safe. With a friend maybe. Sleeping somewhere. In another town. Anywhere.

Just not here.

Not at the bottom of the dark inlet in the eelgrass.

There's movement in one of the inflatables. A yell. The tender's arm shoots up. The hooded head of a diver breaks the surface. Constable Tanaka. His goggles glint in the bleak light.

My jaw tightens. My heart beats faster as I scramble along the boulders, trying to get closer. A gull cries. Rain beats down harder. The horn from the pulp mill ferry sounds mournfully in the mist.

"Camera!" calls the diver to the tender. A camera is floated out to Tanaka, along with a Pelican marker. Tanaka uses the marker to indicate where he found something. He goes down again. Bubbles rise to the surface. Ripples fan out. He's going back down to photograph in situ whatever he discovered, before bringing it up. I know that the divers approach a scene below water as a detective would on ground. The police diver's initial observations can become key in a case. A postmortem investigation begins the instant a diver locates a body, and the diver needs to understand the intricacies of submergence, drowning, and death investigation.

"Panties," the tender calls out to me as Tanaka brings up an item of clothing. The panties are covered in dark-gray silt. They are bagged. "And cargo pants," he calls out as Tanaka brings more clothing up.

Leena was last seen wearing camouflage cargo pants with pockets on the sides.

My mouth goes dry. Sexual assault is now a horrible possibility. I think of how I am going to break this to Pratima and Jaswinder Rai.

"Tide's coming in," says a voice at my side.

I start. It's Tucker. He's returned. He's still holding my coffee.

"I think they're close," I reply quietly.

Another yell from the boat.

Everything then seems to fall silent apart from the pattering of rain on water. Another Pelican marker is floated out. Both divers surface. They've got something big. They're coming toward the bank, bringing it through the eelgrass. Slowly.

"Is everyone off the bridge?" I ask quietly, my gaze fixed on the divers.

"Yeah. Cordoned off."

I swallow. It's her. A body. The men are floating her toward where I stand. Emotion blurs my vision. I move closer, crouch down.

Between the divers is Leena Rai. Bobbing on the tide, facedown, arms out at her sides. The divers are standing now as they carefully walk and float Leena in through the reeds. Her body is mostly covered by the rise of the cold water. Her black hair fans out around her head like velvet. Her naked buttocks barely break the surface. A camisole is tangled up around her neck.

My body feels numb. The men turn her over.

An invisible current shocks through us all as we stare in horror.

RACHEL

Cold leaches through my chest as I watch the podcaster and her assistant struggling through the mud as they make their way up to a red van parked on the road. I deleted Trinity Scott's voice mails. All five of them, over the course of a month. I thought she'd gotten the message. A movement in the attic window catches my eye, and I glance up at the house. Granger, watching from his office. He obviously saw the visitors.

Your partner, Granger, told us when we drove out last week that you wouldn't want to speak to me, and I can understand your resistance.

Anger sparks through me. I know he's looking out for me. I know how the case messed me up, and how he was the one who helped heal me. But he should have told me that Trinity and her sidekick had come all the way out to Green Acres.

Detective O'Leary is in hospice care. He's lucid only some of the time.

For a moment I can't breathe. I count backward from five. Four. Three. Two. One. I suck in a deep breath of cold air, exhale slowly, and shake the memories. Still, as I make my way back to the farmhouse, my gum boots squelching in the mud, Scout following in my wake, I feel the presence of the hidden mountains around my slice of land in the valley. And I feel as though they are pressing in, along with the dense cloud, the rain. The looming winter. And I can't quite shake the feeling that something has been awakened, and is being churned up from where it has been lying dormant in the black soils of memory and time.

Inside the mudroom I tug off my boots and shuck off my rain gear. I grab a towel and rub Scout. He squirms with glee, but where I usually find my dog's delight infectious, now it just sharpens my agitation.

Granger has come downstairs. He's sitting in his leather recliner by the fire, reading glasses perched atop his nose, a manuscript in his lap. He critiques papers for a psychology journal. His area of expertise is treating post-traumatic stress disorder and addictions with hypnotherapy. How trauma lodges in both body and mind, and the mechanisms people use to cope with PTSD, remain his fields of interest.

"You didn't tell me," I say as I make for the kitchen.

He peers over his half-moon glasses. "Tell you what?" He's wearing the nubby sweater I stress-knit for him years ago, before I bought Green Acres, before he partially retired and moved in with me. His hair is messy. Chestnut brown and streaked with silver. Granger has a handsome face lined by weather, time, and the emotions of life. On the shelves behind him books on psychology fight for space with tomes on philosophy and an eclectic mix of fiction and narrative nonfiction, mostly tales of solo adventures, man against nature. He was my therapist before we were lovers. And I know I am lucky to have found him. Granger in many ways is my savior. Which is why I am battling with my anger at his not having told me about Trinity Scott's visit.

"You know what," I snap as I grab the coffeepot. "Why didn't you tell me that podcaster had already driven all the way out here once before already?"

"Do you want to speak to her?"

"Of course not." I fill the pot with water, my movements clipped. "Why on earth would I want to help her sensationalize, monetize, a family's—a community's—pain after so many years?" I fill the coffee machine, splashing water onto the counter. "Entertainment at the expense of others who never asked to be visited by violent crime in the first place? No way."

"So I didn't mention it. Why would I want to upset you unnecessarily?" A pause. I glance at him.

He gets up and comes into the kitchen. "Look, we both know what that case did to you, Rache." He moves a strand of rain-dampened hair behind my ear. "We know what it did to your family—to everyone."

I step out of his reach and grab the coffee tin from the cupboard. I scoop ground coffee into the filter as my thoughts turn to my ex and then to my estranged daughter, Maddy, and my two beautiful little grandkids, whom Maddy will barely allow me to see. I bump the spoon, and coffee scatters across the counter. Tears fill my eyes. Leena Rai's murder changed everything. It changed me. My marriage. My relationship with my kid. It changed the town. Twin Falls lost its innocence the night Leena was sexually assaulted and killed. It was also the beginning of the end of my career as a cop. I never did get to follow in my dad's footsteps and become police chief, as everyone expected I would. I can't even pinpoint the one thing that toppled me.

Maybe it was Luke.

"You need to tell me things like this, Granger."

"I'm sorry. I really am. I love you, and I knew this would bring up bad things. And I honestly didn't think the woman—"

"Trinity Scott."

"I didn't think Trinity would be so stubborn as to return, let alone go around the back of the house and hunt you down in the field. Come to think of it"—he smiles—"she reminds me of someone I know."

I half smile. But disquiet lingers.

"Clay Pelley spoke to her." I watch his face closely. "Trinity claims he's agreed to a series of on-tape interviews, and he's promised to explain why he did it." The change in Granger's eyes tells me. I curse. "You've listened to it. You've gone and listened to her podcast, and you didn't have the guts to tell me?"

"Rache—" He reaches for me. I shove his hand away.

"Damn you. How? How could you listen and not tell me?"

"I was your therapist. I was there firsthand. A person can think they're fine. They can believe they've overcome or effectively compartmentalized negative events, but traumatic memory—it can become locked into the body. And you hearing Pelley's voice, exposing yourself to all this . . . it's unnecessary, for God's sakes, Rache. Just let it go. Leave it alone."

I glower at him as blood drains from my head.

"So . . . you *heard* him speak—you heard his voice?"

Granger remains silent.

"What did he say?"

A small vein swells on his temple. His jaw is tight. "Please, Rachel," he says quietly. "It's not worth it."

I grab the coffeepot and slosh hot liquid into my mug. "What the fuck did Pelley say? Has everyone out there, including Leena's father and her little brother, heard her rapist and killer's voice now?"

He touches my arm. I jerk. Coffee splashes onto my hand and burns. I set the cup down and brace my palms on the counter. I stare out the window above the sink, my heart thumping. Granger is right. Listening to the podcast will not be good for me. Look at what it's doing to me already. I'm being triggered.

"Do you really want my opinion on the first episodes?" Granger asks softly.

I nod, not looking at him.

"In my view, Clay Pelley is messing with the head of a pretty, young pseudojournalist who is hungry to make a sensation and a name for herself in the field of true crime. Trinity Scott is gullible. Or just plain opportunistic. The fact that he's chosen her—it's gone straight to her head, bought her instant notoriety. People are tuning in because Pelley has until now remained silent, and for some reason, Clayton Jay Pelley has started a game."

"Why?" I ask quietly. "Why *now*?"

"I guess the answer to that will become evident as the weekly podcast series evolves, but what is clear after the first episodes—in my opinion—is that Clay is pacing himself. Trinity has apparently been granted a series of twenty-minute sessions with him, and Clay is going to ration his information out. He's going to end each session on some tantalizing hook of information that is not only going to bring listeners back—it's going to bring Trinity Scott back. To him. To his prison. Again and again. A sexy young female in his boring life of incarceration. It could be that simple. A pretty face who hangs on to his every word. It would fit with his pathology of manipulation and power over young women. But whatever his plan is, I don't see that you should fall victim to his sick game, too."

"Maybe he *will* explain why he did it."

"Or maybe he will lie."

"But if he does tell—"

"Then you'll find out. But you don't have to listen blow by blow. You can get the score at the end of the game."

I force out a heavy breath of air.

He comes closer, cups my face. "Promise me you'll try to ignore it."

"When did you listen to it?"

"The day after it first went live."

"Last *week*?"

He looks uncomfortable. I take a moment to breathe in. "Did . . . did he say anything . . . relevant?"

"No."

"How did he sound?"

"Hoarse. Like he's had damage to his throat."

Curiosity is piqued in me. I study Granger for a moment, trying to read his eyes. He meets my gaze, unblinking. I force a smile.

"As always. My rock." I lean up and kiss him.

But as I carry my coffee mug to the fire, I feel a darkness in my wake. My man should have told me. The fact that he didn't unsettles me. And I feel that once more the Leena Rai murder is balancing my life on the cusp of change.

RACHEL

I did it. Okay? I fucking did it. All of it.

Clay's voice from the distant past reverberates inside my skull as I toss and turn in my bed.

I sexually assaulted and then killed Leena Rai . . . I couldn't stand her, what she represented.

I hear Luke's voice echoing through the chambers of time.

Tell us, what did you do? How did you do it?

Then Clay's monotone fills my brain again.

I beat her out of existence. I bashed her away. Killing it, hating it, murdering it. I wanted her gone. Out of my life.

I give up trying to sleep and lie listening to the rain drumming on the tin roof as memories of the interrogation room rise to vivid life in my mind. Clay's gray face. His hollowed-out cheeks. The deep-purple rings beneath his eyes. The sheen of sweat on his skin. The smell of him—old alcohol. My tension. Luke's tight jaw as he leans forward, his gaze lasering into Clay's. The others watching from behind the one-way mirror.

The rain stops. Outside, the clouds clear, and a puddle of silver moonlight pools over our tangled sheets. I can hear Scout snoring and twitching in his doggy bed beneath the window.

I turn my head on the pillow and watch Granger. His breathing is deep and regular as his chest rises and falls in a steady rhythm. The sound has always calmed me. It makes me feel safe. It gives me a sense of home and rightness. He remains a steadying force in my life. A clutch of love tightens around my heart. Yet beneath my love there lies a whisper of unarticulated disquiet, a silently mounting anxiety, something heaving and writhing below in my unconscious. I toss again and punch my pillow into a better shape. I lie back. Trinity's face and words surface in my mind.

He spoke to me.

Quietly, so as not to disturb Granger, I push back the covers. I find my slippers at the base of my bed and reach for my thick robe. Belting the tie around my waist, I go to the window and fold my arms across my chest. I watch the landscape. My farm. Haunting in the silver moonlight. The branches of the hemlocks twist in the wind—hula dancers to a tune I cannot hear. The bare fingers of a birch tick at a windowpane, like a fingernail scratching on glass, trying to get in. I think of the moon that hung over the ghostly peaks twenty-four years ago, that night Leena vanished into the forest and wound up floating under Devil's Bridge. Trinity's voice curls back through my brain.

Our first episode went live last week. The second went on air yesterday. My website address is on there.

I glance over my shoulder. Granger snores and turns onto his side. I sneak quietly out. Floorboards creak as I go downstairs, into my study, where I do the bookkeeping for my farm. I click on a lamp, turn up the thermostat, and fire up my desktop. I hear the click of doggy nails on the wooden floor as Scout enters my office and settles into the dog bed I keep in here. I find the business card Trinity gave me, and I type in the website address for *It's Criminal.*

The podcast is run by a small team. Trinity Scott is the host. Sophia Larsen is the creative director and producer. Gio Rossi is listed as the assistant producer. The rest of the crew includes a writer/researcher, a composer/audio mixer, and an illustrator/media designer.

I click on Trinity Scott's bio, and I study the photo of the young woman. She's striking in an unconventional way. Pale complexion. Pointed chin. Glossy black hair in a pixie cut. Large violet eyes. A doe-eyed look that belies the ferocity, or tenacity, I sensed in person. That was one thing about working as a detective—I learned to read things in people that weren't always immediately apparent. It's a trait that has lingered.

I scan the bio.

"Trinity Scott is a self-described autodidact with a passion for true crime, criminal psychology, and forensic science. She hails from a small town in northern Ontario, and she relocated to the Toronto area after high school, where she joined *It's Criminal.*"

Following the bio is a quote from Trinity that appeared in a newspaper article.

"The world has always been filled with very ordinary people, all of whom are capable of extraordinary crimes. These are the stories that fascinate me . . . Truth is my only guide . . . To paraphrase the great Ben Bradlee, as long as I tell the truth, in conscience and in fairness, I feel I can do a story justice. The truth is never as dangerous as a lie in the long run. I truly believe the truth sets us free."

My neck tenses. My mind turns back to Clay Pelley. To how nice and "ordinary" he once seemed. To how the students and community trusted him.

To how he abused that trust.

To how keeping secrets allowed that to happen.

The truth is never as dangerous as a lie in the long run.

I'm not so sure about that.

I click on the podcast menu. The most recent addition is:

The Killing of Leena Rai—Beneath Devil's Bridge
If it takes a village to raise a child, does it also take a village to kill one?

I bristle. My pulse quickens. I reach for my headphones, put them on, then hesitate, hearing Granger's warning in my mind.

Whatever his plan is, I don't see that you should fall victim to his sick game, too.

If Clayton Jay Pelley is going to play someone, I want to know why. I hit the link for the first episode. Music comes through my headphones, and as it fades, I hear Trinity's voice.

Twin Falls was a tiny mill town in the Pacific Northwest when fourteen-year-old Leena Rai went missing in the fall of 1997. When Leena didn't come home after a bonfire, no one wanted to believe the worst. Girls might be sexually assaulted and murdered in the big city of Vancouver, just over an hour's drive south, or across the Canada-US border in places like Bellingham or Seattle, but not in the closely knit community of Twin Falls, where everyone knew each other.

The resource town was named for the twin waterfalls that plunge from dizzying heights down the granite cliffs of Chief Mountain into Howe Sound, where orcas and whales and dolphins swim. The town itself nestles at the top of the sound and is famed as a gateway to the rugged Coast Mountains, and to wild backcountry. It's now a place of skiing and mountain biking, of soaring eagles, bears, wolves, and salmon that come up the Wuyakan each autumn to spawn. And like every autumn before, in the latter days of the season, the dead fish lay rotting and stinking along the banks of the river on that bleak and misty November day in 1997 when a police diver, feeling his way through murky water, touched his fingertips to the cold, dead body of Leena Rai . . .

THEME MUSIC BEGINS TO PLAY

This is Trinity Scott with *It's Criminal*. Tune in each week as we take you back in time twenty-four years, and right into a penitentiary, and into the mind and soul of self-confessed killer Clayton Jay Pelley, who has not spoken a word about his violent crime in almost a quarter century. But now he's agreed to explain to us why he brutally raped, beat, and ended the life of one of his students. Out of the blue. Or . . . was it? Because that's another question I will put to Clayton Pelley— were there other young women, girls, who he'd hurt and killed? And we will ask the question: If it takes a village to raise a child, does it also take a village to kill one? Was everyone in Twin Falls complicit, even in some tiny way, in the tragic death of Leena Rai?

Heat prickles over my skin. I glance at the door, then bump up the volume.

TRINITY

I focus on keeping my hands motionless in my lap, but nerves bite. I'm sitting at a bolted-down table in an otherwise empty interview room at the correctional institution located up the Fraser River, two hours' drive from Vancouver. It's my first meeting with Leena's killer, and I'm off-kilter.

The red-eye flight from Toronto Pearson Airport drained me. Gio and I grabbed coffees and collected the rental van right after landing. We loaded our equipment and drove straight out to the prison.

I have yet to make contact with Rachel Walczak—I called her several times before flying out west, but she has not returned my messages. Gio and I plan on driving out to her farm and cornering her there in person. The idea of this journalistic format excites me. Releasing information in real time, as it's being uncovered, testing hypotheses in full view of the public, is part of the thrill. It makes the podcast a living, vital thing.

In front of me on the table is my notebook. It contains my first set of written questions for Clayton Jay Pelley. Next to the notebook lie a small digital recorder and a pencil.

I wear black jeans. A simple, loose sweatshirt. Sneakers. No makeup. I removed my smartwatch, earrings, and bracelets before entering the building. Gio waits for me in the van in the parking lot. I was screened, checked in, and brought into this room, where I now await the inmate. Windows with reinforced glass look into the room on two sides. Like a fish tank. A guard stands outside the door. Visiting allotments are only twenty minutes long, but Clayton Pelley has agreed to a series of visits. I worry that if things do not go to his liking, he will renege on his agreement with me. I will need to tread carefully, read him well from the outset. Pace my questions.

What Clayton Jay Pelley did to Leena Rai was bestial. He's a monster. But he's also been a model prisoner from day one, I've been told. There's so much about him that doesn't add up—things I want to know. Like, what made him snap that night? Why pick Leena Rai? Why did he plead guilty instead of fighting for a better sentence and letting the Rai family have their day in court? Who is Clayton Jay Pelley when he's alone inside his head? Did he hurt girls before Leena?

I grow edgier. I check my wrist before remembering I removed my watch. There's no clock in the room. It feels hot. Airless. Time is stretching. I begin to jiggle my leg. I'll need the bathroom soon. It's the nerves. Or the coffee I consumed on the way. Or the fact that Pelley hasn't been brought in yet, and it's making me anxious.

Meeting face-to-face with Clayton Jay Pelley will be my big break. I know it in my bones. I wrote to him several times, requesting an interview. Just as I did to a handful of other incarcerated convicts— all killers—whose crimes I felt might make worthy subjects for *It's Criminal*. Pelley finally replied. It shocked me, then fired me up in ways I can't quite articulate yet. I filled in the requisite application forms, navigated through all the right channels. Made the plans to come out west. Did my research.

The day is finally here.

Perhaps he's going to bail. Is *that* his game? To bring me all the way out and turn me away? Will he then expect me to beg? What will I do if this happens? I check my wrist again and curse—force of habit. The fact that I cannot tell the time is pressuring me. Along with the smell of this place. The sounds. I run through a mental checklist in order to calm myself.

The door opens.

I stiffen. My heart begins to thud.

He enters and stops just inside the doorway, with the guard behind him. He studies me. Predatory. Assessing. He looks nothing like the old photos I found of him, taken from before he went into prison. Before he murdered Leena Rai. His complexion is pale, where in the photos he's tanned. Reportedly once a keen outdoorsman, he had a sun-bleached mop of unruly brown curls. He was almost boyish in his handsomeness. But he was only twenty-seven when he was incarcerated. Now he's fifty-one. Leaner. Harder. Meaner. His eyes are sharp. Dark blue. His hair, what's left of it, has been shorn close to his scalp in a tight buzz. A tattoo of a spiderweb wraps around the left side of his neck, which is thick and muscled. I notice a puckered scar across his throat. His prison shirtsleeves are rolled up. Ink covers his forearms and the backs of his hands.

Focus. Don't show fear. Don't give anything away, not yet. You're here to catalog him. Describe him in your mind so you can do so for your listeners later. Concentrate on how you want the first episode to play out. Get a couple of good sound bites. The power dynamic will be set in these first few seconds. Give a strong first impression.

"Trinnnnity Scott," he says, lingering on the *n* in my name as his gaze locks with mine. The way he holds the letters of my name inside his mouth feels indecently intimate, as though he's taking control. "So you came."

He walks slowly to his chair, his gaze not breaking from mine for a second. Taking his time, he sits. His voice is a quiet rasp, and I wonder

31

if the scar across his throat has something to do with an injury to his vocal cords. Perhaps fellow inmates didn't like the idea of him sexually assaulting a fourteen-year-old girl and bashing her to death. I try to swallow against the dryness in my mouth.

"Thank you for seeing me." I swear inwardly as my voice hitches, giving me away.

Seconds tick. The guard waits just inside the doorway as Clayton Jay Pelley seems to swallow me whole, absorbing me. Consuming me. Every last molecule. I feel powerless to stop him. I need to take back control.

"Does the guard need to be in here?" I ask.

He crooks up a brow, glances at the guard. The guard looks at me. "It's okay," I say.

The guard steps out, closes the door, and stands on the other side, where he can watch through the glass.

"You look like your online pictures, Trinity Scott."

"You have access to internet, then?"

A slow, sly smile. "You'd be surprised what inmates can access."

His gaze moves to my notebook and the recording device on the table.

"Mr. Pelley, Clayton . . . Can I call you Clayton?"

"Be my guest. Did you have a good trip?"

I'm cognizant of my twenty minutes sifting away.

"Fine. Do you mind?" I nod to the digital recorder. "I'd like to have your voice on air. When you're ready, of course."

He moistens his lips, his gaze going to my mouth. "Go right ahead."

I click the recorder on. The red light glows—a tiny cyclops observing, documenting. I become acutely conscious of my potential audience's point of view, and of the need to frame my questions to solicit the responses I hope for. I'm alert to different narrative arcs that might present themselves, and how best to run with them. I'm aware of the fact that I am an actor in this production.

I clear my throat. "As I mentioned in my letter, my podcast is—"

"I know about your podcast," he says in his low, scratchy voice. "I've listened. I know about *you*."

"I, yes, I . . . wasn't sure that you could get access to things like that."

"There are a lot of things you don't know yet, Trinity Scott." He leans forward suddenly and slaps his palms on the table. I jump.

He grins. Then laughs. A hoarse, whispery sound. "But, young Trinity Scott, I will do my best to educate you."

Resentment swells in my belly, twisting into anger and then fingering down into something much deeper and darker and more complex. My mind steels.

"Like you 'educated' Leena Rai?" I say, my gaze locked on his. "You were her guidance counselor, and you tutored her after school. English literature."

He runs his tongue along his bottom lip. "I did indeed. A rewarding student. So tell me what you want to know."

I shift slightly in my chair, pick up my notepad and pencil, and glance at my list of questions because they've fled my mind. I'm running out of time already, and I need a quote. I go straight for the big fruit.

"Why now, Clayton? Why've you never spoken a word of your crime, and why are you choosing to do so now?" I pause. "And it's not like you haven't had plenty of requests over the years, from academics to journalists to writers of true crime. So why me?"

He leans back and hooks his hands behind his head. It shows his muscles. The body language screams dominance. "You mean why this green and pretty little podcaster? Is it because old Clay Pelley wants to look at some fresh, live female, have her come to him, because he's bored in his prison cell after all these years—because he's had nothing since fourteen-year-old Leena?"

Heat flares into my cheeks.

He leans forward. "Why do *you* think?"

Careful now.

"Power," I say. "Your silence was your last hold on some kind of power, control, over Leena and her parents. You denied them their day in court. You denied the press answers. Your silence was some kind of last bid for control over the community of Twin Falls, over the school, the students. Over the detectives who went after you, arrested you, and locked you up." I pause. "But over time that power has waned, because no one is coming to you anymore with hat in hand, begging for you to talk. You've been forgotten. Lost in the monotony of incarceration. Then suddenly true crime podcasting finds its day in the limelight, and you get my offer. And . . . well, it offers a diversion. It once more promises you a degree of control over something." I narrow my gaze. "Control over a young woman."

A smile quirks across his face. He angles his head. "But you also get something in return, no? Tell me, Trinity, what is *your* goal? Ratings?"

"More people listening to my podcast. Bigger audience. And . . . this case intrigues me."

"My case is not that unusual. Male sexually assaults and kills young female. It happens. All the time."

"It's not every day that the assailant is a teacher. A husband. A father. It raises your stock."

"I think I'm going to like you, Trinity Scott." He smiles. Deeply. The sexual undertones are thick. And suddenly I feel ill. Too much coffee, not enough sleep, too much adrenaline. And I don't like him. Disgust rises in my throat, and for a rare, wild moment, I question what I'm even doing here. But time is ticking. I'm committed. I have sponsors. I need to see this through for so many reasons.

"Let's start with Leena," I say firmly. "Why her?"

"You mean why pick her out of all the other girls at school?"

"Yes. I've obtained copies of all your case files, and from the police transcript of your confession, Leena wasn't just an opportunity that presented itself on Devil's Bridge that night. Drunk and alone. In the dark with no one to see. You cultivated her. You *targeted* her. The finale beneath the bridge was the result. So why Leena?"

"She wasn't like the others."

"How so?"

An odd look changes his face. He lowers his scratchy voice. "Why wasn't she like the others? I think you know the answer to that. I think everyone knows. Leena wasn't one of the sexy, pretty girls. She was . . . *Plain* would be an understatement, right, Trinity?"

I feel my blood heat. "So her looks made her an outsider? Did this make her an easier target?"

"Go on, say it," he taunts. "Leena was ugly. That's how she used to refer to herself, anyway. It's what other girls and boys at school called her. They called her names. Fatso. Biggo. Weirdo. Freak." He watches my eyes. "She was bullied."

"So this made her easier to manipulate, because she was starved of affection? An outcast?"

"Leena was socially awkward, and yes, hungry for affection. Needy for it. But she was also gifted. It's why she was moved two grades up in her English class, and it's why I was helping tutor her. I think these days she'd probably be diagnosed on the autism spectrum. Talented poet. Beautiful soul deep inside. People couldn't see past the rest into that beautiful soul."

Shock ripples through me.

"So you *killed* her? Because she was an outsider and a beautiful, gifted soul?"

Silence. A vein pulses at his temple. He's weighing me, perhaps reevaluating what he's going to tell me, changing his mind.

I aim for the chink that I glimpse in his armor.

"Did you like Leena?"

A flicker of emotion darts through his eyes. It strikes me like a blow—Clayton Pelley actually liked the girl. I'm intrigued, and my fear filters away.

"She liked *you*, Clayton. According to the handful of pages of her journal that were found. She wrote that you counseled her on the concept of a Jungian shadow. She wrote that both you and she had dangerous shadows."

He fiddles with the edge of the table.

I lean forward and say, "She had dreams of getting out of Twin Falls. You were the only one who understood her, according to her words."

Silence.

"She *trusted* you, Clayton."

"I'm a bad person, Trinity."

My gaze holds his. I sense something has changed. The atmosphere in the room presses in. It's hotter. Airless.

"Is that what you want to hear? That I am sick? Because I am. I'm a sick, sick man. And I belong in here."

I regard him. Slowly, quietly, I say, "At what point did you formulate the idea to sexually assault and kill Leena? Or did you initially just want to rape her? But then, as you confessed to the detectives, you hated what you'd done, so you bashed her away, out of your life? A form of projection?"

Silence.

The guard taps on the window and holds up two fingers. Two more minutes.

"Not pretty, is it, Trinity?" he rasps.

I need a sound bite. I need a cracking hook. Time is leaking through my fingers. Quickly I say, "What do you want the world out there to know about your crime? What should listeners take away after the first episode of the podcast on killer Clayton Jay Pelley?"

The door opens.

"What I want the world to know, Trinity Scott, is yes, we all have our darkness. That shadow. Even you. But I did *not* sexually assault Leena Rai." He watches me. My pulse quickens. My mind races.

He lowers his voice.

"And I did not kill her."

Excitement knifes through me. I have my sound bite, my hook. I can play this like an unsolved cold case, pose the question: Did the wrong man go to prison? I force myself to remain calm, to not break his gaze, to not even blink. I don't even want to begin to acknowledge what this means to me personally. My eyes water.

"If . . . if you didn't, who did?"

"Time's up, Pelley," says the guard. He takes hold of Clayton's arm and brings the inmate to his feet. "Come on, let's go."

Clayton resists. Quietly, with a glint in his eyes, he says, "Whoever did, her killer is still out there."

The guard ushers him out. The door swings shut.

I sit stunned. Outside the window, as he's being led away, Clayton glances back over his shoulder and laughs. I hear his laughter as he disappears down the corridor. And I hear the echo of his words.

Her killer is still out there.

RACHEL

Silence rings in my ears. I sit back, shocked, my headphones still on. *What in the bloody hell?* I rewind the final clip of the podcast episode and play it again.

CLAYTON: I did *not* sexually assault Leena Rai. And I did not kill her.

TRINITY: If . . . if you didn't, who did?

GUARD: Time's up, Pelley. Come on, let's go.

CLAYTON: Whoever did, her killer is still out there.

THEME MUSIC STARTS SOFTLY

TRINITY: You have been listening to the voice of convicted killer Clayton Jay Pelley. Did the Twin Falls PD homicide investigation team put away the wrong man? Did Clayton lie when he confessed in 1997? Or is he lying now? Could it be true that Leena Rai's killer is out there? Free? Living and working among the residents of Twin Falls, or perhaps he went on to hunt young girls elsewhere? Did detectives Rachel Walczak and Luke O'Leary allow a dangerous monster to slide through their fingers?

THEME MUSIC INCREASES IN VOLUME

TRINITY: Tune in again next week when we take you back to 1997 and we ask, Who was Leena Rai? And how did a community fail her? How did a monster manage to move undetected among the citizens of the small Pacific Northwest town? We also hope to bring you a first-hand, blow-by-blow account of the investigation from Detective Rachel Walczak, who is now retired and living the life of a recluse on her organic farm in the mountains, not far from the town where she hunted a killer.

Numb, I stare out the window above my desk. Through my reflection, dawn bleeds a lambent grayness into the sky. Wind stirs the trees. It looks as though it might snow.

"Rachel?"

I jump and turn in my chair.

Granger. He stands in the doorway to my office, his hand on the doorknob. I yank off my headphones.

"Why on earth didn't you knock? What do you want?"

"I did knock." His gaze goes to my computer. The web page is clear to see on the monitor. The words *It's Criminal* are emblazoned across the top. White letters against a black background are underscored with yellow crime scene tape.

"I had to," I say quietly. "How could I not?"

He inhales, his features tight, disappointment in his eyes.

"Clay claims he didn't do it," I say.

Granger curses softly. "I told you, Rachel, he's playing a game. He—"

"You didn't tell me *this*." I point to the screen. "I asked if he'd said anything relevant. You said—"

"Relevant? That's not *relevant*, Rachel. That's a lie. A blatant lie." He swears again and rakes his hand through his shower-dampened hair. "Do you honestly think that if Clay Pelley was innocent of the crime, he'd have sat silent in prison for twenty-five—"

"Four. Twenty-*four* years."

"Right. Twenty-four years. The evidence against him was irrefutable, and copious. Plus he confessed, giving intimate, firsthand knowledge of exactly how Leena Rai died—information that no one else but the investigative team had. Not only that, but he pleaded guilty. He's messing with Trinity Scott. He's messing with Leena's family. He's messing with *you*. With all of us. And it pisses me off, okay?"

"Trinity mentioned my name, Granger. She put it out there, reminding everyone that I was the lead detective on the case. And now she's raised the question, Did we put the wrong guy in prison? And she's made it clear that she's inviting me to be a part of this thing. It's going to raise questions when she announces that I have refused to comment."

He regards me as if bracing, anticipating what I'm going to say next. And I say it.

"Trinity told me that Luke is dying. He's in a hospice." My voice betrays me.

He pales and his features tighten.

"Did you know?" I ask.

"She . . . mentions it in the next episode."

"So you know Luke O'Leary is dying. And you never said a word to me."

Granger stares at me.

"I guess that's not relevant, then, either?"

He remains silent.

I swear, get up, and push past him, aiming for the kitchen to make some coffee. Instead of following me, he calls out behind me, "I'm going into town. Going for breakfast at the Moose."

His tone sends a chill through me. The Moose Diner is at least a forty-minute drive away. The front door bangs shut. The sound echoes through the wood house. A few moments later I hear the growl of Granger's Harley starting up, then the rumble of his bike as it roars down the gravel driveway and then fades into the distance along the wet and twisting valley road.

I brace my hands on the kitchen counter and hang my head down, trying to breathe calmly. But I have a migraine starting. In my heart I know why he never told me about Luke. Of course I know why. Because now that I've been made aware of the fact that Luke O'Leary is dying, I will go and see him. How can I not?

Stories do not end. Anaïs Nin wrote that.

Clearly the story of Leena Rai is not done yet. I was fooled into thinking we'd all found some kind of closure. But we haven't. All we did was bury the whole episode under the earth of time, and there it lay dormant and silent over the seasons, and now Trinity is digging it up, exposing it to air, and shoots are beginning to awaken, unfurl, and reach up toward the light.

If it takes a village to raise a child, does it also take a village to kill one? Was everyone in Twin Falls complicit, even in some tiny way, in the tragic death of Leena Rai?

I leave the kitchen and make for a door that leads down into the basement. I hesitate at the door, then creak it open. I click on the light at the head of the stairs and begin to descend carefully. At the bottom I flick on a bare bulb that dangles on a wire. It sways, and shadows in the basement leap to life. They dart and duck behind me as I make my way toward steel shelving along the back wall. A damp, musty scent fills my nostrils. Disturbed dust motes float in front of me.

I wipe spiderwebs off the storage boxes on the shelves, checking labels. I find the box I am hunting for. It contains old binders, police notes, copies of the Leena Rai autopsy report, transcripts of witness interviews, the interviews with Clay Pelley, duplicates of photographs— I kept them because the case had consumed me.

I drag the box off the shelf, carry it upstairs, and take it into my office. I set it on a table and lift the lid. It comes off with a poof of dust that makes me cough. The document lying on the top is the postmortem report.

My mind slides back into the murk of time. Slowly I reach for the report.

Case number 97-2749-33. Deceased female.

RACHEL

The morgue is in the concrete bowels of the big hospital in Vancouver. The dead are sent here from other health facilities in the Greater Vancouver area, on the Sunshine Coast, and in the Sea to Sky corridor. The morgue pathologist also conducts autopsies requested by the BC and Yukon coroners' services.

I'm gloved and gowned, with slip-on booties over my shoes. I'm here to observe, to take notes, and to accept into evidence whatever comes off the body. Standing beside me, similarly gowned, is Sergeant Luke O'Leary, a homicide detective with the Royal Canadian Mounted Police. Twin Falls PD chief Raymond Doyle has asked for RCMP assistance in the murder investigation. It's high profile. Attracting relentless and national media attention. Reporters are clamoring to know how the juvenile teen was killed, and by whom. There's a violent killer out there. Our community is frightened for its young women. And our Twin Falls department is tiny. We have limited homicide expertise and scant resources. With Sergeant O'Leary come RCMP forensic techs, the use of RCMP crime labs, plus any other additional experts and manpower we might require.

Luke is a burly, gruff-looking cop with sandy hair and bright-blue eyes. A veteran homicide investigator who started his career as a K9 officer. He told me on the drive into Vancouver that he still volunteers with search and rescue teams around the province, helping handlers train search dogs. I figure Luke to be in his early forties. The attending pathologist is Dr. Hannah Backmann, a silver-haired woman who appears well past retirement age. She's being assisted by a young male diener and a female medical student. Tucker is present to take photos.

Leena lies on the slab in front of us. She's naked apart from her bra and the cheap-looking camisole still tangled around her neck, as we found her. A stand supports her head. Her face is smashed and lacerated beyond recognition. A knot fists in my stomach. My jaw tightens. I haven't attended a postmortem since police academy. I need to get through this without losing my breakfast. I must do it for Leena.

For her parents.

For Leena's little brother, Ganesh, and her beloved older cousin, Darsh, who adores her. For her devoted uncle and aunt, who sponsored Leena's mom and dad when they came from India fifteen years ago. I must do this for the kids at Twin Falls Secondary. For the teachers. For my town. For my own career if I am going to follow in my dad's big footsteps and prove that I can lead the police department into the future, as he expected me to.

For my own daughter, who is the same age as this girl lying violated on the slab.

"You okay?" Luke says quietly. I nod without looking at him.

A somber mood presses down, heavy like the dismal November weather outside. Dr. Backmann commences her external examination, narrating her actions into an overhead recording device as she goes.

"Case number 97-2749-33," she says in a gravelly smoker's voice. "Deceased female. South Asian in appearance. Measured, the girl is five feet, six inches. She weighs one hundred and eighty-two pounds."

The girl.

That's what Leena has become.

A case number. The decedent. Reduced to a general appearance and measurements.

"It's apparent the decedent received a very severe beating," Backmann says. "Most severe on the front of her face. Bruising, lacerations, swelling—it forms almost a complete mask . . . Her nose appears to be broken. There's some debris in the epidermis—bits of stone, soil."

The pathologist proceeds to examine the tender skin along the insides of Leena's arms. She's gentle in her touch. "No needle marks evident. No overt signs of drug use." The camera flashes. "There are abrasions on the outside of the arms."

"Defensive wounds?" asks Luke.

"Would be consistent, yes," says Backmann. She examines Leena's hands, fingers. "Broken and torn nails." She moves her attention down the rest of the body. "No external indication of disease. Healthy-looking girl."

The camera flashes again. I notice that Tucker's hands are trembling. The skin on his brow shines with sweat. I can smell the stress on him, beneath the layers of formaldehyde and disinfectant that permeate the cold room.

Dr. Backmann's hands, however, remain steady, her demeanor calm. She's well respected in her field. On the drive from Twin Falls, Luke told me Dr. Backmann gained her expertise in stab wounds by studying puncture holes in pigskin. She learned how to identify signs of drowning by poking at the lungs of drowned cats. The parallels with how a serial killer might study and perfect his craft with small animals are not lost on me. As Luke informed me of these things, he glanced at me and smiled. And I realized that despite his grizzled exterior and macabre experience, Sergeant O'Leary was a sweet guy with a sense of humor, and he was trying to put me at ease. It helped. A little. It also didn't help. Because I hate that I'm such an open book, that he can so obviously read my discomfort and tell that I am way out of my professional depth.

"The body is intact," the doc says in her gravelly tone, "but the skin on her hands and feet is starting to slip away." Another flash of the camera. "I estimate she spent about a week in cold water."

I clear my throat. "So she likely went into the river shortly after the bonfire, on November the fourteenth—the night she was last seen?"

Dr. Backmann glances at me. "Or the early hours of November the fifteenth. This would be consistent with my initial external observations."

Scrapings are taken from under Leena's nails. A number of swab samples are taken from the mouth and vaginal areas. Then, with the help of her assistant, the pathologist removes Leena's bra and carefully disentangles and cuts away the camisole twisted around the girl's neck. The camisole and bra go into evidence bags to be signed for by me. They will then go to the RCMP crime lab.

"Bloody discharge in her nostrils. Hmm—" She brings her magnifying glass down. "Seems to be some kind of thermal burn just inside the left nostril." She leans closer. "And a circular red mark almost in the center of her forehead. Made by something hot. A round shape." The camera flashes.

"Like a lit cigarette?" asks Luke.

I glance at him.

"Seen it before," he explains quietly. "Usually on the insides of arms. Often on kids, sadly."

Dr. Backmann nods. "Injuries are consistent with cigarette burns."

"Someone stubbed a cigarette out on her forehead?" I ask.

"And possibly inside her nostril," the doc says, pointing.

Silence fills the morgue. I feel sick.

Dr. Backmann reaches for forceps and begins to extract debris from the abrasions on Leena's cheeks and forehead. "Small stones, dirt, some pine needles, and . . . pieces of bark. Stringy bark." She puts the extracted bits of debris into a metal basin that the diener holds out for her.

I say, "Forensic techs found blood on the base of a cedar tree growing under Devil's Bridge on the north side. Could that be cedar bark?"

"We'll know soon enough if it's a match to the tree, and whether the blood on the tree is a match to Leena's," Luke says, his attention fixed on the body.

"Bruising along the collarbone," Dr. Backmann says as she continues the external appraisal. "A large bruise on the left side of the voice box. This bruise appears to be from a karate chop–type blow," she says. "There are red marks on the tops of both her shoulders . . . an odd symmetry to these marks . . . almost a circle on each side." The pathologist opens Leena's mouth. "The teeth are clenched. Her tongue is clenched in her teeth."

I feel time stretch as the examination for sexual assault commences.

"Evidence of genital trauma—vaginal tearing."

My thoughts whip back to my own daughter. Anger tightens my throat. "So . . . she was sexually assaulted?"

"Signs are consistent with rough intercourse shortly before death."

"Semen?" asks Luke.

"Lab results from swabs might tell us more," says the doc. "But she's been in water for a week, and if a condom was used . . ."

"Might be nothing of use left," finishes Luke.

Dr. Backmann asks her assistant to help turn over the body.

"Extensive bruising also apparent on the decedent's back. There's bruising that shows a pattern of what looks like a shoe or boot imprint . . . consistent with stomping." She measures the bruise. "Eleven inches." The camera flashes. Tucker moves around for a better angle, shoots again.

My anger sharpens to a white-hot point in the middle of my own forehead. My skin feels hot and clammy, despite the coolness in the morgue.

"She has luxurious, long, dark hair," the doctor says softly, dropping her clinical facade for a moment. The chink in her professional armor, the sudden glimpse of tenderness, nearly undoes me. I hold my mouth tightly shut in an effort to keep in my emotions as the diener begins shearing off the dark tresses. The hair falls away from Leena's skull. In my mind I see her hair floating like velvet on the dark water, among the eelgrass. An Ophelia in the reeds, among the dead fish.

"Oh, what have we here?" The doctor moves her magnifying light closer. She motions to Tucker and points to a glint of silver.

"Tangled into her hair—" She extracts a pendant of some sort. It hangs on a broken chain. The pathologist holds it up with her forceps for us to see. It's a locket.

Blood drains from my head.

The locket is about the size of a quarter. It has a purple stone in the center, set into a nest of filigreed silver.

"Looks like a crystal, an amethyst," Luke says as he leans forward to study the find. "The silver work around the stone—it's in the shape of multiple Celtic knots." He glances at me. "My mother had a pendant in this design. She got it in Ireland. She said a lot of the tourist shops sell similar trinkets. The Celtic knot supposedly represents eternity, or continuity, or, in my mom's case, it represented the Holy Trinity—the Father, Son, and the Holy Ghost. She was a devout Catholic."

For a moment I can't breathe. My pulse begins to race. I clear my throat.

"Leena's parents never mentioned this locket in their description of what their daughter had been wearing when they reported her missing."

"Not uncommon," Luke says. "Parents think they know more about their children than they do. I mean, do you know what jewelry your daughter is wearing today?"

I turn my attention to Leena's freshly shorn skull. "No," I say quietly.

Dr. Backmann drops the locket into a little metal basin shaped like a kidney. The diener puts the basin to one side.

The doc continues. "There's also a clear imprint pattern of a shoe—or boot—sole on the back of her head. Same size and pattern as the one on her back. Consistent with another stomping kick."

I begin to feel dissociated from my body.

Leena is x-rayed. The examinations show no broken bones, apart from the nose. No dislocations.

The doc readies her blade. My brain scurries down tunnels in an effort to escape as the sharp edge is pressed to dusky flesh. In my mind I see Pratima's dark-brown, tormented eyes. I see the tightness of Jaswinder's jaw, the way his hands fisted and unfisted as I told them how we found their daughter in the river.

An incision is made from one shoulder bone to the other, then a cut is made straight down to the belly button to complete a Y shape. They peel Leena open, snip her ribs out. They come out in one big butcher slab.

"Considerable damage to the liver and pancreas is apparent," says Dr. Backmann. "Evidence of multiple blows sustained to the abdominal area . . . Layers of her abdominal wall are severely bruised in a number of locations." Claustrophobia tightens. My vision grows fuzzy. The doctor's words begin to blur. "Organs crushed. Separation of fatty tissue from muscle tissue. Most severe damage at torso . . . Evidence of internal bleeding in the chest and lower abdomen . . . consistent with a forceful kicking or stomping in the abdominal area . . . Damage to pelvis, stomach, liver, pancreas . . . Mesentery torn away. The mesentery is the organ that attaches the intestines to the posterior abdominal wall in humans." The doctor looks up.

I force myself to focus.

Quietly she says, "This is similar to what I'd expect to see in a crush convulsion injury. Which is something that often occurs with car-crash victims. This girl went through hell. It's like she was extracted from a vehicle wreck that crashed over that bridge."

Leena's heart is removed and weighed, and so is her brain.

"Brain is swollen. A substantial degree of general hemorrhaging and trauma. Sufficient concussive injury to cause unconsciousness."

The lungs, too, are removed, weighed.

"Internal examination of the lungs shows a frothy white substance," says Dr. Backmann. "This is consistent with death by drowning."

The doctor looks more closely at the lungs. Her body stills. She says quietly, "There's something delicate, hidden by the white froth . . ." The doctor removes four small pebbles. They make a plinking sound as she drops them into the metal basin being held at her side. She finds another five pebbles and drops them into the basin as well. She looks up at us over her half-moon glasses. "The small stones were likely inhaled into her lungs with the agonal gasp." A pause. Her eyes watch us over her lenses. "She likely took her last gasp for life with her face pressed down into the bottom of the riverbed, where all the little stones lie. Those circular marks on her shoulders . . . could have been made by knees. Holding her down."

"She was drowned," I say. "Someone straddled her, knelt on her shoulders, holding her head underwater, until she inhaled pebbles."

"Death by drowning will be my conclusion on my report," says the doctor. "But if the decedent had not gone into the water, it's likely that the assault trauma, the brain swelling, would have killed her anyway. But she was definitely alive when she was forced underwater, and held there." She hesitates, and her demeanor cracks. "Whoever did this . . . is a monster."

RACHEL

NOW
Thursday, November 18. Present day.

I close Dr. Hannah Backmann's autopsy report, but the morning in the morgue is alive in my mind. Leena's body was released later that day, but the full analysis and final report took another two weeks. I set the report on the table and glance at the clock on the wall. Granger is not back yet. Nor has he called to say when he will return. I've disappointed him. But he has also irked me. He should have known better than to try to hide things from me, especially in relation to this case. And after listening to the first episode of the podcast, there is no way in hell I can stuff this genie back into the bottle.

Clay's raspy voice snakes through my mind.

I did not kill her . . . Whoever did, her killer is still out there.

I have little doubt that Clay is dabbling in some perverted game with Trinity, but I cannot suppress a darker, more subterranean worry worming into me. What if he *is* telling the truth? What if we did make a mistake, miss something?

From the box I remove binders full of three-hole plastic page protectors that hold transcripts of the interviews we did with students, friends, parents, teachers, family members, other witnesses. The binders also contain transcripts of our interrogations of Pelley, the transcript of his confession, photos of the evidence, copies of lab reports, copies of the few pages torn from Leena's journal, plus pages from my own notebooks and Luke's notes.

I start spreading these out over the table, organizing them, then stop as I catch sight of the photograph that Leena's parents provided the Twin Falls PD when they first reported their daughter missing.

I lift it up and stare at the face of the dead girl. My mind spirals back to the day when Luke and I exited the morgue into a fine drizzle and drove back to Twin Falls to inform Leena's parents exactly how their daughter had died.

This same image of Leena was in a frame on the mantel above the fireplace in the Rais' modest home.

I put the photo down and pick up another. A group of six school-girls aged fourteen and fifteen, arms wrapped around each other, heads together, all laughter and smiles. It's a professional-looking shot, and it was not part of the police evidence, but I added it to this box. The girls were captured beside a bonfire. I can see skis burning, flames shooting orange sparks into a velvet sky. The light on their faces is gold from the fire. The forest behind them forms a black backdrop of silhouettes and shadows.

I stare at the image captured in time. Their laughing, bright eyes. The promise of youth literally shimmering and glowing around them. It was the night Leena vanished, not long after this image was shot. The night everything changed. A cool thread curls through my chest as I look more closely. Then, carefully, I set the image aside.

I empty out the rest of the box's contents and find what I am look-ing for. The locket. Still in the evidence bag, which has found its way to the bottom. I pick up the bag, open it, and slide the locket into the palm of my hand. It's cool. Oddly heavy. The broken chain dangles through my fingers. The purple crystal winks in the light.

The stone is an amethyst, a violet variety of quartz. It's supposed to offer spiritual protection. It's said to cleanse the wearer's energy of negative or dark forces by creating a protective shield of light around the body.

It did not protect Leena.

And the locket is the one item that Leena's parents did not want returned to them.

TRINITY

I exit the prison with excitement zipping through my veins. Gio is waiting in the van. He sees me hurrying over to the parking lot toward the vehicle, and he gets out. He looks worried.

"Everything go okay?" he asks.

"Fuck me, we've got a scoop! We've freaking got a *scoop*." My whole body is pumped, my brain ablaze.

"What happened?" Confusion chases through his features.

"Get in. You drive. I'll tell you on the way up to Twin Falls." I reach for the door handle on the passenger side.

Gio hesitates, then climbs into the driver's seat. He starts the van engine. I buckle up, then put my head back and laugh.

"Jesus, Trin, spill."

I meet his gaze. I can see Gio thinks I've lost it. But he doesn't get just how much this means to me. I haven't even begun to explain it to myself. "Clayton Jay Pelley said he did *not* sexually assault, or bludgeon, or drown Leena Rai."

"What?"

"He said the killer is still out there somewhere."

He stares. Blinks. "Pelley said that?"

"Yeah."

"On tape?"

"Yes."

"Well, shit." He pauses. "Do you believe him?"

"It doesn't matter, Gio! Don't you see? It gives us exactly the hook we need. It hands us this whole series on a plate. It's no longer just a true crime story about why the seemingly normal and nice schoolteacher did this to his student. It becomes an unsolved cold case."

"But if he's lying—"

"Like I said, it doesn't matter. That's the premise we start from. I can pose the question: Is he lying now, or did he lie then, when he confessed? If he's telling the truth now, what did the cops get wrong all those years ago? Why did he confess to them? Did they coerce him somehow? Was it a true confession? And why did he plead guilty to a judge? Why has he remained silent for so long? And why is he speaking now, after all these years?"

"But if he's lying now—"

"That's exactly what people will tune in for: Is Clayton Jay Pelley lying now, or did the two lead cops on his case screw him over? Or plain screw up?" I grin. "We get to play the detective in real time, and our listeners come along. Like them, we don't know the ending, either. Releasing information as we uncover it—it's the new realm of true crime storytelling."

"And Pelley pulls the puppet strings."

I laugh. "It doesn't matter, does it? If he's playing us, that's part of the entertainment. We have a breakout here, Gio. Pure and simple."

He smiles slowly, and his eyes turn bright. He looks alive. Sexy. Beautiful. It's like I've touched him with my own electrical wire of excitement, and now my energy is crackling into his eyes and over his body. Mirroring my emotions back at me. For a nanosecond I feel attraction. But I quickly kick it away into the cold place where I keep most of my true feelings. Gio is an empath. When I feel blue, he'll echo that back at me, too. It's too much work. Too much responsibility. As much as I know that he loves me, I can't offer him anything in return because that sort of relationship will not be good for me. This is something I understand on a gut level. And I've learned the hard way. But Gio is also the best damn producer I could hope to work with, and he'll do anything for me, which is why I keep him close.

"Go on, drive," I say. "I'll play you the audio on the way."

Gio reverses the van. We exit the parking lot and enter a stream of traffic. Gio puts on the wipers as the ever-present rain of the Pacific Northwest begins to fleck the windshield.

I connect the audio to the van's speakers via Bluetooth, and we listen in silence as he drives.

He remains silent for a long while after the interview ends—Clayton's last words, his laughter, ringing inside our brains. We're entering the City of Vancouver now. Anticipation is awash inside me. And as we get a little closer to Twin Falls, something else surfaces in my heart. A whisper of fear perhaps. Of the unknown—of what I will find. But that should be a good thing. I *should* feel the fear and do things anyway. That's supposed to be my mantra.

As if he's thinking out loud, Gio says, "He did it. He had to have done it. It's absurd to think otherwise. We've seen all the transcripts, the photos of evidence, the crime lab results. It all adds up. The evidence matches his confession."

"Apart from the things that don't add up." I turn in the seat. "There are dropped threads. There are still unanswered questions."

"Because he confessed. Why pursue the investigation if . . . well, if it was a wrap? The bad guy said he did it, and he told the cops exactly how, blow by blow."

"Still, there's his story about the jacket, which sounds . . . off. That locket. The facts around that were never resolved. The rest of Leena's journal has never been found. Why were pages ripped out of it? And even if he *did* do it, the crime was so violent, so brutal, with so much apparent rage, it's hard to imagine that the once seemingly benign man cracked to that extreme. It's . . . like he'd have to have done it before. Built up to this. There could be others."

"Oh, now you're being sensationalist."

I grin broadly and lean back in the seat. "Maybe. Yeah. But it makes for great podcast material."

We head over the bridge. Below us tankers skulk on the gunmetal-gray waters of the Burrard Inlet. Puce clouds tumble down the North Shore mountains. Another hour's drive along the highway that twists and turns above the waters of the sound, and we will be in Twin Falls. Finally. After all my research, I get to visit it in person. I will interview as many people as I can find who were part of the case, or who knew the main players. Between interviews we will head back and forth to the prison with further questions for Clayton Pelley. And during it all, we will air the episodes.

In my mind I test out script ideas for the various episodes. In addition to the first session with Clayton, we already have an earlier interview in the bag, with one of the police divers who discovered the body. We did that interview in Toronto before flying out west. Perhaps I will start with the discovery of the body, and feed back into a segment that asks: Who was Leena Rai?

RACHEL

"Was . . . my daughter raped?" Jaswinder Rai can barely utter the words, but his need to know outweighs his fear of knowing. He sits close to Pratima on a floral-patterned sofa opposite me. Luke has taken an ornate chair to my right, and he dwarfs it in a fashion that would be comical if our news wasn't so awful. I feel him observing me. It's just past noon, but we're tired. At least I am. It was an early start, and we drove directly from the morgue to deliver the cause of the Rais' daughter's death in person.

"There are signs of sexual assault, yes," I say gently.

"What do you mean, *signs?*" Pratima asks. Her voice quavers. Her whole body is shaking, and it makes the chiffon scarf over her hair tremble about her cheeks.

"Some . . ." I clear my throat. "Some vaginal tearing that indicates rough intercourse."

Pratima covers her mouth with her hand. Her eyes glisten. Her husband places his hand on her knee. His eyes, coal black and fierce beneath his red turban, bore into me. Barely bottled rage pinches his face.

"And then after she was assaulted, she was bludgeoned, kicked, and drowned in the river?"

"We're not sure yet of the exact sequence, but yes, the cause of death is drowning. I'm so sorry."

"So this . . . this was the motive for the attack?" Jaswinder asks. "Rape?"

"We're working on that assumption right now," I say. "Given the timing, the fact that Leena was alone and vulnerable, it was likely a crime of opportunity. Your daughter could have just been in the wrong place at the wrong time."

"Why, *why*?" laments Pratima. "Why *my* Leena . . . How could anyone *do* this . . ." She begins to rock back and forth. A moaning sound starts low in her throat. Animal. Raw. I feel a visceral response in my own body to her maternal reaction. I don't know what I'd do if it had been my baby girl, my teen, my Maddy. I glance at the framed photos on the mantel. Family groupings. A cute picture of Leena's six-year-old brother, Ganesh, in a canoe. One of Leena herself. Gazing at the camera with a belligerent expression. Her complexion is darker than her mother's or father's. Her black eyes are set close, on either side of a large nose that seems to dominate her face. A mole marks her chin.

Pratima's gaze follows mine. Tears slide silently down her cheeks. And I feel her unspoken words.

We should have watched over her better, been more strict, more careful.

I also feel a wash of guilt at my relief that it's not my child in that morgue. Because it *could* have happened to Maddy just as easily. Or to any of the girls in town.

I clear my throat.

"Would it be okay if we ask you some more questions? It will help with our investigation."

"You *will* find who did this," Jaswinder says. It's not a question. I meet his fierce gaze.

"Yes. We will. I promise."

59

Luke shifts in his chair, and I sense admonishment. He probably would not have made a promise he might not be able to deliver on. But what else can I tell these parents? "We'll do everything in our power to get justice for Leena," I say as I remove two photos from the folder on my lap. I set them on the coffee table and turn them to face the Rais.

They are glossy images of the silt-covered cargo pants and panties that the divers found near the body.

Leena's mother makes a choking sound. She nods. "Yes, yes, those are Leena's. The underwear . . . Fruit of the Loom. From Walmart. They . . . they come in a three-pack. I . . ." Her voice breaks on a sob.

"Yes," says Jaswinder, taking over from his wife. "And those camouflage pants, Leena wore those nearly all the time. She liked the pockets on the sides."

"Can you confirm which jacket Leena was wearing when you last saw your daughter?"

We have not yet located the jacket that everyone claims to have seen Leena wearing at the bonfire. The divers did not find it in the river, and the crime techs and search parties did not locate it along the banks of the Wuyakan.

"It was a big khaki-colored jacket," says Jaswinder. "They call them military surplus jackets. Lots of zips and pockets, and some kind of numbering on the front pocket. It wasn't Leena's. When I asked her about it, she told us she'd borrowed it."

"From who?" asks Luke.

"She just said a friend," says Pratima, reaching for a tissue from the box on the table.

"A male's jacket?" I ask.

"I would say it was definitely a guy's jacket," Pratima says. "It was too big for Leena, and she isn't—wasn't—a petite girl. She was always dieting, trying to be smaller. She . . . she'd lost some weight, and she was so proud . . ." Tears pour afresh down Pratima's cheeks. She swipes at them with the tissue.

"Did Leena have a boyfriend?" I ask.

"No," Jaswinder says immediately. Firmly.

My gaze ticks to his. "Any boys she was interested in, perhaps?"

"No."

I nod. "We found some journal pages in the water near Leena, and a small address book that was inside the left thigh pocket of Leena's cargo pants." I place more photos on the table, showing the wet pages and the address book, both open and closed. The address book is slim, and it has a pale-blue plastic cover. "This book was wet, like the journal pages, but the lab is working on drying it all out so that we can preserve the contents and ink as much as possible."

Her mother leans forward and picks up the photo of the wet journal pages. "That's Leena's writing. Yes." She passes the image to her husband and reaches for the photo of the address book.

"This is not Leena's. I've never seen this book."

"Are you certain?" asks Luke.

She nods.

"Any idea who it might belong to, then?" I ask.

A strange look enters Pratima's eyes. She hesitates, then shakes her head. "No."

"It contains phone numbers of some of the kids in Leena's grade," I offer.

"It's not hers."

I regard Pratima for a moment. She's holding something back. I glance at Jaswinder. His gaze is locked on me. Beneath their grief, I sense another kind of mounting tension. It prickles my curiosity.

I say, "You've already identified the key that was found in her backpack. Her wallet. And the Nike sneakers. Have you come up with any ideas who the book of poems could belong to, or what the initials A. C. might stand for?"

"No," Jaswinder says. "But Leena borrowed books. She was doing a higher grade in English literary studies. She was seeing a tutor. He sometimes loaned her books. And so did some of the other teachers at school."

"And her cousin, Darsh," says Pratima. "He lends Leena books."

"Not poetry books," says Jaswinder. "Darsh doesn't read poetry. He reads popular novels."

"Darsh also gave Leena those Nike sneakers," says Pratima. Her lip quivers. "She . . . Leena wanted them so badly, but they're expensive, you know? And he surprised her with them for her birthday."

"Darsh and Leena were close?" asks Luke.

Pratima nods, her eyes filling with tears again. "He was good to her. Very good. Leena . . . struggled with friends. Darsh was always there for her. When she ran away last year, she went to him. He gave her a place to stay for a few days. He told us behind her back that she was safe, so we let her be for a little while, and then she came home again."

A memory fills my mind. Leena sitting hunched over and alone on the bleachers in the school gym, eating from a bag of potato chips while the other girls on the team finished their basketball drills. I'd arrived early to pick up Maddy. As I climbed the bleachers to sit and wait beside Leena, a group of kids passed below the bleachers on their way to the locker room. They were discussing Leena, loudly enough for Leena to hear their words.

"If she hadn't tried to block me like that, she wouldn't have fallen and twisted her ankle. It's her own damn fault . . . I don't even know why she's on the team."

"Maybe Coach feels sorry for her."

"Boo-hoo. Maybe she should try bhangra dancing."

Laughter.

"She'd break both ankles, she's so freaking big and clumsy."

"Just watch her father go and blame me for blocking her."

"He's a freaking bus *driver—what's a bus driver going to do? Sue me?"*

"Hey, he's scary. Have you seen his eyes? I bet he has one of those curved knives to go with his turban . . ."

Snickers and giggles follow the girls out of the gymnasium door. The door swings slowly shut.

I glance at Leena, my blood pounding. She munches sullenly on her chips, looking directly at the basketball court, as if she's oblivious. But she has to have heard.

"You okay, Leena?"

She nods without looking at me.

I notice a dark bruise around her wrist, and another along her forearm. "Did you fall?"

She flicks a glance at me, surprised. "I . . . just tripped and hurt my ankle. It's not bad. Coach told me to sit out."

"What about those bruises? Did you get those from doing drills as well?"

"I slipped on ice on our stairs the other day."

A person didn't get bruises like the circle around her wrist from falling on ice. I'd opened my mouth to question her further when Maddy came running over to the bleachers, her sneakers squeaking on the gym floor. She was all bouncy ponytail, pink cheeks, and smiles, and begging me to hurry so we could get to the library downtown before it closed for the evening. She had a project due the following morning.

I'd forgotten about that day in the gym. About Leena on the bleachers eating her chips. Until now. Until sitting in this modest, neat home. With her broken parents. And I regret deeply that I never followed up, reported the racial slurs, the bullying words. This kind of thing would isolate a young teen, make her vulnerable. And possibly lead her to move alone in her world, without a support group. It could be why Leena was solo on the bridge. And suddenly I realize I was wrong. What happened to Leena was less likely to happen to a girl like Maddy who moved in a pack of close friends.

I rub my mouth. "Do . . . you have any idea where the rest of Leena's journal might be?"

"No." Pratima's voice breaks again. "Leena was always writing. She wanted a job as a writer when she left school. She wanted to travel.

Maybe even become a foreign correspondent. You can look in her room again."

"Thank you, we'd like to do that." I hesitate, feeling the heat of Luke's scrutiny. He's waiting for me to finish showing the photographs. I take a deep breath. "We . . . also found this." I place the picture of the Celtic locket on the table. "It was tangled in Leena's hair. The chain was broken."

They both stare at the image. Jaswinder slowly shakes his head. "I have not seen her wear that."

I turn to Pratima. She looks almost afraid. "I . . . I haven't seen that before."

"Are you *sure*?"

"It's not hers." Pratima shifts and angles her knees away from her husband. She glances downward.

"Possibly you just didn't notice it, under her clothes?" I prompt.

Silence.

Pratima rubs her thigh, her gaze still downcast. I make a mental note to circle back to this, but Luke leans forward before I can move on. He taps his finger firmly on the image of the locket.

"These filigree designs in the silver—they're all in the shape of Celtic knots," he says. "Never-ending knots. The Celtic knot is known to symbolize love, or a never-ending commitment. Or some Christians see the knot as representative of the Holy Trinity—"

"Not Leena," snaps her father suddenly. Luke falls silent and studies him.

Jaswinder's eyes crackle with fire. "She wouldn't wear something like that." He wags his hand at the photo. "It's not hers."

I exchange a quick glance with Luke, but his features give nothing away.

"Why . . . why would anyone do this?" Pratima wails again. *"Why, why, why?"*

"Sometimes people just do terrible things, Pratima," I say. "Sometimes we can never really understand what darkness drives a person. But I promise we will do everything in our power to find and arrest her assailant. And when we do find him, perhaps we will learn more about why."

I turn to Luke. "I'll go upstairs with Pratima and take another look at Leena's room."

I'm going to separate her from her husband.

He holds my gaze. Nods.

RACHEL

Pratima watches me from the doorway of her daughter's room. I'm acutely conscious of my boots on the pale carpet. When I'm on a job, it's not protocol for cops to remove work shoes at front doors. Outside the bedroom window, the sky is wintry. It will be dark soon, the kind of darkness that creeps in earlier and earlier each afternoon until the winter solstice brings us into the deepest night of the year.

Upon Leena's dresser are two glossy brochures advertising volunteer work with a mission in Africa. I'm reminded of the picture we found in her wallet. The photo of a mercy ship.

Clearly this kid wanted to escape this town.

"These mission ships are run by a Christian organization?" I ask, picking up a brochure.

Pratima folds her arms defensively over her chest. "It didn't mean anything to Leena what the faith was. It was more a vehicle for her to get away. She wanted to do good. To help disadvantaged people. She . . ." Pratima's voice hitches. I glance up.

She struggles to continue. "All Leena wanted was to go someplace where she felt valued. We . . . all just need to feel worthy, don't we? To be loved. To belong. Because if we don't feel that we belong somewhere, how can we ever call it home? Isn't it a most basic survival thing, because to be cast out of a group, or a herd, can mean death?"

I stare at Pratima. And I wonder for a moment if she might even be talking about herself. About her own immigrant experience. I wonder if this bereaved mother feels all sorts of pain that I can't even begin to understand. I wonder if she can talk freely to her husband. If she's lonely.

"Pratima, did it worry Leena's father—the fact that his daughter was interested in pursuing work with a Christian group?"

"Jaswinder is a devout follower of the Sikh faith. He was also very strict with Leena. She was going through a period where she would reject things just to defy him. She was rebelling against his control. She eschewed anything to do with her own cultural background. She . . . she was just trying so hard to fit in with girls at school."

"A typical teenager," I say softly.

She glares at me. Guilt washes up into my chest. I turn back to the dresser. Beside the brochures is a basket of jewelry and other trinkets. I lift up, examine, and replace a few items. Rings. A bracelet. Earrings. A necklace with a shell pendant. Leena's mother enters the room and comes up behind me. Close. She lowers her voice.

"The picture of the locket that you showed us—the one with the Celtic knots. I . . . need to tell you something."

My heart beats faster. This is it. This is what she was keeping from her husband downstairs, the thing that was making her uncomfortable.

"It's the same with that lip gloss you found," she says. "And maybe even the book of poems and address book."

"What's the same?"

"She . . ." Pratima inhales and blows out a shaky breath. "Our Leena used to take things."

"What do you mean, 'take things'?"

"She stole, or borrowed them without permission. Jaswinder forbade Leena to buy any makeup, so she took it from other girls. She developed a habit. Sort of . . . collecting things." Pratima hesitates. "The manager of the Twin Falls Drug Mart, he called a few months ago . . . for us to come and get Leena. He wanted to talk to us. She'd stolen some mascara and eye shadow. She promised she'd never do it again, and he didn't press charges, or report it." Her cheeks flush deep red. "I don't know if she stopped. I think that lip gloss and the address book and the poetry book belong to other students. And the locket, too."

I feel an awkward rush of relief. "Are you *certain?*"

"No. But I thought you should know that it's possible the items could belong to other girls."

"This really helps, Pratima. Thank you for opening up like this." I waver. "Can . . . Do you recall seeing any of Leena's friends wearing the Celtic locket, or one that looked similar?"

She regards me. Time stretches. Wind blows the branches of a tree against the window. I feel a drop in temperature as the weather changes. A storm is coming.

"You don't seem to understand, do you, Sergeant? Leena did not have any friends."

Her statement hangs. I think again of that day in the school gym.

"What about those photos pinned on that corkboard over there?" I go closer to the board on the wall. I saw these photos the last time I was in here, when Leena Rai was still just a missing persons case. Held in place by yellow pushpins is a selection of photos of classmates, taken both in and out of school. Among the faces are many I recognize, including my own daughter's and that of her best friend, Beth. Some of the faces have been circled with a red marker. "Aren't any of these kids her friends? Or why does she have these photos pinned up here?"

"I think it's people she wished were her friends. Sort of like . . . a vision board. She could pretend."

"Why are some of these faces circled in red?"

Pratima remains quiet.

I glance at her.

She inhales again. "I don't know. All that I do know is Leena wanted to be like those particular girls. She wanted to belong."

I frown and take a closer look, noting who all has been circled in red. Beth. Maddy. Cheyenne. Amy. Seema. The popular girls.

Twin Falls has only one elementary school and one high school. One class per grade. Most of the town's children who met in the kindergarten class have moved up through the grades with the same cohort. They all went to the same birthday parties. Shopped in the same stores. Attended the same sporting events and community barbecues. Such is the nature of small towns. And it strikes me that it must truly be hell if you don't fit in, or feel you can't belong. Or if you are disliked. Because there is just no escape.

I moisten my lips and say, "Is there anyone you know—any one of these kids in these photos who was a tiny bit closer to Leena than the others? Someone who might be able to help us figure out what happened to her between the point she was last seen at the bonfire to when she ended up in the river?"

"If there was, she never told me." A pause, and Pratima's big, dark eyes glisten. "We think we can keep them safe if we order them what to do, if we control them. We think that if we keep them busy with sports, they can't get into trouble. But we're wrong."

Suddenly I catch a glimpse of a little dark head peeping around the door. Ganesh. The six-year-old's eyes are wide. He's watching. Listening. Learning.

His mother spins around to see what I am looking at.

"Ganesh! Out!" She points. "Get out. How can you stand there listening like that?"

The child scurries away down the hall. I hear a door slam. Pratima slumps onto her daughter's bed and drops her face into her hands. She starts to sob.

◆ ◆ ◆

As Luke and I walk back through the biting wind to our unmarked cruiser, I feel watched. I glance back at the house. Upstairs in a lit dormer window there's a small shadow. Ganesh again. Observing us detectives. I stare up at him and feel a bolt of sadness. What must the boy be thinking? What did he hear us say? What does he comprehend about the death of his big sister, and how will this forever change him?

I raise my hand to wave, but he vanishes. And I see Luke regarding me from the other side of the car. I lower my hand and climb into the driver's seat. Without meeting Luke's eyes, I put on my seat belt and start the engine. It begins to rain as I drive up the road that will take us to Amy Chan's house. She's the girl who reported seeing Leena on Devil's Bridge around 2:00 a.m. on the morning of November 15.

"We got a call from the lab while you were upstairs," Luke says. "The journal pages have been dried. The ink is legible. They're sending copies over to the station."

I nod. Tense. "Leena stole things," I say. "Pratima feels the address and poetry books, the makeup, the locket—it all could have been 'borrowed' from other kids. She says Leena shoplifted as well."

"So that's what Pratima was holding back from her husband downstairs?"

"Looks like." I turn onto the boulevard that leads up the mountain and into a high-end subdivision. We're heading for the Smoke Bluffs—a granite ledge upon which the Chan house stands like a columned white wedding cake amid similarly ornate homes. "The locket is a common-enough trinket, right?" I glance at him. "Could belong to anyone."

"We'll bring the kids in for questioning again," he says.

"Do you have any children?"

"Never really got around to it. Then our marriage collapsed, and it was too late."

I throw him another glance. "You're divorced?"

"Married to the job. Always have been." He laughs. "It's an occupational hazard, especially in homicide. My ex, understandably, grew tired of playing second fiddle. It was a fairly amicable separation in the end, as far as these things can be amicable."

Rain suddenly begins to drum down heavily. An autumn monsoon. Water runs in a sheet down the steep road, and raindrops squiggle up my windshield as I drive, as though they are racing to rejoin each other in the sky. Normally the incessant fall monsoons are background noise in my life. Today it feels different. The raindrops splatter with an urgency, an insistence, as if they have something to say.

I think of loss. Of the everyday gaps left behind. Leena's Nike shoe. Her bloodied sock. Her wet backpack and book of poems lost between rocks on the riverbank. The floating pages of a journal. A girl full of dreams. Gone. Her plans silenced.

"This Darsh Rai, do you know him?" Luke asks as I turn into the Chans' street.

"Yeah. Good-looking guy. About twenty or twenty-one years old. Works at the pulp mill across the water. Never been in trouble with cops. From all accounts a nice person. Smooth dresser. Passion for restoring old sports cars. Girls flock around him."

"We'll need to speak to this gift-giving cousin Darsh." Luke checks his watch. "We should pay him a visit this evening, after we've talked to Amy Chan. Before word gets around that Leena drowned."

As with the rain, there's a sense of urgency about Luke. I understand. In the early days of a homicide investigation, time is of the essence, and we've already lost plenty.

"There's also something off with the father," he says. "We need to check into his background."

Surprise surges through me. "Jaswinder? Off?"

"Hmm."

I turn into the Chan driveway. "Jaswinder might come across as authoritarian and a bit gruff, but he's a good man, Luke. And he's hurting. Hell, I don't know what *I'd* do if someone did that to my kid. He works for the local transit company. Drives a regular bus route.

Everyone on that route will tell you he's a nice man. An honorable man." I bring the vehicle to a stop, and I remember Leena's bruises. "You can't think *he* had something to do with his child's death?"

He watches my face. Quietly he says, "You know them all, Rachel. Personally. All the players. They're part of your community. It's why Chief Doyle wanted me on the team, as an outside eye. It's tough to be objective when you've lived in a town a long time. It's the reason the RCMP transfers members to new communities every five years—so they don't become too invested and lose objectivity. And while I'm not thinking Jaswinder Rai is in any way responsible, anything is always possible. Statistically most violence done to women is done by someone they know well. That includes male family members. And something is off there. I can feel it."

TRINITY

NOW
Thursday, November 11. Present day.

Gio and I sit side by side at the small dining table in the motel room we've rented for the duration of our project. The motel stands near where the old Twin Falls police station used to be in 1997, in a more industrial part of town with a view of the granite walls of Chief Mountain. The Chief reminds me of El Capitan in Yosemite, and it's well known among the international climbing fraternity. Chief Mountain is also the one constant in this story—it looms like an omniscient sentinel over the town. It's seen everything over the years. But it stands silent. Watchful. Forbidding in the cold light.

The first time I ever saw a picture of the Chief was when I came across an old news photo of Clayton Jay Pelley, smiling in front of the thundering falls.

Gio and I are listening to—and mixing—audio we obtained with police diver Tom Tanaka. Tom now works with the Ontario Provincial Police. He moved east when he married a woman from Toronto.

> TOM: After we floated Leena to the shore, Sergeant Rachel Walczak instructed us to go back underwater to see if we could find anything else.

TRINITY: Like what?

TOM: Like the military surplus jacket the victim had last been seen wearing. Or a weapon that could have been used to bludgeon the victim. The trauma to her face was extensive. When we rolled her body over . . . it . . . We were all shocked silent for a few moments.

TRINITY: Can you take us back and describe in detail what you saw underwater that November morning?

I smile to myself as I reach for a slice of pizza. I like the tension in Tom Tanaka's voice. To be fair, I know it's ghoulish to ask for a blow-by-blow description of finding a week-old corpse floating under murky water, but this is true crime. The spectacle—the theater of murder—is what listeners come for. And I am still beside myself with excitement that Clayton Pelley claims he is innocent of the crime. I chew on my mouthful of pizza, listening to Tom, thinking about how I felt seeing Clayton in person for the first time, how it changed something inside me as the story shifted focus.

TOM: The water was icy. The visibility was almost nil. At times I couldn't even see my hands in front of my face. The two of us were basically diving blind, just carefully inching our way forward and feeling with our hands through the thick murk, touching things— slimy reeds, silt, rocks, bits of metal, old tins, broken bottles, shopping carts, a bicycle—hoping all the while that we wouldn't cut ourselves on something sharp. We desperately wanted to find the girl, but at the same time you don't want to find her under there. The whole time while I was looking, there was this fear that her face would suddenly come up against mine—that I'd swim into it before I realized it. That her eyes would be right there, in front of mine. Open. Looking at me. Her skin pale, luminous like a ghost in the dark water . . . You never quite get rid of that anxiety, that edge of tension . . . And then I did touch her. With my fingertips. Her hair was floating out around her head. Long. And it got in my face, across my goggles. I thought it was weeds before I realized it was her long hair. She had nothing on, apart from her bra and the camisole tangled around her neck.

SILENCE

TRINITY: How did you decide where to begin the underwater search?

TOM: We figured if she went into the river below the bridge, where her belongings had been found, she couldn't have gone far. Leena was heavier than an average female drowning victim, so with the river depth at around twenty-five feet, and the slowness of the current, we figured she'd be heavy enough to resist much movement. Basically, if a diver can swim easily against a current, it's unlikely that a drowning victim will be moved far. So you generally begin at the point last seen. And then you adjust your buoyancy so you are negatively buoyant, and you let yourself sink to almost the bottom, and you hang there, prone, just above the bottom, and then work your way forward. We found her not too far from the bridge trestles. She'd gotten caught up in the eelgrass.

TRINITY: And you found items of her clothing.

TOM: Yes. Her cargo pants and panties. No jacket was found. And when Sergeant Walczak asked us to go down again, I was thinking maybe we'd find a base-ball bat, or a tire iron, or something heavy that could have been used to deliver that kind of blunt force trauma . . . I mean . . . I . . . She looked like victims we've found who've gone over bridges in car wrecks.

TRINITY: That's what the pathologist also said.

TOM: Yes. But because we were looking for a weapon, when I saw the loose journal pages just hanging there, waving softly to and fro in the watery gloom, like three ghosts, I was . . . sort of spooked. And when we brought them up, the pages appeared pretty pristine. The words were still there. Ink is generally permanent, and if the pages have not been in water too long, and if the water is cold like it was, when they're dried out, the writing is legible. Most words survive.

TRINITY: They were from a journal?

TOM: They looked like they'd been ripped from a jour-nal, yes.

Gio starts feeding in the theme music softly. I take another bite of pizza, thinking as I listen.

TRINITY: Jaswinder and Pratima Rai confirmed the writ-ing was their daughter's. They said Leena liked to write, and that she wanted to be a writer someday, possibly even a foreign correspondent. I received copies of the torn pages along with the other case evidence. And here is Leena, in her own words:

MUSIC INCREASES SLIGHTLY IN VOLUME

TRINITY: "We spend most of our lives afraid of our own Shadow. He told me that. He said a Shadow lives deep inside every one of us. So deep we don't even know it's there. Sometimes, with a quick sideways glance, we catch a glimpse of it. But it frightens us, and we quickly look away. This is what fuels the Shadow— our inability to look. Our inability to examine this thing that is in fact our raw selves. This is what gives the Shadow its power. It makes us lie. About what we want, about who we are. It fires our passions, our darkest desires. And the more powerful it gets, the greater we fear it, and the deeper we struggle to hide this Beast that is us . . .

"I don't know why He tells me these things. Maybe it's a way of obliquely bringing out and addressing his own Shadow. But I do think our Shadows are bad— his and mine. Big and dark and very dangerous. I don't think our Shadows should ever be allowed out."

The other two pages, seemingly torn from random places in the journal, have a few jotted lines of thought in this vein. In one place, Leena wrote this:

"He believes in me. It's the one thing that keeps me holding on. He makes me feel smart, and real, and valuable, and I love him. He loves me, too."

And in another line she wrote these words: "He told me it's all very well to want to leave, but I need an exit plan that is more than just an exit. I think I have one . . ."

The last phrase in the ripped pages is this: "He told me about a military term today. MAD. Mutual assured destruction. Like when two powers hold nuclear weapons that would totally annihilate the other side, and it keeps each side in check. He said that's what keeping big secrets is like. He meant huge, dark secrets. Like knowing-the-truth-of-someone's-Shadow kinds of secrets. Secrets that become nuclear weapons. A form of deterrence. And each side is scared into silence. Until they aren't. Until they both act, and implode the relationship. Total mutual destruction."

And that's it. That's where the page ends on a rip. That's all that remains of Leena Rai's words. So far. For the rest of the diary has never been found.

MUSIC GOES LOUDER.

So who was the "He" that Leena loved? Was it the man who ended up in prison? Or was it someone else? Someone closer in age to Leena? Someone who perhaps still lives in town? Someone with a shadow, a truth so dark it got Leena killed for knowing it?

Why were the ripped pages floating in the river with her body? Why were they ripped at all?

And where did the journal go?

Loose pages. Loose ends. They leave too many unanswered questions. Questions the detectives on the case dropped. A trail we will follow.

DISSOLVE TO THEME SONG.

I swallow my mouthful of pizza. "I think maybe we should introduce the clip we recorded this morning on murder being entertainment," I say. "Can you play that one for me again?"

Gio finds the clip, clicks.

TRINITY: Murder and the legal process that follows is a kind of theater, a theater of the macabre. The act of murder forces a spotlight onto the pathologies in our communities. We are drawn to watch because murder reveals elements about ourselves, things we can't look away from. We recognize the various murderers' vices buried deep within each and every one of us— deviant desires, mental illness, urges toward violence, righteous rage, prejudice, racism, frustration, malevolence, greed, envy, cruelty . . . All of this is the stuff of high drama. And to understand a society's murders is to learn a great deal about the tensions that lie beneath the surface of a town. Murder also reveals the authority of a government and the ultimate power it holds over the lives of its citizens. The power to take away freedoms, to lock someone away. To punish. And to even kill in retaliation in the form of capital punishment. But sometimes the authorities get it wrong.

Sometimes it's left to a citizen journalist to find the truth. And sometimes uncovering the truth can start out like the divers underwater, in the murky darkness, just feeling their way, inch by inch, until their fingers touch something.

"Yes," I say. "Yes, let's lead into Tom's interview with that clip."

RACHEL

"Amy Chan is fifteen?" Luke asks as we approach the front entrance to the Chan house on the cliffs. Already their Christmas lights have been strung up. From this vantage point, through the shifting mists, we can see the valley in the distance, where the commercial hub of Twin Falls nestles between rivers and ocean. I can also see pricks of lights from the pulp mill across the sound. The wind is blowing in our direction from the mill. It carries the stench of the sulfurous chemicals used in the pulping process. At times the stink can be nauseating.

"Just turned fifteen." I reach for the doorbell. "Only child. Her mother brought her into the station to make the statement about seeing Leena on the bridge."

The doorbell gives a hollow chime.

The door opens.

Amy, a pretty and petite teen with dark-brown eyes and shoulder-length hair, stands in the white marble hallway. She wears a soft pink sweatshirt and leggings. Socked feet. Behind her a round table of glossy, dark wood holds a vase of blooms that have got to be fake. Or a very extravagant greenhouse import at this time of year.

"Hello, Amy," I say. "How are you doing?"

"Good." She's nervous. Shifting weight from foot to foot.

"This is Sergeant Luke O'Leary. He's helping with the investigation into Leena's death. We'd like to ask you a few more questions about that night you saw her. We'd like to see if you remember anything else. Is either of your parents home?"

"My mom."

"Can we come in?"

Amy steps back to allow us inside. Her mother, Sarah Chan, appears in the entrance hall. Surprise widens her eyes at the sight of us. She's an older echo of her daughter, but with a chic bob that swings at her jawline. She, too, appears edgy. I explain why we've come, and she invites us into a living room with plush cream carpeting, white furniture, and a view over town. In the distance I can see the silver gleam of the Wuyakan River, and a chill sinks through me. Leena was floating in that water for more than a week before Amy came forward. Floating while people looked out their windows at the river, drove over the bridge in cars and school buses.

Luke and I sit gingerly on the very white chairs. Amy and her mother take a seat together on the sofa, much as Pratima and Jaswinder did. Close together for moral support.

I note their clothes, their overt comforts, and I think of the cheap camisole tangled around Leena's neck. No Fruit of the Loom value-pack undies for the Chan women, I'm sure.

"Can I get you tea, coffee, anything?" Sarah asks.

"No, we're fine," I say. "We'd like to once more run through what Amy saw on the bridge that night, if that's okay?" I take out my notebook and pen.

The Chan women both nod. Once more, Luke slips into the role of the outsider looking in. Assessing. And I get the strong feeling he's weighing me and my reactions as much as he is the witnesses, which unsettles me.

"So, Amy, you came with your mother into the station on Friday morning, November twenty-first."

Amy nods. Her hands fidget in her lap.

"That's almost a whole week after Leena Rai was reported missing. Why did you wait so many days?"

Amy glances at her mother. "I . . . I'm so sorry. I . . . didn't know she was dead. I—"

Her mother places a hand over her daughter's. Amy falls silent.

"Okay, let's dial back a bit." I consult my notebook. "You told the officer on duty that you were with your boyfriend, Jepp Sullivan, at around two a.m. on Saturday, November fifteenth, driving over Devil's Bridge, when you saw Leena Rai stumbling along the sidewalk, is that right?"

"Yes," she says in a small voice.

"What were you doing on the bridge at two a.m.?"

Another nervous glance at her mom. Her mother nods. "Go ahead, love. It's okay."

"We'd been to the bonfire in the woods, at the grove. Jepp and I left the fire around one thirty a.m. He was driving, and we were on our way over the bridge to Ari's Greek Takeout—they're always open late, and they . . . It's like a thing to go get donairs after parties and stuff."

"Good hangover food," offers Luke.

Amy says nothing. Ari's is well known to the Twin Falls PD as a late-night joint. Breaking up drunken brawls outside Ari's is not uncommon. Which is why Ari Gamoulakos had CCTV installed. I make a mental note to check whether the footage from that night is still available.

"Jepp has his own car?" I ask.

"Well, it's sort of Darsh Rai's. Jepp has a deal with Darsh where he's paying it off to own it. Darsh got it cheap and fixed it up."

"Had you guys been drinking?" I ask.

"Jepp was fine to drive. He only had one beer the whole evening. He's really good that way. He's training hard and all. He wants a basketball scholarship."

"Okay, run me through what you saw as you guys drove over the bridge."

"There was a full moon. Big. It was clear. And there was a really, really cold wind blowing off the sea. That's what struck me—the sight of someone walking in that freezing wind. I saw long dark hair blowing. And then I saw the shape of the jacket, and the person, and I realized it was Leena."

"There is no doubt in your mind it was her?" I ask.

"I . . . You could totally see it was Leena. She—it's her shape. Leena is—was—tall and big, and she had a certain way of walking that people made fun of. Sort of lumbering. But it was more marked because Leena had been drinking a lot that night, or at least she looked totally drunk. Falling around and grabbing on to the railing. And then a truck went by. The headlights lit her up. And I said to Jepp, 'Hey, that's Leena,' and I turned around in the seat, to watch."

A tightening begins in my chest.

"So she was alone?"

"I . . . I think so. I didn't look farther back or anything to see if anyone was behind her, and then we were past, and off the bridge."

"You didn't think to stop, to see if she was okay, stumbling along the bridge like that? All alone."

Amy's eyes gleam. "I . . . Not really."

"Did Jepp see her?"

"No, he was driving. He noticed someone but not that it was Leena."

"Which direction was Leena walking in?" I ask.

"The opposite way to which we were driving."

"So she was going north?"

"Yeah."

I glance at Luke. Leena's backpack and belongings were found on the south bank of the river, beneath the bridge. But her Nike runner and bloodied sock were discovered on the north bank under the bridge, where we also found blood on the trunk of the cedar growing there.

"Was she carrying her backpack?"

"I . . . No. I don't think so. I can't recall her carrying anything."

"But she *was* wearing the jacket?"

"Yeah. Definitely the jacket. The same one she'd been wearing at the bonfire."

I make another note in my book. We're still searching for that jacket.

"What kind of truck was it that passed Leena?"

"I . . . Just like a regular pickup. I can't remember the color. It was dark, and . . ." Her voice fades.

"Any other cars?"

"I . . . Maybe one other went by." She wrinkles her brow. "I don't know. I don't really remember. I . . . I wasn't paying that much attention—" She looks at her mother, distress twisting into her face.

"Were you drunk, Amy?" I ask.

She nods. A tear plops onto her thigh and leaves a wet mark on her leggings. She swipes at her eyes. "I'm sorry. If . . . if I'd been more focused, maybe . . . maybe we'd have stopped . . . maybe Leena would be alive. Maybe I would have said something more to Jepp."

"But you didn't. You took a whole week," says Luke, leaning forward. "Why?"

"I . . . I didn't think it was an issue."

"Not even after you heard she was missing?"

"We all thought Leena was just being, like, Leena, and that she would show up."

"You didn't think it was an *issue?*" Luke repeats. He's trotting out his bad-cop persona to my friendly one.

Amy flushes deep red. "I . . . I . . ."

"She was worried that I'd find out she lied to me," Sarah snaps. "Amy had informed us that she would be sleeping over at her friend

Cheyenne's house on the night of the bonfire. But she spent the night at Jepp's. She didn't want us to know. She thought she'd get in trouble, and she did. She was grounded."

In a tiny voice, Amy says, "Jepp's mom works the night shift at the hospital. She's a nurse. His dad doesn't live with them. So his parents didn't know I was there."

I know Barb Sullivan, the nurse. I know Jepp's parents are divorced. That much is true.

"But when I started hearing the rumors at school that Leena was probably dead and floating in the Wuyakan River, a victim of some serial killer, I . . ." Amy begins to cry in earnest now. "I told the guidance counselor at school that I'd seen her on the bridge that night. He took me to the principal, who called my mom. And my mom brought me to the station. And we went to the station to make a statement."

"Who told you Leena could be floating in the river?" I ask.

"It was just like a rumor. Everyone was saying they'd heard it from someone else. No one knows who started it."

"So you cannot remember which person at school, specifically, told you?"

"I . . . I think it was the girl who has the locker next to me. She said she heard it from someone in her class, who heard it from someone else."

"And when you got to Ari's Greek Takeout, what did you do there?"

"Bought donairs. We ate them outside. There was a bunch of people there who'd been at the bonfire."

"Who did you see there?"

Amy picks at an invisible thread on her leggings. "I . . . I don't know. I wasn't really focused. Sort of out of it. Kids from my class, and some seniors. Tripp Galloway. He was talking to Darsh Rai. Um . . . Cheyenne. Dusty. Some others."

"Darsh was there? And you didn't think to tell him that his little cousin was stumbling drunkenly along the bridge in the dark alone? You didn't think he might be worried?"

She shook her head.

"You didn't tell *anyone* you saw Leena?"

"No, why would I?"

"Why indeed," I say with distaste. "She was just an outsider. Irrelevant. Stumbling alone along the bridge in the dark. Is that right, Amy?"

Amy starts to sob.

"That's enough," snaps Sarah. "Amy has said she's sorry—she made a mistake." The mother rises to her feet. "This interview is over."

Tight-mouthed, Sarah shows us to the door. As we exit, she calls behind me, "What about *your* daughter, Rachel? Did *she* come home that night?"

I stop, turn. Stare at her.

"Did Maddy tell *you* there was a big bonfire planned? Or did she lie to you, too?"

I hold her gaze.

"Right. I didn't think so. People in glass houses and all that." Sarah closes the door in our faces.

Once we're back inside the car, I say to Luke, "She makes me sound like I'm a bad mother, but I'm a cop—I'm the *last* person in town anyone would tell about an illegal gathering in the woods. My daughter already gets flak for being the cop's kid. She would have been under more pressure than the others not to spill the beans." I start the engine and reverse out of the driveway.

"I can imagine," he says. He's quiet the rest of the way back to town. Then, as we enter the downtown area, wipers squeaking, heater blasting, he says, "I'll handle the interviews with the kids when we go to the school tomorrow."

I shoot him a glance. "Because my daughter will be among them?"

"Yes."

Worry snakes through me. Something is stirring beneath the surface. Changing. I feel it in my bones.

RACHEL

It's late morning as I load my mountain bike into the back of my truck. Granger has still not returned or called. There's a break in the weather, and I need to get out, think, burn off some pent-up anxiety. I also want to warn those close to me who are linked to the old case. Maddy is not answering her phone, so I intend to stop by her house before meeting up with my friend Eileen. As I navigate the twisting valley road, I listen again to parts of the second episode of the Leena Rai podcast.

> TRINITY: When Leena Rai's mother reported her daughter missing, the rumors began instantly. One of Leena's classmates, Seema Patel, who spoke to me on the phone from where she now works as a sales manager in Calgary, said each story grew wilder than the last as their young minds sought to fill the gaps.
>
> SEEMA: Perhaps it was to placate fears, because not knowing can be scarier than knowing something, even if it's bad. Part of it was also just the excitement

of sensationalism. Our town was boring for us teens back then. It's like we created crazy stories about the Leena mystery as a strange sort of entertainment, each story topping the last. It started with rumors of a bear attack, because Leena at first seemed to have disappeared into the woods, and no one recalled seeing her after the rocket in the sky. Someone said she'd been dragged off by a bear when she'd gone to the bathroom down a trail. Others claimed it was a cougar, or wolves. Some believed she'd fallen into a ravine nearby and was hidden by vegetation near the bottom or being eaten by wildlife. Then some smartasses said it was a UFO thing, tied to the rocket event, and that aliens had snatched Leena for research. Some claimed she'd run away with a man who'd been lurking around the bonfire. Or perhaps she was hiding and doing a Leena thing . . . Leena had not come home before, and she often lied. She was needy. She was like a stalker. Jealous. And . . . well, she was always talking about leaving Twin Falls anyway, getting out of town. I actually thought she'd finally done it. I was kinda impressed, because God knows, I sure wanted to leave myself. I hated the place, hated school. Then, when the days stretched into a week, I heard at school that she'd taken her own life. And I figured that was possible, too.

TRINITY: So when did the rumor about Leena floating in the river emerge?

SEEMA: About two days before they found her, I think.

TRINITY: Who started that particular rumor?

SEEMA: We never found out. Cops didn't, either.

TRINITY: But someone had to have known she was in the river, and dead. Because it was true. She was.

SEEMA: At first I thought it was just another wild story. But yeah . . . it was true. Someone knew something.

TRINITY: How well did you know Leena?

SEEMA: I . . . Not well.

TRINITY: I hear your parents knew hers?

SEEMA: Only because they came from the same part of India. But that didn't make our family friends of theirs.

TRINITY: You sound defensive about this.

SEEMA: Just because you come from the same place doesn't mean you are the same. People try to paint you all with the same brush. It's called prejudging. Based on skin color or cultural background.

TRINITY: So you're saying you were different from Leena, better?

SEEMA: I resent that. I was different from her, that's all. We had nothing in common. Leena didn't fit in. She didn't know how to.

TRINITY: But you did.

SEEMA: I had friends.

I hit STOP. I'm entering the outskirts of Twin Falls, which has grown tenfold in the last twenty-four years, segueing from a mill and logging resource community into a recreation mecca for hip young families with a passion for the environment and a penchant for tele-commuting. My thoughts go to Pratima and what she said to me in Leena's bedroom.

We think we can keep them safe if we order them what to do, if we control them. We think that if we keep them busy with sports, they can't get into trouble. But we're wrong.

Pratima was right. I know firsthand. A mother can do everything in her power to make sure the lines of communication with her kids stay open. And it goes wrong anyway. I was a difficult kid myself. Pretty much right up until the time I fell pregnant with Maddy at twenty-two. That's when I went back to my parents, hat in hand, to ask for help, because neither Jake nor I had a job or money, and we were in a tight spot. Jake had come west from Ontario to hike mountains, ski, and party. I fell hard for him and joined him as a ski bum. My dad, who was already police chief at the time, helped find Jake a job in construction with a friend of his. And my mom babysat Maddy while I started my police training. Jake and I grew up pretty fast from that point. I joined the Twin Falls PD, thanks to my dad, and Jake eventually started his own small construction business. Maddy, however, never settled emo-tionally, even after she married Darren Jankowski from her class. Or after they had their two girls. My grandbabies.

I turn into a street of suburban homes, all similar in design. It's one of the newer developments above town, higher up the flanks of the mountain. At the end of the cul-de-sac lies Maddy and Darren's pretty white double-story with green trim. Jake helped them build it.

As I spy the house, my neck goes tight. I feel my stomach brace.

I pull my truck into their driveway, kill the engine, and stare at the house with its quaint dormer windows. Next door a male neighbor is stringing Christmas lights around a fir tree that grows in his front yard. A toddler, all bundled up, watches from a stroller on the porch. Smoke curls from their chimney.

I get out. Wave. The neighbor's gaze darts toward Maddy and Darren's front door, and he hesitates before returning my wave. Is that how foreign I look? Like a stranger in my own kid's yard? Or does he know full well who I am, and that I am not welcome in this green-trimmed house?

I knock on the front door.

Darren opens it. Shock chases across his face, but he quickly controls it and offers a smile. "Rachel? What . . . what're you doing here?"

I slide my truck keys into my back pocket as I see little Daisy peeking around the corner.

"Heya, Daisy." I crouch down. "How are you, kiddo? How's your little sister?"

Daisy, four years old, smiles coyly, comes forward slightly, and holds on to her dad's jeans as she leans into his legs.

"Say hi, Daize," Darren says. "It's your grandmother."

"Hi," she says shyly, twisting against her dad's leg, cheeks blushing.

I feel a sharp pang of hurt. I am alien to my granddaughters, and Lord knows I've tried to change that, but Maddy puts up roadblocks any way she can.

"I brought you something." I take a small Snickers bar from my pocket and hold it out to her.

"Maddy doesn't want the girls to have candy." Darren manages to look apologetic. "Especially if it has peanuts."

I slide the candy back into my pocket. "Well, then, I'll have to bring you something better next time, okay, Daize? Where's Lily?"

"Thleeping." Her lisp is adorable. It squeezes my heart, and emotion shoots to my eyes. I come erect.

"Is Maddy home?" I ask Darren. "I saw her van in the garage."

He looks trapped. Her van is clearly there, the garage door open. He can hardly pull a Granger and pretend his wife is not home.

"Who is it?" I hear Maddy's voice before she comes around the corner into the hallway.

She appears, sees me, and freezes, her hands tightening on the sides of her wheelchair. Her face changes.

"Hey, Mads," I say.

"Who died?"

"I was passing by. I stopped to . . . I came to say hi to my grandchildren."

"Right."

"Can we have a word?"

"Whatever you want to say, you can say it here." In the entrance hall. With the door right behind my back.

"I got a visit from a woman named Trinity Scott. She's producing a podcast on the Leena Rai murder."

Maddy stares at me. Time stretches. Abruptly she spins her chair around and heads out of the hallway, disappearing from sight.

Darren jerks his head and says softly, "Go on through."

I find my daughter in her kitchen, washing dishes in the sink, her back to me. Above the sink is a window with a clear view of the north face of Chief Mountain. The rock face gleams with moisture and is streaked through with shades of gray. I see two specks of color in a crevice. Climbers. I feel sick. I can't understand why my daughter wants to live in a house with such a prominent view of the granite mountain against which she used to hurl herself so hard and so often, tackling one climbing route more challenging than the last, as if defying the Chief to shrug her off. Almost as if wanting it to. And then the mountain did. Two years ago, not long after she'd given birth to Lily. The Chief finally shrugged a shoulder, as if vaguely irritated with the human flea attacking it, and a slab of stone separated with Maddy holding on to it. Everyone said it was a miracle she hadn't been killed. A secret part of me believes my daughter really wanted to die, and I have not been able to fully understand why, or where it all started to go so wrong with my once-happy little girl. Or why most of her anger is focused on me. Yes, I had a brief fling. But her father did a lot worse. Yes, she is angry at her dad, too. But it's me she seems to want to really punish.

"Trinity wants to interview me," I say. "About the investigation that put Clay Pelley behind bars."

"So?" Maddy doesn't bother to turn to face me. "Is this just an excuse for you to come see the girls?"

I seat myself on a bar stool at the kitchen counter. "Trinity says she's going to try to talk to everyone who was involved. Detectives. Leena's parents. Her classmates. The people who saw Leena at the bonfire."

Maddy gives a shrug and sticks a plate in the rack. But I can see her shoulders have stiffened. I realize Darren is standing in the doorway, also listening, with Daisy on his hip.

"I . . . just thought I'd give you a heads-up, Mads. In case Trinity calls you, or stops by."

Silence presses into the kitchen as she washes a knife, then jabs it violently into the cutlery basket on the drying rack.

"Why? Because you think it will upset me?"

I say nothing.

She spins around. Her eyes glitter. "You think it might hurt me to be reminded of how you broke up our family during that investiga-tion? How your affair with that cop ruined our life? How Dad had to leave—"

"Your father was already having an affair of his own, Maddy." My voice comes out clipped, and I realize she's already baited me. And I swallowed it, hook and all. My blood pressure instantly shoots sky-high.

"So that makes what you did right? Dad only started seeing someone because you'd already cut him out of your life. You cut us both out. It was always work first. And then came the Leena case. And it was an excuse for you. You were more worried about a dead girl than your living family. It was all *Leena, Leena, Leena*, but really, it was all about Luke O'Leary, wasn't it? All those long nights? The excuses about working late—really just excuses to fuck your colleague. And you weren't even subtle about it—"

"Maddy," Darren warns from the door.

She ignores him. My daughter is back on her bitter roll, her gaze locked fiercely on to mine.

"You were seen by my own friend and her mother in that alley. You literally drove Dad to drink. Are you afraid I will tell all that to Trinity Scott? That you were a shitty cop, and a shitty mother?"

"Jesus, Maddy," Darren says.

"Oh, back off," she snaps.

"It's all right," I say. "I'm leaving." I come to my feet. But Maddy has turned her back to me again and is facing the sink, looking at the two climbing specks on the granite mountain that forever looms over our town. And our lives.

"The first two podcast episodes are already live," I say quietly. "Clayton Jay Pelley spoke."

"Clay *spoke*?" Darren asks.

I keep my gaze on the back of Maddy's head. "Yes. Clay said he didn't do it. He did not assault and kill Leena. Clay said the killer is still out there."

Maddy doesn't move a muscle. Not even a twitch. From my pocket I take Trinity Scott's business card. I place it on the counter and say softly, "The website addy for the podcast is on this card. You can also download it from iTunes."

Still she doesn't move.

"I can show myself out," I say to Darren.

As I open the front door, I hear Darren and Maddy beginning to argue in the kitchen, their voices going louder. As I step out the door, I hear Darren telling his wife that she could at least *try* to be nice to her mother. I hear him saying to Maddy that she's being unreasonable.

Stories do not end . . .

I drive away from their perfect-looking house in the perfect-looking subdivision that sits in the shadow of Chief Mountain, and I try to remember exactly when it all started to go wrong. Were things wobbling off the rails between Maddy and me before I started working Leena's case?

Or did it happen because of what had been done to Leena?

RACHEL

THEN
Monday, November 24, 1997.

It's almost 5:30 p.m., and Luke and I are waiting in our unmarked vehicle at the Laurel Bay ferry dock. We see the lights of the small ferry coming in through the mist and darkness. Rain continues to drum down heavily on the roof. Behind us is the Twin Falls Provincial Park. We can hear the thundering of the falls.

"The mill is not accessible by road?" Luke asks.

"No. Back in the twenties there was a settlement around the mill, complete with a school, but families have long since moved away."

The ferry horn sounds as it comes in to dock. The gangway goes down, and foot passengers start disembarking. They come toward the parking lot in small groups. Several mill workers sport turbans. Other employees wear coveralls and ball caps, or lined jeans with suspenders, plaid shirts, and heavy jackets. Some carry lunch pails and look tired as the lights catch their faces. Especially the old-timers. The younger ones are easy to spot—they still have pep in their step. These mill workers represent the changing demographics in this town, new immigrants mixing with those who were born in BC and grew up in and around the forestry and railway industries.

"That's him." I put on my cap, point. "The tall guy. Black hair."

Darsh Rai strides a head taller than the rest. His hair is glossy and wet with rain as it catches the light from the lamps along the causeway. We exit the car and make for him.

He aims toward the employee parking area.

"Darsh?" I call out as we approach.

He stills, turns. Emotions scurry across his face as he realizes it's me, the cop who found his dead cousin. He shoots a glance at Luke, and I introduce him.

"Are you here about Leena?" Darsh appears anxious. "Have you got results from the postmortem?"

"Is there somewhere we can talk out of the rain?" I ask.

He hesitates.

"How about over there?" Luke points to a picnic table under a wooden gazebo near the ferry café. I buy coffees, and we sit under the cover, listening to the rain as workers get into their vehicles and start for home. The nearby roar of the falls is loud out here.

"Do you have the cause of death?" Darsh asks.

"We don't have the official report yet," I say, "but Leena was drowned. I'm sorry, Darsh."

"Drowned." He repeats the word softly. His eyes glisten in the reflected light. "Why would someone drown my little cousin?" His features harden. "Was she sexually assaulted?"

"There is trauma consistent with sexual assault," I say. "We're waiting on lab results to ascertain whether there was semen present."

His hands fist upon the picnic table. His mouth flattens. He looks away. I can see his pulse beating in his neck. His muscles are tight. He's an image of bottled rage and pain. A powerful, passionate powder keg of a young man. His volatility is almost tangible in the damp air.

"Darsh," Luke says, leaning forward, his arms on the picnic table, "we need to ask you some questions. Is that okay?"

"Yeah. Go ahead."

"You were close to your younger cousin?"

He nods and looks away again, clearly struggling to compose himself. Slowly he turns back to face us. "People misunderstood Leena."

"How so?" Luke asks.

"All she wanted was to be liked, to be respected. Maybe admired a little."

"Leena told you that?" Luke asks.

What Darsh is saying echoes what Pratima said about her daughter. I let Luke run with the questions. It's giving him a read on Darsh Rai.

"She never said it in so many words," Darsh says. "But it was obvious. You could see."

"Because she wanted brand-name shoes?"

His eyes narrow. "The Nike sneakers? The ones I bought for her? The ones you found on the bank with Leena's bloody socks in them?" His voice gets louder. "You think *I* had something to do with her death? Is *that* what you're getting at?"

"I'm just trying to learn more about who your younger cousin was, Darsh," says Luke. "The more we can learn about a victim, the more we understand her movements, her thoughts, her friends—it can help us figure out what happened to her. For example, it could tell us why she was staggering along that bridge alone in the first place. And why Amy Chan didn't tell you that she'd just seen your cousin in trouble on Devil's Bridge when she and Jepp Sullivan ran into you at Ari's Greek Takeout. What was it that made Leena a target that night? Who might have singled her out? Or was it a crime of opportunity that presented itself, because she was—"

"Stop!" He slams his hands down on the table. "Please. Just . . . stop." He inhales deeply and rakes a hand through his damp, thick hair. "I'll tell you about Leena. My cousin wanted the Nike shoes because she wanted to wear what the other girls wore. Same brands. Same styles. She thought it would help her fit in. But her parents couldn't afford the brand-name clothes, so she had to wear the cheap stuff. She wanted to listen to the same music as the popular kids.

Watch the same movies . . . On summer evenings, when the weather was nice, she would wait for me here at the ferry dock, and she'd beg me to take her for a drive in my yellow Porsche convertible—which I basically rebuilt myself. She loved that car. She'd want me to put the top down, and she'd ask me to drive us past the Dairy Queen on the main road where all the cool kids hang out on some afternoons. She'd plead with me to drive by three or four times in a row. With the music blaring, bass thumping." His voice hitches. He rubs his jaw, struggling to compose himself.

"So I did it. Drove her up and down past the Dairy Queen, even though it was so obviously pathetic. Everyone could see what she was trying to do—I mean, who drives up and down past Dairy Queen four or five times in a row? Leena just wanted to be one hundred percent certain that the popular girls saw her with me. And that boys like Darren and Johnny and Jepp saw her in the Porsche." He pauses. "I'm sure everyone has told you by now that Leena did stupid, stupid things, and that she had no idea how desperate it made her look. Sometimes . . . she just had trouble reading people."

"Yet you indulged her," Luke says. "You gave her shelter when she ran away last year. You bought her nice stuff."

"It's the least I could do. Her father . . . he's very strict. And I mean very. Her mother . . . Pratima just does what Jaswinder wants. Like I said, they don't have much money. Jaswinder drives a bus and Pratima doesn't work."

"And you have money?"

He makes a scoffing sound. "Would I do this job if I had money to burn? Would I go to that stinking pulp mill, breathe in those fumes, feed those logs into stripping machines day after day, if I didn't need the income? I get some nice extra cash on the side for my hobby repairing and remodeling cars, though. I have dreams, like Leena had dreams, of getting out of here one day. We share—shared—a cultural heritage steeped in traditions that don't always fit this place we're in now. So it's not easy, you know, in a town like this. Just look around you. Me? I understood Leena's loneliness. Maybe I needed her friendship, because she understood me in the context of my background. We're family. We stand by each other."

I hear his bitterness. I hear love. I see a young man fighting for some ideal. Darsh in some ways is like Twin Falls itself, struggling with bringing a past into the present, and looking into the future as it diversifies. And sometimes this causes conflict. In more ways than one.

"So yeah, if you think Leena's oddness made her a victim, it did. She was always on the outside of the pack, trying to get in. And not wanted. And the harder she tried, the more ridiculous she could look, and the more fun people would make of her. So if she was alone on that bridge that night, it doesn't surprise me, and it shouldn't surprise anyone. She didn't have the best judgment. And if she'd been drinking . . ." His voice fades. Then he says, "Amy should have told me. Maybe she'd be alive if I'd been told." Another long pause. "I'm pissed at Amy."

I say, "You were at the Ullr sacrifice, Darsh. When Leena didn't return home, you told police that you'd seen her there."

"Yeah." He rubs his face, clearly tired.

"Why did you go that night?"

"To the bonfire? Everyone went. To meet girls. Get wasted. Get high. Chill. Be seen. Not much else exciting happens in town."

"Who did you go with?"

"Why are you asking me this?"

Luke says, "It's about getting as full a picture as possible of that night, and the events that could have led to your cousin's death."

He moistens his lips. "I drove up to the grove where the bonfire was held with a couple of my friends who work in town. We went in my car. We got there about eight. I did see Leena, and I tried to talk to her, but she went the other way and got lost in the crowd."

"Did you see her with a guy?" I ask.

"I did, briefly. On the other side of the dancing crowd. It was dark, though, and she was in shadows, near the forest, on a log with him. I didn't register who he was."

"But it was a he?"

Darsh nods. "That's what I assumed. Tall. Big dark jacket. A black hat, and black scarf that kinda hid his face. Gloves. It was really cold, and everyone came dressed warm. Thing is, I was happy to see her with someone. Happy that she wasn't actually going to try and latch on to me that night."

"And cramp your style," says Luke.

Darsh glowers at him. "Yeah. Exactly. And I will live to regret it for the rest of my life, okay? But Natalia was there, and I was hoping that would be the night where she and I got together. So I hung with her and her friends, and forgot all about my little cousin." He holds Luke's gaze. "And now she's dead."

Luke regards him steadily. Time stretches. Wind gusts and rain blows at us. It's getting colder and I'm beginning to shiver.

"Who is Natalia?" Luke says finally.

"Natalia Petrov," I say. "She's from Russia. She lives at the group home with her little sister, Nina, who is in Leena's grade. Nina knows Maddy. The sisters lost their parents in a car accident a year ago."

"Yeah," says Darsh. "Natalia works at the Chans' grocery store downtown, and she's always looking after her little sister. Are we done now? Because I'd like to get home."

"What time did you leave the bonfire, Darsh?" Luke asks.

"Right after the rocket in the sky. Natalia had work early the next morning, and she wanted to be up early. I gave her and Nina a ride back to the group home, and then I went to Ari's Greek Takeout to meet up with Tripp Galloway."

"Thanks, Darsh," I say. "And again, I'm so sorry to bring you bad news."

"Yeah. Whatever." He gets up from the bench and stalks off into the rainy darkness without another word. We watch him go.

Luke checks the time. "We should get back to the station. The copies of those journal pages should have come in by now. Want to grab some takeout on the way?"

I hesitate. I'm exhausted. Maddy and Jake are waiting for me to join them for supper. Or, more likely, they're waiting for me to make supper. I'll need to phone them from the station, tell them I'll be working late. "Sure," I say. "There's a Mexican place on the way."

As we get back into the vehicle, I say, "Have you got a place to stay locally?"

He grunts. "Yeah. Super Saver Motel." He opens his notebook and scribbles something down.

I start the car and reverse out of the parking spot.

His gaze flicks toward me. And I feel my cheeks heat for my even thinking about where he will sleep after he clocks out for the day.

If one ever clocks out of a murder investigation.

RACHEL

When I finally arrive home after examining copies of the ripped journal pages with Luke and Tucker, I find Jake drinking beer in front of the television. He's watching a hockey game. The sound is loud. His socked feet are up on the coffee table, and I can see three empty beer bottles on the little table beside him in addition to the one in his hand.

"Hey," he says without looking at me.

I shrug out of my jacket. "Who's playing?"

"What?"

Louder, I say, "Who's playing?"

"Canucks and Oilers." Still he doesn't look at me.

I hang up my jacket. There are dirty dishes in the kitchen sink. I see only one plate, one set of utensils.

"What did you guys have for dinner?"

He glances over his shoulder. From the flush on his face it's obvious he's had a few. "Leftovers, like you suggested when you called."

"Just you?"

"Mads called to say she was going to be late."

"Where is she?"

"Beth's—she said something about working on a project." He turns back to the game as one of the teams scores. He whoops, pumps his fist in the air, then takes another swig from his bottle.

A bolt of irritation slides through me.

Thanks, honey, yes, my day was rough. Thank you for asking about the autopsy. You knew how anxious I was about attending the postmortem of a girl the same age as our daughter. Her classmate. Talking to her parents. The investigation into a local child's sexual assault and her beating and drowning is heavy going, thank you. You know how hard I'm working to prove I can fill my dad's shoes down the road, how he told me before he died that it was his fervent wish for me to become chief.

But I'm partly to blame for Jake's indifference. I've helped cultivate this distance between Jake and myself because I often work cases that I can't really talk about. Especially in a small town like this. Sometimes, after a rough day, I also just want to sit and have a drink, and be silent, and process. Or watch some mind-numbing show while my body and brain take a breather. Sometimes—especially when I'm tired—the weight of my father's ambition for me feels too onerous, as though he's set the bar too high, and I struggle with what I perceive as resentment among some at the PD.

I open the fridge, grab a bottle of white wine. I pour a glass, take a deep sip, then another. The warmth through my chest is a relief. I top up my drink, put the bottle back into the fridge, and make for the stairs.

"I'm going to run a bath," I call to Jake.

"Yeah." Another score. Another whoop. I'm not sure which is better. His ignoring me or the affair he had a few months back. My husband says he has stopped seeing the other woman, but it seems he's replaced his vice with beer and TV, and it feels like he's punishing *me* for having called him out for sleeping with someone else.

Upstairs, I use the phone in the bedroom to call Eileen Galloway. Beth's mother is a purchasing manager for the Twin Falls hospital.

We're also mountain-biking buddies. I take another sip of wine as Eileen picks up.

"Eileen, hi, it's Rachel. Is Maddy at your place?"

"No. Beth is alone, upstairs studying."

I hesitate. But then I think of Sarah Chan's parting jab.

What about your *daughter, Rachel? Did* she *come home that night? . . . Or did she lie to you, too?*

"Listen, did Maddy sleep over at your place on the Friday night of the Ullr bonfire?"

"I . . . Beth told me she slept at *your* house."

"Okay. I . . . Thanks. I was just wondering."

"Rache, is . . . is this about . . . the Leena thing? Is everything okay? I'm so worried. Is it . . . Was she murdered? Or did she fall in drunk or something?"

I close my eyes, see the body floating. Velvet hair. An Ophelia in the black water. Leena being rolled over. The gut punch at seeing her bludgeoned face. I hear the wishful thinking in Eileen's question. No one wants to think there is a killer in our town. I reach for my drink, take another deep slug, and say, "It's a suspicious death, yes. We've brought in a guy with experience in homicide. We're working on finding who did this. And . . . I'm guessing at this point no kid went home from the bonfire. It seems from the debris left behind that some of them might have camped out there overnight, and no one's telling the truth about where they were."

"So it's definite that she was murdered?"

"It's an active homicide investigation. And . . . I really can't talk more about the case."

A beat of silence.

"Are you . . . Do you need me to help you find Maddy?" Eileen asks.

"She's probably at the library or something. I'll give her another hour." But we both know the library is closed at this time.

I hang up. Disquiet threads through me. Rain ticks and splats against the window. It sounds as though it's turning to sleet. I swallow the rest of my drink, set the glass down, and make for Maddy's room.

I hesitate at the closed door, my hand on the doorknob. The noise from the hockey game downstairs is loud. I hear no movement on the stairs. I inhale, open the door, click on the light, and enter my daughter's bedroom. I shut the door quietly behind me. I pause, absorbing the little-girl things Maddy still has in her possession. The teddy bear on her bed. The large, frilly pillow she got one Christmas years ago. A soft yellow blanket she can't part with. My heart squeezes. No matter how much we pretend otherwise—mothers, daughters, grandmothers—there is always a part of us deep down inside that remains the little girl we once were. Whether we are fifteen or forty or eighty, that little person still lurks beneath everything we do, or think, or try to become, or fight against. She's always there. My pain for Pratima Rai is suddenly acute. It steals my breath. My eyes prick with emotion. I know that emotion is partly generated by fatigue, and the wine. But God, what I'd do if that body had been Maddy's . . .

I go up to her dresser. Tentatively I touch the lacquered box with the gold clasp on top. I waver as a bolt of guilt washes through me. I shouldn't even be in here. Not like this. But a deeper, more powerful need forces me to open the box. Once it's open I am moving fast. Quickly I rummage through the trinkets and jewelry inside, opening and closing little boxes. I can't find it. I hear a car outside, and I freeze. Lights flare past the window. The car goes on.

I tip out the box, spreading all the necklaces and bracelets and rings over the top of the dresser. My skin goes hot. Maybe I missed it. It *has* to be here. But I cannot find it. I open her drawers, her closet, going through everything as fast as I can. Inside the small drawer beside her bed, I see a glossy photo. I pick it up, stare. A group of girls. Maddy among them. I recognize the others: Natalia Petrov, Seema Patel, Cheyenne Tillerson, Dusty Peters, Beth Galloway. It's been shot in the dark. A professional-looking image. Beautifully in focus, all of their faces. Pink cheeks. Behind them a massive bonfire roars, shooting orange sparks into the dark sky. I can see skis and snowboards burning among logs.

My pulse quickens. I swallow. This was shot at the bonfire.

"Mom!"

I spin around, gasp. "Maddy?"

"What in the hell? What are you *doing*?" She storms up to her dresser, stares at the scattered contents. Her mouth opens in shock. She glares at me, her backpack still on her shoulder. "What are you looking for? These are *my* things." She drops her backpack to the floor and starts scrabbling to gather her trinkets and jewels back together, tangling them in a pile, stuffing them back into the lacquered box. Her hands are shaking.

I touch her arm, trying to calm her. "Maddy, stop. Please. I can explain."

She shoves me away. Her long, dark hair—an echo of my own—smells of cigarette smoke. I also smell alcohol, and something sweet like strawberry.

"What the hell? What do you think you're doing? Why're you going through my things? How *dare* you?"

I stare at my girl. All I can think of is Leena. Snuffed out. Raped. Beaten to a pulp. Drowned. Tiny pebbles deep in her lungs. Her cut-out heart on a scale in the morgue.

Maddy's face changes as she reads something in mine. It dials her back a little. A look of wariness steals into her features.

"Mom? What's going on?"

"The locket that your grandmother gave you, the gift from her trip to Ireland, where is it?"

"What?"

"Just answer me, Maddy," I snap.

"What's the *matter* with you?"

"You always used to wear it. Where is it now?"

"I haven't worn it for ages."

"Maddy, *just tell me*! *Where in the hell is it?*" My voice comes out shrill. I'm coming unstrung. My heart races.

Fear widens Maddy's eyes. She glances at the door, as if she needs to ensure an escape avenue. "I . . . I don't know."

I struggle to tamp myself down. "What do you mean, you *don't know?*"

"I just told you, I haven't worn it for ages. Why are you even asking?"

"It was special—you used to think it was special. Because it was from your gran. And after she died you used to wear it all the time."

"I don't know where it is. I haven't worn it, and it's probably in my room somewhere. I just haven't seen it for a while, okay?"

I bite my lip.

"Besides, you have no right to come in here and do this. Why did you? Why didn't you just ask me?" Maddy returns to putting her trinkets back into the lacquered box. Then, as it seems to strike her, her hands go still. "Why are you asking about that locket anyway?"

"I was just thinking about your gran, and I needed to see it, that's all." I drag my hands over my hair. "Look, I'm sorry, Mads. I'm sorry— it's just been a rough few days."

"Whatever. Just don't do it again," she says quietly without meeting my gaze. "Now get out of my room."

"Where were you this evening?"

"I was with Beth."

"You weren't. I just spoke with Eileen."

She turns slowly to face me. I feel a chill at the look in her eyes. "You *called* her? To find out if I was lying?"

"Maddy—"

"You know what, it's none of your business. *You* didn't come home for supper, either."

"I have a job. Someone died—was murdered. A classmate of *yours*. There's still a killer out there, Maddy. Every parent in this town is worried about their girls being out alone in the dark right now, including me. Someone has to find out who did it, and lock him away. *That's* why I was late. And will be again. Until he's behind bars. And you lied to me about where you were. You're grounded. For one week. You go to school and come straight home. You understand?"

"Get out, Mom." She flings her arm toward the door. "Get the hell out of my room."

I exit. The door slams shut behind me. My heart pounds in my chest. I realize that I slid the photo of the girls into my pocket.

RACHEL

About ten minutes after I left Maddy and Darren's place, I pull into the gravel parking lot at the top of a logging road high above the valley and town below. The lot is empty. I'm surrounded by towering cedars, hemlocks, spruce, and mountain peaks draped with tattered clouds. It's cold. Wet. But the sky has clear spots, and when the sun pokes through, it offers some warmth.

I pull on my biking gloves, wondering if Maddy has listened to the podcast yet and whether Trinity will contact her for an interview. Perhaps Trinity has tried already. I wouldn't put it past Maddy to pretend she hadn't. I shrug into my waterproof jacket, grab my helmet off the passenger seat, and exit the truck. The sound of the nearby river is loud. It's swollen as it thunders through the gorge. As I take my bike out of the back of my truck, Eileen's red Volvo wagon pulls up, her tires crunching on the gravel. She parks next to me.

Beth's mom is sixty-three now. Three years older than I am, but she's still a firecracker of energy and whip fit. Eileen powers down her window and pops out her head of strawberry-blonde curls. When she started going gray, Eileen began dyeing her hair, and her once deep-red mop is now a more muted shade.

"Hey, woman," she says brightly. "How in the hell are you, and why have we waited so long to do this again, huh?"

I laugh. She has that effect. Her effervescence is contagious.

"Yeah, well, farming keeps me busy," I say as I set my bike down and the tires give a small bounce on the gravel.

She gets out of her Volvo, starts taking her mountain bike off the rack on the back. Wind gusts. Eileen's hair blows. I think of Beth, who looks like her dad and not at all like her mom. Beth is willowy tall and almost white blonde. Her once-waist-long hair is as straight as a pin. Beth is married to Johnny, Granger's son. She and Maddy used to be the tightest of friends, but they gradually grew apart over the years since the murder of their classmate. No one was left untouched, and we're all still inextricably linked to that past.

I feel uneasy as I watch Eileen and consider how to broach the topic of the podcast with her. I figure I'll do it once we have some miles in our legs.

The trail starts out easy—nice and undulating on a firm bed of needles and packed dirt. I feel my limbs warming and my body limbering up as the trail begins to twist and climb toward a campsite that lies along the shores of Lake Wuyakan. I'm out of breath in no time. My muscles burn and my chest heaves. There's no room for talk now, and it feels good this way.

Not long after a super-steep pitch, we reach the campsite and the turquoise waters of the lake. Panting, sweating, we stop. I unclip my water bottle, take a swig, and grin.

"Feels good, right?" says Eileen, unclipping her own bottle. She points it at me. "You and Granger should come on our group rides. We're still meeting every Saturday, at least until it starts snowing." She takes a deep swallow of water. "The late snow this year has been a gift. Maybe we'll . . ." She sees something in my face. "You okay? Too much too soon?"

I replace the cap on my water bottle. Hesitate, then say, "You haven't heard about the podcast yet, have you?"

I've known Eileen since our girls were in kindergarten. That's how I met her. She'd have mentioned it off the bat if she knew. Outspoken Eileen never minces her words, or her thoughts. She takes no prisoners, pulls no punches.

"What podcast?" she asks, slowly closing her water bottle as her gaze holds mine.

I tell her. "The first two episodes are already live. Apparently Trinity Scott will be loading new ones as soon as they're ready."

"You have got to be kidding me."

"'Fraid not. And Clay Pelley is talking. Trinity is doing a series of interviews with him. Apparently, according to the blurb on the *It's Criminal* website, he's granted her twenty-minute sessions until she gets what she needs from him."

Eileen pales. "You listened? You *heard* him? His voice?"

"He claims he didn't kill Leena."

"Oh, you cannot be serious . . . Are you serious?" She stares at me. I watch her face intently. I think of our girls, and how the stress of that time seems to have jabbed a wedge between them, and they were never again as close.

"Yeah, Eileen, I'm joking. I've always been such a big joker."

"This asshole was our kids' basketball coach. He was their guidance counselor. He was the prick who provided them with health informa- tion that included *sex* education, drug and alcohol abuse prevention. He was supposed to tutor them in healthy lifestyles, emotional health, antibullying . . . and he was a freaking perverted alcoholic pedophile himself!"

I say nothing.

She looks away, out over the still waters of the lake. Her chest rises and falls as her breath comes out in rapid puffs of white. Finally, quietly, she says, "Is that why you invited me for a ride?"

"No. I needed to burn off some steam after listening to him. After thinking about it all again." I pause.

She turns to face me.

"I needed a friend." I give a half shrug. "And they say you shouldn't ride alone."

She gives a soft snort.

"And I couldn't not tell you."

"Yeah. Yeah, I see." She glances at the lake again and is silent for a long while. "So this podcast is online? I can go listen?"

I nod. Take another swig.

Wind ripples suddenly across the incredible blue surface of the lake. Like a sign. A warning. I notice another sort of warning, this one nailed to the tree behind Eileen:

BEWARE. COUGARS IN AREA. KEEP SMALL CHILDREN CLOSE.

She follows my gaze and smiles. "A selfie?" she asks. "Of us two cougars. In front of the sign, for Instagram."

I climb off my bike and wheel it over to the tree. I prop it against the trunk, and we put our heads close together. We fake-grin with wide-open mouths, like we're doing something way cool. Eileen makes a rock-on sign with her index and pinkie fingers raised as she clicks.

"It should say, 'Caution, jaguars in the area,'" I say as she pockets her smartphone. "Because we ain't no cougars."

"You mean panthers. Isn't it panthers for over sixty?"

I laugh and straddle my bike. Slowly I begin to cycle back toward the trail while Eileen mounts her bike. My thoughts turn to the photograph I kept in my box, of our two daughters and their friends at the bonfire that night twenty-four years ago, and I think how different it was in those days before every kid had a cell phone. Before everything was captured or recorded for social media. How much easier it was to hide things.

"Does Maddy know?" Eileen calls out from behind me.

"Yeah," I yell over my shoulder. "I told her on my way here."

We fall silent as we pedal harder and the incline grows steeper and the switchbacks sharper. I know Eileen is wondering if Beth and Tripp, her son, know. And Johnny.

I, too, wonder if Johnny knows—whether Granger has informed his son. Or if he'd even bother, since clearly Granger believes Trinity and Clay Pelley are wasting our energy.

Whether we like it or not, Trinity Scott is going to dredge up bad memories. Her podcast is going to be like a big rock hurled into a still pond, and the impact will ripple through people in this town who thought they'd moved on. As the pitch grows steeper and I pedal harder, I wonder just how big those ripples could get.

REVERB

THE RIPPLE EFFECT

NOW

re·verb

/'rē͵vərb, ri'vərb/

noun

To a producer or a sound engineer, reverb—short for reverberation—is an acoustic phenomenon, or audio effect. Put simply, reverb happens when a sound or signal bounces off various surfaces in a room, causing numerous reflections to reach the listener's ear so closely together that they cannot interpret them as individual delays. This result is magnified in larger rooms, where it appears that the sound continues long after the source has stopped . . . But in true crime podcasting, reverb can also refer to the story itself.

—Gio Rossi, *Toronto Times* interview

When you investigate a crime in real time, on air, you have this problem of reverb. The reporting you do today will influence the interviews and responses you get tomorrow, because your subject will have heard your episode, and will know your doubts, and suspicions, and theories, and thoughts. They will know what others have told you. And it will influence what they in turn tell you. That's fine for fiction, but it's a serious problem from a journalistic standpoint, the telling of a story influencing the story as it's unfolding. It's bait and switch. It's unfair to the listener. You have your footprints and fingerprints all over the story in a very postmodern way. The risk with that—the reason news organizations don't do it—is that you'll find inconsistencies. You'll find people lied to you. You'll find you overlooked a piece of information, and you may have to reassess or revamp your story. I'm not saying it's unethical per se, just that there are these potential pitfalls.

—Mark Pattinson, journalism professor,
on the ethics of true crime podcasting

Thursday, November 18. Present day.

Maddy is in her home office. She fingers the business card her mother left on the kitchen counter as she listens to the first podcast episode. The sound of the voice she once knew sucks her down, down, down, into the past, back into her schoolgirl persona . . . all the way back to that night of the Ullr fire.

CLAYTON: What I want the world to know, Trinity Scott, is yes, we all have our darkness. That shadow. Even you.

But I did *not* sexually assault Leena Rai. And I did not kill her.

TRINITY: If . . . if you didn't, who did?

GUARD: Time's up, Pelley. Come on, let's go.

CLAYTON: Whoever did, her killer is still out there.

THE SOUND OF A DOOR SHUTTING. MUFFLED LAUGHTER.

Mr. Pelley's words echo in her head, bouncing back louder each time.

Her killer is still out there.
Her killer is still out there.
Her killer is still out there.

"Maddy?"

She jumps, spins her chair around. Darren is in the room. Standing just inside the doorway. He's been listening. The look in his eyes makes her scared.

"What if he *didn't* do it?" Darren says. His voice sounds strange. "And like Trinity Scott says, if he didn't, who did?"

"This is stupid!" Maddy flings her arm toward the speaker. "This is so fucking stupid. It's gratuitous. It's exploitative. He's flat-out lying, and that Trinity woman—she knows it. She *has* to know it. And she's making a story out of his lies, sensationalizing it all. And I'll tell you what—she got one thing right. *It's Criminal* is criminal. Her whole bloody podcast is criminal. You shouldn't be allowed to do shit like that. It's defamatory. Libelous."

"She hasn't defamed anyone if—"

"Not yet. But she's laid the groundwork for new theories on who did it, all based on a sociopath's lies. And in so doing, she's going to start raising unfounded suspicions about people in this town. People we know. People who still live here."

"Will you talk to her, when she calls? Because it's just a matter of when, not if."

Maddy regards Darren. "I . . . Will *you?*"

He smooths his hand over his hair. "Maybe cooperating will be better than not talking. Look at how your mother is going to come across if she refuses to be interviewed. It's going to appear as though she has something to hide. It might be better if she *did* tell her side, explain how the investigation unfolded. At least if we all give our sides of the story, it'll set Trinity straight. The fewer people who talk, the more it's going to fuel a person like her. And the more listeners will buy into the idea there was some conspiracy."

Maddy holds her husband's gaze. Tension is thick in the room. It feels as though a paradigm has shifted, and the world they were once comfortable in—or complacent about—no longer offers the same guardrails.

Across town, Johnny Forbes listens to the Leena Rai podcast as he runs errands en route to the brewery where he works. His mind turns to the military surplus jacket the divers couldn't find. He wonders if what he always thought to be true is maybe not true at all. Perhaps he's been comfortably hiding from the real questions all these years. Perhaps it's because it was just easier to bury his head in the sand. Perhaps they all have. He pulls into the parking lot of the Raven's Roost pub to check how much beer the establishment needs to order. The building is just up the street from the brewery, and he can see his father's Harley parked outside.

Inside the pub, Johnny finds Rex Galloway, his father-in-law, talking quietly across the bar counter with Johnny's dad, Granger. They're drinking coffees.

"Johnny?" Granger says as both he and Rex look up. "What are you doing here?"

Johnny nods to their mugs. "Checking in on your order. Seems I'm just in time to join you guys for a coffee."

As Rex pours him one, Johnny seats himself on a stool beside his father. "You guys hear about the podcast?" he says, taking a sip from his mug.

"We were just talking about it," Rex says.

Granger adds, "Rachel is pretty pissed about it. And at me, for trying to keep it from her."

"You did?" asks Johnny.

"That case led her down a bad path all those years ago. Even she will admit that. I didn't want her to start reliving it all blow by blow." Granger finishes his coffee, sets the mug down. "It was misguided of me. Of course she was going to find out. And now I've made it worse." He gives a rueful smile. "So I'm giving her space to cool off."

"Do you believe what Clay Pelley says?" Johnny asks.

"He's a liar," says Granger. "And he's a sick man. Always has been."

"No kidding," adds Rex. But he looks uneasy. Johnny feels disquiet, too.

Two blocks over, in the industrial part of town near the old log sorting yard, Darsh Rai listens to the podcast on a speaker as he tinkers under a vehicle in the auto shop he now owns. Ganesh appears in the garage doorway. Ganesh now works for him. He's a younger, even more handsome echo of both Darsh and his father, Jaswinder. Ganesh's eyes burn hot and angry beneath his thick black hair.

"Why in the hell is she doing this, putting us all through this again? There should be a law against this. Does she not know what this did to our family? To my mother, my father?" Ganesh asks.

Darsh rolls out from under the car, comes to his feet, and wipes oil from his hands. He reaches for his phone on the workbench and hits the STOP button. "Maybe Clayton Pelley *didn't* do it. Wouldn't you want to know for sure? I mean, there wasn't even a trial. Why was that?"

Ganesh's gaze locks on his cousin's. He steps closer. "You can't be serious."

Darsh tosses the oil rag onto the workbench. "I don't know what to think. But part of me is glad she's opening this all up again. I've always believed those cops dropped the ball. Trinity Scott is right. There were too many loose ends just left hanging in the wind when that bastard confessed and pleaded guilty. There's more to this. I've always known there's more to this."

In a different part of town, Liam Parks, who runs Parks Photography and Design, climbs the ladder to his attic after listening to the podcast episodes. Up inside the attic space, he dusts off a storage box and opens it. Out of it he takes some old prints that he developed in the school lab. He sifts through them. Images of faces locked in time. Classmates. Girls. Boys. Laughing, smiling, partying. Playing sports. At school dances. In the hallways. He comes across the pile he was looking for. Images he shot on that night they all saw a rocket fall in pieces through the sky. He finds the one he's after. A group of girls, laughing, arms around each other. He shot them in front of the bonfire that night. He stares at the youthful faces, the pretty smiles. Memories shimmer to life—memories that make him uncomfortable.

He wonders what he should do with these images now.

Jaswinder Rai sits alone in his heavily silent living room. It's dusty. He should clean it. Pratima always took care of things like that. He's so lost without her. He stares at the photos on the mantel. Pratima died two years ago. She choked on food in a restaurant. Perhaps it was because nothing was easy for her to swallow after their baby girl was brutally assaulted and killed. He's relieved Pratima doesn't have to hear this podcast. It would have been too cruel. But a part of Jaswinder is edgy. Clayton Pelley's raspy voice crawls through his head, as if echoing and bouncing off other thoughts in there, getting louder and louder.

I did not kill her . . . her killer is still out there.

Clayton Jay Pelley lies on his back in his prison bunk, his hands hooked behind his head as he listens again to Trinity's voice through the buds in his ears. He's listened to the podcast episodes over and over and over. He can't get enough of listening. Of hearing her voice. He thinks of all the things he might have done right in his life, and of all the things he has done wrong. But there's one thought, one feeling, that surfaces above them all. He's regained some autonomy. He's wrested back a degree of control over things, over people. Even from inside this miserable institution of rules and bars and gates and barbed wire. Once more he feels a sense of power. He smiles. It's been a long, long time since he's had this feeling.

This is now in his control.

RACHEL

"Nanaimo bars!" proclaims Detective Dirk Rigg with a flourish as he saunters into the Twin Falls PD conference room carrying a plate of dessert bars. Tucker enters behind Dirk, ferrying a tray of takeout coffees.

Dirk sets the plate down on the table and removes the cling wrap covering the iconic custard-and-chocolate-ganache bars. I get a whiff of the stale cigarette smoke that always clings to his clothing. When it's combined with the strong smell of the coffee, the airless room suddenly feels nauseating.

Or perhaps I'm just unwell after the long day yesterday that started with the autopsy and ended with my fight with Maddy.

"Merle is trying to quit smoking again," says Dirk, helping himself to a Nanaimo bar. "So naturally we now have way too many baked goods in the house, and extra pounds adding up on the scale." He gestures for everyone to take one, and he bites into his bar, talking around his custardy mouthful as he takes a seat at the conference table. "I figured you guys could do with some breakfast, since we have so much."

Luke reaches for a bar.

"Merle is Dirk's wife," I explain to Luke. "She's worked at the post office forever. She's also always trying to quit smoking, but the fact Dirk smokes makes it hard, right, Dirk?"

He grins. "She's trying hypnosis to quit the habit this time." He pops the rest of the custardy goop into his mouth and reaches for his coffee.

It's very early morning, and outside it's still dark and snowing softly, dusting everything white that was black and gray and dying. I'm worried about my kid. I need to be here and want to be here. I also want things to be normal and happy at home. When I knocked on Maddy's bedroom door before I left this morning, she told me to go away. I made her breakfast and left it on the kitchen counter. I check my watch. She's probably not even up yet. Jake promised to make dinner for her tonight if I'm late again. My thoughts go again to the locket her gran gave her as a gift a few years ago.

The locket that is missing.

Chief Ray Doyle strides into the room, his girth preceding him. He carries an armful of files. "Morning, everyone." He plops the files down at the head of the table and takes a seat. Behind Ray's chair is a whiteboard that Luke wheeled in. He's using it as a crime board. It reminds me of every detective show on TV. We've never used one, but Luke seems attached to the form. Perhaps it's a homicide thing.

Tucker sits opposite me. He's silently nursing his coffee. His complexion looks gray under the unflattering fluorescent lights in the room. One of the lights flickers ever so faintly. I believe I can hear it emitting an electronic buzz. This part is not at all like TV. This kind of scene would be depicted in moody, shaded lighting. But policing in this tiny detachment is all harsh lights, stains on the ceiling, an ever-present scent of dampness, and faded blue squares of carpet beneath our boots.

"Nanaimo bar, Chief?" Dirk pushes the plate toward Ray.

Ray helps himself, bites into his bar, and opens the top file folder in front of him. "Okay, what've we got, guys? Rachel?" he says around his mouthful.

"The autopsy report is still to come, but the cause of death is drowning." I get up and go to the whiteboard.

I point to one of the autopsy photos. "These circular marks on her shoulders here are consistent with someone having straddled the victim to hold her down underwater." I explain the rest of the postmortem findings, the stones in her lungs. "Dr. Backmann says that if Leena had not been drowned, the blunt force trauma and the resultant swelling of her brain would have resulted in her death anyway."

"Anything found at the scene that could have been used as a weapon?" asks Ray.

"We found no weapon, but the victim's body is imprinted with two patterns of a shoe, or boot. Size eleven. Someone stomped on her and kicked her." I point to another photo on the board. "And there was bark found in her skin here—on her face and head. The forensic ident guys also found blood on the trunk of a cedar tree growing on the north bank of the river, near where Leena's Nike shoe and bloodied sock were located. The cedar bark on the tree looks to be a match to the bark pieces found in Leena's skin. We anticipate lab results will prove the match. And we anticipate the blood evidence on the cedar will be a match to Leena's blood."

"You're saying she went head—face—first into a tree trunk?" Dirk asks.

"She could have been forced headfirst into the tree," Luke says. "Multiple times."

Dirk whistles softly and reaches for another Nanaimo bar. Tucker looks ill.

I point to another photo. "This is an image of the shoe, or boot, imprint. We have techs running through the sole patterns of various brands. The goal is to identify the brand. And then try to match the brand and size to a potential suspect. There are also indications of aggressive sex—vaginal penetration and some tearing. So far there's no evidence of semen present, so it's possible a condom was used. We're also awaiting lab results on hairs and fibers, from nail scrapings and from the blood on the sock, plus the blood evidence that was found on her backpack strap."

Ray takes a sip of his coffee and says, "So the victim's backpack, and what appears to be contents from the pack, were found on the south bank, but her Nike shoe and sock were found on the north bank, where the bloodied cedar tree is?"

"Correct," I say. "Amy Chan witnessed Leena stumbling northward along Devil's Bridge around two a.m. Amy claims Leena was not carrying a backpack at that point. Leena could have left it on the south bank for some reason, or had it ripped from her there."

Tucker clears his throat and says, "So if she was on the south bank and lost her backpack and contents there, why was she going north? Just . . . confused? Drunk?"

"Or she wasn't stumbling because she was drunk," offers Luke. "Perhaps she was stumbling because she'd already sustained a violent attack and was in severe pain, or shock."

Silence hangs. A chill seems to enter the room despite the heaters blasting.

"Was there anyone else seen on the bridge?" Ray asks. "Following her?"

"Amy didn't see anyone else. But she also stated that she was under the influence herself, and distracted, unfocused," I say. "It's possible Leena was drunk, lost her backpack on the south bank, but then ran into real trouble on the north side. Either when she came across someone, or perhaps someone in a vehicle saw her and stopped."

"Perhaps she stumbled down the path that led under Devil's Bridge on the north side because she was drunk and disoriented and looking for her pack, and that's where she encountered someone," Dirk says.

"Any signs of a blood trail on the bridge?" asks Ray.

Luke says, "Too much time, too much heavy rain, too much traffic over the bridge in the week before she was found."

"We got video footage of the onlookers that lined the bridge the day the divers found her body," I say. "Tucker will be going through the footage today to see if anything unusual jumps out. There's also the CCTV coverage from outside Ari's Greek Takeout, where Amy Chan and Jepp Sullivan joined a group of other kids who'd also been at the bonfire. All those kids would have had to have crossed Devil's Bridge at some point to get from the bonfire to Ari's takeout. Perhaps someone saw something they didn't realize was important at the time." I glance at Luke. "Luke and I will be heading up to the school this morning. We'll be reinterviewing all the students who saw Leena at the bonfire. The last time we canvassed them, it was in the context of a missing persons case. We need to talk to them all again. This time Luke will handle the interviews. I'll observe, take notes." I clear my throat. "It'll offer a fresh eye, a fresh perspective."

"We need to know more about the male who Leena was apparently seen with in the grove," Luke says. "We need an ID on him. We need to talk to him." Luke points his pen at the image of the journal pages on the board. "And we need to know who the 'He' is that Leena mentions in those ripped journal pages. We need to figure out why the journal was ripped like that. Were the pages already torn, and inside her pack before being dumped out? Did Leena do something with the rest of the journal herself? If so, where is it? And where's the military surplus jacket she was wearing, because Amy Chan stated that Leena was wearing it when she was stumbling without her backpack northward along the bridge."

Dirk wipes custard off his stubbled chin. "And there's the address book. Plus the poetry book and that locket."

"Leena's parents claim the address book and locket are not hers," I say. "Her mother said Leena used to steal or borrow things without permission. We'll be showing students the images of the address book, the poetry book, the locket, and the other items we found in an effort to locate the rightful owners." I inhale deeply. "We also need to find out who started the rumor that Leena's body was floating in the Wuyakan River."

"Was there anything inside the locket?" Ray asks.

"Negative," says Luke. "We'll see what forensics shows up."

I glance at him. "Like what?"

He looks up from his notes and frowns at me. "Like prints, microscopic fibers, blood evidence. I'd also like to run a background check on the father. And we should keep an eye on the cousin, Darsh."

"Whoa," says Tucker. "You don't think . . . Her cousin? Or her own *father* had anything to do with this?"

"The violence to her face—it feels personal to me," Luke says. "It smacks of rage. Temper. That girl wasn't just killed, her face was smashed out of existence. And from observing Jaswinder, and listening to Darsh talk about his uncle . . . I hope I'm wrong, but I get a feeling Jaswinder Rai could be pushed too far if his convictions are challenged."

"But there's the sexual assault," says Ray.

Luke says, "We should keep an open mind."

I recall the words of the gaggle of girls who passed below the bleachers in the gym on that day I sat beside Leena.

Just watch her father go and blame me for blocking her . . . He's scary. Have you seen his eyes? I bet he has one of those curved knives to go with his turban.

I think about the bruising I saw around Leena's wrist.

Silence presses into the room. Outside, a pale dawn seeps into the sky. Behind the veil of falling snow and fingers of mist, Chief Mountain gleams wet.

"Right," says Ray, closing his folder and coming to his feet. "Let's get to it. Media pressure is on. I'll be making a statement to the press later this morning."

RACHEL

As Luke and I enter the Twin Falls Secondary School foyer, Clay Pelley, the guidance counselor and sports coach, comes striding down the hallway toward us. He's in his twenties. Good-looking. Fit. Tanned. A head of wild curls that lend him a devilish or mischievous air.

"Rachel." He shakes my hand, then turns to Luke. "And you must be Detective Sergeant O'Leary? I'm Clay Pelley." But as he shakes Luke's hand, I notice Clay stiffens and winces slightly, and I see that the back of Clay's right hand is bruised, with cuts that are healing but still red. My gaze goes to his left hand. I see the same on his knuckles.

"I wish we were meeting under better circumstances," he says. "Our principal, Darla Wingate, is on a conference call, so she's asked me to show you into the classroom we've set aside for the interviews. It's this way."

We follow Clay Pelley down a corridor lined with lockers. We pass the entrance to the gym, and I hear the thuds of bouncing balls and the squeaks of gym shoes on the lacquered floor.

"We've commandeered this room." He shows us in. "It's the one I use for CAPP classes—the education ministry's Career and Personal Planning course. Feel free to use any one of these tables. We have the list of names that you sent us, and I'll have the kids brought in one by one as you're done with them." He hesitates. "Are you sure they don't need parents present?"

"It's just a canvass at this point," says Luke. "Just trying to see who all was where at the bonfire. If we need to question anyone further, we can do that at the station with a guardian present." Luke sets his folders and notebook on a table and pulls out a chair, and he nods at Clay's hands. "Your hands look sore."

Clay holds them up and examines the backs. "Oh. Yeah." He laughs. "Stacking logs a few days ago. I ordered a cord of firewood for the winter, and as I was stacking the wood, one of the logs at the bottom of the pile released. When I tried to stop the others from rolling down, I got my hands caught between logs. Stupid move."

"Gloves might help," Luke says, holding Clay's gaze.

Clay's smile fades. "Yeah, well, I'll send in the first student. The list is alphabetical, so I'll send them in that order. I believe you've already spoken with Amy Chan, so I'll start with—"

"You're the guidance counselor who Amy Chan talked to about having seen Leena on Devil's Bridge?" Luke asks.

Clay is stopped in his tracks. "Yes. I . . . Amy came to talk to me after she heard the rumors about Leena being in the river. We approached the principal together. And Darla called Amy's mother, Sarah, who came to fetch Amy, and then took her to the police station to make a statement." He turns his gaze to me, then back to Luke, as if sensing something. "Leena was a good kid." He clears his throat. "She had issues, sure, but what teen doesn't? Leena might have done some silly things. She might have been emotionally and socially arrested in many ways, but she was smart. Talented writer. She wanted to travel. Volunteer."

"So you knew her fairly well, then?" asks Luke.

"She was in my CAPP class. And she was on the basketball team I coached. Plus I tutored her from my home office. English lit. She'd advanced two grades in English, and she wanted to do even better. Her dream was a career around writing, and literature." He pauses. Luke regards him in silence. Clay talks again, as if trying to fill the space. "I do tutoring for several kids. Outside of school. I . . . uh . . . Let me know if you need anything else. Meanwhile, I'll send in Johnny Forbes first."

We seat ourselves at the small table, and Johnny walks into the room. He's tall, almost six feet. Gangly. Sandy hair. Angular features. Good-looking kid. Wearing jeans and a hoodie. He takes a seat, slouches, and stuffs his hands into his hoodie pockets. He starts jiggling his leg.

Johnny is clearly nervous.

"Hi, Johnny, do you know who I am?" I say.

"Yeah. Maddy's mom."

I give him a smile. "Sergeant Rachel Walczak."

His leg jiggles faster. He keeps glancing sideways at Luke. Perhaps it's the presence of the big-city homicide cop that unnerves the kid.

"And this is Sergeant Luke O'Leary. He's from the RCMP, and he's helping with the case. He's going to be asking the questions."

"Are you okay, Johnny?" Luke asks. "Want some water or anything?"

"No, I . . . I'm good." He wipes the back of his hand over his mouth.

Luke asks Johnny to describe the scene at the bonfire. The story is the same as when I first canvassed the kids after Leena initially went missing. Festive atmosphere. Lots of drinking, some drugs. Loud music from boom boxes and amplifiers. Big bonfire with burning skis and snowboards. Plenty of excitement.

"I was hanging in a group, but also mixing around, dancing and stuff. And yeah, there was lots of drinking. I saw Leena, yes, but I don't know who she came with. She was just there. Like all the other kids were there, you know? She was drunk. Really drunk. Wearing this big coat."

"In your earlier statement to the police, you said you saw Leena with someone." Luke reads from Johnny's statement in his file. "You said, 'Leena was with some guy.'"

"Well, I didn't really see who the guy was. Not like in a way that I would recognize him."

"But you *did* see her with a male?"

Johnny gives a half shrug and his cheeks redden. "I . . . uh . . . Well, that's what the other kids were saying. You know, after she didn't turn up at home or at school. That she was with some guy."

"So you're saying now that you, personally, didn't see this guy?"

"I didn't see him." He looks down, rubs the knee of his jeans.

"Are you sure, Johnny?" I ask.

Luke casts me a look that says, *Let me handle this.*

"Yeah, I'm sure."

"What time did you leave the grove?" Luke asks.

A shrug. "Not sure. Late. We were going to camp there for the night, so we hung around there for a while, but it got super cold. And I went home like . . . early morning on Saturday."

"Over Devil's Bridge?"

He shakes his head.

"How did you get home?" Luke asks.

"Got a ride with Tripp Galloway."

Luke and I exchange a glance. Tripp was seen at the Greek takeout place on the south side of Devil's Bridge. He'd have had to have crossed the bridge.

"Did you go *anywhere* else after leaving the bonfire site?" Luke asks.

"I . . . No. I went home."

"What time did you get home?" Luke asks.

"I dunno. Like maybe one or two in the morning."

"Will your parents confirm this?"

"I sneaked into the house, so I don't know if my dad heard me. My mom died a while ago. It's just me and my dad."

"Who is your father?"

"Granger Forbes. He's a psychologist."

Luke makes a note. "So you didn't go and get donairs at Ari's takeout?"

Johnny looks nervous. Confused. "No."

"What if Tripp Galloway, your chauffeur, was reportedly seen outside Ari's takeout around two thirty a.m. on Saturday morning?"

"Then he must have gone to Ari's after he dropped me off. I fell asleep on the way home from the bonfire, in his van. I was wasted. Or maybe I was still asleep in the van when he stopped, and I don't remember being there, or never woke up."

We show him the photos of Leena's belongings. "Recognize anything?"

He frowns, shakes his head. I write in my notebook:

Johnny Forbes—lying? Confirm with father what time Johnny returned home.

"What about the rumor that went around school, the one about Leena floating in the river?" Luke asks.

"I . . . I never heard that rumor. The first I knew of it was when news broke that Leena's body had been found."

Next in is Beth Galloway. She enters with her shoulders squared and a sway to her long blonde ponytail. My daughter's best friend. Tripp Galloway's sister. I tense.

"Hey, Rachel," she says.

"Beth. This is Sergeant Luke O'Leary. He's going to be interviewing you today."

It knocks her back that I won't be the one asking the questions. She sits, looks hesitant, then flashes her pretty smile at Luke.

Luke doesn't return the smile, and it undercuts her a little further.

Beth describes the same scenario as Johnny. She claims she spent most of the time on a log near the bonfire hanging with Dusty Peters, Darren Jankowski, Nina and Natalia Petrov, Darsh Rai, Cheyenne Tillerson, Seema Patel. And Maddy, of course.

"So you weren't with Amy Chan and Jepp Sullivan, or your brother, Tripp?" Luke says.

"No. I mean, we were all there, but . . . Yeah, I saw them around."

"What about Leena?"

"Saw her. She was with some guy on a log at the far side of the bonfire, near a little trail into the woods that leads past the outhouses. I don't know who he was. And I didn't see her after the rocket in the sky."

"Did you know everyone else at the fire?"

"There were some people I didn't recognize. Maybe from out of town."

"What time did you leave?" asks Luke.

Beth glances at me. I keep a neutral expression. But I feel that she knows I called Eileen, and that I'm aware Beth lied to her mother about sleeping at my house. And that Maddy in turn lied to me that she was sleeping over at Beth's.

"We camped out there until early morning, when my brother, Tripp, came to fetch our group in his van, and we all went for breakfast at the Moose Diner."

"What about Johnny Forbes? Was he also at the Moose for breakfast?" Luke asks.

She lifts her eyes to her right and appears to be thinking hard. "No. Tripp said he took Johnny home earlier. That's right. He basically dropped Johnny at his front door. The guy was pretty much passed out."

"Recognize any of these?" Luke spreads out the glossy photographs of the items found along the river.

Beth's jaw tightens as she studies the prints on the table. She flicks another glance at me. I see Luke notice.

"That's mine." She points at the image of the slim, pale-blue address book. "Did *Leena* have this? I . . . I've been looking for it."

"You sure it's yours?" Luke says.

"Hundred percent. It's my book, that's my writing. Those are my friends' phone numbers."

"How do you think Leena got it?" Luke asks.

"I . . . I don't know. She's been to my house. She came with a group of girls about two or three weeks ago. And Leena's locker is near mine. I . . . really don't know." She looks stricken.

"Why would she take it?" Luke asks.

"I don't know! Maybe because she knows I have all the cool guys' phone numbers in there? She did weird things like that. Can I have it back?"

"It's evidence right now. Do you recognize anything else in these photos?" Luke says.

She scans them again, more carefully, shakes her head.

"What about this locket?" Luke asks.

My pulse quickens. Beth glances at me again. She shakes her head. "No," she says softly.

And I wonder how it is that Beth doesn't appear to recognize a locket that looks just like the one Maddy—her best friend—used to wear more often than not. Until it apparently went missing.

Luke says, "Can you tell us when you first heard the rumor that Leena was probably floating in the Wuyakan River?"

"I heard it in the cafeteria. Everyone was talking about it. I don't know who started it."

Beth leaves. A few moments later Clay enters with Darren Jankowski.

"I know Tripp Galloway is next on the list," says Clay, "but Tripp went home sick about an hour ago. Dusty Peters isn't at school today, either. She bounces between living with her alcoholic mother and the local group home, and every now and then she hits trouble at home and doesn't attend school for a few days."

Luke and I exchange a glance as Clay leaves and Darren takes a seat in front of us at the table. He looks beat. In need of a shower. Possibly hungover.

His story is exactly the same. He also ended up at the Moose for breakfast. No, he doesn't know who started the rumor. No, he can't recall who actually told him.

"Everyone was talking about it."

Darren doesn't recognize any of the belongings in the photos. But the topic of photographs makes him look up. "Liam Parks was taking photos at the bonfire," he says. "Maybe he got a picture of Leena and the guy on the log."

"Liam is the unofficial school photographer," I explain to Luke. "He's on the yearbook team. He does work in the school darkroom and uses the school cameras."

Luke makes a note and dismisses Darren.

Liam is next on the list. He's skinny and pale with deep-set, dark eyes. I've heard Maddy refer to him as "the geek." Liam's recollection of the bonfire is identical to the others'. I jot in my notes: *Did the kids coordinate stories?*

Liam says he doesn't recognize any of the items found on the riverbank.

"Did you shoot photos at the bonfire, Liam?" Luke asks. "Of the crowd?"

His eyes flicker. He nods.

"Can we see them?"

He looks at his hands in his lap.

"Liam?"

"I . . . I lost the camera, and the film inside. I . . ." He raises pained eyes. "I got wasted, and I woke up in a tent, and the camera was gone. It was a school camera. I'd signed it out, and it had been stolen."

"Are you *sure?*" I say.

Liam shoots a look at me. I'm thinking of the print I found in Maddy's drawer. I can see distress in Liam's eyes.

"It's gone. I'm sure. I asked everyone. No one saw anything, or knows anything. It never showed up in lost and found, either."

"What about the film?" Luke asks. "Had you removed any rolls? Developed anything at all?"

A redness creeps up his neck and into his face. His mouth is tight. He shakes his head.

"So who might have stolen your camera? Why?" Luke asks, leaning forward.

"It's . . . a valuable piece of equipment. I suppose that's why."

"So you *never* developed any prints of that night?"

The redness deepens and rises high into his cheeks. He shakes his head.

"Did you—just maybe—shoot images that someone didn't want seen, and that's why the camera was taken?"

"I just shot the usual party stuff. I dunno. I suppose maybe someone didn't want to be seen drunk or making out . . . or whatever . . . but I didn't get threatened or anything."

Liam claims to know nothing about how the rumor started, either.

Seema Patel, whose parents run the Indian restaurant downtown, enters the room after Liam leaves. She's stunningly pretty. Petite. Delicate. Graceful. She moves like the dancer she is. Although her family shares a cultural background with the Rais, Seema is everything that Leena was not. Seema is able to fit into the mold.

"Yeah. I saw Leena that night. Army surplus jacket. Camouflage pants. She was with a guy. Don't know who he was. There were quite a few people from out of town—skiers and boarders. Older local kids no longer in high school. Guys like Darsh who work at the mill."

I think again of the photograph of the girls, Seema in it.

"Anyone take photos of your group?" I ask.

She shakes her head. And I write in my notebook: *Why are they lying? What are they hiding?*

Seema recognizes the address book in the photo as Beth's. "Leena stole things," she says. "She took some makeup from me once, when I left my bag on the bench in the locker room to take a shower. One of the other girls saw her taking it. We confronted her, and she gave it back. That was about two months ago."

"Why would Leena take the address book?" Luke asks.

"I don't know. She did stupid things, for, like, attention, you know, and it usually backfired. Maybe she wanted to phone Beth's friends and talk smack about her, or call some of the boys. She'd do stuff like that."

"How about the locket—recognize that as belonging to anyone?" Luke says.

I watch her face carefully. She pulls her mouth sideways, frowns. Scratches the back of her hand, shakes her head.

"Are you certain?" I say.

"I don't think I've seen it before."

As Seema exits the room, Luke says, "And of course she doesn't know who started the rumor, either."

"Remarkably consistent," I say.

"Suspiciously so."

Nina Petrov's statement is also consistent. And her account meshes with Darsh's—he drove Nina and her older sister, Natalia, back to the group home early.

Jepp Sullivan, a senior like Tripp, is very tall. He has broad shoulders, olive-toned skin, and tightly cropped dark hair. His eyes are a pale green in contrast. He dwarfs the seat he takes in front of us. Jepp confirms the version of events put forth by Amy, his girlfriend. No, he didn't notice Leena on the bridge, although Amy did tell him that she'd seen Leena. And yes, they went to Ari's Greek Takeout for donairs. He chatted to Darsh while there. He didn't even think to mention to Darsh that Amy had seen his younger cousin alone on Devil's Bridge.

"It wasn't like . . . a deal. Not at the time anyway. I'm sorry," he says. "I'm really sorry we didn't realize it was a big deal." Jepp appears anguished by the fact that maybe, just maybe, he could have saved a girl's life if he'd said something, or gone back to check if Leena was okay, or to see if she needed a ride.

"See? That's the thing," Jepp says. "No one really cared about Leena. She . . . It's like she did these things to herself, and now it's gotten her killed. I've spoken to other students, girls, who said *they* would never have ended up alone on that bridge, wasted like that, but it's not true. They all get as wasted. But Leena was there by herself because . . ." He breaks our gazes and looks at the floor. "She was lonely."

Cheyenne Tillerson echoes the exact same refrain as the other girls. When Cheyenne, an attractive redhead with freckles, leaves the room, Luke says, "Definitely feels rehearsed. Like they've gotten their stories all lined up. Question is, Why? What are they covering up?"

Maddy is next, and when she enters and sees me, her lips purse tightly. She plops herself into the chair and sits, sullen.

"Maddy, this is Luke O'Leary. He's with the RCMP and is helping us with the investigation."

She nods at Luke.

I remind myself to keep my mouth shut and to take a back seat as a mother in an observer role. This is tricky ground. In fact, it's all tricky ground in a small and tightly connected town. You can't turn around in the supermarket, or the hardware store, or the post office without being connected to some thread that weaves through the fabric of Twin Falls.

"Yeah, I saw Leena. I saw her on the log."

"With a male?"

"Yeah."

"Do you know who he was, Maddy?"

She says nothing.

My pulse quickens.

"Maddy?" Luke says calmly, voice deep.

She doesn't meet his gaze. She looks unusually pale. Tension coils in my gut.

"You need to tell us if you recognized the male, Maddy. Leena disappeared after that rocket went through the sky. The next time anyone saw her, she was dead. Floating in the river. Sexually assaulted, murdered. If—"

"It wasn't all just kids there."

"What do you mean?"

She looks up and meets the intensity in Luke's gaze. "There . . . there were adults, too."

"Which adults?" Luke asks.

She inhales shakily.

"Maddy?"

"I . . . I . . . Before the rocket came, I needed to pee. I'd had a fair bit to drink, and . . . I didn't want to miss the rocket, so I hurried into the woods, along the trail to the outhouses. When I passed around the back of the fire, Leena wasn't there anymore. When I reached the outhouses, there was a group of people waiting to use the facilities, and I *really* needed to go. Plus I didn't want to miss the lights in the sky. I had my headlamp with me, so I put it on, and I went a bit deeper into the woods along a smaller trail that leads away from the washrooms. And as I crouched down to pee in some bushes, I heard . . . things."

"What things?"

"Sort of heavy breathing, snuffles. At first I thought it was a bear, and I quickly pulled up my pants. But then I realized it was . . . it was people having sex." She swallows. "I inched forward and peered over the berry bushes and ferns, and I . . . I saw a light. They had a little camping light with them. It made a halo. I saw . . ." She clears her throat. "I saw it was Leena. Under . . ." Tears pool in her eyes and begin to leak down her cheeks. She swipes at them. I can barely breathe. Luke is wired.

Quietly he says, "Go on. Who did you see with Leena?"

She makes a strange noise.

"Maddy," Luke says.

"I . . . I . . . It was Mr. Pelley," she blurts. Her face goes red. "He was having sex with Leena."

"*Clayton Pelley?*" I say.

"You mean the *teacher*?" Luke says. "Your guidance counselor?"

Maddy's face goes hotter. She fidgets her hands in her lap. Nods.

"Are you certain?" Luke says. I'm struggling to process. I feel tension pulsing from Luke in waves.

Maddy nods again. And anger swells through me. I don't trust myself to speak.

"Maddy," Luke says slowly, his voice deep, "was Clayton Pelley the guy on the log with Leena?"

She nods, her eyes downcast.

"How come you're the only one who saw who he was?"

"I . . . I needed to pee." Her voice is soft, small. "And I was in the bushes, right there. I caught them in the beam of my flashlight when I parted the bushes, and he had his hat off. They both looked right at me."

"Did you tell anyone?" Luke asks.

She nods.

"Who did you tell?"

"I don't want to get anyone in trouble."

"Just tell the truth, Maddy," I snap.

She swallows. "I told Beth. The other kids also know that the guy on the log was Mr. Pelley. They just didn't want to tell the cops he was there, because Mr. Pelley . . . he's *nice*. He would get into trouble from the school. He was like . . . a friend of the kids. We all told him things."

My mouth drops open. I glare at my daughter. My own kid. She kept a secret like *this*?

"He wouldn't kill her, though," Maddy says, hysterically now, fear flashing through her eyes. "He would not do that. There's no way."

Motive.

It's lying right there in front of us now. Plain as day. Ripe and fat and ready to burst, and Luke and I are positively shimmering with tension.

Clayton Pelley is just down the hall. He's in a position of power over all these kids. Good-looking and oh-so-friendly wanna-be-cool Mr.

Pelley who is only in his early twenties and thus not much older than some of the seniors at this school.

My daughter begins to shake. And cry harder.

"Maddy," Luke says calmly, quietly, "do you recognize anything in these photos?" He spreads the photos of the items found along the river.

Maddy sniffs, wipes her nose, and nods. "That's Beth's." She points at the address book. "She was looking for it."

"How about this locket?" asks Luke.

Her jaw tightens. She refuses to look at me. "I . . . I had one like it."

"Had?" Luke asks.

"I haven't seen it in a long time." She's silent for several beats. My skin goes hot. "I . . . I always wondered if Leena maybe took it."

"When and how could she have taken it?" Luke asks.

"She came to our house like maybe a month or more ago. To borrow a book for homework."

I feel like a cigarette. I haven't had a smoke in years, but I feel like I need one now.

RACHEL

Pelley sits on the other side of his desk in his office. Behind him is the window, and outside snow continues to fall heavily. On a bookshelf beside him is a framed photo of his wife, him, and their new baby.

He looks bloodless under his otherwise-tanned complexion. He squeezes his fist repeatedly around a stress ball. Squeeze, release, squeeze, release.

"That firewood really did a number on your hands," Luke says, watching Clay's hand squeezing.

"Oh, this ball is for an old sports injury. Physiotherapist recommended it. For tendon lengthening. What can I do for you? Everything go okay with the kids?"

"Well, it's you we'd like to talk to." Luke says it calmly, like he wants to discuss a sports game.

Clay's expression changes. Even though his hand keeps squeezing, a stillness seems to come upon him.

Luke flips through his notebook, as if searching for some notes. "You're the guidance counselor?" He continues flipping.

"Like I said. Yes. I teach the CAPP classes, and some phys ed."

"Right. And you mentioned tutoring in a private capacity."

Clay's hand stops moving. He says nothing.

Luke glances up. "You have quite the position of trust. Clearly the students—*kids*—look up to you."

"Do you have a question, Detective?"

"Yeah . . . On November the fourteenth, between five p.m. and nine p.m., where were you?"

Clay regards us. Outside, snow thumps off the school roof into the parking lot. He clears his throat. "Why?"

"Getting a picture of where everyone was at," Luke says.

"I . . . was probably home. With my wife, Lacey. I'd have to check my calendar. Sometimes I go to the gym after school, or work late."

"It was the night of the Russian rocket," Luke prompts. "It went through the sky at nine twelve p.m. It was forecast to happen that night, and everyone seems to know exactly where they were when they saw it." He pauses. "Things like that have a way of anchoring memories."

"Right." Clay hesitates. "Like I said, yes, I was home. Pretty sure I was home at that time."

"Your wife, Lacey, will verify?"

"Yes." He rubs his mouth.

My gut is tight. Adrenaline zings through my blood. Either Maddy is lying or Clay Pelley is lying. And right now, my money is on Maddy having told the truth. And it was clearly a struggle for her to do so, to have voiced the thing she witnessed in the dark woods. It would explain her weird reactions and mood at home.

"We have several witness statements that you were at the bonfire." Luke is bending the truth to see what pops out. "And you spent time with Leena on a log."

Clay's face loses all expression. His eyes go utterly blank. Silence swells into the office.

"So? Which is it? You were at the bonfire, or at home?"

Pelley taps the edge of his desk. "Oh . . . Wait, yeah . . . I did briefly go up to the bonfire first, before heading home, just to do a quick check on what was up. You know, I'd heard about it—the students tell me things. And one of them told me it was going down, and—"

"Which student?"

"I . . . I can't even recall."

"Was it Leena?" Luke asks.

Clay sits lower in his chair. He looks like he's coiling. As if he might suddenly expand and bolt. I shift position, readying myself, in case he actually does try.

"Okay," says Luke. "Let me see if I got this right. You drove twenty minutes. Up into the mountains, along a dark logging road, in the cold, and all the way out to an area called 'the grove,' to quickly check on some students?"

"Yeah. I drove up there, in and out, went home. Kids seemed to be okay. No obvious trouble brewing."

Sick bastard. I try to swallow the distaste filling my mouth, but it sticks in my throat. I want to nail this man to the wall.

"And why didn't you mention this earlier?" I ask, my voice clipped. "When Leena went missing? When we were all looking for her, and I asked if anyone had *any* information about her movements that night?"

"Look." He leans forward, his gaze fixing on me. "*You* know what it's like, Rachel. The Ullr festival was outlawed, banned this year. By *you* guys—"

"It was a town council decision. The PD works for the town."

"Well, the kids didn't want authorities to know they were celebrating on their own, for obvious reasons. It would have gotten them shut down, and because I'd been told about it, it put me in an awkward position. I want to keep their trust. And yes, with something like this, a lot of booze, other drugs, it has a potential to get out of hand, dangerous—"

"It did get dangerous," I say darkly. "For one child. Leena. She was sexually assaulted and murdered." My gaze is locked on his.

He swallows.

A school buzzer sounds in the hallway. I hear kids' voices as they exit classrooms, growing in volume. Feet running. Laughter. A few yells. Locker doors slamming.

Luke says, "So when Leena was reported missing, you still . . . what? Just forgot to mention you were there that night, that you saw her?"

"You didn't need me to tell you that she was at the bonfire. Others saw her, and said so. I honestly figured at the time that Leena would show up. She played games like this for attention, and I didn't think it was anything serious. Plus I didn't want to lose the hard-won trust of my kids. If they trust me, it keeps the lines of communication open. It puts me in a position to help if a red flag does go up. Like when Amy Chan told me she'd witnessed Leena stumbling along Devil's Bridge. Straightaway I took her to the principal's office, and her mother was contacted, and Amy did the right thing. She went into the station with her mother to report it."

Luke inhales slowly, deeply, and I can see he's ready to blow. Very quietly he says, "So you spent time with Leena at the bonfire?"

"I chatted with her a bit, while sitting on a log."

"What were you wearing that night?"

"A black jacket . . . a toque—black. Jeans. Work boots. Scarf. Also black. Gloves."

Luke leans forward, getting into Clay's personal space. "Mr. Pelley, did you have intimate relations with Leena Rai?"

"*What?*"

"Just answer the question."

He goes white. Then two hot spots form along his cheekbones. "Hell no. Are you *mad?*"

"What if I told you that a student witnessed you getting intimate with Leena in the bushes, shortly before the Russian rocket went through the sky?" He pauses. "Sexual intercourse. With a student. A minor."

He stares at us. His mouth opens. Words seem to have deserted him.

The noise of kids increases outside the door. Time stretches.

"I don't believe this," he says quietly. "What student said this?"

"Is it true?"

"Of course not. Whoever said that—she's lying."

"What makes you think it was a she?"

His eyes shine. "She. He. Whoever said it is a liar. And it's their word against mine. And if you claim otherwise, I'll have your asses sued from here to high heaven for defamation."

"What size boots do you wear, Pelley?" Luke asks.

"I'm a size eleven. What's this got to do with—"

"We need you to come down to the station," Luke says. "We should do this officially, on the record. Are you good with that?"

"What, *now?*"

"Yes. Now."

Clay glares at Luke, then me. He surges suddenly to his feet. I come to my own feet.

"This is ludicrous," he says in a hiss of a whisper. "Are you *arresting* me?"

Luke remains seated. "We'd like to clear some things up in a formal setting, get an official statement on the record."

"If I'm not under arrest, I'm not going anywhere with you. And I'm not saying another goddamn word to either of you without my lawyer present. Now get out. Get the hell out of my office."

TRINITY

NOW
Thursday, November 18. Present day.

I find Dusty Peters at the Last Door Addictions and Wellness Centre, where she works as a counselor. It's a residential facility on rural land just outside of Twin Falls. Dusty is one of the first of Leena's old classmates who responded to my outreach. She was not interviewed at Twin Falls Secondary along with the other kids because she was absent that day. Dusty was, however, questioned later, and her statements in the transcript match what the other students said about the bonfire night.

"We treat both adults and teens," Dusty says as she shows me into an office with a view of the forest. We sit on comfortable chairs in front of a flickering gas fire as rain falls on the brooding conifers outside. "It's a refuge, and it's not only for addictions. It's about rebalancing."

"From group home to wellness center," I say. "That in itself has a nice full-circle balance about it, Dusty."

She smiles. Dusty is strong, stocky-looking. Her hands are those of a farmer or laborer. She has a scar across her cheek. Her eyes are kind. I sense that life has dealt Dusty more challenges than most, and that she's found a way to overcome and give back. I'm here to learn more about who Leena Rai was.

"Do you mind if I record our conversation?" I ask.

"Go right ahead." As I click my digital recorder on, she says, "I honestly never got to know Leena that well. And it's one of my regrets. She had a tough time, was an outcast. And I of all people should have understood, because my own life was a mess. My father was deceased. I had an alcoholic mother and an abusive uncle. There was violence in my family. We had no money, and I was in and out of the group home, where Nina and Natalia Petrov also stayed for a while. All of that made me insecure. Angry. It made me need to belong somewhere, and I tried everything to belong to a group of girls at school. That group, in a sense, became my family. We were tight. And in order to belong, it felt like . . . like I had to be loyal in picking on someone like Leena, who'd become our target. It was, I suppose, a way of validating ourselves. Something that united us."

"What was Leena like?"

Dusty heaves out a sigh. "Socially awkward. Did dumb things to get attention, and it usually backfired."

"And Clayton Pelley's relationship with her?"

"Well, that's the thing—he seemed to care for her. Like a good teacher would. He . . . seemed protective. He admonished us from time to time for our bullying behavior. Which is why I was so shocked to hear what had happened."

"Did you see Clayton Pelley on the night of the bonfire?"

"Yes, with Leena on the log. I never saw them having sex, but I heard about it. Which totally shocked me. Horrified me. Ironically, not the fact that he'd had intimate relations with a student, but that it was Leena."

"Because she wasn't what you'd have thought of as sexually attractive?"

"That's what I thought at the time, I'm afraid. But the murder, the violence . . . we couldn't see that. That was really hard to believe, or understand."

"Do you think it's possible Clayton could be telling the truth now? That maybe he didn't do it?"

Dusty falls silent and considers this. She rubs her brow.

"I don't know. Honestly, I just don't. When I listened to the first episode, the question I kept circling back to, if he didn't do it, is, Why did he confess and plead guilty?"

"For argument's sake, if he didn't do it, was there anyone around town that you girls thought was . . . weird, perhaps? Any guy who ever gave any of you trouble? Anyone who ever followed any of you, or stalked, or watched you in ways that made you uncomfortable?"

Dusty casts her mind back. Rain streams down the windowpanes behind her, and the wind picks up, bending and swirling the trees in the dense forest.

"I don't know. I mean, there were men who'd look when we went by. Workers from the mill. Construction guys. Before Clay Pelley confessed, I thought Leena's killer could have been a truck driver who was going through at night, and saw her alone, and pulled over. Something like that." She frowns. "The only other . . . I guess you could say—" She glances suddenly at my recording device. "Can we talk off the record for a second?"

"Is that necessary?"

"I don't want to get sued. I have a reputation here as well. I . . . I don't even know if I should mention it."

My pulse quickens with interest. I reach forward and click off the device.

Dusty hesitates, then says, "There was a cop. He was stationed outside our school after the detectives left. They'd been to interview all of us again, and the two detectives had been inside Clayton's office, talking to him. After they left, this cop car arrived and parked in the lot. We saw it from the classroom window. Beth told us the guy inside had harassed her once. He'd forcibly kissed her, and followed her home one night."

My mouth goes dry as my heart races a little faster. "Which cop?"

She regards me in silence, as if taking my measure. "This is sensitive," she says quietly. "You need to do your own research. Is that understood?"

"Okay. Yes."

"He's the police chief now. His name is Bart Tucker."

RACHEL

Tired. That's the word that comes to mind when Lacey Pelley opens the peeling front door of her tiny clapboard house near the railway. She stares dully at me and Luke in our coats. Wind blows hard from the sea, northward up the sound. It swirls with the snowflakes and smells of salt. A lone gull cries in the mist. I notice that a layer of ice covers a dog's water bowl on the front step. A Beware of the Dog sign clacks in the wind on the front gate, but no hound has come to the door, barking.

Just inside the door, in the mudroom, I can see a recycling bin piled high with beer cans and hard-liquor bottles.

Lacey is reed thin. Very early twenties. Stringy, dun-colored hair that could use a wash and some brightening. Ashen complexion. Hollows underscore her eyes.

With her hand on the door, she says, "What do you want?"

"Lacey, hi, I'm Rachel Walczak," I say, shivering in my down coat. "I don't know if you remember me? We met once at a school function. I think it was after a basketball game. Coached by your husband. My daughter, Maddy, is on the team."

Clay's wife glances at Luke.

"And this is Sergeant Luke O'Leary from the RCMP. He's helping with the Twin Falls PD investigation into the death of Leena Rai."

We've come straight from Clay's office. Tucker has been dispatched to the school to watch Clay. He's been tasked with sitting in a marked vehicle in the parking lot and has been ordered to follow the teacher if and when he leaves.

Something hardens in Lacey's features. I hear a baby beginning to cry inside.

"If it's Clay you want, he's not here. He's at work," she says. "At the school."

"Why would you think we're here for your husband?" I ask.

"I . . ." A wariness enters her eyes. I can see the wheels of her brain ticking over.

"You said the Leena Rai investigation. Leena was one of his students, and he tutored her, so . . ." Her voice fades.

"He tutored Leena from his home office, here?" Luke asks.

"He converted the garden shed into an office. We need the money."

The woman appears to have no filters left.

"Can we come in, Lacey?" I ask.

"It's a mess." She stands unmoving in the doorway.

"That's okay." Luke starts forward, crowding Lacey so that she steps backward and inside.

I follow them in.

"Dog okay? Saw the sign," Luke says.

"Dog's at the pound looking for a new home. And before you go judging me, I just can't. I can't look after it. It needed walks. It barked the whole time. It shat in the house. It chewed everything. Clay is always busy with work, coaching, the extra tutoring. Janie . . . she doesn't sleep. I . . . We don't even have the money for the dog food."

Toys lie scattered all over the living room floor. The sofa is ripped, presumably the dog's doing. In the kitchen, dishes are piled in the sink. The baby is strapped into a portable chair and is now screaming, her face crinkled and bright red. The infant is wearing a bib covered in orange shmoo. The same color as the streaks on Lacey's T-shirt. Lacey picks up her crying child and jiggles her, patting her back. The crying continues unabated.

"Here," I say gently, reaching out. It's not kosher, but I can't help myself. "Let me hold her while Luke asks you some questions, okay?"

Emotion shines in Lacey's eyes. She hands me the sour milk–smelling infant.

"How old?" I ask over the cries.

"Seven months."

"Got clean diapers? She smells and feels like she could do with a change." I make a face, trying to convey alliance, friendliness.

"In the next room."

I go to change the baby. In the room I see a pacifier on a table alongside the changing pad, and a packet of disposable diapers. I lay the infant down on the changing pad and place the pacifier in her mouth. She quiets and starts sucking intently. Her big watery eyes with wet lashes fix on me.

I smile. "There you go. You just need a change and something in your tummy, I bet."

Little sucking noises ensue. The baby's gaze remains locked on my face. I reach for a fresh diaper and start changing little Janie.

I note the crucifix hanging above the crib. It's the sole piece of decor on the walls. Lacey is religious? I'd never have guessed this about her husband. But then, why should I have?

"There you go, sweetie," I whisper. "I'm surprised I still remember how to do this, you know that?"

Janie makes a noise. I smile again. And I wonder if I will ever have grandchildren of my own, which turns my thoughts to my daughter. Worry rears back up inside me. As I strap the fresh diaper onto baby Janie, her chubby legs kicking, I wonder about motherhood, and just how far we mothers might go to protect our babies. Our children. Our teens. Our grandbabies. Our families.

I pick Janie up and snuggle her close, stealing a moment of babyness. As I do, I hear Luke say in the next room, "Do you recall what you were doing on the night of November fourteenth, Mrs. Pelley?"

"One day runs into another. They all seem the same at the moment. I don't get out, so I was here."

"It was the night of the Russian satellite."

"Oh . . . I . . . Yeah. I remember that day. Janie had colic. She was screaming nearly all day."

I enter the living room with Janie.

Clay's wife is not a heck of a lot older than some of the kids at Twin Falls Secondary. I figure she's around twenty-one or twenty-two years of age, young enough to be at bonfires herself, doing hedonistic dances, making sacrifices to snow gods, waxing her skis, or prepping her snowboard or mountain bike. But here she sits while her husband hangs out with the youth. And worse.

All I know about the Pelleys is that Clay married Lacey in Terrace, a small community farther north in BC. He was teaching at a school there, met his wife there, and Lacey was heavily pregnant when Clay took the new guidance counselor position at Twin Falls Secondary. Janie was born soon after at the Twin Falls hospital. I know that Clay has degrees in psychology and English literature. He's sporty and apparently loves the outdoors. But I know very little about his wife.

I begin to wonder if she was ever a student of his.

Lacey doesn't bother to look my way as I take a seat with Janie on the chair near the sofa.

"Did you see the rocket, Lacey?" Luke is using a gentle, avuncular tone.

"No." She wipes her forehead. For a moment she looks as though she's going to cry. Clearly she's struggling to hold a myriad of emotions down under an exhausted, fragile facade of control.

"How about your husband? Did he see it? Was he home?"

Her eyes widen slightly, as if it's hitting hard and fast for the first time why we might really be here. Her gaze darts around the room, as if searching for the correct response.

"He . . . Clay called from the school to say he was meeting a friend for a catch-up. A drink. Before coming home."

"A catch-up where?" Luke asks.

"The Raven's Roost."

I know the pub. It's owned by Rex Galloway, Eileen's husband, Beth's father. It's a bit of a biker hangout. Rex loves his Harley and the lifestyle that goes with it.

"Which friend?" Luke asks.

"An old friend from the university. Clay went to UBC. He got his degree there. He said he was seeing a guy from the psych department. He didn't give a name."

"What time did your husband arrive home, then, Mrs. Pelley?"

She hesitates. "What did he say . . . Have you spoken to him?"

"Can you just answer the question, Lacey?" Luke says.

Now she looks nervous. "I . . ." She swallows, flicks a glance at me. "It was late." She rubs her knee.

"How late?" asks Luke, patience still steady in his tone.

"Late, like . . ." Her voice comes out strangled, hoarse, as if reality has suddenly gotten its grip and is digging fingers into her throat. "Early morning. Like 3:42 a.m. He . . . stumbled into the bedroom." With a shaking hand she swipes tears that begin rolling down her face.

"That's a very precise time, Lacey," I say.

"I was watching the clock. I was lying awake. I noted it. I . . . I planned to confront him about it the next day. So I made a point of remembering."

"He was stumbling, as in drunk?" asks Luke.

Mouth tight, she nods. "He drinks a lot."

I think of the recycling bin in the mudroom.

She inhales a shuddering breath. "I . . . I'm trying to keep up the breastfeeding, but it's not working." Another swipe at her tears. "But I haven't had a drink since I fell pregnant. And he . . . still . . . he . . . he drinks to pass out. Every night. Every. Single. Night. Blackout drunk. He doesn't remember things he said to me after a certain point in the evening, or what he did once he's consumed a certain quantity. Although he can seem okay at the time, he doesn't recall things. Sometimes he goes out to his shed and comes back inside in the dark hours of the morning."

"Yet he goes to work every day, does his job?" I say.

She nods.

"And he tutors students here? Is he sober when they come over?" I ask.

"Yes. No. I mean, sometimes he has a beer or two before they arrive, so it's like maintaining a base level. He's an alcoholic . . . a functional alcoholic. He starts with a beer the moment he walks in the door." She puts her face into her hands. Her bony shoulders heave as she starts to sob.

"Hey—" I get up and hand the baby to Luke, then go and sit beside Lacey on the ripped sofa. I place my hand on her bony knee. "I can see you're struggling, Lacey. I can get you some help, put you in touch with someone, but first we do need you to help us by answering these questions. Can you do that?"

"Why?" She looks at me, her face tearstained. "What has he done? Has he done something bad? What does this have to do with Leena Rai?"

"We're just trying to ascertain what everyone in the community was doing that night. There might be things that people don't realize are of relevance, so anything can help. The bigger the picture we can paint, the better."

She looks away. Out the window. Trying to marshal self-control. Bare branches nod hard in the frigid sea wind outside. The panes of glass are smeared with grime where the blowing snow collects in patterns. Lacey gives a small shudder. Like a physical release. She faces me, and her gaze locks on mine. I glimpse something raw in her eyes, and it punches me in the belly. My muscles brace.

When she speaks again, her voice is firm, almost strident. Clear.

"He was really drunk that Saturday morning when he came home. More than usual. From the way he was stumbling and knocking about. He fell over when he was taking off his pants. He smelled . . . he . . . smelled like sex. I . . . He's come home a few times smelling like that, and I . . . He's having an affair. He denies it. But I am sure of it."

I meet Luke's gaze. His eyes, intense over the baby's head, hold mine. He's jiggling the baby on his knee. If the mood weren't so dark, I would find it comical. But my heart hurts for this young woman. And at the same time, my anger at Clay is hot. I reach for Lacey's cold hand.

"I understand," I say very softly, not intending the words that follow out of my mouth, but they come anyway. "I know what it feels like. To be married to someone who is being unfaithful."

She holds my gaze, almost not breathing.

I feel Luke's interest. It's instant and keen. I can't put the words back now. I realize at this very moment just how much Jake's affair has been hurting me. I clear my throat. I take a deep breath.

"Do you know who your husband might be sleeping with, Lacey, if that is the case?"

She shakes her head.

"No idea?"

"No. I . . . was thinking maybe one of the other teachers. Or someone from the gym."

I feel she might be lying, hiding her true, deeper suspicions.

"How many students does Clay tutor here?" Luke asks, awkward with the infant, who seems mesmerized by him and is now staring silently at his face, sucking her pacifier as he continues to bounce her on his knee. "Apart from Leena."

"About four others. Off and on."

"Females? Males?"

"Females." She looks sick. Like she's going to throw up. Like Luke's questions are taking her mind where she doesn't want it to go. She reaches for a tissue from the box on the table beside her chair and blows her nose.

"I think one is Dusty Peters. She's sort of a problem student at school, with trouble at home. And Nina. She's from Russia, and English is her second language. There's a girl called Suzy, and a Melissa. But Clay hasn't told me anything about them."

"Are those work boots in the mudroom the ones your husband was wearing on the night he came home so drunk?" I ask.

She looks confused. "Why?"

"Just helps to eliminate things," I say.

"I'm not sure. Maybe."

"Can we take a look at them?"

Her eyes darken. She swallows. "Okay. Sure."

I go into the mudroom, pick up a boot, turn it over. My adrenaline kicks. It's the right pattern. It looks like the bruise imprints on Leena's body. I reenter the room and nod to Luke.

He says, "Do you mind if we take those boots?"

She says nothing for a long moment. She clears her throat. "Is this to do with Leena?"

"We're investigating all avenues right now."

"Take them," she says, voice clipped. "Take the damn boots. Take anything you want."

"One more thing, Lacey," I say as I put the photos of the evidence found in and near Leena's backpack on the coffee table. "Do you happen to recognize anything here?"

She moves to the edge of the sofa and leans forward, studying the images carefully. She points.

"That book of poems, *Whispers of the Trees*, it's Clay's."

"How do you know?"

"The inscription there, on the title page, *With love from A. C., UBC, 1995*. A. C. is Abbigail Chester. She was a friend of Clay's when he was at UBC. She gave him the book. He told me." She looks up. "Where did you find it? Are these other things Leena's?"

"They were found at the scene," I say.

"Maybe Clay loaned Leena that poetry book," she says.

"Yes. Probably," I say.

While Luke continues to hold baby Janie, I go out to the vehicle, fetch an evidence bag and gloves, and return to collect the boots. Then I write a name and number in my notebook, tear out the page, and hand it to Lacey.

"I want you to call this number. This is someone who can help. And I'm also going to phone someone and get them to come and check up on you, okay?"

"You mean like a social worker? I'm a good mother. I don't want anyone thinking I'm not a good mother. I'm doing my best."

"I'm sure you are. But we all need help. Raising a child . . . it's not a thing that should be done alone." Another thought hits me as I recall the crucifix in the baby's room. "Do you go to church, Lacey?"

She nods, blows her nose again.

"Which one? Because I know some people who can help from our local faith communities, too."

"Our Lady of the Hills."

"Okay. I know someone with the Catholic Church. I'll give them a call to see if they have some solutions to help, okay?"

She nods and takes the piece of paper from me.

Luke gets up and hands her the baby. He says, "Can we take a look inside Clay's tutoring shed?"

She stiffens. Panic chases across her features. "I . . . It's always locked. With a padlock. And don't you need to ask him, or have a warrant or something?"

"Fair enough," Luke says. "But we might need you to come down to the station, to make an official statement. We can get someone to bring you in. Is that okay?"

She nods and sees us out the door.

◆　◆　◆

As we duck into the car and out of the blowing snow, I say, "So Clay Pelley has no alibi. He lied to his wife. Mr. Nice Guy is a shit husband."

"Or worse," says Luke as he reaches forward to start the engine.

I curse as I buckle up. "She's just a kid herself. Barely older than some of the seniors at school. And clearly struggling."

Luke glances at me. "Do you believe your daughter is telling the truth about what she saw?"

"I do. It was hard for her, but yes, I believe her."

"We'll have to bring the kids in again. Officially. Into the station with guardians this time. Grill them on record about whether they saw their teacher at the bonfire. And we'll get those boots to the lab. Could give us enough for an arrest warrant, or at the least a search warrant for his home and shed."

Luke reverses out of the driveway. The tires spin and bump over the mound of snow left by the plow that has just driven along the road.

"Is it true?" he asks. "What you said about your husband?"

"That's not your business, Luke."

"You made it part of an interview."

I say nothing. He doesn't pursue it.

As we round the corner, I glance back through the misted car window. I see Lacey exiting the side of the house in a big coat. She's heading through the blowing snow, aiming for the shed in her backyard.

TRINITY

I find Beth Galloway Forbes at the hair salon she owns in a new strip mall. It's after lunch. Gio and I stopped at a fast-food place on our way back from visiting with Dusty Peters. Gio once more waits for me in the van in the parking lot. When I phoned Beth early this morning, she said she'd be happy to be interviewed—she'd already listened to the first two episodes. She said her mother, Eileen, had called to tell her about the podcast. Eileen had listened, too.

Beth's salon is upmarket and trendy-looking, and Beth is model glamorous. Her blonde hair is cut in a sleek platinum bob that swings cheekily at her jawline. She's on the tall side of average height, wears a sleeveless blouse made of some chiffony fabric, and has delicate tattoos of roses and other flowers along one arm.

She takes me into a small office at the back of the store. The place smells of shampoos and the ammonia of hair dyes.

"Can I get someone to fetch us coffee?" she asks in a rich voice. "Got a great coffee shop down the mall."

"I'm fine, thanks. And thank you for agreeing to see me. I spoke with Dusty Peters at the wellness center this morning, and I'm hoping to connect with more of Leena's classmates."

"Yeah. I haven't spoken to Dusty in, like, ages. She phoned me to say you were going to be meeting with her. It's kind of bringing us all together again. Have you spoken to Maddy?" Beth asks as she takes a seat behind a glass desk. I sit in a chrome chair to her side.

"I've left messages. She has not returned my calls yet."

She gives a soft sigh. "I tried to call her. To talk about it. Mads has been isolating herself since that climbing accident put her in a wheelchair. I mean, Maddy and I were once super tight, but something changed in her that fall Leena was killed, and we gradually drifted apart after that." She falls silent for several beats. I hear the sound of a hair dryer in the salon. "It sort of changed everyone. Leena's murder. Changed the whole town."

"Do you mind if I record this?"

She hesitates, just fractionally, then says, "Of course not. I agreed to talk. You sure you don't want a coffee?"

"I'm sure." I click my digital recorder on, reach forward, and set it on her glass desk. "Feel free to chat casually. We'll edit out any extraneous chitchat."

"Sure. Okay."

"Are those your kids?" I nod to a frame on her glass desk, trying to set her more at ease.

She smiles. "Douglas and Chevvy. Doug is six, and Chevvy is four. They're with my mom today."

"Nice to have helpful family close." I smile and angle back to my purpose. "Dusty said she never really got a sense of who Leena was, other than she was an outsider and picked on. No one really understood her, apart from, perhaps, your teacher, Clayton Pelley?"

"Which is weird. I mean, Mr. Pelley—Clay—did seem to like her, and he acted to protect her from meanness, so knowing that he did what he did, assaulted and killed her . . . it's a real shocker." She pauses, her eyes going distant. "I guess we never really can know people, can we? Then again, another part of me was not surprised, I suppose."

"How so?"

"Clay was a charmer. He had a way of making us girls feel . . . special. When he singled one of us out with a flattering comment, it's like we were the chosen girl for the day. Like some golden light had been shined on us. He was sexy. Experienced. I . . . I suspect every one of the girls might have dreamed about being with him."

"So it was a surprise to see him with Leena?"

"You mean the sex? Well, I didn't see them in the act. Maddy did, and she came running up to me at the bonfire to tell me. She was flushed and horrified-looking, her eyes wild. She'd been to the bathroom, and had come across them off the trail, in a tiny clearing. She hurriedly told me what she'd seen, and I ran with her down the path to go look. We got there in time to see Mr. Pelley helping Leena up off the ground, and he was buttoning up his shirt and zipping his jacket back up. Leena's clothes were also all in disarray. He helped her zip up the coat she was wearing. He then put his arm around her and started leading her along a trail that led up to the logging road where his car was parked. She was wobbling because she'd been drinking a lot."

"So if you heard the first podcast episode, you heard Clayton Pelley denying that he raped Leena and that he killed her?"

She nods.

"Is it even vaguely possible, in your mind, that he could be telling the truth now?"

She thinks for a long while.

"Honestly, I don't know," she says quietly. "I really don't know anymore. He said he did it—killed her. So we all believed he did. And he had all those details about exactly how she died."

"Tell me about Bart Tucker."

Her eyes flash wide, and her gaze locks on mine. She tenses. "What about him? Why?"

"He was one of the handful of cops on the case. Did he ever harass you when you were a student?"

She swallows, glances at the digital recorder. "Can we turn that off?"

"Must we?"

She says nothing.

I reach forward and click it off.

"Tucker—we all call him Tucker—he's the police chief now."

"I know."

"He was young and totally handsome back then. He looked cool in his uniform. I'd seen him about. I . . . Some of us girls used fake IDs to get into a club once, and he was there. Out of uniform. Kind of tipsy, having a good time. He showed an interest in me. I told him I was nineteen. I was all dressed up, and I could pull it off. We . . . kissed, and stuff. And in the following days, he tried to see me. Then he learned how old I really was, but I still caught him driving slowly by my house once or twice. One night he parked across the street, watched my window when I was getting undressed. I saw his car out there, and I yanked the drapes shut. Another time he followed me slowly in his car when I was walking home one night. He rolled down his window and asked if I wanted a ride. I agreed. I thought he was going to try to kiss me again when we got to my house, but my dad was arriving home on his motorbike from the club, and I panicked and got out of the car."

"It was a small town—he truly didn't recognize you as a fourteen-year-old from school?"

"Twin Falls had a population of around fifteen thousand back then. Not everyone knew all the kids and which grades they were in. And I was totally dressed up. Full makeup, high heels. It was dark in the club. Like I said, he was a bit drunk. I believed at the time I was pulling it off that I was nineteen."

"Did Tucker ever get pushy? Aggressive in his interactions with you, or anyone else?"

"Maybe . . . maybe a little. But that was a long time ago. I've never heard anything else weird about Chief Tucker. And I confess I did go all out to seduce him that first night. He was a man who wore a uniform. And I mean, I did lie to him about my age."

"He still stalked you, watched you. That's problematic, and his behavior is *not* your fault."

"I know that now, of course, and yes, it makes me angry. But . . . back then, I confess it was a kind of thrill."

When I leave Beth's salon and climb back into the van, I say to Gio, "This is good. Really good."

"So why do you look so grave?"

I turn in the passenger seat to face him. "One of the cops who was on the 1997 case, he was Clayton's age at the time of the investigation. He also had a sexual interest in young female students. And he followed at least one of them at night, watched her changing in her bedroom." I hold Gio's gaze. "We have other possibilities, other suspects we can raise. A cop involved in the investigation would also have known details of how Leena died."

"What—you mean he could have told Clay, given him the details?"

"Maybe something happened during the confession."

RACHEL

THEN
Tuesday, November 25, 1997.

"Where is your father, Maddy?" I ask, shrugging out of my coat and hanging it on a hook. I'm beat, and I need to talk to Jake about what Maddy said she saw on the night of the bonfire. He needs to know. He'll need to be with her when she is questioned further.

Maddy is at the dining room table, busy with her homework. The television is on in the living room.

"Out." She doesn't make eye contact.

"Out where?"

"Don't know."

"Maddy?"

"What?" She still refuses to meet my gaze.

"Look at me, Maddy."

Her mouth flattens. Slowly she raises her eyes. They're red and puffy. She's been crying. My heart spasms as my latent anger slams into fear, and confusion, and love. I'm walking a tricky tightrope working this case with my daughter being a key witness. I'm not sure how long I can actually stay on the case if things develop further with Maddy. But a deep, driving part of me also *needs* to see this through now. The pressure is on, especially if I am to take the role of chief when Ray finally retires.

I want to bring this bastard to justice. For the kids. For my own child. For other parents. And for the Rai family.

I remind myself that this is a small town. *Everyone* is connected to some degree.

I sit at the table. My child's shoulders are tight. I try to breathe in calmly, breathe out. Softly I say, "Why didn't you tell me earlier about Mr. Pelley being at the bonfire?"

"Because exactly this would happen." She slams her pen down on the table. "You, the cop, would start some stupid manhunt! Because the bonfire was not legal, and kids were drinking, and *he* knew. And it would get him in trouble."

My heart thuds as incredulity swirls.

"Maddy, you told a homicide detective from the RCMP that you saw your teacher having sex with one of his students—one of *your classmates*—shortly before she was brutally murdered."

She glowers at me. Her eyes gleam with moisture. Her mouth quivers.

"Are you *certain* you saw what you claim you saw?"

"I'm not lying," she snaps. "I saw what I saw. And Beth and the other kids saw Mr. Pelley going to his car with Leena, and he had his arm around her."

"So they *all* lied to us? They all knew that the male with Leena on the log was Mr. Pelley?"

Maddy bites her lip. Hard. Her eyes look wild.

"Did Mr. Pelley ask you all to keep silent about his presence at the bonfire?"

"Is this police business you're doing right now? Are you officially questioning me again? Shouldn't your *partner* be present, because don't you have a conflict of interest? Shouldn't this be done at the station when I go in tomorrow?"

"I just cannot understand why you'd even want to keep something like this quiet. Do you realize that what Mr. Pelley did is criminal? It's rape at the very least, even if he had nothing to do with what transpired with Leena under the bridge."

Her face drains of all color. Her eyes are shiny and her breathing is shallow. She's deeply stressed.

I take another slow, measured breath. "You're my daughter, Maddy. I'm a mother. Like Pratima is a mother. I'm just worried other girls could be in danger, or perhaps they have already been in some kind of danger with that man." I lean forward, arms on the table. "Is there *anything* else you are keeping secret from me?"

She doesn't respond. The distant wail of a siren reaches us. Probably another accident on the highway in this first big snowfall of the year.

I moisten my lips. "Liam took photographs at the bonfire—did you know that?"

No reaction. My neck tenses as I think of the image I took from her drawer.

"Did he shoot any pics of you and your friends?"

Her eyes flicker. And I know. I just know that the photo I found in her bedside drawer was shot by Liam.

"Who cares if he took photos? He always shoots everything. He's always following girls around with his camera, like some freak stalker. He is a sicko pervert." Abruptly she gathers up her books and papers and comes to her feet. "I'm going upstairs to finish my homework."

"Maddy?" I call after her.

She stops at the bottom of the stairs but does not turn around.

"Are you sure that you don't know what happened to your locket with the Celtic knots?"

"I *told* you. I haven't worn it for a long time, and I haven't seen it."

"You saw the photos of the items found with Leena's body. The—"

"If the locket that was found with her was mine, then Leena stole it ages ago. Just like she stole Beth's address book. Just like she stole things from everyone. Like I told Detective O'Leary, she was in our house, and she could have taken it then."

"When, exactly, was she in *our* house?"

She spins round. "*Like I said*, a month or so ago. When you were at work—and when are you not at work? Even Dad says that. Always trying so damn hard to get Grandpa's job that you don't even know what is going on in your own house. Leena came to borrow a book for some homework." She thumps up the stairs.

I press my hand to my sternum. I feel nauseous.

TRINITY

"Chief Tucker!" I call out as I run after the Twin Falls PD chief, who is striding across the parking lot to his vehicle. He stalls, turns.

I reach him, out of breath. I'm under my umbrella and the light is fading. He's standing bareheaded in the rain. I've ambushed him outside the station. "I'm Trinity Scott, I—"

"I know who you are. I told you on the phone, I can't participate. You have all the old case files." He reaches for his car door handle.

"I do, thank you," I say quickly. "But I'd also love to ask you some questions about the town back in the day, and your personal observations about the investigation."

"It's against PD protocol. Speak to our press officer." He opens his car door.

"And I'd like to ask you about your past friendship with Beth Galloway Forbes."

He stills and stares at me through the rain.

"What about Beth?"

"The two of you dated?"

"We did not. Beth lied to me. She claimed she was nineteen. Nothing happened between us once I found out, and . . . Why is this even an issue? Why is this coming up? Did *Beth* put you onto this?"

"Did you ever follow the female students, Chief? Twenty-four years ago. Ever park across from their houses, and watch them through their windows while they changed?"

His broad face darkens. He lowers his voice and leans toward me. I smell mint on his breath.

"I don't know what you think you're doing, Ms. Scott. An honest true crime story is one thing. Tabloid sensationalist schlock at the expense of good people's reputations is another." He pauses. And his eyes bore into mine. "It was a solid investigation. Solid detectives working the case. It cut us all up—that horrific murder. Every last one of us. And if you go making insinuations like this, you're going to be looking at the sharp end of a serious lawsuit. Be careful," he says. "Tread very, very carefully here. And consider where you're getting your information. From a self-professed sex offender? A violent killer? A convict? And a bunch of girls who were infatuated with him?"

He gets into his car and slams the door.

Rain drums on my umbrella. I watch his car pull out of the lot and turn into the street.

RACHEL

I perch my butt on the edge of my metal desk. It's almost noon, and there are five of us in the "bullpen." Chief Ray, Tucker, Dirk, Luke, and me. Luke balances himself against another metal desk in front of his crime board. Leena's photo watches us from the top. The heaters are on, the windows are misting up, and outside the snow is turning to ugly slush.

Luke spent the morning reinterviewing the students, who were brought in one by one with parents. Maddy was first, at 8:30 a.m., accompanied by Jake.

Jake acted like this was all my fault. Maddy wanted nothing to do with me. I watched from behind the one-way glass with Ray, Tucker, and Dirk while Luke peppered Maddy and the other kids with questions about what they'd seen in the woods.

Maddy claimed that after she witnessed her teacher fornicating with Leena, she ran and told Beth immediately. Beth and Maddy hurried back to the small clearing in the bushes. They saw Clayton adjusting his clothes, helping Leena to her feet, putting his arm around her, and walking her along a narrow trail to his vehicle.

Beth confirmed Maddy's account.

Both said they were too shocked and too afraid to mention it when Leena was first reported missing. This is something I cannot understand. It could be a form of denial. Compartmentalizing and burying something so horrible that the kids didn't have any kind of narrative with which to deal with it. So they just blocked it. Until pressed. But it's eating at me. My own daughter couldn't talk to me.

The other students who got a good look at the man on the log with Leena all confirmed it was Clayton Pelley, but they had been "afraid to say." There'd been a conspiracy of silence.

"Okay, let's run it through," says Ray. "The RCMP has dispatched another forensic ident team to the grove, this time to search near the outhouses for corroborating evidence of the sexual liaison between Clayton and Leena. But chances are slim of finding anything given the passing of time and snow at the higher elevation. Luke, you spoke with the BC Prosecution Service?"

"Just got off the phone with a lawyer," says Luke. "Plus warrants are in hand to search the Pelleys' house, his shed, his office at school, and his vehicle. We've got enough to arrest him for further questioning, but the prosecutor would like something more solid in terms of evidence for an ironclad charge and conviction. Let's see what those search warrants yield. So far Pelley has admitted he was at the bonfire. The lab says his boot imprints are a match to the marks on Leena's body. Pelley cannot account for the time between when he was last seen leaving the bonfire with his arm around Leena and when he arrived home at 3:42 a.m. in a severely inebriated state, according to his wife, Lacey."

"She also claimed her husband smelled of sex," I say.

Tucker clears his throat. Ray crooks up his brow. "So Pelley had opportunity," Ray says.

"Both opportunity and means," I say. "And if he slept with a student who threatened to rat him out, he also had powerful motive."

"Anything else from the lab yet?" Ray asks.

"Still waiting on results to see if the soil on Pelley's boots is a match to the soil under Devil's Bridge. That would put him at the scene. We're also still awaiting results on the nail scrapings from under Leena's nails. Plus some of the hair and fiber evidence."

Ray says, "So far we have only one witness—a young teen—who claims she actually saw Pelley having sex with Leena Rai in the woods. Unless the lab coughs something up, or the warrants do, or those ident guys find something—a used condom, fibers, hairs—we need more."

"What I don't get," says Tucker, "is why in the hell those kids kept silent about their teacher being there in the first place."

Dirk says, "Kids do weird things. I've lived and worked in this town long enough to know how powerful those pacts of silence can be when it comes to a cohort that bonded in kindergarten and has moved all the way through the school system and into young adulthood. It's like a pack. A herd. And that unit can display more powerful connections to each other than the kids have with their own families and parents. They will keep secrets and do things for each other that can be hard to understand."

I think of Maddy. Her tight friendship with Beth, and with the rest of her group, and I know Dirk is talking truth. We all know it. While a small town can be wonderful, the lack of diversity presents other unique challenges.

"Well, yeah, maybe," says Tucker. "I mean, I grew up here. I *know* this. But not mentioning a fellow student being sexually abused by a teacher? And not just a teacher, a friggin' guidance counselor who's supposed to guide them through this weird period of sexual unrest in their teens?"

We all stare at Tucker. His face goes red.

"Sorry, but it works me up," Tucker says. "Just because this kid—Leena—was an outsider, she's left to the wolf, and no one says a goddamn thing because she's not one of them."

I inhale deeply, look down, and study the tattered carpet squares. This is my child they're talking about. My failure as a mother. Perhaps my failure as a cop, too.

"What about the ripped journal pages?" Ray asks with a nod to the copies on the board.

"The 'He' that Leena writes about could easily be her teacher. It adds up," I say. "If she was infatuated with Clay Pelley, in love with him, he could have abused that. Taken sexual advantage."

"But why were they ripped from the journal? Why were they at the river?" Dirk muses.

"Maybe he wanted her to get rid of them, because the pages implicated him," I say.

Luke adds, "The two could have gotten into some kind of fight where he tried to grab the pages. And it escalated into him hitting, then beating, then needing to silence her by drowning."

Dirk rubs his chin. "The autopsy report shows vaginal trauma. Tearing. That doesn't square with consensual sex in the woods."

"It might—if the sex in the woods was rough," I say.

"I dunno," says Dirk. "Perhaps we need additional input on that postmortem evidence. Whatever happened to that girl, it was violent."

"Pelley's temper could have cracked over journal pages, and then he went over-the-edge crazy," Luke says. "The damage to Leena's face—that feels like rage to me. And very personal. It would fit."

"And the CCTV footage from outside the donair place?" asks Ray.

"Darsh Rai's account of events holds," says Luke. "So does Tripp Galloway's. It also fits Amy Chan's and Jepp Sullivan's stories."

"And still no sign of the jacket or the rest of the journal?" asks Ray.

"Not yet."

"Okay, let's execute those warrants and bring the bastard in," says the chief.

But just as we begin to move, the door to the bullpen swings open, and Bella, our civilian admin assistant, with her big blonde hairdo, pokes her head into the room. "Rachel—there's someone at the front to see you."

"Can it wait?"

"She says it's urgent."

"Who is it?" I ask, voice clipped.

"Wouldn't give her name. She's in the waiting area."

I stomp through to the reception area, then freeze in my tracks as I see—on the other side of the counter, sitting in the waiting area on a plastic chair—a thin, ragged woman in an oversize coat. Her hair is stringy and she's white as a sheet. On her lap is a stuffed gym bag. She's clutching it tightly as she rocks back and forth.

Hurriedly I open the half door that divides reception from the waiting area.

"Lacey! Are you okay?"

She surges to her feet, looking like a terrified deer caught in headlights. She hugs the gym bag tightly to her tummy. Her whole body is trembling. "I . . . I need to talk to you. Right now. I . . . need to show you something."

I take her arm, lower my voice. "Where's baby Janie? Is the baby all right?"

"She's with a woman from the church. It's about Clay," she whispers. "I think . . . He did it. My husband killed Leena Rai. He . . . he killed his student."

RACHEL

THEN
Wednesday, November 26, 1997.

"Come, come this way, Lacey." I usher her behind the counter and lead her quickly down a corridor toward an interview room. I open the door. "We can talk in here. Please, take a seat. I'll be right back."

Lacey sits gingerly on the edge of a plastic chair, still clutching the gym bag to her belly as though her life depends on it. I shut the door. Adrenaline courses through my system as I stride back to the bullpen.

"It's Lacey," I say. "She has something to show me. She says her husband did it. Killed Leena. I think I should talk to her alone."

Luke gets to his feet, glances at the chief.

"We'll observe," says Ray.

I head back into the interview room with my notebook and take a seat opposite Lacey.

"Are you sure your baby is okay, Lacey?" I'm concerned for the woman's mental health.

"Janie's with Marcia McLain from the Catholic Church women's group. I . . . I don't have long. My husband, Clay . . . he . . . called into work sick, and he went to see his doctor. He'll be home soon. And if he finds I'm gone. I . . . I . . . ." She abruptly upends the bag on the table.

A jacket tumbles out.

Khaki. Ironed. It has creases where it was neatly folded. Numbers and letters on the pocket.

I stare at the jacket. Jaswinder's words surface in my brain.

It was a big khaki-colored jacket. They call them military surplus jackets. Lots of zips and pockets, and some kind of numbering on the front pocket . . . She'd borrowed it.

My gaze shoots to Lacey.

"It's Clay's." Her voice is thin, tight. "I know Leena went missing in a jacket of this description. I heard it on the news, when she first vanished. I remember thinking, *Clay has a jacket like that.* But then right after she'd been reported missing, he brought it home from school. It was inside this gym bag. And it was all laundered and ironed and folded. Like this."

Slowly, quietly, I say, "What day did he bring it home, Lacey, do you remember?"

"It was Tuesday evening. The eighteenth. When he returned from school. It was the day after I heard on the radio that Leena Rai was missing. I didn't think much of the fact that Clay had a jacket that matched the description, because there must be plenty of jackets like that, and there was talk that Leena would show up. But when I hung the clean jacket in the hall closet, I noticed these dark stains." With trembling hands Lacey spreads the jacket out on the table for me to see. She points at the dark areas on the fabric. I'm conscious of being observed through the one-way mirror. I can almost feel the tension in the others behind the glass.

"These marks did not come out in the laundering process," she says. "I thought it was weird, and I asked Clay about them, and I also asked why he'd had the jacket laundered instead of bringing it home to put in the machine. I mean, we don't have money for a Laundromat."

"What did Clay say?"

"He said it was mud, and blood. He slipped and fell on a trail near the school, and he cut his hands on something sharp in the mud. He said he dropped the jacket off at the Laundromat because it was big and bulky, and our machine isn't an industrial one, but I've washed his jackets in our machine before. It was strange, but I forgot about it until . . ." She swallows, and emotion pools in her eyes. "Until Leena's body was found, and you guys came around asking those questions about Clay and his boots. That's when I knew."

"Knew what?"

"That the blood could be Leena's." She smears a tear across her cheek with a bony hand. "Everything . . . adds up. Him coming home at that time. Drunk like that. The jacket. The boots . . . The fact that Leena used to come around to be tutored in the shed . . ." Her words die, and she stares blankly at the jacket on the table.

My heart accelerates. I don't touch the jacket. Not without gloves.

"Why did you wait until now to tell us? Why didn't you mention it yesterday?"

"He's my husband. I . . . For better or worse. I . . . I didn't want to believe it was possible. I *couldn't*. But then . . ." Her voice fades.

I think of the crucifix on her child's bedroom wall, above the crib. This young woman, barely out of her teens herself, is a wife, and a mother, and deeply religious. Her belief in the wedding vows made in church, in front of her God, are powerful. *Till death do us part.* She's fighting a cognitive dissonance, turning in the father of her baby, even believing he could be evil.

"But then what, Lacey?" I prompt gently.

"Then I went into his shed. After you left. I took the bolt cutters. I broke in, and . . . and what I saw . . . it's a sin. Evil. God will punish him. He will burn in hell."

"What did you see, Lacey?"

"It's in the bottom of the bag. It's one . . . just one of them. I . . . couldn't bring the others. I . . ." She falls silent and sits like a woman awaiting a guillotine. Dead still. Resigned. Head bent forward. She arrived coiled like a spring, and now that she's delivered her message, she's spent.

"Can you wait here a minute?"

She looks at me blankly.

"I'll be right back. I just want to get some gloves."

I fetch a pair of crime scene gloves and return to the room. Tentatively I open the bag. My pulse kicks.

Disgust fills my throat.

RACHEL

NOW
Friday, November 19. Present day.

It's 3:45 p.m. and dark outside as I walk down the quiet hospice corridor, looking for Luke O'Leary's room. I find it—his name card is in the holder outside the door, and the door is ajar. I hesitate. Afraid. There's a small glow from inside. A curtain hangs partially across the doorway. I ease back the curtain and enter quietly.

My heart stalls for a moment.

I don't recognize the man propped up in the hospital bed with his eyes closed. He's impossibly thin. Gray complexioned. His veins, deep purple, are ropy and visible through translucent skin. A drip from the side of his bed leads into his arm. Oxygen tubes feed into his nostrils. The machine makes a hum. My stomach tightens. The once burly and gruff-looking detective who was married to his homicide job is a ghost of the man I once knew. And maybe once could have loved.

Careful not to wake him, I move quietly around the bottom of the bed and sit in the chair beside him.

He turns his head slowly, sensing a presence. His eyelids flutter open.

My heart quickens. I lean forward.

"Luke?" I say softly. "It's me—Rachel. Rachel from Twin Falls."

He stares at me blankly, and then he appears to slowly recognize who I am.

"Rachel." His voice is hoarse. Quiet. A smile curves weakly across his mouth, but the rest of his body doesn't move. "You finally came to see me. About bloody time." He pauses, inhales slowly. "Now I know what it takes . . . to get your attention." He sucks in another breath, struggling. "I've got to go and die, huh, and then you come?"

I give a soft, sad laugh. "I see you haven't lost your sense of humor, then, have you, Luke?" My voice hitches as emotion suddenly explodes in my chest. I fight to hold back tears, be brave. I have nothing to give to help him with what he is battling through. And I suddenly, desperately, don't want him to die. I reach forward and take his hand. His skin is cool, dry.

"Bloody thing, this cancer," he says. "Thought I could fight it, you know? So who told you I was checking out, eh? Who broke the news?"

I debate whether I should even mention it. But suddenly I *need* to talk to someone. Someone like Luke. Someone who was there. Someone who, in truth, I think maybe I did actually love. Maybe I still do, in a strange way. Or perhaps the emotion I'm feeling is far more complex, and it's another kind of bond that we share. A knowing. A mutual understanding. I know what makes him tick, and he knows in turn what makes me tick. And he once cared.

He cared when Jake didn't.

"Well, it's kind of a long story," I say.

"I have a bit of time. I think."

I inhale deeply. "There's a young woman who is doing a true crime podcast on the Leena Rai murder."

His eyes close. He's silent for a long time, and I wonder if he's gone to sleep. Or worse. Panic licks at me. I lean forward. "Luke?"

"I'm here. I'm here." He tries to moisten his lips, struggles to swallow.

I reach for the plastic water cup next to his bed. It has a bendy straw inserted into the lid. I offer him some water. He sits up a bit, and I hold the straw to his dry lips. He sips with difficulty. Water dribbles down his gray-whiskered chin. I reach for a tissue, wipe it away, and my eyes flood with emotion again. I smooth his hair back off his forehead. His brow feels hot. Clammy. He doesn't smell so good. And I wish—wish with all my heart—that I'd seized life by the horns all those years back and not let Luke go. That when Jake walked out, I'd followed Luke to Vancouver.

But I had Maddy.

I was, and still am, a mom.

Even though Maddy wanted nothing to do with me then, and even less now. She moved in with her father when Jake left me for the other woman. I figured if I remained in town, I could still be there for Mads, and she'd eventually grow out of whatever strange phase she was going through. I truly believed she'd come around and learn to love me again. But it was futile.

"How is your family, Rache?"

I wonder if he's lost the conversation thread. Or if he's reading my mind.

"Alive." I offer a smile that feels false. "Maddy ended up marrying Darren Jankowski, from school. He was one of the kids you interviewed back in the day, about the Leena Rai case. I don't know if you remember him?"

"Not really. Are they happy?"

I look away.

I owe Luke the truth. His days, hours, are numbered. There is no place left for lies in this fragile space between life and death. Pretending otherwise is just me trying to save face. He deserves more than that. If it were me in that bed, I'd want honesty. And maybe I just need to say it. To someone. Get it out of me.

"I don't know if my kid has deep-down happy genes, Luke. She loves her family and being a mother, but I don't know if Maddy is actually capable of finding true inner peace. She fights against everything, all the time. Especially me. There's like . . . a bitterness in her. A permanent rage that simmers perpetually just below the surface. She . . ." My voice fades as Luke's eyes close and his breathing deepens.

"Go on," he whispers, eyes still closed. "I'm listening."

"Sometimes I feel as though she's been trying to self-destruct since her early teens, you know? She almost succeeded when she had a climbing accident and suffered a spinal cord injury."

His eyelids flutter open. He stares at me.

"Paralyzed from the waist down."

"So she took up rock climbing?"

I nod and moisten my lips. "From about the age of sixteen. She tackled more and more complicated and technical climbs over the years, and then started attacking the north routes on Chief Mountain like a fiend, every free moment she could. Like she *needed* to fight that granite mountain. Or dare it to kill her. And it almost did. She fell shortly after her youngest daughter was born. Now she no longer climbs, yet chooses to live in a house where she can see that rock face taunting her, lording over her, from every damn window in her house."

He's quiet for a long while. "So she has kids. You're a grandmother."

"On paper I'm a grandmother. Two girls. Lily, who is three now, and Daisy, who is almost five. They barely know me. Maddy never forgave me for . . ." Suddenly I can't say it.

"You mean for me. For us. That one time."

I nod, fiddle with my fingers. "She fights me harder than she fought Chief Mountain."

Luke reaches for my hand. I take his and hold. The contact settles something in me, and I fall quiet.

"Tell me about the podcast. Is that why you came?"

"I came to see *you*, Luke. The podcaster—her name is Trinity Scott—she broke it to me that you were in hospice. I didn't know."

"It's all the rage, isn't it, these crime podcasts." It's more a statement than a question. "Did she say why she picked the Leena murder? What's the angle?"

"Clay Pelley is talking." I watch his face closely as I say it. "He's on tape, saying he didn't do it. He said he did not assault or kill Leena."

He squints at me, then pulls a wry mouth. "Even if Pelley is lying, even if no one believes him, it sure gives fodder to a true crime narrative," he says, barely audible. "Why in the hell is he suddenly talking now, anyway, after all these years?"

"I don't know."

"Have you been interviewed?"

"I declined."

"She's going to drag you into it, Rache. If you don't talk, it's going to make him look sympathetic. Maybe you should tell your side of the story."

I sit silent for a while.

"What's there to lose, really?" he asks. "Or . . . is there something I don't know?"

Anxiety rises inside me. "What do you mean?"

"I always felt . . . that you were keeping something from me. Protecting someone."

My heart beats faster.

"That's why it never did work between us, isn't it? You had barriers up, blocking something. It locked me out."

"That's not true. I had a teenager. I was a mother. I had future job prospects with the Twin Falls PD."

"Yet you were passed over in the end. You were groomed and pegged for chief, yet Ray Doyle brought in a shiny new guy from the Vancouver PD. Why do you think he did that?"

"You know why. It was the stress leave I ended up taking, the therapy I needed. I . . . I suddenly wasn't such a good prospect. Perhaps I *should* have left the PD back then. Maybe, deep down, that part of me that wasn't a mother wanted to follow you—should have followed you."

He smiles sadly and closes his eyes. He's silent for several minutes, and again I worry that he might have stopped breathing.

"What if he's telling the truth?" he whispers finally.

"Clay? You cannot be serious."

"I'm too far gone to not be serious." He opens his eyes, takes another strained breath, and when he speaks, his voice is weak, fading.

"We had loose ends with that case, Rache. In more ways than one. Questions that were never answered because he confessed. There were things I wanted to know, like—"

A nurse enters, so silently that she makes me jump. "Evening, Detective O'Leary," she says cheerily. "Are you ready for your meds top-up?" She's holding a syringe as she goes over to the drip next to his bed.

"Morphine," explains Luke.

"Who's your lovely lady friend?" the nurse asks, giving me a wink as she feeds the syringe contents into a tube.

"My old girlfriend," he says.

She laughs. "Right. Sure. She's far too good-looking for you, Detective." Then she says softly to me, "He'll go to sleep as soon as I've administered this."

I nod. "I'll wait with him."

The nurse exits.

"Bye, Rache," Luke whispers, his eyelids going heavy. His words begin to slur. "Thanks . . . for coming to say farewell. Live a little while you still can. Get . . . to know those grandbabies of yours. Life—the little moments, the now—it's all we've got."

Emotion wallops me. I try to swallow it down as tears pool in my eyes. I kiss him on his brow and whisper near his ear, "I'll be back. I'll tell you more about the podcast. I'll download it for you. Okay?"

He squeezes my hand. He whispers again, so quietly I need to lean close to his mouth in order to hear. "Follow the truth, Rache. Even if it hurts. Even if it takes you where you don't want it to go. It's not too late."

"What do you mean?"

His eyes shut. "The truth . . . sets you free." His breathing changes. He struggles to get his next words out. "It's . . . the secrets that fester. You . . . think you've buried them, gotten rid of them somehow, but they're like this damned cancer. The minute you're down, the second you grow tired, it starts to grow again, and it catches up with you."

I swallow. I watch his face. My pulse is racing.

"Luke?"

Silence. He's asleep.

I hesitate, then kiss him again on his brow and whisper, "I'll come again. I promise."

I go to look for Luke's nurse and find her in the nursing station. I ask her about his prognosis.

"It's doubtful he'll last the night," she says gently. "One can never really tell, but there are signs, and they are there. I'm sorry."

Tears slide down my face.

"Will you be okay?" she asks.

I nod because I can't speak. I go sit for a while by the gas fireplace that flickers in the living room area of the hospice. I need to gather my wits before the long drive back home in the darkness. At a table in the corner of the room, a man sits with a woman who is bent forward. She is reed thin and has a blanket wrapped around her shoulders. The man holds her hand. I imagine she's his mother.

The pain in my heart is suddenly unbearable.

About twenty minutes later, the nurse finds me.

"I'm so sorry," she says. "He's gone."

I am completely lost for words. I can only stare at her.

"Would you like to see him?"

I hesitate. Nod. And come to my feet. I feel disoriented as she leads me back down the corridor. The door to Luke's room is now closed. A ceramic butterfly hangs on the door handle.

He's free.

She sees me staring at the butterfly.

"We hang that there so staff knows the occupant has passed. So people don't enter and get a shock."

The nurse reaches for the door handle, and suddenly I say, "No. I . . . I did see him. I saw Luke. What's inside there—he's gone." I turn and march hurriedly for the exit and push out into the cold. I stop in my tracks, and take a deep, shuddering breath. My hands are shaking. Wind gusts and swirls fiercely about me. Dead leaves clatter along the walkway. I glimpse the moon between gaps in the scudding clouds. I think about the moon in the sky and the burning Russian rocket on the night Leena died.

This is it.

No more secrets.

No more walls.

The now is all we've got. I want truth. The whole truth. I'm no longer afraid of looking too deep. I'm ready no matter what I find.

RACHEL

"There! He's pulling in!" I point as I see Clay's beat-up old Subaru turning into the driveway, his headlights painting the rain silver.

Luke keys his radio. "Go. Go. It's him."

Sirens engage, and officers—most of them RCMP—move fast. One vehicle, its light bar flashing, pulls into the driveway behind Clay, blocking his escape. A second vehicle parks across the driveway on the road. A third goes around the back of the block, in case Clay tries to run through to his backyard and jump the fence. Luke and I exit our unmarked car wearing bullet suppression vests. We are armed. We stride down the driveway toward Clay's vehicle. My heart pounds with a primal kind of rage as I hold in my mind that photograph Lacey brought to the station in the bottom of Clay's gym bag. It showed a girl of around eight years of age being sexually abused by an unidentified older male.

Lacey's words circle in my head.

It's one . . . just one of them. I . . . couldn't bring the others.

Clay flings open his car door and exits into the rain.

"What the hell—"

"Clay Pelley, you're under arrest," I say. "Turn around, put your hands up on the roof of your car."

"What in the hell for?"

"Turn around. Hands on car. Spread your legs. Now."

Slowly he turns, places his hands on the roof of his Subaru. Rain drums down on us as I pat him down, then cuff his hands behind his back.

"Clayton Jay Pelley, you're under arrest for the possession of child pornography and for statutory rape of a minor." I turn him to face us. "We have warrants to search your shed, your home, your office at Twin Falls Secondary School, and to impound and search your vehicle for evidence in connection with the death of Leena Rai. You have the right to retain and instruct counsel," I say. "And you have the right to silence, but anything you do say can be used as evidence against you. Do you understand?"

"This is ridiculous. I—"

"Do you understand what I'm saying, Clay?"

"I—" Clay curses viciously. "Yes. But this is—"

"Take him away," I say to the officer nearby. And to another I say, "Impound the Subaru. Tow it."

Luke waves the other officers toward the house.

"I want my lawyer!" Clay yells as the officer ducks him into the rear of the marked vehicle with the light bar pulsing red and blue through the streaks of rain.

"Knock your socks off," I say. "We'll see you at the station."

With flashlights, Luke and I make for the shed in the back garden. Fury fires through my veins.

There are two officers in the shed already. They've brought in klieg lights. The interior is awash with harsh, unforgiving light that exposes every corner.

Four file boxes are open on a table near a desk. Beside the boxes are a computer and printer. An officer steps back for us to see.

"Must be hundreds of images in the boxes," he says quietly.

I stare. Deep down inside my belly, I begin to shake. The cop is correct. The boxes contain hundreds of glossy photographic prints. All of pornographic acts, some more awful, more violent, than others. Graphic images that show unidentified men with young children. *Girls.* Inside one of the boxes is a fat manila envelope with a return address. It, too, seems to be stuffed with photographs.

I turn slowly and study the shelves along the back wall. A camera rests on one. Lighting equipment on another. I try to imagine Clay tutoring Leena and other girls in here. My hands tremble as I watch the officers begin to carry the boxes and computer equipment out to the vehicles.

Luke puts his hand on my shoulder. "You okay?"

Quietly I say, "How can anyone be okay with this? Those . . . those are children in those photos. Young children. What is this? Is he part of some pedophile ring that shares child porn via mail? And what's in those film canisters on that shelf there? Did he also take pictures of the kids in this shed, while he was allegedly tutoring them? Has he shared those?"

Luke rubs his mouth.

My voice cracking, I say, "He did it. I'm sure he did it. He killed Leena. I'm going to nail his dick to the wall."

RACHEL

Clay's lawyer is Marge Duncan, a woman from Twin Falls who tradi-
tionally handles minor criminal cases like DUIs and shoplifting. She's
probably all Clay Pelley can find at this time. She looks uncomfortable.
It's 7:32 p.m., and Marge sits beside Clay on one side of the interrogation room table. Luke and I sit opposite them. We've run through the
preambles. The interview is being recorded.

"Where's Lacey?" Clay demands again. "Was she home when you
invaded? Did she see? Where's my baby, Janie? Is she all right?" Clay's
skin shines with sweat. His clothing is disheveled. His pores exude a
stale alcohol stink.

"Lacey and Janie have been put up in a motel," I say tightly. "Her
parents are driving down from Terrace to fetch her."

Clay's head drops forward. I am ramrod erect, simmering after what
we found. Now that I know what darkness lives inside this man's head,
I can barely tolerate him. I have an urge to beat him. To kick the shit
out of him. This man who taught and coached my daughter and her
friends. The others watch from behind the one-way mirror, including
a prosecutor. This case is blowing up. Media attention is going to go
global. I've been instructed to let Luke do the interview.

"Okay, Clay," Luke says. "By your own admission, and confirmed by nineteen witnesses, you were at the Ullr bonfire on Friday night, November fourteenth. You sat beside Leena Rai on a log. You spent considerable time talking to her, and then shortly before the Russian rocket hit the earth's atmosphere at nine twelve p.m., you went with Leena Rai down a trail toward the outhouses."

He glances at his legal counsel. She communicates something to him with a whisper in his ear. He remains silent.

Luke continues. "You made a statement that you left the bonfire before the rocket and drove directly home in your Subaru. However, your alibi doesn't hold up. Lacey, your wife, has made a statement that you arrived home at 3:42 a.m. on Saturday morning, November fifteenth. She says you were intoxicated."

He looks up. His eyes widen. "No. That's not right." He glances at his legal counsel, panic beginning to show. "That's not what happened. I was home. Lacey saw—"

"You don't have to answer, Clay," Marge says. "You—"

"But it's *not* true. I went straight home."

Luke calmly glances at the notes in his folder. "Another witness, one of your students, Maddison Walczak, stated she saw you and Leena Rai engaging in sexual intercourse in bushes off a trail near the outhouse. This was shortly before the rocket went through the sky."

Clay stares. He pales. "*Maddy* said that?"

"Did you engage in sex with your student, Leena Rai?" Luke asks.

Clay's gaze flares to mine. His features are twisted with what looks like fear. His eyes shine.

"It's a lie. No way in hell is that true."

"Maddy says it's true. She saw your face clearly with her headlamp."

"It's a blatant lie! It never happened. And it's her word against mine."

"Maddy ran straight to tell her friend Beth Galloway, who was at the bonfire. Maddy and Beth returned quickly back down the trail

193

in time for Beth to see you helping Leena up off the ground, putting your arm around her, and walking her back to your Subaru, which was parked on the logging road. We have several other witnesses who also saw you walking up that trail, holding Leena." Luke pauses, and he watches Clay closely. "Where were you taking Leena, Clay? Where did the two of you go between nine twelve p.m. and two a.m. the following morning, when Leena was seen stumbling, alone, along Devil's Bridge in your jacket?"

Clay regards Luke intently. Silence fills the room. I can smell him— his scent is stronger, sweat permeating the stale alcohol stink with an acrid stench of fear.

"Clayton?" Luke prods.

He swallows and glances at his lawyer.

Marge nods.

"I gave her a ride back into Twin Falls."

Adrenaline spikes in my blood. I feel the waves of silent energy rolling off Luke, but he remains outwardly calm.

"You gave Leena Rai a ride? In your vehicle—the Subaru?"

He nods and inhales heavily. "She was very inebriated. I was worried about Leena. I feared for her judgment and safety. And that is the truth. She . . . I liked Leena. I was fond of her."

"I'm sure you were," I say.

Luke fires a hot glance at me. I hold my tongue. But I remain wound like a spring. I want to tear his throat out. He has a struggling wife, a tiny child. This bastard with boxes of child porn in his shed, where he tutored Leena and others.

"So you drove Leena back to town, after you had sex with her."

"I never had sex with Leena. We sat on the log and talked. Like I said, she was very drunk. I told her I was going home, and I offered her a ride. I . . . I told her she'd be safer if she came home with me, rather than hang around alone in that group."

The irony hangs in the close atmosphere of the padded room.

"I'll play along," Luke says. "You drove her back into Twin Falls. Where did you drop her off?"

He rubs his face hard with both hands. "I was going to drive her to her home, but when we reached the intersection on the north side of Devil's Bridge, she wanted to get out of the car. I said no, I was taking her to her house, and she started getting belligerent and opening the door while I was driving."

"Why was she getting belligerent?" asks Luke.

"I *told* you, she was very drunk. Obstreperous. She wanted to go to Ari's Greek Takeout, which is across the river. I wanted to go the other way, to her house and then my home. But she insisted, so I let her out."

"You let a very drunk student—a fourteen-year-old girl—out into the dark, alone?"

He nods.

"Could you speak your answer out loud for the recording, Clay?"

"Yes. I did."

"So let me see if I've got this straight—you were worried about Leena's judgment and safety at the bonfire, and then when you get back into Twin Falls, right near Devil's Bridge, you are suddenly no longer concerned about those things?"

Silence.

"What changed, Clayton? Did Leena say something that made you mad? Did she threaten to reveal that you had sex with her, maybe?"

"That's enough, Detectives. My client has—"

"I did *not* have sex with Leena. Maddy is a liar."

I tighten my fists in my lap.

"Did you ever talk to Leena about a shadow, Clay? A Jungian-type shadow?"

He looks worried. Confused. Unsure where Luke is going with this.

"Uh . . . yes. Part of a literature study of global mythologies."

"Did she ever profess her love for you?"

His eyes flicker. He looks cornered. He fiddles with the edge of the table. "She . . . Leena had infatuations. She misread things."

Luke takes a page out of his folder. He begins to read from it.

"'We spend most of our lives afraid of our own Shadow. He told me that. He said a Shadow lives deep inside every one of us. So deep we don't even know it's there. Sometimes, with a quick sideways glance, we catch a glimpse of it. But it frightens us, and we quickly look away . . . I don't know why He tells me these things. Maybe it's a way of obliquely bringing out and addressing his own Shadow. But I do think our Shadows are bad—his and mine. Big and dark and very dangerous. I don't think our Shadows should ever be allowed out.'"

Clay looks down at the table.

"Is this what you tutored Leena about?"

"It's possible this is how she interpreted it."

"Are you the 'He' that Leena refers to in her journal text?"

"It's possible."

"Did you know what was in her journal, Clay? Did you and Leena fight over it? Did the fight get physical under Devil's Bridge?"

"No. None of that. I dropped her at the bridge. I never saw her journal. I didn't know she'd written those things."

"Why did she write that you both have very dangerous shadows?"

"I have no idea what was in her head when she wrote those words."

"What about her backpack? Did you drop that off with her, too?"

"It was on the back seat of my car. I handed it to her when she got out. And then I drove through the intersection, and went home."

"What time was that?"

"I'm . . . not sure."

"If you left the bonfire around nine p.m., did you go elsewhere? Because Lacey said you only returned home at 3:42 a.m."

"I told you, that's untrue. I went home. I started drinking, and I could have gone into my shed, then stumbled into bed at 3:42 a.m. But I was home."

"So where did Leena go, between when you dropped her off and when she was seen staggering along the bridge around two a.m.?"

"I have no idea."

Luke sits back. He assesses the suspect. "Clay, why did you not tell us this when she was first reported missing?"

"I . . . knew how it would look."

"We could have searched in the Devil's Bridge area right away," I say. "Instead, we had to wait a week before Amy Chan came forward."

Luke casts me another warning glare. I fall silent. My heart is thudding. My rage is building.

"Did anyone else know that you drove Leena to the intersection, Clay?" Luke asks.

"I don't think so."

"Do you recognize this jacket?" Luke slides toward Clay a photo of the jacket that Lacey brought in earlier.

"That's mine. I loaned it to Leena a couple of weeks before the bonfire. It started raining while she was with me for a tutoring session. She didn't have a coat with her. My jacket was hanging on the back of my shed door, and she asked if she could borrow it, and she just sort of kept it."

"How did you get it back?"

"I don't know."

"You don't know?"

"It was just there, in my office on Tuesday morning after the bonfire weekend. Laundered. Just left there in a plastic bag. I actually thought it was Leena who had returned it, until it became clear that she was truly missing."

"Right. And these dark stains?"

Silence.

"Tell me again how you cut and bruised your hands."

Silence.

"Look, the RCMP crime lab has your jacket now, Clay. If these stains here"—Luke taps the photo—"are from Leena's blood, the lab *will* find the match. If that blood on the backpack is either yours or Leena's, they will find that out, too. If there is any fiber evidence in your car—"

Clay goes white and makes a strange noise. He's almost hyperventilating. His pupils are dilating. He looks confused, drugged.

"Something you want to say, Clay?" Luke asks.

He makes the noise again, and he shakes his head rapidly, as if trying to banish an image, or a memory that is suddenly surfacing and that he can no longer fight.

"Clay?"

"It's my blood. On her backpack. It's my blood."

Luke goes rigid. "Why is it your blood?"

"I told you . . . I cut my hands while stacking a woodpile. And I bumped the wounds in the forest while at the bonfire, and my hands started to bleed again. And when I reached into the back of my car to grab Leena's pack, I could have gotten my blood on the straps."

Clay still doesn't look right. He appears dazed. My gaze ticks to Luke.

He takes another photo from his file, and slides it toward Clay.

"This is a photograph of the title page from a book of poems found with Leena's things alongside the river. It's titled *Whispers of the Trees.* Your wife identified it as your book, Clay, and the initials A. C., your wife says, are the initials of a woman named Abbigail Chester. Who's Abbigail?"

"A friend. From university days. She's dead."

"What happened to Abbigail?"

He looks worried. His eyes dart to his lawyer. She looks confused, troubled.

"They . . . they say it was a home invasion that went bad."

"See? Here's what we've now learned from my RCMP counterparts, Clay. Abbigail Chester did in fact die in what appeared to be a home invasion. But she was also sexually assaulted. Violently. Then bludgeoned to death." Luke pauses, regards Clay steadily for a few moments. "Bit of a coincidence, don't you think? Finding a book that Abbigail Chester gifted you near the body of a young woman who died under remarkably similar circumstances?"

"My client has no knowledge of the Abbigail Chester crime," Marge says. "You're on a fishing expedition."

Luke pushes another photo toward Clay. It glares up at us. Hairy male body. Aged hands. The soft skin of a young girl. Erect penis.

We all watch Clay. He seems to swell with an invisible electricity. It crackles around him. It changes his face. His eyes take on a dark and strange look as he studies the image.

Softly Luke says, "This is one of hundreds found in your shed, Clay. Do you know who brought this photo in to show us?"

He swallows, but refuses to meet Luke's eyes.

"Lacey brought it in. *Your wife.* She found the photos in your shed."

His gaze flares up. It locks on to Luke's. Clay's entire body seems to be vibrating. Like bottled rocket fuel ready to blow. His lawyer looks increasingly nervous, out of her depth. Her attention darts between the horrific pornographic image and her client.

"Lacey found a babysitter, Clay. And she brought this jacket and that photo into the station. She told us what was inside your shed. She asked us to keep her safe. From *you.* Your own wife. She turned you in. She *saw* what you kept under bolt and key inside that shed where you tutored girls."

A tear leaks from Clay's eye. It dribbles down his cheek. He casts his eyes down, looks at his hands in his lap.

Luke slams his hand on the table.

Clay jerks, but still doesn't look up.

"Clay, I'm going to ask you again, did you have sex with a minor? Did you have intercourse with Leena Rai in the grove on the night of the Ullr bonfire?"

He makes a blubbering sound. More tears flow down his cheeks. His nose begins to run.

"Did you take Leena Rai beneath Devil's Bridge?"

He swipes his wrist across his nose, smearing snot.

"Did you assault Leena under the bridge? Did you—"

"Stop!" he screams. Luke, the lawyer, and I jerk back, taken off guard. He surges to his feet.

"I did it. Okay? I fucking did it. All of it." He glares at us.

"Clay, please, sit down," Luke says. I'm wired, ready to move to block the door, restrain him.

Clay stands, unmoving.

"Sit, Clay."

He clears his throat. Slowly, as if in a trance, he sits.

"Tell us, what did you do? How did you do it?"

In a slow, quiet monotone, he says, "I sexually assaulted and then killed Leena Rai. After I raped her, I couldn't stand her, what she represented. Because she represented everything I hate about myself, everything horrible I've done, all my addictions—my addiction to pornography, my arousal around children, young girls. I beat her out of existence. I bashed her away. Killing it, hating it, murdering it. I wanted her gone. Out of my life."

I swallow. The lawyer is as pale as a ghost. I can feel the tension of the others watching from behind the mirror. I'm aware of the camera and audio recording this. I feel surreal.

"How?" Luke says softly. "Tell us exactly how it happened, step by step. How did you kill Leena?"

He closes his eyes for several long beats. The smell of him in the room is thick. Again, in that soft monotone, Clay speaks. "I had sex with Leena in the grove, off an overgrown trail near the outhouses. I know Maddy saw us. She had a headlamp on. Her beam lit on our faces. I tried to call out to Maddy, but she ran away, along the trail, back toward the bonfire. Leena . . ." He looks confused for a moment, closes his eyes again, and he begins to rock back and forth. "She was upset, crying. I reached down to help her up. That's when I heard people in the bushes. Possibly watching us. Leena was wobbling, drunk. I put my arm around her to assist her back to my car. I . . . I was going to take her home."

He glances up at the camera near the ceiling, then turns his gaze back to us. "On the way home, she got more and more agitated. She started to say she was going to report me, because Maddy had seen us already, and Maddy would tell anyway. Leena said she'd written about me in her journal, which she had in her backpack. Instead of taking her home, I drove her to a lookout, to try and talk her down, and to try and sober her up a bit. She fell asleep for a while. We were parked at the lookout for a few hours. She woke up and seemed more reasonable. I then started to drive her home, but when we reached the intersection near Devil's Bridge, she got riled up again and asked to be let out. I handed her her backpack, watched her go, then panicked. I parked my car off the road, behind some trees, and I followed her over the bridge. I guess this was sometime around two a.m. On the south side, I grabbed her and forced her down the path that led under Devil's Bridge."

He falls silent.

"And then?" Luke asks.

"I ripped the pack from her back and tried to take her journal. She fought me. The pages ripped. I struck her across the side of the face. She fell onto the gravel path. I stomped my boot onto the back of her head. I . . . raped her there. She got up, got away, staggered across the bridge, heading north. I followed, but I held back because some vehicles went by, and I didn't want any witnesses to link me to her. Then on the other side of the bridge, where it was dark, I grabbed her again and dragged her back down along the trail under the north end of the bridge this time. I hit her head with a rock. I stomped on her back. I grabbed her by the collar, dragged her over the stones and boulders. The jacket came off while I was dragging her, and her shirt, too, because I was pulling the sleeves, tugging, and she was fighting me. And a shoe came off. Leena staggered to her feet, and I got hold of her, and I ran her face-first into the trunk of a tree. And again. And again. And again. And she still wasn't gone, still wouldn't die. She was still breathing. So I dragged her body over the small rocks into the water. Her pants came off while I was pulling her. She was limp, and very heavy, and kept getting snagged up in the stones. I dragged her thigh deep into the water. It was cold. And then I straddled her, and sat on her, using my body weight to press her down into the small stones on the bottom of the river. I used my knees, forcing them into her shoulders. I held the back of her head underwater with both hands. Until she was gone. I killed—I drowned—Leena Rai."

Clay absently examines the bruises and healing lacerations on his hands, as if seeing them for the first time. "From hitting Leena, I guess," he says quietly. "Punching her."

Silence fills the room. Time elongates and shimmers. Then in his quiet, strange monotone, Clay says, "I left her there. Floating facedown in the reeds. Under Devil's Bridge. And no one even noticed for a week. The bus that her father drove—his route went right over that bridge every day. Several times a day. And the school bus that she wasn't on, it went over the bridge twice a day, too. And no one saw her down there. Floating in the eelgrass, until she sank. The forgotten girl."

RACHEL

I walk into the Raven's Roost pub with Luke and the rest of the team. It's almost midnight. We have charged Clay Pelley. He's been transported to a remand facility in the Lower Mainland to await further processing.

The pub is buzzing, and we're all pumped to burn off steam. A local band plays on a small stage, and the music is loud and upbeat. Bikers and cops mix with loggers and climbers and other local townsfolk. Chief Ray has commandeered a long table of thick wood and is ordering beers and whiskeys and pizza for us all.

Bella with the big hair is opening a bottle of sparkling wine. She shrieks as the cork explodes out of the bottle and fizz spouts over the table. Tucker hurries to put champagne flutes under it.

Ray takes my arm, leans his mouth near my ear. "Your dad would be proud, Rache. This is exactly what you were cut out for."

I smile and accept a glass of bubbly from Bella. Ray's words mean more to me than he can imagine. I want desperately to do my dad proud. To prove I have the mettle. Especially after he and my mom supported me as a young mother going through police training. My life goal is to follow in his footsteps and lead the PD, this town, into the future after Ray retires. Luke scoots over on the bench to make room for me at the table. As I slide in beside him, my thigh presses against his. His muscles are solid. His body is warm. Everything about Luke is solid and warm. Comfortable and strong. I glance at his face. His eyes meet mine. For a moment we are locked in an instantly private and silent bubble, erotic, suspended in time. My skin tingles. I feel heat in my belly. I swallow, break his gaze, and raise my glass along with the others, but the feeling of electricity still crackles through me.

"Well done, everyone," says Ray.

As the drinking and revelry and raucous joking progress, as the alcohol takes effect, I find myself falling into myself and going quiet. I'm worried about Maddy again. I should have gone straight home. But it's late, and she'll be in bed anyway, and tomorrow will be a new day with no more working on the Leena Rai case. I know the trial will come. And so will the associated tension with Maddy being deposed and testifying. But that could be a year out, or more, from now.

Tomorrow Luke and I will visit with Leena's parents. Tomorrow I will turn all my free attention to Maddy's needs.

But there is more. Something deeper down that cooks silently inside me.

My mind returns to the photo I took from Maddy's drawer. The one that is now in an envelope and locked in a box of my own things. I think of the locket. And of Leena's beautiful written words, so full of longing and exploration. And I wonder where the rest of that journal is now. On further questioning, Clay couldn't answer that question for us. When Luke asked him if Leena had been wearing that locket we found in her hair, he said he couldn't recall. He couldn't explain to my satisfaction the thermal burns on Leena's face, either. He said he thinks he must have lit some of Leena's cigarettes from her backpack and done it.

My pondering turns to Liam Parks. And his allegedly stolen camera and film. I take another sip of sparkling wine, then tense as I feel Luke's hand on my thigh.

"You okay?"

His mouth is close. He needs to lean forward so I can hear him over the music and rambunctious laughter and chatter around the table. My body goes hot in spite of my cool inner thoughts and lingering questions. I watch his lips as he speaks. For a moment I can't breathe. I clear my throat and say, "I . . . was just thinking . . . there are loose ends. Like where is her journal?"

"They'll be resolved. When this goes to trial, I'm sure all these things will come out in discovery, and via testimony in the court case itself."

I nod.

"Want to get out of here?"

I hesitate. I should know better. But I say yes.

We take our leave, and as we step out into the bracing cold, we see the night sky is clear and full of stars. An icy wind blasts off the sea. It clears my head.

"I should go home."

He looks disappointed, but just briefly. "Yeah, I could do with some sleep, too. I'll walk you to your car."

"When are you heading back to the city?" I ask as we proceed down the sidewalk.

"I'll check out of the motel tomorrow. Drive back after we've gone to see Pratima and Jaswinder. I can tie anything else up from the Surrey office." We enter a short alley that leads between buildings to the parking lot on the other side. It's dark. Shadowed. He hesitates. I stop to look at him. Moonlight catches his strong profile. His eyes glint in the light.

"Want to come to the motel, for a nightcap?"

I open my mouth, then shut it.

Luke takes my hand. Logic deserts me. He draws me closer, and I let him. He tilts up my chin, whispers over my lips, "Come back to the motel, Rachel."

He bends closer, and I lean up and kiss him. At first it's tentative, then suddenly it's fierce, wild, blinding. He's cupping my buttocks, drawing my pelvis hard against his. His tongue is in my mouth, and my hand goes between his thighs. I feel the erect length of him, and my legs seem to melt. A groan escapes his throat as he leans his erection into my hand.

A light suddenly shines at the end of the alley. Headlights flare brightly on us, exposing us like actors in a spotlight on a dark stage. A raccoon scuttles away and tins clatter. The car turns, and the headlights pan away. I tense, pull back, heart hammering, reality slamming back into my brain.

The sound of the vehicle fades into the distance. I should go home. I need to go home. I must. But to what? Maddy, who is sound asleep? Jake, who no longer loves me, and in some ways started the process of abandoning our marriage, our partnership, months ago?

"Coming?" he asks softly, near my ear.

And I go.

I cross that line.

I go with Luke to the cheap motel on the highway. The same bloody motel where Jake used to cheat on me.

Perhaps that's why I go.

Perhaps it's an unconscious form of revenge. Or proving to myself I can do what Jake did.

Perhaps it's because I know I won't see Luke again. And I can't quite let him go. Or maybe I need to tap into his solid energy, feel loved, feel desired, just one more time. And I *need* sex. I need to feel human, like a beautiful woman again. I need to make love in the face of the death and ugliness we've witnessed on this case. And he's an opportunity that presents. An ally. No complicated strings.

As we back into his motel room, kissing, stripping the clothes off each other's bodies, and as we make hot and desperate love, I know I must never see Luke again. Not like this. Because it will take apart what is left of my marriage. And the good girl in me knows I should do what I can to save it.

For Maddy.

TRINITY

"Clayton, I obtained all the police transcripts along with other case records, and I have a copy of your confession right here with me." I push the copy toward him. The digital recorder rests on the table between us. "Can I ask you to read this part of the transcript of your confession for our listeners? If you could start from where you said that you did it, that you raped and killed fourteen-year-old Leena Rai."

"I didn't."

"That's what you claim now, but it's not what you claimed then, in 1997. Can you read what you said, word for word, so our audience can hear what the two detectives heard in the room that day?"

He pulls the document closer.

"Please start from the part where you say to Detective O'Leary and Detective Walczak, 'She woke up and seemed more reasonable.'"

I watch him as he scans the text, finding the right point. A strange look overcomes his face. His energy changes. I feel the atmosphere in the room shift, and for a moment I feel scared, and I'm acutely aware of where the exit door is in relation to my chair in case I need to bolt or need help. Because Clay suddenly seems to be becoming someone else.

He begins to read in a scratchy monotone. Slowly. Quietly. It sounds unreal. Like he's rehearsed it for all the years that he's been in prison, and he's sort of dissociated from it.

"'I then started to drive her home, but when we reached the intersection near Devil's Bridge, she got riled up again and asked to be let out. I handed her her backpack, watched her go, then panicked . . . I grabbed her again and dragged her back down along the trail under the north end of the bridge this time. I hit her head with a rock. I stomped on her back. I grabbed her by the collar, dragged her over the stones and boulders. The jacket came off while I was dragging her, and her shirt, too, because I was pulling the sleeves, tugging, and she was fighting me . . . Then I straddled her, and sat on her, using my body weight to press her down into the small stones on the bottom of the river. I used my knees, forcing them into her shoulders. I held the back of her head underwater with both hands. Until she was gone. I killed—I drowned—Leena Rai.'"

He looks up.

"And you left her there, floating in the reeds, beneath Devil's Bridge. 'Floating in the eelgrass . . . The forgotten girl.'"

He shakes his head. His eyes hold mine. I feel more than see the little red light blinking on my recording device. I feel my future audience listening, expectant.

I prompt him. "Detective O'Leary asked you exactly how you did it, Clayton."

"It . . . I made it up. It's not true." For a moment he actually looks confused. And I think I know what's happening. He's not so much lying to me about not having killed Leena. He's deluded himself. And now he's being confronted with the black-and-white printed reality of what occurred in that interrogation room twenty-four years ago.

"You told the detectives, with your lawyer present, *exactly* what the autopsy report also told them."

"It's not true."

"Clay, how did you manage to make up information—forensic details—that only those close to the investigation knew?"

He stares at the printout.

"Go on, Clayton," I urge gently. Adrenaline zings through my blood. This is awesome. Ratings will be insane. But beneath my excitement, another sensation is building. Something I don't want to—can't—think about right now.

Suddenly Clayton seems to go utterly vacant. He's a shell, just sitting there. Empty. His eyes have gone distant, as though his whole being has slid down a wormhole in time to a place in the dark and cold under Devil's Bridge twenty-four years ago.

"Clayton?"

He blinks. Then rubs his chin.

"How could you have known all those details if what you said wasn't true, if you didn't do it?"

"It . . . just came to me like that. Came into my head. And I wanted to say it. All of it."

I glance at my recorder to make sure it's still working, and say, "Why did you want to say it? What made you plead guilty? Why no trial?"

"I wanted to go to prison."

I stare at him. Out of the corner of my eye, I notice the guard outside the window checking his watch. The guard motions to me, two minutes. Tension torques.

"Why?"

"I'm a bad man, Trinity." He looks at me so intently that I feel as though he's trying to get inside my head. Into my body. I'm uncomfortable in my chair. I glance at the guard.

"I'm a sick, sick man. Sick with addictions I cannot control."

"Addiction to child porn?"

"And alcohol. I used drink in an effort to numb the arousal I felt around girls, young teens. I used it to blunt that part of myself, that beast—the monster—that lived inside me, and controlled me."

"The shadow that Leena wrote about?"

He nods. "I was in two halves. The evil shadow part of me that was aroused, and wanted the bad things. And the good part of logical me that knew my desires were bad, wrong. The good part of me sought medical help from a professional to kick the addictions. But it was to no avail. There is a devil inside me, Trinity. An evil. A sick ooze. And when . . . when my own sweet Lacey, whom I'd let down, saw those child-sex photos, I . . . I couldn't even begin to try to go back to her. To my old life. There was no way on earth I could wipe that slate clean and attempt to start over. And I looked at those detectives who could see the devil inside me, who wanted to lock me up, and suddenly I knew. I had to go inside. I had to go behind bars. I *wanted* to be locked away. To save those around me. To save those kids. To protect my own child. To cut myself off from the temptations of evil."

I swallow, suddenly filled with a strange sense of compassion that makes me feel deeply uncomfortable. I clear my throat.

"So . . . you confessed? You just made up these details about killing Leena Rai?"

He nods. There is real pain in this hardened man's eyes. Is he playing me? The guard taps on the window. Tension whips tighter. Quickly I say, "And why no trial?"

"Because the trial could have exposed my lie. Because I wanted to go straight to prison. Because I never wanted to talk about any of the bad things again. I wanted to die. But I also didn't want to die, because that was too easy. I . . . That part of me that sought help? That part wanted me to be punished. For a long, long time."

"So why now, Clay? Why're you telling the world this now? What do you want?"

The door opens.

"Time's up, Pelley," barks the guard.

"Is it because you want to go free? You want to get out of prison now?"

"I just want the truth out there." He holds my eyes. "I want everyone to know there is still a killer on the loose who has not paid for what he did. Maybe he's even killed again."

The guard marches Clayton out. The door swings shut. I watch them through the glass. He looks back over his shoulder. Just for a minute. Before they round a corner and disappear.

Either he's playing me like a fiddle.

Or it's the truth.

And he just wants me and the world to know it now.

REVERB

THE RIPPLE EFFECT

NOW
Friday, November 19. Present day.

Darren stands in the doorway of his wife's study. The lights inside have been dimmed, and a gas fire shimmers in the hearth. She's replaying the third episode of the Leena Rai murder podcast series, which has just gone live. Darren is worried. It's the fourth time she's replayed that episode. His wife appears wholly, completely absorbed by the whispery, papery sound of Clay Pelley's voice. She doesn't notice that Darren is there. Or perhaps she is aware of his presence and just doesn't care.

Their daughters are asleep upstairs.

His stomach knots.

Confused, conflicting emotions churn and heave through his chest. He's loved Maddison Walczak since he can remember. Maybe even since kindergarten. In a kindergartner's kind of way. Most definitely in a more male, sexual kind of way since he was about twelve. To him Maddison was always the prettiest, smartest, funnest girl around. Even through her popular-girl-ego phase, when she made fun of him, or totally ignored him. Even then, he'd dreamed fervently that Maddy would be his first sexual conquest. That wasn't to be, but he'd won her hand in the end. She'd finally come around to his hidden charms.

His wife leans forward suddenly and turns up the volume on the speaker.

> TRINITY: Why now, Clay? Why're you telling the world this now? What do you want? Is it because you want to go free? You want to get out of prison now?

> CLAYTON: I just want the truth out there. I want everyone to know there is still a killer on the loose who has not paid for what he did.

> *THEME MUSIC STARTS SOFTLY*

> TRINITY: So if Clayton Pelley truly did not engage in sexual intercourse with Leena Rai on the night of the Ullr bonfire, why did Maddy Walczak lie? Why did she say she'd seen them having sex?

Maddy hits the STOP button. Sits in silence.

Darren walks into the room. He places his hands on Maddy's shoulders.

"He's lying," Darren says. His wife's neck muscles feel tight, hard as metal. He starts to massage them, and she sits motionless. He expected her to pull away. But she doesn't. This is unusual. The anxiety in his chest snakes up into his throat. He feels as though time is folding in on itself as their memories are being sucked back to that day they were called, one by one, into Mr. Pelley's classroom to be interviewed by Rachel and Detective Luke O'Leary. And then later when they were summoned to the station to make official statements.

"Did you lie in those interviews, Maddy?" he asks quietly.

She looks up at him. "Did *you?*"

He swallows.

She spins her chair and wheels out from under his touch. She goes out of the room. He stares after her.

He knows he lied.

He knows why he lied. Because Maddy had asked him to.

Darren grows even more worried. Because he doesn't know what endgame Maddy is playing now.

Eileen Galloway listens to the third podcast episode. She's alone in the house. Her husband, Rex, is at the pub, as he usually is at this hour. Eileen is knitting furiously, a scarf that is getting longer and longer. Too long. But it helps with stress. She's a high-strung woman to begin with. And now she's fretting over this podcast story. Because she's always felt that her daughter, Beth, and the others were hiding something. They were protecting some male. She's certain of it. She knits faster. One purl, one plain, one purl, one plain . . .

> TRINITY: You have just listened to Clayton Jay Pelley's confession. Word for word in his own voice, read from a copy of the police transcripts. Those words are a record in black and white. They are the exact replica of what Clayton told Detectives Rachel Walczak and Luke O'Leary that night in the interrogation. There is audio and visual to accompany them.
>
> *THEME MUSIC GROWS LOUDER*
>
> So I ask you all this question: Do you think it's actually possible that Clayton made a false confession in order

to protect his wife and child from himself? In order to lock himself behind bars, to seal himself off from worldly temptations that could cause him to hurt children in the future? Was this addiction of Clayton's an illness, a scourge, that he truly tried to fight by seeking medical help, but failed? Is this the extent of it? That Clayton Jay Pelley, in his twenties, was a secret child porn addict and a functional alcoholic who played cool-guy teacher at school? A young and vibrant and handsome man who tutored Leena Rai, and who was idolized by her? But he never sexually assaulted her, or murdered her?

THEME MUSIC INCREASES IN VOLUME

And if this is the case, if he's telling the truth now, if he did not engage in sexual intercourse with Leena Rai on the night of the Ullr bonfire, why did Maddy Walczak lie? And if Maddy Walczak lied, does that mean Beth Galloway did, too? What about the other kids, who at first all tried to get their stories straight?

And once again, I must ask: Why is Clayton talking now? What's in it for Clayton Jay Pelley?

Someone out there listening might know the answer. Someone has to know something. If you have any input, please call. And tune in next week—

Eileen reaches forward and jabs the STOP button. She sits for a long while, thinking. Then she reaches for her phone. She calls Rex at the pub.

◆ ◆ ◆

Granger is back at the Raven's Roost. He's had dinner there and is drinking yet another beer at the bar with Rex Galloway and a few others. Their heads are bent forward as they listen to episode three of the podcast, which recently went live. Granger is disinclined to go home. This whole affair has sucked his partner back into a strange place. He knew the podcast would do that to her. He's also unhappy. Edgy. He wonders if Rachel has gone to see Luke O'Leary at the hospice yet.

"Bloody woman," Granger mutters about Trinity as the episode ends. He's had more than a few beers, which means he probably won't be able to ride his bike home now, and he'll have to bunk down in town, and things will get darker between him and Rachel at a time when he should be focusing on being better and being there for her. "Dragging this all up—it's messing with the collective psyche of this town."

Rex gives a slow, rueful smile. "Spoken like a drunk shrink."

"Is Beth listening to this?" Granger asks. "Is she participating?"

"Yeah, she already spoke with Trinity. She said Dusty Peters did, too."

"Beth already spoke to Trinity?" Granger repeats. "Johnny never told me."

Rex shrugs. "I guess those interviews are yet to be edited and aired. Eileen is listening, too. I'm sure the whole town is tuning in by now."

"Along with half the country, who listens to these kinds of things in the name of entertainment." Granger takes another sip. "What do you think that wanker in prison is going to say next? Do you think he's going to offer up some conjecture about why Maddy supposedly lied?"

"Hell knows. What about Rachel? Has she been interviewed yet?"

Granger swallows the last of his beer, plunks the empty on the counter. "No. And she won't be."

"And Maddy?"

"I have no idea. Maddy does her best *not* to communicate with us."

Rex holds his gaze, and Granger feels his body itch.

"Is Maddy still messed up about the affair Rachel had all those years ago? With that RCMP cop on the Leena Rai case?"

Granger grunts. "Whatever it is, it just seems to get more bitter over time. And this podcast surely must be dredging up those old feelings in Maddy, which can't help."

During therapy sessions with Granger, Rachel spoke to him about her broken marriage. About her feelings around Jake. About how much she'd really cared for Luke O'Leary. Granger knows this much. He also knows that Rachel struggled deeply with the dissolution of her marriage. It undercut her very identity. Her sense of self. And it was all exacerbated by the Leena Rai case. Because of it all, she began to struggle with her focus on the job. She made some stupid decisions, lost her temper more than once. It compounded problems at work. Resentments about her being fast-tracked for police chief started to surface. Staff began to sabotage her—or so she believed. And suddenly one day Rachel found herself unable to get out of bed. She was diagnosed with clinical depression. Put on disability leave. Therapy was mandated. Therapy with him. It cost her the promotion. In the end she quit.

She put everything she owned into buying that piece of land out in the valley and building Green Acres with blood and sweat into an organic farm. She started selling vegetables at farmers' markets in the summer. She began to find peace from whatever inner demons taunted her. Granger asked her out for a drink one hot summer's day when he came across her stall at the farmers' market downtown. He'd fallen for her during therapy, but had refrained of course from acting on it. But their doctor-patient relationship was over. She looked tanned and so naturally beautiful that day. Happy. One thing led to another. Eventually Granger partially retired and moved out to Green Acres to live with her.

And right now, in his inebriated state, it feels like it was all just hanging there on a thread, waiting to be crushed by Trinity Scott's knock on the farm door and the resurfacing of the Leena Rai case.

Rex is called into the pub kitchen, and Granger sinks deeper into his morose thoughts.

His mind tunnels back to that day he found his son washing a military surplus jacket that wasn't his. Johnny was putting it into the washing machine on the Monday afternoon after the bonfire weekend, the day after news broke that a student, Leena Rai, had gone missing. There was blood on that jacket. Mud and blood.

When Johnny arrives home that night, Beth is asleep. He climbs into bed and snuggles close, putting his arm around his wife.

"Did you listen to episode three?" she says into the darkness.

Johnny is quiet for a long while. Outside, the wind blows. He wonders if it will bring snow by morning. Finally he says, "Did Maddy lie, Beth?"

He feels his wife's body tense. She remains silent in the darkness. Wind whistles louder outside. A shutter bangs somewhere.

"Did *you* actually see Clay Pelley having sex with Leena?"

"Fuck you, Johnny," she whispers.

Shock ripples through him.

She turns onto her back, glares up at the ceiling, her eyes shining in the darkness. "How dare you even ask me that?"

"I mean, maybe Maddy lied to you. Or—"

"Or what? We both made it up? Do you honestly think I would lie about something so very serious? That I'd sit here all these years knowing a man went to prison in part because I fabricated something with my friend?"

"Mr. Pelley went to prison because he confessed, Beth. Not because of you. And now everyone is talking about whether it was a false confession, that's all. Maybe he never slept with Leena in the woods. Maybe Maddy did lie."

"He was a pervert. He was—is—a pedophile. A kiddie porn addict. A sex offender. You heard him say right there in the podcast that he's aroused by girls and young teens. He . . . he made a pass at me once."

"You never told me."

"I wanted to forget it."

"Did you ever tell anyone?"

"No. I didn't."

"Not even Maddy?"

"Especially not Maddy. But Leena? She was easy. She needed love. She needed to be needed, and that creep took advantage of that. I totally believe the confession was true. Word for word." She's quiet for a while. They listen to the wind. "But you know that Leena was easy, don't you, Johnny?"

"What is that supposed to mean?"

"She was so desperate to be liked that she'd do anything, open her legs for any boy who was so hungry to lose his virginity that he didn't care who he did it with."

Johnny feels sick. "I cannot believe you just said what you did."

Silence.

He closes his eyes. His world seems to be spinning in a slow black spiral. He feels like he's a piece of debris in water swirling around a sink, being sucked toward a drain, whirring in ever-tightening circles as he nears the plughole.

He thinks of the day he realized his father was watching him from the doorway as he stuffed the military surplus jacket covered with mud and blood into the washing machine.

Meanwhile, across the country, in a town along the sprawling out-skirts of Toronto, Jocelyn Willoughby, a woman in her early seventies, sits with her daughter, who is in her late forties. The senior fingers a rosary as she listens to the Leena Rai murder podcast. She's always been addicted to true crime. The rosary beads are just there for comfort, something to do with her hands as she listens.

The younger woman—her daughter, Lacey—is in the latter stages of early-onset dementia. She's in a care home now. Lacey no longer recognizes members of her own family. She's having trouble swallowing and eating. She can no longer walk. Outside the home, a blizzard rages and piles snowdrifts against the low windows, which is why Jocelyn is staying overnight in her daughter's room. Public transit stopped running hours ago.

A nurse enters the room. She murmurs hello to Jocelyn and goes over to check her patient. She takes Lacey's pulse.

Lacey doesn't respond. She's sleeping soundly. Jocelyn removes her earbuds and musters a smile for the nurse. The nurse checks the drip feeding into Lacey's arm.

"What's that you're listening to?" asks the nurse in a friendly, conversational tone.

"Podcast. True crime. The killer of a young teen is in prison, and he's finally talking about the case."

"Oh, you mean that murder out west? In Twin Falls?"

Surprise washes through Jocelyn. "Yes. The Leena Rai murder."

"One of the day nurses was telling me about it. It got me hooked. Everyone is listening. I think Clayton Pelley is telling the truth. I bet those cops were hiding something. I bet they forced his confession or something, and it's going to come out."

Jocelyn doesn't even consider the words before they tumble out of her mouth—she just says them, needs to say them. "Lacey was married to him."

The nurse's hands go still. She flicks her gaze to Lacey in the bed, then back to Jocelyn. "Are you *serious*?"

She nods.

The nurse stares. "I . . . Wow, that must have been so difficult. How . . . I mean—"

"It's okay. You don't need to say anything. I . . . I've just never spoken about it. And now . . ." Her voice fades as she looks at her daughter. Now Jocelyn just needs to feel a connection. To somebody, anybody. Even if it's just the night nurse.

"So Clayton Jay Pelley . . . he's your son-in-law?"

"Was. He and Lacey met in Terrace, where we used to live. They met at a Christian youth camp Clay was helping run. Lacey was nineteen at the time, just out of school, basically, and she was smitten by him. My husband and I—we worried about the intensity of the relationship. But like the girls said on the podcast, Clay was a charmer. I mean, like Ted Bundy was a charmer. These narcissistic sociopaths with paraphilia . . . they can make you see and believe things that are totally false. They make you trust."

"Was Clay an alcoholic back then?"

"He occasionally drank heavily at social occasions—barbecues. A picnic. A country fair. But a lot of people in our community at that time did. We never worried that it had become a real problem at that point." Jocelyn sits silently for a moment as she watches her daughter breathe in her sleep. "It all got bad in Twin Falls. I guess a human being can only pretend and hide a sickness for so long until things start to devolve." She clears her throat. "After Clay was arrested and charged, we took Lacey and the baby home to Terrace, and then we packed up and all moved east. To start over."

"Wow. I . . . I'm sorry." The nurse glances at Lacey again, and Jocelyn wonders if the woman is thinking that Lacey could have lost her memory, her mind, because of all she has gone through. Perhaps it is the case. Perhaps early dementia is just Lacey's way of finally escaping.

The nurse says, "When I said I think he didn't do it, I—"

"I don't think he did it, either." Jocelyn falls quiet. The nurse doesn't leave. It's as though she senses there is something more that Jocelyn wants to get off her mind.

"Lacey lied," Jocelyn finally says, very quietly. "She told me that she lied to the police."

"What do you mean?" The nurse sits down slowly on the edge of the chair beside Jocelyn. She's hooked. She leans forward with interest.

"Clay gave Lacey as his alibi. He told the detectives he was home around nine on the night of the bonfire. And he was. He got drunk at home. In his shed. Lacey lied when she told the detectives he only arrived home at 3:42 a.m. the following morning."

"But . . . if he was home, he couldn't have killed Leena."

"I know."

"Why did she lie?"

"She needed to protect herself. She needed him taken away."

The nurse stares. A gust of wind ticks snow pellets against the window. Softly she says, "Have you *told* anyone?"

Jocelyn looks down at the rosary in her hands. She's convinced God will smite her for this secret she's kept all these years. But Clay Pelley is a sinful man with evil desires. It was right he went to prison. Even if the reasons for it were not exactly right.

The nurse presses. "What about the baby—Lacey's little daughter, Janie Pelley? Does *she* know? I mean, this podcast—everyone's talking about it. If she doesn't know, it could come out who her mother is, and that her mother lied about her father."

"If it comes out, then maybe that's the Lord's will."

The nurse sits in silence, watching Lacey in the bed. Time seems to stretch. "The truth always has a way of coming out." She glances at Jocelyn. "Why did you tell me?"

Jocelyn inhales a deep and shaky breath. She's not sure why. She just did.

"Sometimes," says the nurse, "secrets are too great and too heavy to keep inside forever. The body needs to release them. The body finds a way even if the mind is unwilling." The nurse reaches for Jocelyn's hand. Her touch is soft. "We all need to do what we can to survive and to protect our daughters. In the best ways we can at the time."

"You're a mother?"

She nods. "Two girls."

◆ ◆ ◆

Liam Parks fetches a box of negatives down from his attic. He carries the box into his photographic studio. He clicks the light on in his light box and sits at his bench. He takes out a strip of film, reaches for his loupe. He puts the little magnified lens on the film, bends over, and puts his eye to the loupe. Slowly he moves it across the strip of film. The past comes to life in negative shades. A group of boys in front of a bonfire. Images of a moon over Diamond Head. Comet-like streaks from the Russian rocket that hit the earth's atmosphere at 9:12 p.m. on Friday, November 14, 1997. The night of the Ullr sacrifice. The night Leena died.

He's been listening to the podcast again. It's eating at him.

As he scans another strip of negatives from the many rolls of film he shot that night, Detective Luke O'Leary's voice shimmers to life in his mind.

Did you shoot photos at the bonfire, Liam? Of the crowd?

I . . . I lost the camera, and the film inside. I . . . I got wasted, and I woke up in a tent, and the camera was gone. It was a school camera. I'd signed it out, and it had been stolen.

He stops his loupe over an image of Leena and Mr. Pelley sitting on a log. He thinks about the voice he's been listening to on the podcast.

CLAYTON: I did *not* sexually assault Leena Rai . . . And I did not kill her.

TRINITY: If . . . if you didn't, who did?

GUARD: Time's up, Pelley. Come on, let's go.

CLAYTON: Whoever did, her killer is still out there.

Liam looks even more closely at another image of a group of girls. In it are Maddy Walczak, Natalia Petrov, Seema Patel, Cheyenne Tillerson, Dusty Peters, and Beth Galloway. He frowns as his magnifier suddenly brings into focus a pendant. It has a purple stone nested into silver filigree. The stone catches the light from the bonfire. Liam sits back.

Just hours after he shot this photo, Leena Rai was sexually assaulted, bludgeoned, and then drowned. And he knows from the podcast that there was a silver locket with a purple stone tangled in the dead girl's hair. But it's not Leena who is wearing it in this photograph.

Liam's heart thuds in his chest. Is that why Maddy asked him to pretend his camera had been stolen? She offered up one of her girl-friends as his date to the prom if he did as she asked. So he lied. How else was a kid like him going to get a girl? Back then, he was not about to look a gift horse in the mouth. He also wanted to please one of the most popular and cool girls in the school. Maddy.

What should he do now?

RACHEL

NOW
Saturday, November 20. Present day.

It's midmorning, and Granger still has not returned home. He called late last night to tell me he'd had too much to drink and would be bunking in the apartment that Rex keeps above the club.

I'm oddly numb about this as I stick a photo of Leena at the top of my new crime whiteboard. I think of Luke and the board he created back in 1997 when the Twin Falls PD station was still located near the water and the railway yard. My heart hurts. I'm glad I saw him, but it's made everything feel raw and alive in my chest.

Under the photo of Leena, I stick the picture of the locket found in her hair. Beside the locket photo, I put up the image of the girls at the bonfire that I took from Maddy's drawer. I reach for a Sharpie and draw a line between the locket and the girls. And beneath the image of the girls, I write: *Liam shot this? Lied? Why? What other photos did he shoot?*

Next I stick up photos of the jacket, the journal pages, the book of poems, the bloodied backpack, Leena's Nike shoe, and images of the other items found either in the pack or among the rocks. I follow these with some of the autopsy images, including the boot print on the back of Leena's skull, and the thermal burns on her face.

I step back to examine my work, but Luke is still filling all the space in my brain. And heart. My whole body.

Maddy blamed the breakup of our family on my brief fling with Luke. What made it so easy for Maddy was the fact that it had been Cheyenne and her mother in that car that had turned in front of the alley. The car whose headlights had illuminated Luke and me like actors on a dark stage. And we'd stared into those lights like guilty lovers. Which we were. Briefly. And Cheyenne, of course, told Maddy at school the next day. And Maddy told Jake. It was just the excuse he needed to blow up at me and return to his own fling.

And now Jake and his squeeze are gone anyway. All the way to New Zealand, where they eventually got married and now live, near his new wife's parents. And Jake has new babies around the same age as Maddy's kids. It all fed into Maddy's bitterness.

Perhaps it really all began with my need to prove myself to my own dad and my spending too much time on the job at the expense of nurturing my family. Would I feel this same way if I were a guy?

Maybe some marriages just go wrong, and there is no one particular thing that can be blamed.

I stare at the image of Maddy and her girlfriends with the light of the bonfire glowing golden on their skin. Pretty young dragonflies locked in the amber of time. Full with so much promise. So many dreams. Like I once was.

Follow the truth, Rache. Even if it hurts. Even if it takes you where you don't want it to go. It's not too late . . . The truth . . . sets you free. It's . . . the secrets that fester. You . . . think you've buried them, gotten rid of them somehow, but they're like this damned cancer. The minute you're down, the second you grow tired, it starts to grow again, and it catches up with you.

Luke was right. This case has seeded some sickness in all of us. And even though we might have thought we'd moved on, the cancer is back.

Suddenly I'm struck by something. The photo of the packet of Export "A" cigarettes. And the lighter. Clay Pelley didn't smoke. Not that I knew of. So how did Leena get those thermal burns?

Did she light up under the bridge? Did Clay grab the cigarette from her and then stub it out in her nostril, or on her brow? Which came first? Whichever it was, surely the action of pressing the lit end of the cigarette into her skin to cause those deep burns would have extinguished the cigarette? Leena would surely not have lit another for Clay to burn her again. Or maybe she did. We didn't retrieve any cigarette stubs or butts at the scene. Even if we had, DNA was not used in 1997 in the way it is today. But one thing I do know is that Clay never explained the burns satisfactorily. And that Clay was not a smoker.

I reach for a notepad and make a note of this. I make another note about the jacket. I want to ask Clay why he washed it and brought it home for his wife to hang up if the bloodstains were still visible. I want to know why he didn't try to dispose of it somewhere instead. Because it's not adding up in my brain.

I hear scratching at my office door and realize I closed Scout out. I open the door and let him in. I ruffle his fur, then reach for my phone as he settles into his doggy bed.

I do a search for Parks Photography and Design. I find the contact number, check my watch, then dial.

The call is picked up on the second ring. "Liam Parks here."

Adrenaline sparks down my veins as I'm suddenly thrust fully back into old investigation mode. I'm reopening this case. At least in my mind. And when I have my questions lined up, I'm going to drive out and see Clay Pelley.

"Liam, hi, it's Rachel Hart. I used to be Detective Rachel Walczak, back when Leena Rai was murdered. Detective Luke O'Leary and I spoke with you at the school about the bonfire night, do you remember?"

There is a long silence, so long that I think he might have hung up.

"Liam?"

He clears his throat. "I know why you're calling," he says. "I've been listening to the podcast. We all have. I . . . I heard Clay Pelley say that he didn't do it, and . . . I always truly believed he *had* killed her, but then I got to wondering . . ." His voice dies off.

"Liam? Are you still there?"

"Yeah. Yeah, I am."

"What did you get to wondering?"

"Well, it's funny you called. Because I realized last night that there is something I need to get off my chest, and I have no interest in talking to Trinity Scott. I really don't. I'm not into that sensationalizing stuff. And I learned from the podcast that Luke O'Leary is in hospice, so I couldn't talk to him. And—"

"Luke passed yesterday."

Another long beat of silence. "I'm so sorry."

"Me too."

"I . . . Wow." He inhales. "You know, time has a way of changing things. I'm not that insecure little geeky kid I was once. And I decided last night that I need to tell someone because . . . just . . . it's been bottled up and festering for such a long time. After I listened to the podcast episodes, I went up into my attic." Another pause. "I still have the film I shot that night."

Quietly I say, "So your camera and film were not stolen?"

"I'm sorry."

I moisten my lips and stare at the photo of the girls on the board. "You developed some of the film, didn't you?"

"One roll. Yes."

"You gave some of the prints to the girls?"

"Yes. I was going to give them one each."

"Why them?"

"They were—I was attracted to them. I wanted to get in with them. They were the hottest of the hot girls at school. The popular girls."

A coolness leaches into my chest. Tension squeezes a fist around my throat. I want to ask my next question, but I'm not certain I'm ready for the answer. I hear Luke's voice close to my ear, almost as though he's with me now, in this room, laying a soft shadow of a touch on my arm, whispering to me.

Follow the truth, Rache. Even if it hurts. Even if it takes you where you don't want it to go.

"Why did you lie about the camera and film being stolen, Liam?"

"Maddy asked me to."

I close my eyes. My heart races. "Why?" I manage to say.

"She said something about Mr. Pelley not wanting it to get out that he was there."

"When exactly did she ask you?"

"The morning after the bonfire."

"There was no school. It was a Saturday."

"She cycled over to my place. Knocked on my door. I gave her the print, and she told me to get rid of the others, and the rest of the rolls of film, and to pretend I had lost the camera. She said the police had learned there was an illegal Ullr sacrifice, and that they would probably be asking kids about it, and we shouldn't tell anyone that Mr. Pelley was there. I didn't understand at the time. Not until I heard Leena was missing. But at the time I believed her because she was the cop's daughter, and I figured she had insider information. She also promised if I did what she asked, Cheyenne would go to the prom with me."

I suck in a slow, deep breath. "So you still have the negatives?"

"Yeah. I do. Do you want to take a look at them? Or should I take them to the Twin Falls PD? Or maybe the RCMP? I don't really know if it would even be of interest to the cops now. But like I said, I'm not going to go giving them to Trinity Scott."

My gaze ticks back to the image of the girls on the board. I have what I need. I've always had what I needed. It was in my face, even

230

though I refused to fully see it. I think of appearances, and how it might be interpreted if Liam gave the film to me. Especially now.

My thoughts go to Maddy. And truth. And lies. And how bottling secrets, stuffing down guilt, can make a person ill and bitter. I think of our failed relationship.

It's . . . the secrets that fester . . . They're like this damned cancer.

"You should call the RCMP, Liam. You should hand it all over to them. You need to tell them that you were asked to lie."

I kill the call and slump into my chair. Perhaps I've done a terrible, terrible thing. A wrong thing. But how far should a mother go to protect a child? When should she stop?

What if protecting a daughter ends up hurting everyone around her? What if it leads to the wrong man ending up behind bars for almost a quarter of a century? Even if he's a disgusting, evil man?

I rub my brow. Clay confessed. I *have* to remind myself of how it went down. I bought it. We all bought his words. Why should we not have? The forensic evidence matched.

I surge to my feet. Pace. Clay had no way of knowing exactly how Leena had died unless he'd been there and done it.

I pace up and down, and then stall dead in my tracks as something I heard on the podcast strikes me. I grab my phone and find the episode I'm looking for. I fast-forward, searching for the words. I click PLAY.

> CLAYTON: —the good part of logical me that knew my desires were bad, wrong. The good part of me sought medical help from a professional to kick the addictions. But it was to no avail.

I fast-forward some more, then click PLAY again.

CLAYTON: I wanted to die. But I also didn't want to die, because that was too easy. I . . . That part of me that sought help?

I swear out loud, then replay, just to be sure. I set down my phone and scrabble through the case binders. I find the copy of the transcript of our interview with Clay. I read through it carefully.

Nowhere in the transcript did Clay mention seeking medical help for his addictions. It's not that we ignored it. He never told us. I sit back.

My heart thumps hard against my rib cage. I feel blood pounding through my body. If Clay was getting medical—professional—treatment for addiction in Twin Falls, a tiny town, there were very few professionals at the time who handled that kind of thing.

We had loose ends with that case, Rache.

I read through the transcript again, and the scene comes alive in my mind. I can smell the room again. I can feel the tension. I recall the strange look on Clay's face. The odd monotone delivery. It sounded like the same tone when he reread his confession for Trinity on the air, except that time there was that strange rasp in his voice.

I reach for my phone again and find another section of the podcast. I hit PLAY.

TRINITY: How could you have known all those details if what you said wasn't true, if you didn't do it?

CLAYTON: It . . . just came to me like that. Came into my head. And I wanted to say it. All of it.

I write on the board: *Who was treating Clay for addiction to child porn?*

I check my watch again. Perhaps if I can find Lacey Pelley, she will talk to me after all these years. She might tell me who was treating Clay in 1997.

I sit down at my laptop and start googling. But all I find are some old newspaper articles that have been digitized. It appears from the articles that Lacey Pelley moved back to Terrace with their baby. I imagine Lacey would certainly not be using the Pelley name any longer. I find an article that mentions the last name of Lacey's parents. Willoughby. Jocelyn and Harrison Willoughby. There's also an old photo embedded in one of the articles that made national news—Lacey carrying baby Janie. Some paparazzi-style photographer snapped her hurrying from her car toward a supermarket entrance, holding her hand up to shield her face. And something else strikes me. What about Janie Pelley? Where is she now? Do Lacey and Janie know about this podcast? What about Lacey's parents—the Willoughbys? Are they still alive? Do *they* know about the podcast? It must be bad enough for Jaswinder and Ganesh and Darsh to be hearing all this now, but what about them?

I reach for my phone and call an old friend who was once a cop like me.

He answers almost immediately. "Joe Mancini here. Pacific Investigations and Skip Tracing."

"Joe, it's Rachel Hart, well, Rachel Walczak, ex–Twin Falls PD."

"Holy Mother, Rache? How in the hell are you?"

We exchange pleasantries, then I get straight to the reason for my call. I tell him about the podcast.

"I'd like to use your services, Joe. I'd like to locate and talk to Lacey Pelley, and possibly her daughter, Janie Pelley. I can't find anything via simple googling, and I know you have access to all the good tools, and I'm looking for fast results. My bet is they're not going by the Pelley surname." Like I am no longer using Walczak.

"Yeah. I bet."

"Her maiden name was Willoughby, so possibly she used that."

"Leave it to me. I'll get back to you as soon as I have something. Shouldn't take long if any name changes were legal."

I hang up, and I try once more to call Maddy.

She doesn't pick up.

Neither does Darren.

I chew the back of my pen, wondering if they've listened to the three podcast episodes by now. Wondering where Clay is going to lead Trinity next. I hear the growl of Granger's bike coming along the farm road, growing louder as he turns into the driveway.

A few moments later he knocks on my study door and enters. Scout rises from his basket, wiggling his tail.

"Sorry about last night, Rache." Granger crouches down to hug and ruffle Scout. He looks up, then goes still as his eye catches my crime board. Slowly he comes to his feet. He goes toward the board.

He reads my questions.

His shoulders go rigid. He's silent. I watch him. He turns his head, and his gaze locks with mine.

"Was it you?" I ask.

"Me what?"

"You know what. There was no one in town twenty-four years ago doing what you did. Was it you who treated Clay Pelley for addiction?"

RACHEL

"I don't believe it." I say the words quietly, slowly, as I stare at Granger. It's like I'm suddenly seeing a man I don't know. "So Clay *was* seeing you?"

"You're jumping to ridiculous conclusions."

"How many *professionals* were there in Twin Falls in 1997 who treated addictions? It was your big schtick. Using hypnotherapy to help break patterns of addiction. You put patients into a hypnotic state in order to 'talk directly to their unconscious,' where you could seed suggestions that would be activated by triggers once they were out of the trance and fully cognizant again." I know because Granger used this technique to help treat my PTSD.

"Jesus, Rache, what has gotten into you? Why all this anger? This . . . this is exactly why I didn't want you to listen to that goddamn podcast! This is *exactly* what I expected to see—you going off the rails via some guilt trip because you'd start second-guessing everything you did, including sleeping with Luke O'Leary and screwing up your marriage. And now it's messing with *our* relationship. And you're attacking *me*."

"I can't believe you just said that."

"Oh, for chrissakes, I don't mean *I* think your sleeping with Luke messed up your marriage. It's what you told me *you* think. We worked through this, remember? In therapy. All of it. You and me. I helped you work through it. And Clay Pelley . . . He could have been going for treatment anywhere in the city, Rachel." He flings his arm toward the window and points. "It's a one-hour drive to North Vancouver, where there is—and was—a huge hospital and a surrounding neighborhood that houses all manner of medical and psychology and psychiatry professionals. Plus it's just a short drive over the bridge from there into Vancouver, where there are more huge hospitals, and where psychologists, therapists, and addiction specialists are a dime a dozen. Now. And then. How dare you?"

He looks hot. Hungover. Edgy. His hair is ragged. Stubble shadows his jaw. He drags his hand over his hair as he registers me weighing him, and he tempers himself, lowering his voice. "Look, I appreciate that this thing has you on edge, but just leave it alone. She'll wrap up her podcast. Whatever happens with Pelley, it doesn't matter. Your record on the case is solid. He confessed. Leave it at that."

But now I really, really need to know who Clay Pelley was getting treatment from. Because something deep inside me, evil and ugly, has taken hold. And it's crawling up into my chest and into my throat, and it's closing my throat, strangling my breathing, and blurring my vision, and it's not going to let go of me until I can prove it wrong.

"I need to know who he was seeing."

"Why? What difference does it make who was treating him?"

"Because if—just *if*—Clay is telling Trinity the truth, then somehow, from somewhere, he got the details—the exact, minute autopsy details—not only of how Leena Rai was murdered, but in what sequence these events occurred, and how the homicide investigation team was interpreting that autopsy information and the crime scene evidence."

He glares at me. The tension is thick. "So why do you think it was me? You think I somehow passed information on? Because that's absurd.

You and I didn't even know each other back then. I mean, I knew you by sight. I knew you were old Chief Hart's daughter, and a cop, and Maddy's mother. Because Maddy was friendly with Johnny, and I'd seen you around the school. But that's all. I had zero to do with the case."

I hold his gaze. My brain is whirring. I sense there is something I am missing, something I know in my unconscious, but I haven't managed to surface it yet. And I don't like what I see in Granger's eyes. It scares me.

Follow the truth, Rache. Even if it hurts. Even if it takes you where you don't want it to go.

Very quietly I say, "I'm going to go see him. I'm going to ask him directly who his therapist was, and where he could have gotten police holdback information. If I can't get the answers anywhere else, I'm going to ask him to his face."

"Pelley?"

"Yes." I make for the office door.

"You can't just show up and see an inmate, Rachel. There's a process."

"Then I'll start it. I still have contacts who could help speed things up." I stop in the doorway, face him. "I'll pack a bag. I might have to stay overnight near the institution. I'll call to let you know. Can you look after Scout?"

"Of course I can look after Scout," he snaps. "But I think it's a fucking stupid idea. He's going to mess with you."

I blink. Granger doesn't use profanity with me. His eyes are furious, flashing. That unarticulated fear threads deeper into my core.

"He already did mess with me, Granger," I say softly. "He messed with all of us. A long time ago. I need to finish this once and for all, so I can let it go."

◆　◆　◆

It's almost 2:00 p.m., and I am driving over the Second Narrows Bridge on my way to the Mission correctional institution when my cell rings. I answer it on speaker so I can keep my eyes on the traffic. The highway is heavy with commuters. The pelting rain doesn't help.

"Rache, it's Joe."

"You got something already?"

"Easy as pie. Just need to know where to look with the right tools. Lacey Ann Willoughby Pelley legally changed her name in 1998. Which coincided with Jocelyn and Harrison Willoughby's move from Terrace to a small town in Northern Ontario called Shackleton. Lacey and her daughter moved with them."

"So Lacey changed her name back to Willoughby?"

"No. Fresh new start, it seems."

Energy sparks through me. I slow for a car to feed into my lane, my wipers squeaking. "What name?"

"Lacey Ann Scott."

I go ice cold. Then my heart kicks and jackhammers. I allow another car to pass into my lane. My throat is dry. "Her . . . daughter's name is . . . Janie Scott?"

"Actually Trinity Jane Scott. It was always Trinity Jane. I guess they just liked to call her Janie. I have a mate whose parents call him by his middle name, too. It's a thing."

I suck in a long, slow, steadying breath, then put my indicator on and take an off-ramp. "Hang on, I'm going to pull over." Up ahead I see a turnout leading into an industrial area. I pull into a parking lot outside a flooring store and come to a stop.

"Trinity Scott is Clay Pelley's daughter?" Then I swear and hit the wheel as the scope of it dawns on me. "It's not Clay who's screwing with us all. It's not Clay who's playing Trinity like a fiddle. It's her. She's playing *him*. She's playing us.

"So that's going to be her big reveal," I say quietly. "That Clay is her daddy. *That's* her bloody game."

REVERB

THE RIPPLE EFFECT

NOW
Sunday, November 21. Present day.

Most of the men are watching the television mounted on the wall. The news is on. Clay watches only half-heartedly. He sits at one of the bolted-down tables, and he's trying to reread Nabokov's *Lolita*. He gets away with it under the pretext of furthering his literature studies. Or perhaps the guy managing the library just doesn't know what it's about. Clay is in medium security because he's been a model prisoner. He's even taught others through a special program—English as a second language, literature studies, and classes in basic business writing skills and grammar. He's also furthered his own psychology degree. After a few very early missteps that got him cut across the neck, which damaged his vocal cords, he learned quickly where his bread was buttered and which factions to align himself with. He rubs his neck, where the spiderweb tattoo now forms a network of inked lines over the neck scar. The tat marks him as a member of a particular gang. He does favors for the gang leader. He gets little favors in return—they watch his back. That's the biggest thing. Survival. Being part of a herd ensures his safety.

Even some of the guards are in on the game. The power dynamic on the inside is intricate. And it can be deadly.

Guards observe the convicts from behind a window in an observation booth. Cameras watch from all angles. Clay is having trouble focusing on the words in the novel. His thoughts are on Trinity Scott, who is coming to see him again later today. He's considering what he should tell her in the next twenty-minute session, how much to reveal so he can hook her, keep her coming back hungry. He cannot even begin to articulate what it means to have her coming to him, to watch her pretty face, those big eyes. To smell her. To be near her. It's awakened something wild and a little dangerous in him. He will need to be careful.

He thinks back to when he told her about Maddy Walczak. About why Maddy lied. Clay knew a lot about teenage girls. They liked him. They used to flock to him. Like flies to honey. He understood enough about the psychology of the young female mind to know that their inner lives were complex and sometimes feral places. Unpredictable passions. Needy. Demanding. Intoxicating. Powerful. Sweet. Mean. Balanced on the razor's edge between childhood and adulthood, they craved experiences. Sexual mostly. But they were not always ready for what came.

"Pelley! Hey, you're on the news!"

He startles. His focus zips back to the television. Everyone else in the room has suddenly turned full attention toward the TV, too. A strange hush falls over the men. Out of the corner of his eye, Clay sees the two guards in their station also watching the news through their windows. Clay feels a charge going through the room, and it makes him uneasy. Living among caged men requires an animal awareness. No man ever feels truly safe at any given moment. No man is ever certain who is predator, who is prey, and who is circling. But Clay's wilderness senses are suddenly alive and prickling.

On the screen is Trinity Scott. The camera zooms in on her. Pinked cheeks, her short, dark hair blowing in the wind. She's talking to a reporter right outside their prison. It's a rare look at their cage from the outside, and to the men it's a sudden and shocking reminder of a landscape right beyond these walls that lock them in. Clay swallows at the close-up of young Trinity.

The reporter says, "Some of those children in the pornographic photographs that Clay Pelley had in his shed were as young as five years old. They were being sexually abused in those photos."

"I know," says Trinity. "By his own admission, Clayton Jay Pelley is a sick man."

An inmate abruptly rises from the bench in front of the TV and comes to sit at Clay's table. He begins clenching and unclenching his fist, which makes the spiderweb tat on his bulging forearm appear to be expanding, then shrinking. Like it's breathing. Alive. A web of lungs inhaling, exhaling. The man's name is Ovid, and Clay realizes Ovid is watching not the television, but him. Intently. One of the guards has also now turned his attention to Clay.

Clay keeps his eyes aimed toward the screen. But he knows. There's been a shift. He can feel it. Creeping. Rippling. Crackling. An invisible and silent energy. Something is happening.

The blonde reporter is saying, "Do you believe him?"

The camera zooms right in on Trinity's face. "I do believe he's a very sick man," she says, eyes watering in the wind. "From all the evidence, from his own words, he was addicted to child pornography. The evidence found in his shed went to a federal task force, and it did help to crack an international pedophile ring being run out of Thailand but with most of its business in North America. But as to whether Clayton sexually assaulted and murdered Leena Rai, I'm still waiting to hear what else he says. For me, the jury is still out."

Smart, Clay thinks. *Trinity is using the newscast to do marketing for her podcast. She's hooking viewers right there, whether she believes what she's saying or not.*

The reporter says, "Does he show remorse?"

"For the pornography, yes. For the rest, he claims he confessed to killing Leena Rai because he believes he *should* be behind bars. He says he did it to protect his wife and child." Trinity wavers. "I . . . I think I believe him. I think he actually cared for, maybe loved, his wife and child."

"Or you want to?"

"Maybe. Perhaps I want to believe that monsters can also be human. That a bad man can do things that are good. That he still has feelings for the people around him. If you've listened to my podcast, you'll know he tried to get treatment for his paraphilia. He wanted it to stop. He knew it was wrong. But as research has shown, the recidivism rate for this kind of offender is high. Clay *is* safer inside."

"Or rather, children are safer with him inside."

"Yes," says Trinity.

"Pedo," someone whispers loudly in the room. Clay's stomach tightens. He tries to swallow without showing his fear.

"Kiddie fiddler," whispers someone else from the other side of the room.

Clay turns to look. All the men are now regarding him. Both the guards, too. Fear climbs higher inside his throat.

Ovid says, "Doing a fourteen-year-old who is going on fifteen is one thing, Pelley, but jacking off to a photo of a five-year-old? Fucking pedo. *Children? Babies?* You think you're safer in here?"

The reporter says, "Is it difficult to talk to a man like him, when you know what sickness, what evil, lives inside him?"

"I don't pretend to understand the deviance that can afflict people," says Trinity. "But I think it can be useful to try. I think it can also be instructive. Understanding the enemy, knowing him, is always better than the unknown, the unseen."

"Is he using you and your podcast, Trinity? Is he playing some kind of game because he's bored?"

"I believe he has something he wants to say. He needs to get it off his chest. I'm the vehicle, the opportunity that presented itself for him to do so."

"And what do you say to Leena Rai's father, who is still alive, and to her little brother, and her cousin? What do you tell those who criticize you for exploiting their pain for your own gain, your own ratings?"

Trinity turns to the camera, and suddenly it's like she's looking right into the prison, right into Clay's eyes.

"To Leena's family, and to everyone listening, and to anyone who might be hurt or confused by this, if there has been a miscarriage of justice, I think you all deserve to know it. Truth is my driver. Only the truth. I want the truth of what happened to Leena Rai."

The door of the guard's cubicle opens, and the guard steps out. "Pelley, I need you to go collect a bucket and mop from the supply store. Someone threw up in one of the corridors."

Clay stands, hesitates, glances at everyone watching him.

"Move it!" barks the guard.

He walks slowly toward the door and waits. The buzzer sounds as the door unlocks. He exits. The door shuts and locks automatically behind him. He makes his way down the corridor toward the caged storage area. He glances up at the CCTV cameras near the ceiling as he goes. It's quiet. He's alone. Too alone. He rounds the corner and makes his way to the end of the long corridor, where the supplies are kept behind a metal fence. Two of the fluorescent lights at the end of the corridor have gone out. A third is flickering and humming. He stops as he notices something else. A white substance has been smeared over the far camera near the gate to the supply area.

Clay takes a step backward, begins to turn. But a shadow comes fast, seemingly from nowhere. He tries to run, but another man rounds the corner and strides fast, purposefully, silently, toward him. His arms are out at his sides. Something in his right fist. It's partially tucked up his sleeve.

Clay steps backward, in the other direction, and bumps into the man behind him. The inmate in front of him keeps coming. Clay recognizes him now. It's Ovid. That's when he knows the guard is in on it—the guard ordered Clay to come here to clean up the alleged puke. And Ovid was let out of the room right behind him. That's also when he knows he's done. Ovid is upon him, reaching forward like he's going to give Clay a hug. The man behind him holds him in place. Clay feels the thrust of the blade in Ovid's fist like a punch to his stomach. Shock explodes through his body. He doubles over, winded. His assailant withdraws the shank, pulls his arm back, and punches it in again. Right at Clay's liver, and he angles the blade up. He yanks it out. And then the men are gone.

Clay clutches at his stomach. Blood pulses, oozes, hot through his fingers. His knees buckle under him. He tries to cry for help, but no voice comes. He staggers sideways, leans his body against the wall, but he can't stand. Dizziness swirls. Slowly he slides down the wall, leaving a bright-red streak. He slumps to the floor. Blood pools out from under him. He watches it. Shiny and thick and red. It spreads and turns into a river on the antiseptic-smelling tiles.

RACHEL

NOW
Sunday, November 21. Present day.

The road into Mission parallels the long, brown, lazy Fraser River. There is no rain here, but heavy clouds scud across the sky. It's midmorning, and time is ticking. Anxiety winds tightly inside me as I fist the wheel of my truck. I need to speak to Clay, get information from him before Trinity does. Now that I know who she is, I'm worried about her endgame. I fear that any half-truths she might broadcast before they can be properly followed up and validated could wreak serious damage. What is her ultimate intent? Does she actually believe her father is innocent of murder?

Does she want to exonerate him?

Or is it revenge she's after?

Is she gunning for *me*? Or my family? Or does she just want a cracking podcast that will have a stunner of a climax when she reveals on air that she is baby Janie Pelley?

Does it even matter at this point? Should I have listened to Granger and just sat back and let unfold what may?

I clench my jaw. No. It *does* matter. I need the truth, too, now. The whole truth. Luke was right. There were, and still are, unexplained loose ends. It's time to close off those ends, no matter what comes. For starters, I need to know which therapist Clay was seeing. I want to know what happened to Leena's journal. And if Clay didn't kill Leena, we all need to know who did.

Because if it wasn't Clay, the real rapist-killer could have been hiding in plain sight, right in Twin Falls, all these years. Living and working among the community. Shopping for groceries, recreating, eating in restaurants, going to the doctor and dentist, borrowing books from the library. Or perhaps he was a transient and moved on. Or maybe he was a resident who left and went somewhere else, where he could have killed again. More than once. And we'd possibly let it happen by putting the wrong man behind bars.

I see a road sign. I'm nearing the prison. My pulse begins to race as I take the off-ramp.

Once I recovered from the shock of learning who Trinity Scott was, Joe Mancini told me that her mother, Lacey Scott, was in the advanced stages of early-onset dementia. He learned this after contacting the number listed for Lacey's mother, Jocelyn Willoughby, and asking to speak to Lacey. Jocelyn said her daughter was in a care home. Joe then contacted the home to inquire about the patient. He also gave me Jocelyn's number.

While parked outside the flooring store, I called her. She told me she could no longer keep Lacey's secret. She said her daughter had lied to us. Clay *had* come home early that night, as he'd initially stated. Lacey lied in order to protect herself and her daughter. She *wanted* her husband taken away, especially after she found the child porn in his shed. In truth, said Jocelyn, her daughter had really wanted to kill her husband. Setting him up to take the rap for murder by lying about what time he came home was easier. It was an opportunity that had presented itself to a distraught young wife and struggling mother. Jocelyn said Lacey had, however, been telling the truth about the jacket showing up laundered and ironed. She also believed Clay had been sleeping with Leena.

My fists tighten on my truck wheel. I turn down a road. The correctional institution looms ahead.

What I don't know yet—what Jocelyn Willoughby doesn't know—is whether Clay Pelley is aware that Trinity Jane Scott is his child. As far as Jocelyn knows, her granddaughter, Trinity Jane, has not yet told him.

I pull into the prison parking lot, come to a stop, and stare at the building, the walls, and the fences topped with coils of barbed wire. It's like all roads suddenly lead here.

All the answers are in there.

I don't have an appointment, but I plan to get one. I reach for my wallet, then freeze as I catch sight of two people near a red van. *Trinity and Gio.*

What renders me motionless is not the fact that they are here, but the emotion in the vignette itself. Trinity's producer is hugging her, stroking her back, and she seems to be crying and gesticulating frantically toward the prison building.

My heart, which was running fast to begin with, beats even faster as I think back to the call I got this morning.

Her daughter's name is Janie Scott? Trinity Jane Scott.

Wind gusts and leaves blow across the parking lot.

Trinity puts her face in her hands. Gio draws her closer. She rests her head on his shoulder. Her body heaves. She's sobbing.

My gaze remains locked on them as I reach for the door handle. I exit my truck. Slowly I walk toward them, the wind tearing at my coat, my hair, my scarf. A sense of doom unfolds in me, dark as the thunderous clouds muscling across the bleak sky.

They see me. Both go still. They stare. Their faces are white, their eyes wide as if with shock. Leaves clatter, crisp and frozen with frost.

"What happened?" I say as I reach them.

Trinity shoots a glance at the correctional institution, the coils of razor wire.

"What are you doing here?" demands Gio.

"He's gone," Trinity says. "Clayton is gone."

My heart kicks a double beat. "He *escaped*?"

"He's dead. Someone killed him. Shanked."

My jaw drops. I feel slammed into a wall. "What do you mean, 'He's dead'?"

"He was murdered this morning. Found in a pool of blood near a utilities room. He'd been stabbed twice with a homemade blade of some sort. Someone knew what they were doing. Got his liver. He bled out fast. Too fast for anyone to save him."

"*Who* did it?"

Her eyes water, or perhaps it's the tears.

"They . . . they don't know who did it. They haven't located the weapon. The security cameras in that part of the corridor had been smeared over with toothpaste. So the CCTV was out. They think it's gang related, and they cautioned me that there tends to be a code of silence around these kinds of killings inside. They're hard to solve."

Clay's voice from the podcast echoes through my skull.

Her killer is still out there.

A sinister thought leaches through me. He's been silenced. Someone got to him. On the inside.

RACHEL

NOW
Sunday, November 21. Present day.

"I know who you are, Trinity."

Her eyes lock with mine. Her face is pale, her features tight. I see her pulse beating rapidly at her neck.

We're sitting in a booth in a diner not far from the Mission correctional institution. Outside the diner windows, people scurry, hunched into their coats against the wind. It's late afternoon.

Trinity is rattled, and emotional. I offered to take her for a coffee, but we both sip hot chocolates.

Outside, Gio is in the van in the parking lot. I told him we needed to talk. Alone. And he's giving us space. Or rather, keeping watch. I can see him behind the misted van window. His attention does not leave us.

"So tell me, what is the real purpose of the Leena Rai podcast? Revenge? Or purely mercenary—using your own situation to craft some narrative arc on the backs of other people's pain?"

"I don't know what you mean."

"Of course you do." I pause. "Trinity Janie Pelley Scott."

She swallows, inhales deeply. "How did you find out?"

I sidestep her question. "I've met you before, you know? When you were about seven or eight months old. I changed your diaper when your mother was battling in a home with little money, dirty dishes, and piles of empty liquor bottles in a recycling bin, and you, crying with colic, stopping her from getting healthy sleep. You did fall quiet, though, when Detective O'Leary bounced you on his knee." A bolt of grief sideswipes me. I waver for a moment, my words stolen by the realization that Luke, so big and vibrant, is gone. And time is short on this earth. The small moments precious. I clear my throat. "I think it was in that moment, Trinity, when Sergeant O'Leary and I knocked on your mother's door, that she formulated the intention to lie about what time your father came home."

Trinity's big violet eyes gleam. Her hands tremble slightly as she lifts her mug and sips. I can see she's doing this to think. Her brain is racing as she figures out how to deal with this. With me.

"So is it revenge?" I ask. "Did you start this to get back at your father? Or are you just cashing in on some sensationalist reality TV, Darth Vader is my father–style reveal? Forcing the victim's family to relive hell for your own personal gain?"

She takes another sip, her eyes still holding mine. But they're narrowing slightly. I'm angering her. Good.

"Was it a surprise when he denied that he killed Leena?" I ask. "A nice plot twist that presented itself for you?"

Silence.

I lean forward, my arms folded on the table. "You got him killed, you know?"

She sets her cocoa mug down abruptly. Her eyes turn to flint. "How dare you?" she whispers.

I make a scoffing sound. "It's true."

She hesitates, then says, very quietly, "Maybe it's the truth that got him killed. Maybe someone on the outside is worried that my father was going to expose them."

"Or maybe his participation in your podcast revealed to his fellow inmates just what a sick kind of pedophile he was. That doesn't tend to go down well inside."

Her mouth flattens and she breaks my gaze, stares out the window. After a few moments she asks, "How *did* you find out who I am—what made you look?"

"The fact that Clay Pelley decided to talk to *you*. And no one else," I say, which isn't exactly truthful. But it explains a lot about how the podcast came to fruition. And I'm not prepared to reveal to her my worries about my partner having been her father's therapist. "It was easy enough. Your mother changed her name legally. It's part of the record. Your grandmother's phone number is listed. She told my PI that Lacey was in a care home." I pause.

"So is that why he agreed to do the podcast? You told him you were his daughter? And you were saving this fact for a 'big reveal'"—I make air quotes—"in a later episode? Manipulating your audience? A cheap narrative trick in what is supposed to be true crime, and an alleged hunt for the truth?"

She reaches into a bag at her side and takes out a brown envelope. She slides the envelope onto the table and places her hand on it, palm down. "I didn't tell him who I was. I wrote him several times over a period of eighteen months, asking for an interview. And one day he answered. I don't know what triggered him to reply. It's something I planned to ask him." Her voice hitches. She takes a moment to compose herself. "He—my father—gave this envelope to one of the prison guards last night. He asked the guard, in case something happened to him, to give me this." She moistens her lips. "He must have . . . suspected, had a premonition, or known something was coming down."

She slides the envelope toward me. "Take a look."

I open it and extract a dog-eared photo with tape still stuck to the corners. It's creased. Old. It shows a man in his twenties with wild sandy-brown curls. A broad grin crumples his boyishly handsome face. His eyes are aflame with life. He stands in front of a thundering waterfall that sprays mist up around him. Nearby is an orange Westfalia camper van. The man is holding a tiny baby in a pink woolen hat. It punches me in the gut. There is a second photo in the envelope. It's similarly dog-eared and creased, and it shows a man and a woman with the same baby. The couple are smiling. They look happy, in love.

It's the same photo I saw on the bookshelf in Clay Pelley's office at Twin Falls Secondary School that day Luke and I interviewed him. Memories slam through me—Clay Pelley striding down the corridor to greet us. Clay showing students into the classroom to be interviewed. Me and Luke arresting Clay on that cold, wet night. Clay in our interrogation room smelling of sweat and old liquor.

"These were taken at the Twin Falls Provincial Park," I say quietly. "At the campground below the falls."

"The guard told me Clayton had them on his wall. Above his bed."

I bite my lip as I stare at the photos. The same little baby I held. Janie. Lacey looking happy. The Before Lacey.

"Turn it over—the one with my dad holding me."

I do, and on the back—freshly written, it seems—are the words:

I always knew where you were, Janie. I kept track of you and your mom. You can get any information you need on the inside. I got updates all the time.

I look up and meet her eyes.

"He hired a PI," she says. "The guard told me. Like you said, it was easy to find us if you were looking."

"So he knew?"

She regards me. Uneasy. Unsure. And nods. "Yes," she says softly. "My father knew. But he didn't let on to me. Perhaps he was waiting for me to reach that conclusion via the interviews. Perhaps he wanted me to meet him, and to first learn who he was, and to try to understand. Maybe he just wanted to get to know me. Or explain how he'd tried to protect me and my mother by confessing. He took a rap for murder so we could go free, so we could go somewhere else to start new lives."

"When did you find out who your dad was?"

She glances away, out the window again, and watches the leaves blowing across the parking lot. Flecks of rain start to speck the window.

"For nearly my whole life, I was led to believe I was someone else," she says without looking at me. "A kid with a different dad. A dad named James Scott, who was good and faithful, and who was killed in a tragic hit-and-run when I was a baby in Terrace. That's the story I was told by my mother when I was old enough to hear it. There were photographs of my father, sure. When I asked." Trinity looks down at the images on the diner table.

"Those were two of them. My gran had copies. My mother had none. My gran showed me these in secret. She said it was too painful for my mom to have photos on display, so that's why these were boxed away. That was her story. My gran said it was to be our secret that I'd seen them. She said talking about my dad was painful for Grandpa, too. So 'let's not talk about it, shall we?' And all the while I thought that man in the photos was named James Scott."

Trinity falls silent for a moment. I believe she's telling me the whole truth here, and my heart hurts for her. This poor kid. This baby Janie whose diaper I once changed. Who watched me with big, round tear-filled eyes while sucking on her pacifier in a room with only a crib, a changing table, and a crucifix on the bland wall.

"I was always a big reader of mysteries," Trinity says. "Stories about detectives who solved crimes. And my gran loved true crime. She had all of Ann Rule's books on her shelves. And so many others. And when I spent summers with my gran and gramps, while my mom worked, I started to devour the true crime books on her shelves. Moving on to criminology, stories about FBI mind hunters. Then on to books on abnormal psychology. And all the while I could see my gran watching me in a certain way as I read them. Gramps and her had a big fight one night after he caught me with one of her books on 'killer minds.' I heard them at night. Gramps raging on about her filling my head with ideas. And what if things ran in families. Which started wheels turning deep inside my mind. It did seem odd, given my grandparents' devout faith, yet my gran loving these deviant stories of horrible, evil deeds. The irony is, those true crime books, I think, were my gran's way of trying to understand the mental pathology of her son-in-law, the man her daughter married. My father. But it turned me into a true crime aficionado."

"And that led you into true crime podcasting?"

She nods. "I joined a true crime book club. That led to an online cold case group. We'd pick an unsolved case each month, study it, and then all try to solve it. That led to me cofounding *It's Criminal*. And while I was casting about, looking for old cases to cover—Canadian ones, specifically, because we were planning a Cold North Killers theme—I ran across the 1997 Leena Rai murder. The fact that she was sexually assaulted and killed so violently by her teacher, who was also her guidance counselor, and tutor and basketball coach to boot, well, that was a riveting candidate. It had all the feels. Young schoolgirl. Small and closely knit mill town in the Pacific Northwest. The great big thundering waterfalls, and that mountain that looms like a tombstone over the town. And this killer who'd confessed but had never, ever spoken about what he did. It was like there remained a lingering secret. Something worse, darker. And this could be my narrative angle. So I started digging more. And when I opened up an old newspaper article, I . . . I nearly passed out. There was a photo with the news story, and it was *him*. Clayton Jay Pelley was the same man in my gran's photographs. I was sure of it. So I found more photos. And then there was no doubt in my mind I was looking at the same man."

"So you confronted your gran?"

"Yes. This was maybe three years ago. My gramps had passed two years prior. My mom was already sick, and losing her memory. And that's when my gran told me. She said she couldn't in good conscience keep the secret any longer, not from me. And now the truth could no longer hurt my mom, or my gramps. She told me my mom had lied because she wanted to protect me. From a sick man. So yes, I learned my dad was a kiddie porn addict, a sexual deviant. So how do you think that sat with me?"

"Did you think he might not have been Leena's killer?"

"Other than my mom allegedly lying about being his alibi, I had no reason not to believe he'd done it. He'd confessed. And when I got the transcripts, there was even less doubt."

"Then in episode one—at your first interview—he said he didn't do it."

"That's right." She sips her hot chocolate.

I can understand. Trinity couldn't possibly let this history of her family go. I can see why she's done what she has. With the podcast.

Trinity sets down her mug, but she keeps her hands wrapped around the warmth of it. "And then, the more I listened to him, and the more I spoke to people, I began to think that yes, maybe he did confess to something he didn't do to protect me and my mom. I *wanted* to believe my father, that some part of him loved me, us. But if he didn't do it, his confession had to have allowed someone else to go free."

She pauses. Something hardens in her face. Her eyes drill into mine. "And you let it happen, Rachel. You and Luke O'Leary." Another pause as the look in her eyes sharpens. "See? I think you were aware something was not right. That there *were* loose ends. But you allowed it, his confession, and now I want to know why. My other question, Rachel, is: What are *you* doing here? Right now? Just appearing outside the prison on the very day that my father is shanked, killed?" A beat of silence. "Just how badly do *you* want my father to stay silent? How badly did you want to put him behind bars in the first place, and why? Did you *know* something? Were you protecting someone? Are you still trying to protect them now?"

"That's ridiculous. I—"

"Is it?" Trinity leans forward. "I know how these prison gangs work, Rachel. My father had a tattoo on his neck that marked him as an affiliate of a gang on the inside. A spiderweb. I looked it up, and I did my research. It's a mark of the Devil Riders. A biker gang. Notorious drug trade connections. Affiliations to the Red Scorpions, and the Snakeheads, too. If a Devil Rider member, or a boss, wants someone targeted either on the inside or the outside, they can make it happen. That barbed wire keeps no one safe."

My heart starts to hammer. I can't breathe.

"My father was going to expose someone. Quite simply, someone didn't want that to happen, and stopped him. Dead."

"I just came to ask your father questions, Trinity. Because I now have as much interest as you in finding the truth."

She gives a false little laugh. "I haven't aired everything that I recorded with him. There's more."

"What do you mean?"

"There's one more audio." She holds my gaze. "In it, my father tells us all exactly why Maddy lied."

TRINITY

NOW
Sunday, November 21. Present day.

Rachel's features harden as she assesses me, and my words hang tangibly in the air between us.

My father tells us all exactly why Maddy lied.

I regard the shape of her face, the fine lines around the ex-detective's eyes and mouth. The streaks of silver in her thick, dark, wavy hair. She looks older today than when I first saw her at her farm. Perhaps it's the stark, wintery light that floods in from the window. But she seems tired, and angry. Edgy. Maybe even afraid now. This mother. Who was a cop. Who put my dad behind bars. Who changed my diaper. This woman I watched plowing her land in her green tractor with her dog at her side.

She's coiled in a way that scares me. I don't know if she could be dangerous to me. Or what she might have already done in the past. I'm unsure how far to push her, and whether pushing will unravel and reveal more things that I need to know or shut them down totally. But I'm wounded, too. My shock is morphing into a thumping fury. A rage that fires through my veins. I believe with my whole heart that someone on the outside—someone with connections to the twenty-four-year-old Leena Rai murder case—arranged to have my dad killed on the inside.

And it could've been this woman sitting in front of me.

The reason I believe this is what my father told me during our last session.

"You're bluffing," Rachel says quietly.

"Am I?"

"Or fishing, more likely."

She's poking me, trying to get a read on me. I'm aware of Gio watching us from the driver's seat in the van. He's ready to call 911 if things suddenly turn bad and I give him the signal. Slowly, my gaze holding hers, I set my phone on the table between us and hit PLAY.

My father's voice rises, distant and almost tinny, from the phone speaker. Rachel's eyes narrow sharply at the sound of him. She flicks her glance around the diner. But it's empty, save for an old couple in the far booth near the counter and the server up front.

> TRINITY: In our previous session, Clayton, you claimed Maddison Walczak lied about seeing you and Leena having sex in the woods. You were referring to the fourteen-year-old daughter of the detective who was investigating Leena's homicide, Rachel Walczak.
>
> CLAYTON: She did lie.
>
> TRINITY: If Maddy Walczak did lie, why did she do it?
>
> CLAYTON: Oh, I had sex in the little clearing all right, off the tiny trail near the outhouses. But it wasn't with Leena. It was with Maddy. The cop's daughter fornicated with me. She wanted to. It was consensual. And it wasn't the first time.
>
> *SILENCE*

SOUND OF TRINITY CLEARING THROAT

TRINITY: This is . . . Could you repeat this? Because I'm not sure I heard you right.

CLAYTON: I was seeing Maddy Walczak. We were having . . . an affair.

TRINITY: An affair? With a fourteen-year-old girl? One of your students?

CLAYTON: She was almost fifteen. She was hungry for experience. She was older in many ways than a lot of other girls her age—

TRINITY: That is not consensual. She was *fourteen*. A child. She wasn't capable of consent. You were an adult, and one who was in a position of dominance, of power. Legally, that's rape. That's sexual assault.

CLAYTON: . . . Do I disgust you, Trinity Scott?

Rachel's color drains. She fists her hands, and her knuckles whiten. Her jaw goes tight. She stares at my phone. Unblinking. Transfixed as she listens.

I felt just as shocked when my father said those words. Because he was my dad. And now I also know that he was aware I was his daughter when he said them to me.

TRINITY: I . . . I'm just processing, that's all. I . . . So your story is that you were not having sex with Leena Rai in the bushes, but with Maddison Walczak.

CLAYTON: That's correct. It was Leena who spied us in flagrante delicto. Who interrupted us. Maddy and I were going at it hard . . . and that's how I reopened the cut on my hand. I had already hurt my hands stacking logs, but I was leaning them hard into the dirt as I . . . She was under me. I was on top. And there was some broken glass in the pine needles. Suddenly we heard a noise, a cracking sound in the brush. And I looked up. Maddy looked, too. Right into Leena's eyes. Leena had a small flashlight. Leena bolted. Maddy scrambled out from under me and yelled for Leena to stop as she pulled up her pants. Then Maddy chased down the trail after Leena. She brought Leena back to me, and I saw how drunk and upset she was. Maddy told Leena that she had to promise not to tell anyone. Leena was crying. I told Maddy to go back to the fire. To act normal. That I would take care of Leena, take her home, talk some sense into her on the way. Leena was malleable. She . . . she loved me. I knew this. I used this. I put my arm around her, and I helped a sobbing Leena to my car, which was parked on the logging road.

Rachel's eyes shine. Her stillness is almost terrifying. Sinister. Her whole face has changed. She seems to have aged an additional ten years as she listens.

CLAYTON: I drove back toward town. Leena and I argued on the way. See? I told the detectives this. That part is all true. I was fond of her, but she'd misinterpreted my kindness and attention. She was utterly broken by the fact she'd seen me with Maddy. It was like I'd betrayed Leena personally. I told her how much I believed in her, and how she would become somebody important one day. And that I would continue to tutor her, and help her become great. But she must not tell anyone what she saw. She said she hated me. Started hitting at me while I was driving. She insisted I drop her off near the bridge, and if I refused, she would rat Maddy and me out. She was drunk, getting hysterical. So I took my chances and pulled over. I reached into the back with my bloody hand and grabbed her pack. I handed it to her and drove off.

TRINITY: She was still wearing your jacket?

CLAYTON: Yes.

TRINITY: You never drove to a lookout?

CLAYTON: No.

TRINITY: Weren't you still worried she would tell?

CLAYTON: Yes. Very. And if she did, I was done for. But I gambled with a belief she might keep her mouth quiet once she sobered up. That she would try to protect me.

TRINITY: You were accustomed to the female students doing your bidding.

CLAYTON: I got off on it.

TRINITY: What time did you drop her off near Devil's Bridge?

CLAYTON: I'm not sure. But I did leave the grove before the rocket. And it used to take about twenty minutes to drive from the grove to town. And after I dropped Leena off, I did go straight home. Lacey lied.

TRINITY: So where did Leena go, before she was seen by Amy Chan crossing the bridge around two a.m.?

CLAYTON: I don't know. Maybe she just hung out under the bridge smoking. Maybe she went somewhere else.

TRINITY: So Lacey lied. And Maddy lied. Why would Maddy claim you and Leena had sex?

CLAYTON: By that time Maddy had learned about the murder. Maybe she believed I *had* done it, I don't know. Maybe she believed with all the questioning that one of the kids was going to slip and reveal I was at the bonfire, and up to no good. And maybe she was scared her mother would find out what she did with me. So she threw me under the bus first. To save herself. Because then it would be her word against mine, because Leena was gone.

TRINITY: What about Beth Galloway's statement that she saw you with Leena going back to your car?

CLAYTON: Well, I did go with Leena back to my car.

TRINITY: Beth stated that Maddy told her she'd seen you having sex with Leena.

CLAYTON: If so, Maddy would have been lying to Beth. Perhaps Beth bought her lie. Or perhaps Beth knew everything and was backing her friend up.

TRINITY: How did your jacket get cleaned? How did it come back to you, if Leena was wearing it right before she was killed?

CLAYTON: I don't know. I just don't. It showed up in my office washed. It was inside a plastic grocery bag. At first I thought Leena had left it there. I didn't know at the time she was dead. Only that she hadn't gone home, or come to school on Monday.

TRINITY: So what happened to Leena under that bridge?

CLAYTON: You sound skeptical, Trinity.

TRINITY: I am.

CLAYTON: I really don't know. All I can tell you is that I'm a sick person. I tried to get help. Several times over the years. Like I said, I was like two people in one body. The good Pelley and the bad Pelley.

TRINITY: Who did you go to for help? What kind of help?

CLAYTON: I was seeing a local therapist in Twin Falls. A psychologist. He was trained in hypnotherapy. I first approached him about my alcohol addiction. He then dug deeper to see if I had an underlying cause for the drinking.

TRINITY: Hypnotherapy? He put you under hypnosis?

CLAYTON: Allegedly so he could speak directly to my unconscious. It didn't work for me.

TRINITY: Did the detectives ask you about your therapy? Did they pursue this angle at all?

CLAYTON: They didn't ask me. It never came up. Perhaps they pursued it later.

TRINITY: What was the name of the therapist?

CLAYTON: Dr. Granger Forbes. He was Johnny Forbes's father.

I hit STOP.

Slowly Rachel raises her eyes.

I say, "Can you see now why I asked you how badly *you* might have wanted to silence Clayton?"

"You can't air this." Her voice comes out hoarse. "This . . . this is not the whole picture. You cannot let this go live until we've gotten to the whole truth. If you let this out, it . . . it'll do damage you don't understand."

"That's the problem with secrets, isn't it, Rachel? The deeper you bury them, the more collateral damage they do when they're finally ripped out."

"You can't—"

"I already did." I check my watch. "Episode four went live an hour ago."

REVERB

THE RIPPLE EFFECT

NOW
Sunday, November 21. Present day.

Maddy and Darren listen to the new episode of the Leena Rai podcast while Lily and Daisy play with Legos in the living room. *PAW Patrol* is on TV. Maddy's skin prickles with heat, and she feels faint. Neither she nor Darren make eye contact.

> TRINITY: If Maddy Walczak did lie, why did she do it?
>
> CLAYTON: Oh, I had sex in the little clearing all right, off the tiny trail near the outhouses. But it wasn't with Leena. It was with Maddy. The cop's daughter fornicated with me. She wanted to. It was consensual. And it wasn't the first time.

Maddy hits STOP. She sits, unmoving, staring at her phone. So does Darren. Very slowly she looks at him. What she sees on her husband's face scares her.

"Is that true?" he asks. "Is that fucking true?"

She shoots a glance at the girls in the living room, their little blonde heads bent close together. They're occupied, out of earshot. "Keep your voice down," she says quietly.

"How . . . Fuck, Maddy! How *could* you? What does this mean? Did you—"

"He killed her, Darren. I have not the slightest doubt. I might have slept with my teacher. I . . . I see it now for what it was. That I was his victim. But at the time I didn't view it that way. He . . . he was only twenty-six, or twenty-seven, and it wasn't like he was . . . old. He was attractive and charming and seductive and I was naive and it was a terrible mistake that still haunts me. I lied about that. But he's lying now. He *still* is. He killed her." Tears fill her eyes.

Darren's face is twisted. A thick, sour memory swells between them. It hangs like a sentient, tangible creature. An evil. But neither can voice anything about it. Not even to each other. Darren, as angry as he is, looks as frightened as she feels. Maddy grabs for her phone and starts to wheel down the hall.

"What are you doing? Where are you going?"

"I'm going to call my mother."

"What in the—" He goes after her, and tries to grab the phone from her.

"Darren!" she barks as she tucks it out of his reach. "Leave me alone."

He glowers at her.

The kids look up. Lily starts to whimper.

He hurries toward them in the living room. "It's okay, honey. Daddy is just helping Mommy with something." He lowers his voice and looks at Maddy in the doorway. "What do you think you're doing? You haven't spoken to Rachel in . . . Why are you even calling her? What are you going to say?"

"It's enough, Darren. I . . . I've been thinking. A lot. I can't do this anymore. The guilt, the secrets, it's killing me. It's made me into someone I don't like. I don't want to be this person anymore. I *can't* be this person anymore."

"What in the hell are you talking about, Maddy?"

"My whole life I've been running. Fighting stuff. Hurting. Tempting fate. Taking risks that should have killed me a million times over, and perhaps I wanted them to. I . . . I think I've been trying to kill this thing *inside* me. This guilt. The shame. And I've lashed out at everyone and the world because of it. I . . ." Tears run from her eyes. She swipes them across her cheek. "I just can't do this anymore. I cannot sustain this any longer. Not now. Not with that podcast out there. It's time for the truth. I owe it to my girls. And to my mother. She . . . she protected me. She knew something was off, and she protected me anyway. And because I felt that she'd glimpsed my guilt, I've hated her for it. I've hated myself." She starts to dial.

He comes close, looms over her chair. "How? How exactly did Rachel protect you?"

"The locket. My locket—"

"Stop. Now. Just put that phone down. We need to talk. You need to tell me everything. All of it. Before you call your mom."

Beth is driving. She's going to pick her kids up from her mom's place. She's playing the new episode through the Bluetooth speakers.

TRINITY: Beth stated that Maddy told her she'd seen you having sex with Leena.

CLAYTON: If so, Maddy would have been lying to Beth. Perhaps Beth bought her lie. Or perhaps Beth knew everything and was backing her friend up.

TRINITY: How did your jacket get cleaned? How did it come back to you, if Leena was wearing it right before she was killed?

CLAYTON: I don't know. I just don't. It showed up in my office washed. It was inside a plastic grocery bag. At first I thought Leena had left it there. I didn't know at the time she was dead. Only that she hadn't gone home, or come to school on Monday.

She hits the brakes. A car squeals and skids as it swerves away from her. The driver flips a sign, honks. She's shaking. She didn't even see the vehicle. She pulls off the road onto the verge. She tries to call Maddy. Maddy's voice comes through the speakers. "I'm on a call or away from my phone, so please leave a message."

She tries again. Same message. Beth attempts to call Darren.

No answer.

She gulps in a few big breaths in an effort to calm and refocus herself, then puts her car into gear and pulls back into the traffic. She drives to her mother's house. The front door of her parents' home opens before she even reaches the porch stairs. Eileen stands in the doorway. Beth realizes her mother must have been watching for her car to come up the drive. Her mother's face is white, her features pinched. And Beth knows. She just knows—her mother has heard episode four.

A long-haul truck driver heading north along the 725-kilometer Highway 16 corridor between Prince George and Prince Rupert in British Columbia is listening to the Leena Rai murder series. He's taken to listening to true crime podcasts on these extended trips. They keep his mind alert, and they entertain him. Especially on this highway in the north, where the monotony of trees and trees and more trees along a never-ending ribbon of tar tends to make him feel sleepy. And he's not young. He drops off more easily these days. He can't wait to retire. He's driving for a food distribution company now. He used to work in forestry, driving log hauls through Sea to Sky country. His route used to take him through the mill town of Twin Falls.

As he listens to the host, Trinity Scott, talking about how witness Amy Chan saw Leena Rai on Devil's Bridge on Saturday morning, November 15, 1997, she reminds listeners that it was the night the Russian rocket hit the earth's atmosphere.

> And later, around two a.m. the following morning, Amy Chan saw Leena Rai on Devil's Bridge. These are Amy Chan's words, as per the Twin Falls PD interview transcripts, as she described what she saw. "There was a full moon. Big. It was clear. And there was a really, really cold wind blowing off the sea. That's what struck me—the sight of someone walking in that freezing wind. I saw long dark hair blowing. And then I saw the shape of the jacket, and the person, and I realized it was Leena."

A bolt of energy shoots through him. He sits more erect, and he turns up the volume.

> "You could totally see it was Leena. She—it's her shape. Leena is—was—tall and big, and she had a certain way of walking that people made fun of. Sort of lumbering. But it was more marked because Leena had been drinking a lot that night, or at least she looked totally drunk. Falling around and grabbing on to the railing. And then a truck went by. The headlights lit her

up. And I said to Jepp, 'Hey, that's Leena,' and I turned around in the seat, to watch . . . I didn't look farther back or anything to see if anyone was behind her, and then we were past, and off the bridge."

The image suddenly comes alive in the driver's mind. He drove over that very bridge just hours after that Russian rocket exploded in the sky and trailed comets over the mountains. He was driving his logging rig north. He remembers seeing a girl on the bridge, lit up by his logging truck lights. They bathed her fully. She was a big girl, with long black hair blowing in the wind. She was wearing a big military-style jacket and cargo pants, and she was stumbling drunk. Or he figured she was drunk. He didn't think too much about it. Friday night segueing into Saturday morning in a small Pacific Northwest town where kids were bored and there was probably not much else for them to do on the weekend other than get wasted—it seemed quite normal to him.

When he sees a sign for a gas station and truck stop ahead, he puts on his indicators and takes the off-ramp. He pulls into the truck stop parking lot and stops. The driver reaches for his phone and looks up the tip-line number for *It's Criminal*.

He dials.

He gets a voice mail recording asking him to leave a message.

"I saw her. I think I saw Leena Rai crossing Devil's Bridge that night. I was driving a log haul, and I crossed the bridge with my rig probably around two a.m. I remember because of the rocket. I saw a girl stumbling north along the bridge. And farther behind her, back in the shadows . . . I saw what appeared to be following her."

RACHEL

I drive fast. It's dark already. And there's bad weather coming in. I want to reach Twin Falls before it starts snowing. As I negotiate the Highway 99 twists and turns along the cliffs above the ocean, I listen to Clay Pelley's words again.

> CLAYTON: Leena bolted. Maddy scrambled out from under me and yelled for Leena to stop as she pulled up her pants. Then Maddy chased down the trail after Leena. She brought Leena back to me, and I saw how drunk and upset she was. Maddy told Leena that she had to promise not to tell anyone. Leena was crying. I told Maddy to go back to the fire. To act normal. That I would take care of Leena, take her home, talk some sense into her on the way. Leena was malleable. She . . . she loved me. I knew this. I used this. I put my arm around her, and I helped a sobbing Leena to my car, which was parked on the logging road.

My knuckles are white as I take a hairpin bend too fast, high above the water. I hit ice, slide. My tires squeal as I right myself and get back onto the road. My heart thumps.

TRINITY: Did the detectives ask you about your therapy? Did they pursue this angle at all?

CLAYTON: They didn't ask me. It never came up.
Perhaps they pursued it later.

TRINITY: What was the name of the therapist?

CLAYTON: Dr. Granger Forbes. He was Johnny Forbes's
father.

I call Maddy. Again. She's still not picking up. This time I leave a message.

"Do *not* listen to the recently uploaded episode, Maddy. Please. Just don't. Call me. We need to talk first. About . . . about the locket. About the photo that Liam shot. I need to know. Call me."

I navigate another hairpin bend, both hands on the wheel. My headlights cut tunnels through the mist that rolls down the mountainside. Mouth dry, I make another call. This time I try Granger.

No answer.

I curse.

I try again. Same. So I try phoning the farmhouse landline. The call kicks to voice mail.

I swear again. Another sharp bend appears in my lights. I slow slightly as a semi barrels toward me in the oncoming lane. The truck's massive wheel hurls a wave of blinding spray at my windshield. I engage the wipers at speed. They *clack, clack, clack* as I round the bend.

Granger lied to me. I asked him directly whether he'd treated Clay, and he flat-out lied by evasion. What does that mean? For the case? For us—our relationship? Suddenly our whole life together feels built upon falsehoods. But why hadn't Granger told me? What had he been hiding? Clayton's words flood back into my brain.

He was Johnny Forbes's father.

I navigate another bend. I don't want to go where my mind is going. But Granger is the link. He has to be. I know how his hypnotherapy sessions used to unfold. More than once he inducted me into a hypnotic trance for treatment of my stress-related PTSD. Before putting me into a hypnotic state, he gave me instructions, saying that when I woke up, I would not recall what had transpired during the session. He explained beforehand that hypnotherapy was a powerful tool for activating an autogenic type of healing process in the body. The intent was to break negative thought loops that fed addictions or other destructive behaviors.

Once awakened from the trance, he said, if I was faced with a trigger, I would automatically default to a new way of dealing with that trigger.

I hear his voice again in my head from all those years ago.

Once you're in the hypnotic state, I will be able to talk directly to your unconscious mind. The cortex gets out of the way—sometimes so far out of the way that my subject cannot remember anything that happened during the hypnotic session. But I will be able to seed thoughts directly into your unconscious. When you are awake again, and are faced with a particularly upsetting set of circumstances, this new way of thinking will just come to you. From where I seeded it.

Another sharp bend looms along the Sea to Sky highway. I take it as fast as I dare.

Just come to you.

My mind goes back to that day Luke and I faced Clay in the interrogation room with the others watching from behind the one-way mirror. I recall the strange, vacant look that overcame Clay's face right before he confessed in that strange monotone. I think of the podcast again.

TRINITY: How could you have known all those details if what you said wasn't true, if you didn't do it?

CLAYTON: It . . . just came to me like that. Came into my head. And I wanted to say it. All of it.

It can't be. Granger couldn't have. Why would he?

He was Johnny Forbes's father.

But how? Granger had nothing to do with the 1997 investigation . . . It suddenly hits me. Something Dirk Rigg said when he set that plate of Nanaimo bars on the table in the Twin Falls PD conference room.

Merle is trying to quit smoking again . . . She's trying hypnosis to quit the habit this time.

I find a lookout, and pull into it. My breathing is so fast and so shallow that I'm getting dizzy. I fear I might hyperventilate. I bring my truck to a stop.

Calm, Rachel. Big breath in. Slow out. Again. I open the window. The cool air shocks me back into clarity.

I scroll quickly through my phone to find Dirk Rigg's number. His wife, Merle, is long dead, and Dirk retired years ago. He lives in a retirement home, and I have coffee with him once or twice a year when I'm in town.

I find his number and call. I tap my steering wheel in agitation as I wait for him to answer. He picks up.

"Rachel?"

"Dirk, hey, listen, I know this is abrupt, but I need to know. Way back, when Merle was trying to quit smoking, and you said she was trying hypnosis, which therapist was she seeing?"

"Is . . . this to do with that podcast?"

"Yes. You mentioned in the incident room that Merle was having hypnotherapy."

"There was only one hypnotherapist in town in 1997, Rachel, and you know that."

I close my eyes. A bitter taste crawls up the back of my throat. Softly I say, "Granger."

"Of course. It helped for a while, you know. She quit for about two years. Then she went back to it. Probably because I was always smoking in the house, and it was too much of a trigger for her. I shoulda quit, because . . . well, as you know, the lung cancer got her in the end."

"I need you to be honest with me, Dirk. There can be no more secrets. Do you understand? Did you ever share with Merle the details of Leena Rai's autopsy? Did you talk to your wife about the case, and about how Leena was killed?"

Silence.

"Dirk?"

"Shit," he whispers. "I . . . Does this have anything to do with—"

"Just tell me, Dirk."

"I told Merle things. Always. She was my rock, Rache. She kept my counsel. She never shared what I told her. And I was badly affected by the Leena case, like we all were, especially after I got a look at the postmortem results, and saw what that girl went through, and how she was drowned. Those pebbles in her lungs . . . that did me in. Inhaling those pebbles with her last, desperate gulp for breath. Those photos of the boot imprint on her skull. I needed to talk to Merle. And maybe I shouldn't have, because what I told her messed with her head, too. She had trouble sleeping. She said the images kept coming at her, and her imagination would run with them in the darkness. She couldn't get the whole thing out of her head. It made her reach for her cigarettes again. I . . . I think she asked her therapist for a way to deal with it. The trauma of it. The horrific nightmares. The things that were urging her to smoke again."

Emotion wells in my eyes. I inhale deeply.

"Rache?"

"I'm here." I struggle to moderate my voice. "Thanks, Dirk."

"Did this have anything to do with—I mean, it couldn't have impacted the investigation, could it?"

"Maybe. It's okay."

"Shit," he whispers. "What happened—what's going on?"

"I'm not sure yet. I promise I will let you know, okay? Thanks, Dirk. Thanks for your honesty."

I kill the call and try Granger again. Still no answer. It's like everyone in my close circle is avoiding me. A pariah. I check the time. It's just past 8:00 p.m.

I decide to drive past the Raven's Roost to see if Granger's bike is perhaps parked outside.

When I pull into town and take the small side street around the back of the pub, I see Granger's bike.

Parked beside his motorcycle are two other Harleys. Both display Devil Riders insignia—that distinctive spiderweb design.

I know how these prison gangs work, Rachel. My father had a tattoo on his neck that marked him as an affiliate of a gang on the inside. A spiderweb . . . If a Devil Rider member, or a boss, wants someone targeted either on the inside or the outside, they can make it happen. That barbed wire keeps no one safe . . .

RACHEL

I walk into the bar. It's busy. Sunday night, so there's live music. Plenty of food, specials on drinks.

Rex is behind the bar. He spies me and raises his hand, but I ignore him as I scan the faces of the packed pub. I see him. Granger. Leather jacket. Ruffled hair. He's huddled in a booth in the back corner with his son, Johnny, their heads bent close as they discuss something.

I march toward them, bumping people in my haste.

"Hey! Old bitch. Watch where you're going."

I ignore the jibe. My whole being, every molecule in my body and mind, is focused on the back of Granger's head. I'm zeroing all my mental and emotional energy in on him because I can't even begin to process properly what Clay said about my daughter, and what that means to me as her mother. And right now, my worst fear is that the man I live with not only helped put Clay away twenty-four years ago, but also helped kill him today.

I reach the booth. Johnny stares up at me in surprise.

"Rachel?" Johnny says. "Are you all right?"

Granger turns his head, sees me. Blood drains from his face.

"Did you do it?" I growl at him. "Did you have him killed?"

"What in the hell are you talking about?"

"Clay Pelley. He's dead. Shanked. Did *you* do this? You and your Devil Rider contacts?"

"Jesus, Rachel." He surges to his feet. "Sit down, will you. Lower your voice."

"You were his therapist, Granger. You were Merle Rigg's therapist, too. You took those crime scene details from Merle, and you seeded them into his head."

His face pales further. He grabs my arm. I try to yank free. He grips tighter. He's strong. He pulls me close and puts his mouth to my ear. "Not in here. We'll talk outside. In your truck. Come, walk." He begins to usher me out.

Johnny stares after us, slack jawed, as his father marshals me through the bustling crowd. I see Rex at the bar, watching, frowning. I see Johnny going up to the bar to talk to his father-in-law.

We exit into bracing air. Drizzle comes down, fine as mist.

"Get in," he says as we reach my truck.

I beep the lock, climb in behind the wheel. I'm vibrating. I'm going to have this out with him come hell or high water.

Once Granger is in the cab and the passenger door has been slammed shut, I start the engine so I can run the heater. Windows start fogging quickly.

"Tell me what in the hell you're talking about," he says. "What do you mean Clay is dead?"

"You know he is."

"Rachel, for God's sake. I don't. Bear with me."

"Clay Pelley was stabbed to death at the prison earlier today. It happened shortly before I got there."

He stares at me for a moment. His gaze shifts slowly to the club. He stares at the line of bikes parked outside. He looks afraid. I've never seen him like this. As he's watching the pub doors, Johnny busts through them and comes running past my truck.

Granger powers down the window. "What's going on?" he calls. "Where are you going?"

"Got a call from Darren," Johnny yells. He hesitates briefly. "I—I'll talk to you later." He vanishes behind my truck. My panic—my fight-or-flight response—is so focused on Granger, and the fact that Johnny is Granger's son, and that Johnny was at the Ullr bonfire that night, that the logic center of my brain barely even registers Johnny's words.

"You lied to me, Granger. I asked you outright if you were treating Clay. You implied you didn't, but Clay outed you. You haven't listened to the last episode, have you? Clay told Trinity and the rest of the world that he sought help for his addictions from *you*. And he noted on air that you were Johnny Forbes's father. I called Dirk Rigg, because I remembered him saying Merle was getting hypnotherapy for her smoking addiction. He told me Merle was your patient. He also said he'd shared all the details of the case with Merle, and it had upset her."

Granger is silent for a long while. He swears softly and rubs his face hard with his hands.

"You did it, didn't you? You seeded those details into Clay's unconscious. Something we said to Clay during the interrogation triggered him, and suddenly he started talking in this distant sort of monotone, reciting how he killed Leena. You put it there. I want to know why."

He swears again, sits back, drags both hands over his hair.

"*Tell* me, Granger. Everything. Don't even *think* of lying to me now, because you know what? I've been lied to enough. My own daughter was being assaulted by Clay." I swipe tears away with a shaking hand. "My *fourteen-year-old child*, with her teacher." My voice cracks. I tighten my mouth, struggling to bottle down my emotions, to marshal my wits. "Maddy lied. The rest of the kids lied, or tried to, to varying degrees. Lacey Pelley lied. *You* are lying."

He sits silent. Resigned.

I shift in the seat to face him more fully. "Look, I know I made mistakes myself, Granger. Clearly my failings as a parent are far bigger than I ever realized. I refused to see things back then, or to follow them through, and yes, I stopped thinking about any loose ends in the case after Clay confessed, because it was easier than pursuing the alternative avenues of thought. But the time for hiding is long past. It's out there. It's all unraveling, and there can be no more running from the truth. Not for me, or you, or Maddy, or any of us."

"Whatever you did back then, Rache, it's what a mother does. Protects her children. It's what a father does—what parents do."

"Is that what happened?" I ask quietly. "Johnny. You did it for him? You screwed with your client's head to protect your son?"

His eyes and cheeks gleam. I realize Granger is crying. His face is wet with tears. I've never seen Granger cry.

"Granger," I say more gently, no less desperately, "please, tell me. It's all coming out now. You can't stuff this genie back in the bottle. If Johnny did something . . . What happened? What are you protecting him from?"

He inhales deeply. "When Johnny came home from school after the bonfire weekend, I found him in the laundry room. He was trying to wash a military surplus jacket. It was covered in mud, and what looked like blood. He'd tried to soak it first, and the water was red."

"Clay's jacket? The one Leena was wearing?"

"That's what it looked like. Lettering and numbers on the breast pocket. I asked him what he was doing, and he said he was washing it for a friend because the friend's machine was broken. He said his friend had slipped in mud and gotten cut, which is why there was blood. But I'd heard the description on the radio of the missing girl, and what she was wearing. And . . . I just got a real bad feeling." He blows out a heavy breath of air. "Johnny had been having a rough time since his mom died, and I was working on our relationship, and I . . . I didn't press him. I didn't corner him. He'd already threatened to run away the last time I did, and I knew if he did run, I would not get him back. We were on a cusp back in those days. The jacket came out of the machine, went into the dryer, then vanished from our house. And I didn't think about it for days. Until news broke that the girl's body had been found in the Wuyakan River, and that the jacket was still missing."

My heart thuds against my rib cage. I think of Clay. The podcast.

TRINITY: How did your jacket get cleaned? How did it come back to you, if Leena was wearing it right before she was killed?

CLAYTON: I don't know. I just don't. It showed up in my office washed. It was inside a plastic grocery bag. At first I thought Leena had left it there.

I hear sirens. They invade the hot interior of my truck cab and my thoughts. They grow louder. They are joined by more sirens. They're coming from the fire hall. It sounds as though they're heading up into the residential subdivision on the other side of the valley. I'm thinking of Johnny. And nothing is adding up. Every time I learn something new, a curveball comes my way. How does this piece fit into the puzzle?

"You were treating Clay Pelley. You knew about the child pornography. He was a teacher. He had kids in his care. He had a baby of his own. You *knew* children were in danger. You had an obligation to report this, an ethical obligation. You—"

"Clay came to me for alcoholism. He wanted help with that. Only when I dug deeper in an effort to learn if there were any underlying drivers to his desire to numb himself did it come out. During a session. Under hypnosis. And around the same time, I learned the details from Merle. And . . . Clay was sick, Rache. The recidivism rate for guys like him is—"

"I don't care. What you did was unforgivable."

"And you? Did *you* look the other way?"

I turn my head away from him, stare through the misting window. My heart is jackhammering.

Granger says, "I seeded something in the unconscious of a sick man. *He* was the one who confessed. *He* used those details because he wanted to lock himself away."

Softly I say, "And in the meantime, a violent killer slipped through our fingers and walks free." I face him. "Did you ask Johnny about the jacket again, after the news about Leena's body broke?"

"No. I was afraid to. But that's what I was doing tonight. Just as you barged in. Finally. After all these years, I asked him directly. He says a friend brought the jacket to him at school on Monday morning in a plastic grocery bag, and asked if he'd do them a big favor and wash it and then put it in Clay Pelley's office."

"You believe him?"

He inhales and averts his eyes.

"Did he do it, Granger? Did Johnny kill Leena? Did he sexually assault and kill his classmate?"

Granger's phone rings. He looks down to check the caller ID and holds up his hand. "Just a sec. It's Johnny."

He answers it. "What's up?"

Granger's body stiffens. His eyes widen. His glance shoots to me. *"When?"*

I go cold at the look on Granger's face. He hangs up.

"It's . . . it's Maddy and Darren's house. It's on fire."

RACHEL

I gun the gas as I roar up the road toward the cul-de-sac where Maddy, Darren, and my grandbabies live. Heart in throat, I spin the truck wheel and screech around a corner. Granger braces his hand on the dash as I squeal around another corner. More sirens approach from behind us. I can smell smoke. My heart races.

As I round the next bend, I see the blaze. The house is fully engulfed. Lights from fire engines pulse through the mist. The flames illuminate the whole end of the cul-de-sac. A road barricade forces me to slam on my brakes. A cop in uniform comes running toward my truck as I fling open the door and begin to race toward the fire.

I shove the barricade aside and bolt up the middle of the cul-de-sac. The officer chases me. A firefighter in full gear comes at me from an angle. My attention is fixed on the house. All I can think of is Maddy trapped in her chair. Of Lily, Daisy, their dad.

A blast shatters windows out of the side of the house. Wind is sucked inside and flames roar loudly. I hear crackles and a thundering sound. Another explosion.

The front door busts open. A figure comes barreling out with a jacket or blanket over his head. It's caught on fire. The figure runs onto the front lawn. Firefighters race toward him as he drops on the ground and rolls. One of the firefighters aims the hose to hold back flames beginning to consume the front porch as the other firefighters pull the man to safety.

The firefighter running toward me cuts me off. He grabs my arm.

"Ma'am, you need to stay back." He's panting from his run. "Everyone needs to go back. We're worried about a gas line."

I fight him off me. "That's my daughter's house, she's in there. With her kids. She's in a wheelchair—"

The uniformed cop reaches me. She takes hold of my arm, trying to restrain me. I shake her off, too, knocking her in the face. She staggers backward. I need to get to the house. I am not thinking. The power in my limbs is monstrous.

Another cop arrives. A male. Bigger. Stronger. He tackles me and holds me still. He grips me by the shoulders. "Ma'am. Listen to me, ma'am. *Look* at me."

I stare at the house. The building is so fully engulfed that the firefighters are not even attempting to enter. They're merely holding back and containing the blaze, stopping it from spreading to the neighboring homes and to the forest behind. "My . . . my grandkids are in there."

The female officer has come back up to her feet. Her nose bleeds copiously where I bashed it. She takes my other arm. "I've got her," she says to the firefighter. The firefighter lets go of me and rushes back toward his truck.

"Ma'am," says the female officer, "we all need to get back. We're moving the barricades back. There's a chance the gas line could blow."

But I stand, numb, my gaze fixed on the roaring flames.

The two cops physically turn me around, march me back to the barricade. I see my truck is gone. Granger or the cops must have moved it.

A boom sounds behind us. I wince and crouch reflexively. An explosion rips through the night. I feel the force of it slam into my back, and we all stagger forward. My ears ring. Someone is screaming. Everything seems distant. Black smoke billows. I choke and cough. The blaze roars like thunder.

TRINITY

"Want a beer?" Gio asks.

I glance at him. I'm sitting on the small sofa in the motel room, staring out into the darkness through my own reflection on the windowpane. It's just past 9:00 p.m., and the drive back to Twin Falls felt like an endless series of curves through blackness and time. I'm not sure how to process the death of my father. Whether I should care, or be pleased.

Or grieve.

My thoughts turn to some of his final words to me, and I recall the emotion in his eyes, on his face, as he spoke them. It all takes on a totally new meaning now that I know he knew he was speaking directly to his daughter.

I looked at those detectives who could see the devil inside me, who wanted to lock me up, and suddenly I knew. I had to go inside. I had to go behind bars. I wanted *to be locked away. To save those around me. To save those kids. To protect my own child.*

Was he afraid he might eventually abuse me, too?

Is that what underscored my young mom's actions when she gave him up to the police? Hurt burns into my eyes as a raw, deep longing surfaces inside me. It's a longing for something that could not—*cannot*—exist. A longing for a father's true and healthy love. In some strange, ugly, complicated way, I am jealous of Leena Rai. Of the fact that my father seems to have cared for her. The fact that she knew him in a way I can never know him now. It makes no sense at all for me to feel this way about the victim of a brutal killing. But I am relieved he didn't kill her—I truly believe that whoever Leena's killer is, he's still out there. And my job now is to finish this off. For me. For my mom. For my gran. For my dad.

And mostly for Leena and her family left behind, because they still have not seen justice done.

"Yeah," I say to Gio. "Let's have a beer." I tuck my socked feet under my butt on the sofa and watch him as he goes to the small fridge in the kitchenette, opens it, plucks out two bottles of the local brew, and carries them over.

I like watching him. I like the way he moves. He's wearing low-slung sweatpants and a faded gray sweatshirt. Sure, they're designer brands, but he'd look just as good in thrift store wear. His black hair is mussed. Stubble shadows his jaw. It makes his green eyes look even lighter below his thick, dark brows. I realize suddenly just how lucky I am to have Gio at my side.

"I like when you dress casual," I say as I reach for the cold bottle.

He blinks in surprise and seems momentarily lost for words. Something heavy and hot passes between us. He slowly takes a seat beside me as I look away and twist the cap off the beer bottle. I notice my pulse is beating faster. I take a long, cold swig, wondering what it is about me that scares me away from getting involved with guys. I mean really involved, with men I actually like and respect. Instead of my series of short-term flings, and one-night stands with men who are disposable to me.

He kicks his feet up onto the coffee table beside mine. He takes a long swallow, then says, "I wish you'd told me."

I turn to look at him.

"That Clayton Pelley was your father." His eyes show hurt. I get it. I would be hurt, too.

"I'm sorry, Gio. I . . . I couldn't. I didn't even know how to think about it myself. Going through the interview sessions, I suppose, was my way of trying to figure that all out. Figure *him* out. And to try to understand, or process, my relationship to him." I pause, take another sip from the bottle. "As much as Leena's family probably wanted— needed—to know why he did what they thought he did, so did I. And then when he said he didn't kill her . . . it messed with my head. I began to *want* to prove he didn't. I wanted him to be innocent of that, at least."

"And then he said he confessed in order to set you and your mom free."

I nod. "That, and . . ." Emotion snares my voice and strangles my words. I sit silent for a few beats. Gio places his hand on my knee.

"I understand," he says quietly, in a nonsexual, nonthreatening, dear friend kind of way. It makes the tears come. But he just sits there and lets me cry. And in that moment, I love him. I probably always have, and it always scared me off. Because Gio is good. Too good for me. I didn't want to start something that would hurt us both and screw with our professional arrangement.

"You should call your gran," he says quietly.

"It's late where she is."

"Still, she'd want to know."

I nod. He's right. Gran is probably sitting awake in the care home beside my mom's bed. Alone. Listening to the podcast. Wondering what I am feeling.

"How about I go score us some takeout while you do that?" Gio says. "Sound good?"

I swipe tears from my cheek and give him a smile. "Yeah. Thanks." My gaze holds his, and I feel that rush of warmth in my chest again. I see his pupils darken. He smiles gently. I think we both know in that quiet instant that we will sleep together. Tonight.

"See you in a few?"

I nod.

When Gio steps out the motel room door, and I hear it click shut behind him, I phone my grandmother.

As I wait for her to answer, I listen to a distant, rising wail of sirens, and I try to imagine what it must have been like in Twin Falls twenty-four years ago, at this same time of year. Sirens going to arrest my father. Me being cared for by a woman from the church while my mother gave up my dad. Chief Mountain, omnipresent, looming, lurking, watching from behind ever-shifting curtains of mist.

"Trinity?"

"Gran, I'm sorry I'm calling so late."

"Is everything okay, hon?"

"How's Mom?"

"She's the same, Trin. Are you all right? What's going on?"

"Did you listen? To the last episode?"

"I did. It doesn't surprise me that the Maddison Walczak girl lied, you know?"

"He's dead, Gran."

A beat of silence. More sirens join the distant, wailing chorus. Something big must be happening.

"What do you mean, 'He's dead'?"

"Clayton. It's my fault, Gramma. I . . . My podcast, it got him killed." Complex feelings surge through me like a tsunami as I voice the words. "Either the inmates learned he was a pedophile and took him out. Or someone on the outside who knows who the real killer is had him killed. I'm going with the hit orchestrated from the outside. Because I believe him. He didn't kill Leena. And someone out there did. If I hadn't started this podcast, he'd be alive. *I* did this."

"No, Trin, no. Clayton played his own role. He *wanted* to talk to you. He participated. He wanted to tell his truth to the whole world, through you. You offered him a medium. He *had* to know what chances he was taking in order to share that with you in that way. If you ask me, Clayton might have expected this." She pauses. "Maybe he even wanted it, Trin."

"He . . . he knew who I was. He didn't tell me, but I learned after his death that he's been keeping an eye on me and Mom. He knew where we were at all times."

My gran is silent for a long while. "Well . . . then. He wanted to meet you and see what and who his baby girl had become. He wanted to tell you to your face that he didn't kill that teen. To say sorry in his way. To let you know why he confessed—to save you and your mother."

"My mother helped put him there."

"Lacey had to survive, Trin. She was twenty-two years old. She was locked in a nightmare. She survived. She made you thrive. They both did what they did for you."

Tears flood my eyes again. Very quietly I say, "Thanks, Gramma." I struggle to speak as another wave of emotion swamps me. "Thank you for everything. For taking me and Mom in all those years ago. For helping us all move east. For . . . for telling me the truth." I choke as my throat closes with the sudden pain of loss. "I can only imagine how lonely and how hard it must have been for you. You . . . you gave me what I needed. You helped me learn who I am. And now I need to figure out who I want to be—where I want to go from here."

My gran falls silent again. I feel she is crying. I feel her aloneness as she sits beside my mother, who is, in most senses, gone from our lives. When she speaks, her voice is thick, quiet. "I love you, Trin. Now get some rest. I'm going to sleep. I think I will sleep tonight. A proper sleep."

"I love you, Gramma."

I end the call, and on my phone I pull up the photo of my dad with a tiny me in his arms. I zoom in to his face, his big smile. I touch the image. I hate him and grieve him. But I am glad he didn't kill Leena.

Gio knocks and opens the door. The smell of food, hot and delicious, comes in with him. I'm suddenly ravenous.

"Hey, that smells so good," I say as I get up and go to him. I kiss him on the cheek. But something in his face chills me. I step back.

"You okay? What is it?"

"Those sirens," he says, setting the bags on the kitchenette counter. "The people in the restaurant place—they heard on the radio—everyone was talking in the shop. They . . . they're saying it's Maddy and Darren's place. Their house. It's completely engulfed. And a gas line has ruptured."

Shock, horror, slams me.

"Are they okay?"

"I heard they're inside." His voice cracks. "Maddy and Darren are in the burning house, with their girls. They're all inside."

RACHEL

NOW
Sunday, November 21. Present day.

I sink to the sidewalk at the side of the road and sit and stare blankly ahead. A fine mist of rain descends over me. I can't seem to register or absorb anything. They've taken me to a makeshift command center of sorts, about two blocks away. Traffic to the neighborhood has been cut off. Two ambulances are parked nearby. There are marked police vehicles everywhere. Cops are interviewing people. Someone has given me a coat and a woolen hat. A silver survival blanket has been draped over my shoulders, but I'm still shivering, teeth chattering. Two neighbors are with me. A man and a woman. I don't recognize them.

A paramedic comes over. He wants to put me in the ambulance, but I refuse to go. I have to stay here. I want to know what's happening to the house. To my family. My whole life—my entire world—is burning. Everything that was most precious, that I should have worked harder to save. And now it's too late. I hear another explosion. There is a dark-orange glow in the mist. The smell of smoke is thick. Acrid.

I turn my head slowly. I can't see Chief Mountain in the darkness and clouds, but I sense it there. Looming, watching. Over yet another fire. Like the bonfire all those years ago. Like the Chief watched Leena being beaten up and drowned in the river. Like it watched her body floating in the eelgrass, then sinking. Like it watched me watching the divers searching for her in the murky, dark water beneath Devil's Bridge as eagles soared up high and fish carcasses rotted along the banks.

I think of Pratima. Dead now. Her words echo softly in my skull.

We think we can keep them safe if we order them what to do, if we control them. We think that if we keep them busy with sports, they can't get into trouble. But we're wrong.

And even if we do manage to protect them enough to keep them alive, we still can't make them love us. The very act of protecting can drive them away. Even make them hate us.

Another woman comes over, crouches down beside me.

"Can I get you anything, hon?"

I barely register her. Because as I turn in the direction of her voice, I see behind her, silhouetted by the strobing lights from a police vehicle, Johnny Forbes. He, too, has a silver blanket around his shoulders. Light dances in reflections all over it—red, white, blue, red. Johnny is talking to two officers. I suddenly focus, and I recall Johnny running out of the pub. I remember Granger powering down the window.

What's going on? Where are you going?

Got a call from Darren. I—I'll talk to you later.

Woodenly I get to my feet. I walk toward the vignette.

As I near, I notice Johnny has fresh bandages wrapped around both hands. He has a bandage on his head. I hear him saying to the officers, "The door to the living room was locked. From the inside, I think. I couldn't open it, and then fire burst through the study door, which had also been closed. I . . . I couldn't get to them. Any of them."

I realize in shock that the figure that came running out of the house with the burning blanket must have been Johnny.

Johnny, who rushed to see Darren before the fire started.

Johnny, who was caught by his dad washing blood from the jacket that Leena was wearing when she was killed.

"He's lying!" I yell, going right up to Johnny and punching him in the chest with both fists. He staggers backward and falls against the hood of the police cruiser. I shove him again. "Did you do it? Did you fucking do it . . . Did you start the fire? Is that what happened? Because you were here, you rushed straight here from the pub. Then this is what we find. You came running out of the house . . . It was *you*, wasn't it? You did it! You started the fire. That's why you were inside. *You* did this!" I beat him with my fists.

"Jesus, Rachel, get off me. Get her away from me."

The cops drag me away from Johnny. I struggle to shake free of their hold. I'm shivering. I can't think right. I can't seem to process what the cops are saying to me.

Granger arrives, out of breath. He must have had to park my truck some distance away.

"Rachel? Johnny? What in the hell is going on here?" He turns to the cops, then to me.

"He did it—Johnny burned the house down. He set fire to it with everyone inside. I—"

"Rachel?" Granger grabs hold of my shoulders, turns me to face him. "Look at me. Focus."

I try.

He says, "Johnny went in to try and save them."

I blink.

"Darren phoned me," Johnny says. "He phoned to say it's all over."

"What . . . what is all over?" My head feels thick. I'm confused.

"I don't know. But he sounded wrong. He's been my mate forever, and something was wrong. I . . . He sounded like he was going to end it, his life or something. He was drunk. He . . . I drove right over, and when I got here, I saw there was a fire in the house, and I ran inside. I tried to get to them, but the doors seemed to have been locked. I heard screaming inside the rooms, and banging, but I couldn't get to them."

I stare. I can't believe him. It's just another lie.

"You had that jacket," I say darkly. "Leena's jacket. You told your father a friend had fallen in the mud and cut himself. Who was the friend? Who asked you to wash the jacket, Johnny?"

Johnny stares at me. Red and blue light pulses across his face, giving him an eerie, wild look.

"Who, Johnny, *who*?"

He looks away, inhales, then meets my gaze. "It was my wife. It was Beth. She asked me."

"What?"

"Beth brought it to school in a plastic bag. It was Monday morning. She came to me when I had my locker door open. She asked me to hide it, wash it, and then put it back in Mr. Pelley's office . . . She rewarded me, with her body. It's . . . how we started dating, romantically. I . . . I was a horny teenager. It was too much to pass up—Beth Galloway? Pretty blonde, the queen of the school? It was just a jacket I washed." He pauses. "Until it wasn't."

"Beth?" I can't seem to process what he's saying.

"Darren wanted me to know what my wife was. He wanted me to know the truth. He said he wasn't going down alone, and—"

The cop's radio crackles. Johnny turns. Suddenly people start talking excitedly and moving around me. Someone starts running.

I spin around. "What's going on?"

Granger says, "It sounds like they've got someone. From the house. Out the back. Two of the neighbors pulled one or two of the occupants from the house before the gas line blew. They took the occupants down into the ravine at the back of the house. They're activating a rescue team to reach them, through the forest."

I start to run.

TRINITY

It's just past midnight. Gio and I are sitting in the rental van. Rain comes down. We can see the glow of the fire in the low clouds, and we can hear sirens. There are police vehicles everywhere. Cops stop us at a police barricade at the bottom of the boulevard that leads up into the subdivision. They're not allowing any traffic in or out due to a "police incident." Which tells me this is more than just a fire. Something big is going on.

"You think it's arson?" says Gio. "Do you think it's tied to the podcast somehow?"

"I don't know," I say softly. But I fear it is. "Maybe we've unleashed something terrible. I . . . I feel sick about those two little girls." I face Gio. "What if it's my fault? What if they're dead because of me?"

"If anything is anyone's fault, Trin, this is on those people who kept secrets. Who lied. Who tried to bury this whole case down deep, because that's what this looks like to me—collateral damage being caused by an explosion of truth. And the damage is bad, because the longer the truth remained buried, the more lives that became impacted.

Now it's innocent kids. Being hurt by something that happened twenty-four years ago, long before they were even alive. The people involved are all going to have to accept blame for that." He holds my gaze. "Just like the actions your mother took to protect you. Because of that lie, because you needed the truth in order to live like a normal person, it drove you back here in search of answers. What your mother did, what your father did, what all those students at school lied or did not lie about . . . *that's* what's caused this. *That's* who's to blame. Even those detectives are to blame."

I feel a buzz on my wrist. I glance at my smartwatch, see I have a voice mail via the *It's Criminal* website. I take out my phone, dial in, and click 1 for the lone message.

The voice is male and gravelly.

"I saw her. I think I saw Leena Rai crossing Devil's Bridge that night. I was driving a log haul, and I crossed the bridge with my rig probably around two a.m. I remember because of the rocket. I saw a girl stumbling north along the bridge. And farther behind her, back in the shadows . . . I saw what appeared to be following her."

"Listen—listen to this," I say to Gio as I put my phone on speaker. The gravelly voice fills the inside of the van.

"Behind the drunk girl, staying far back, was a guy with a black toque pulled low. Tall guy. Big jacket. With him was a girl. She stuck out. The moon was full, and my headlights lit briefly on them. It was her hair that caught my attention, the way it glimmered in the light. Long. White blonde. Almost silvery in that moonlight. Blowing in that cold wind. It was waist length."

I swallow.

"Beth?" asks Gio. His voice grows excited. "It *had* to be Beth Galloway."

"Anyway—I was listening to the podcast, and the bit about the rocket, it reminded me. I can recall exactly where I was that night I saw the girl on Devil's Bridge. My name is Daniel Barringer. This is my number where I can be reached."

I stare at Gio. My brain races. But I still can't quite fit the pieces together.

"If it was Beth on the bridge, what was she doing following Leena? And who was the guy with her?"

RACHEL

NOW
Monday, November 22. Present day.

It's after midnight, and I'm at the Twin Falls hospital. Maddy was brought in unconscious. ER physicians are working on her now. The girls are with other doctors. They're alive, but I don't know yet how severe their injuries are. I am scared. I'm pacing, rubbing my arms. Granger is with me, but I cannot look at him. Cannot bear to see his face.

One of the neighbors who helped save Maddy and the girls is in the waiting area. He's the father I saw putting up Christmas lights while his baby watched from the porch when I went to visit. A dad with a young child of his own. He risked his life to assist my daughter and her girls. His wife could have been left a widow and his child without a father. It's weighing heavily on me—these ripples that seem to have fanned out over the years from Leena's murder. When does a story begin? I know it doesn't end.

"Are you okay?" the neighbor asks me.

I bite my lip and nod. "I don't know how to thank you."

"Maddy did most of the work. And that they're alive is thanks enough."

The neighbor and a friend who was visiting him last night smelled smoke. They went outside, saw the fire, and ran around the back of Maddy's house. She'd managed to break a window at the rear of the house, and she'd pushed both her girls out through the broken glass. The men got the girls away from the back of the house while the fire raged at the front. But Maddy was still inside. While she'd been fighting to save her children's lives, a beam had come down, hit her head, and rendered her unconscious. The men broke a sliding glass door, got inside, fought smoke, and managed to find her. They carried her and the girls down into the wet ravine behind the house just before the big explosion. They had to hunker down there while the fire raged until rescue teams could get in to extract Maddy and her kids.

Darren never made it out of the house.

"Why don't you go home?" I ask the man. "Your family probably needs you with them right now."

"I have to know that Maddy and the girls are going to be okay. I mean, really okay. I just . . . I must know."

A doctor comes down the hall. We all freeze and stare at him. I try to read his face. I can't breathe. Can't think.

He zeroes in on me. "Are you Rachel Hart?"

"I . . . I'm Maddy's mother, yes. I'm the grandmother. I—"

"They're going to be fine. The children are both physically fine. A few bad cuts and abrasions. Some minor burns. Some issues from smoke inhalation, but they're going to be okay."

My knees collapse, and I stagger slightly, then right myself. "My daughter?"

He offers a kind smile. "She's going to be fine, too. She took a bad knock to the head. She's got a concussion from the blow, but we've stitched up the gash on her brow. And we've set an arm fracture—she's in a cast. We'll be keeping a careful eye on her for the next twenty-four hours, and over the next few days." He pauses. His gaze flicks to

Granger. "They're very lucky. You can both come through and see them now."

The neighbor has plopped down into a plastic bucket chair and has his face in his hands. He's sobbing with relief.

"I'll be right there," I say.

I go over to the neighbor, sit in the chair beside him, put my arm around him. "Thank you. Thank you . . . I can never thank you enough."

"Thank God. I . . ." His words die on a dry sob.

"You took such a risk going into a burning building. You put your life in danger. Your wife . . . your own child could have lost someone they loved if you'd been hurt."

"Those beautiful little girls. Lily and Daisy. And Maddy, hurt while saving them . . . I . . . I couldn't *not* go in . . . We just acted. Didn't even think. I . . . just needed to hear the doctor say that they were all going to be okay. That I made a difference."

"Do you want to come through and see them?" I ask.

"No . . . no, I'll be fine. I need to get back to my wife and daughter."

"Granger will take you—he'll give you a ride," I say.

Granger's eyes flare to me. I inhale and meet his gaze properly for the first time since we sat inside my truck outside the Raven's Roost.

"I need to see Maddy and the girls alone. I don't want you in there with me."

His features change, tighten with pain. His eyes begin to glisten.

"We all made mistakes, Rache. We all just wanted to protect our kids."

"Is that what you'd say if Maddy and Lily and Daisy had burned to death along with Darren? What about Darren? My son-in-law? How many lives need to be sacrificed because of toxic action a quarter of a century ago?"

He stares at me. And in that moment, with the clinical smell of the hospital around us, the smell of smoke in our clothes, we both know one thing to be true. It's over between us. It has to be. I will not be able to forgive him for what he did. I don't know exactly what part I played—the extent of it—but the fact that I played one means I will probably not be able to forgive myself, either.

The nurse takes me through to see the girls first.

I enter the room and see two beds, two little faces. Scared eyes.

"They've been sedated slightly," says the nurse. "Lily, Daisy, your grandmother's here."

"Gramma?" says Daisy. "Where's Mommy? Where's Daddy?"

My heart cracks, and tears flow. I sit on the bed, gather Daisy in my arms, hold Lily's hand. Through my streaming tears, I say, "Mommy's going to be fine. She's going to be just fine."

Dawn is creeping pale into the sky outside the hospital windows when Maddy's eyes flutter and she slowly comes around. I'm sitting in a big chair beside her bed with the girls on my lap. They both finally fell asleep in my arms. My legs have gone numb, but I haven't dared move for fear of disturbing them. I spent the hours breathing in the scent of smoke on their hair, and another that is the scent of my grandbabies.

The police came and told me during the night that Darren's body was found in the locked living room in the front part of the house. It was clear that Johnny had indeed tried to break down the door but had not been able to get to his friend.

The police want to speak to Maddy when she wakes. They said evidence of arson was clear. There were signs that several fires had been started through the house with an accelerant, one after the other in close succession. It appears as though Maddy and the girls were locked into Maddy's study, and Darren locked himself into the living room. There was a burned-out gas container with him. The police said it appears he might have doused himself in gasoline before starting the fire in the living room. The officers will be returning soon. I hope I can talk to Maddy before they do.

I stir and carefully extricate myself from under the sleeping kids. I place a blanket over them and go up to the bed. I take Maddy's hand.

"Mads, honey?"

She blinks and slowly focuses on me, then suddenly tries to sit bolt upright.

"The girls!"

"They're okay. Look. Shh, they're fast asleep. They've had a mild sedative."

She turns her head on the pillow, wincing as she moves. There's a bruise forming under her eye, deep purple. Above the eye a bandage covers stitches. She tries to move her arm, then seems to realize it's in a cast. With her free hand she tentatively touches her brow.

"You're going to be fine, too," I say softly. "Broken arm. Big bang to the head, some stitches. But you got your girls out the back, and then it seems you were knocked on the head. Your neighbor and his friend broke in and brought you out."

She seems confused, as though she's trying to remember. Then panic widens her eyes.

"Darren?" Her voice is hoarse. She coughs and winces again.

"I'm so sorry, Mads. He . . . he didn't make it."

She closes her eyes and sinks her head back into the pillow. Tears leak from beneath her lashes.

"The police officers will return soon. They're going to ask you what happened."

Her lids flicker open. She's silent for a few moments. Moistening her lips, she says, very quietly, "I want to talk to you, but I . . . I don't want Lily and Daisy to hear."

I nod. "I'll go find a nurse to see if someone can help me get them back to their room and watch them."

Once the girls have been safely relocated, I pull the chair close to the bed, sit, and take Maddy's good hand. For a few minutes she just lies in silence with her eyes closed, and she lets me hold her. My daughter, for the first time in twenty-four years, has not pulled away from my touch. Tears fill my eyes, and I just allow the moment, because I fear it will all change again in an instant.

She tries to moisten her dry lips again. "He started it, Mom. Darren started the fire."

Mom.

My stomach contracts.

I have not heard that word from my daughter's lips in such a long time. And suddenly it breaks me. I struggle to hold in my surge of emotion.

I sniff and say softly, "Why?"

"Because of what he and Beth did to Leena."

"I don't understand."

Maddy inhales a shuddering breath. She closes her eyes again. And when she speaks, it seems to be from a distance, as though she's slipped into a place far, far away.

"I always thought it was my fault. Our fault. All of our faults. I never knew. I . . . None of us knew that Darren and Beth went back. They went back to finish it off."

Cold leaches slowly down into my belly. I don't say a word. I'm terrified to hear what's coming next.

"Me and the other girls, we . . ." She opens her eyes. They're awash with tears. Her voice is shaking. "We swarmed her. Leena. That night. Under Devil's Bridge. Us girls. We beat her up."

RACHEL

"What do you mean, *swarmed* her?" Blood thumps against my eardrums.

"Beth found out that Leena stole her address book. It was the last straw for Beth. Leena had already taken jewelry from us, and makeup. And then when she took the address book, she started calling up boys, and pretending she was Beth, and she said things on the phone that were . . . disgusting. Beth was always on Leena's case, being a bully and kind of sadistic about it, so . . . I don't know, maybe that's why Leena did it. But when Beth found out—it was like a direct attack on Beth, and thus all of us in the group. Beth said we had to teach Leena a lesson."

Maddy falls silent. She reaches with her good arm for the water cup next to her bed and takes a sip.

"Beth phoned Leena the day before the bonfire. She invited her to an 'after-party' under the south side of Devil's Bridge. Beth told Leena there was going to be a nice surprise. Leena bought it. She couldn't even see it for the ruse it was. A trap. A setup. An ambush. Leena was excited. She actually thought Beth was trying to be her friend, and she was pestering us at the bonfire."

The words Darsh Rai uttered to me and Luke that night at the Laurel Bay ferry dock resurface from memory.

I'm sure everyone has told you by now that Leena did stupid, stupid things, and that she had no idea how desperate it made her look. Sometimes . . . she just had trouble reading people.

"We wanted to tell Leena to bugger off at the bonfire, but Beth said we had to play along, or Leena wouldn't come to the bridge."

I am so still, so silent, that Maddy stops to regard me. Her eyes are huge and dark, and she's so pale. She looks like my little Maddy. The young girl I used to love so very much, and would move the earth for. My heart, my soul, is shattering all over again. A part of me wants to tell her to stop. I've heard enough. I don't want to know the rest. A suffocating horror is rising in me. Terror. Of what is yet to come out of my child's mouth.

"Say something, Mom. Please. Say anything."

I'm conscious of the seconds ticking away. The dawn outside is getting brighter. The police will be back soon. I swallow, clear my throat. "And Clay Pelley? Was he at the bridge?"

"No."

I feel ill.

"He was only at the bonfire. After Leena stopped badgering us, she sat with Clay on a log on the other side of the fire." Maddy hesitates. "He had a soft spot for her. A different way of interacting with her. He cared. The part of him that was a teacher truly cared for Leena, I think."

My ass.

"Is . . . is it true what Clay said, on the podcast, Maddy? Did he abuse you?"

Tears leak down her pale cheeks. "I thought I loved him. I thought it was daring, and that I had the most cool secret in the entire world. I thought it made me so special, that he was interested in me like that. I'd have done anything for him. And yes, I was with him in the bushes that night. But Leena came looking for him, and she found us. Doing it." She sucks in a shuddering breath. "It makes me so ill to think about it, how I was emotionally manipulated by a trusted authority figure, and how I could never bring myself to talk about it, to tell you. And the longer I've held on to it, the sicker it's made me in my head, in my soul. It . . . it made me lash out at everything, including you. Mostly you. And I am so sorry. But . . . what Clay said on the podcast was—is—true, Mom. I ran back to the bonfire, while he began taking Leena up the path to his car."

She falls silent. I glance at my watch. Tension torques in my chest. The cops will be here soon. I am weighted down with the realization that I have completely failed in my role as a mother. I wasn't there for my child in the way I should have been. I didn't save her from a very sick man. I wasn't home enough or present enough to realize she was growing troubled. I didn't look hard enough. Until it was too late.

"Maddy," I say very softly, "what made Clay target you? What made you vulnerable to this predator?"

She wipes tears from her cheeks. Her hand trembles. "I didn't think I was a victim at the time. Like I said, I felt I was special to be selected for his attention. It . . . it started when I went to him because I was . . . I was having trouble with things at home."

My throat closes in on itself. My words come out husky, strained. "What trouble, Maddy?"

"You. You and Dad. You always working. Trying to prove to everyone you were going to be a good police chief and fill Granddad's shoes."

My eyes pool with tears. I turn my head and stare out the window. She takes my hand.

"Mom. Look at me, Mom."

I swallow and face my child.

"I am a mother, too, now. Sometimes . . . sometimes . . ."

"Can you forgive me, Maddy? Can you find it in your heart?"

"I can't forgive myself, Mom. For what I did."

"Did . . . did you tell Beth, the night of the bonfire, what you did with Clay?"

She closes her eyes again. "No," she whispers. "But Beth spied us when she went to the washroom. She lost it. She was furious. But in the end we both lied—she lied for me. It was the start of the end of our friendship." She holds my gaze. "You see, it was Beth who invited Clay to the bonfire, who told him about it. I realized—when she got so enraged with me—that she actually thought *she* might seduce Clay that night. She thought *she* was Clay's 'special girl.'"

"Maddy, the locket—"

"I was wearing it on the night of the bonfire." Her gaze locks with mine. "But you know that. Because you stole that photo Liam shot of us girls. The one from my bedroom drawer, where you can clearly see the locket around my neck."

"How did it get in Leena's hair?"

She turns her head on the pillow, away from me.

"Maddy?"

"We waited under the bridge for Leena to come," she says softly. "Me, Beth, Darren, Cheyenne, Dusty, Seema. Dusty was super amped up, and she was accustomed to violence. She experienced violence at home. She'd been violent herself. She struck Leena first. Hard. Across the face. We . . . we all beat her, and kicked her, and Darren stomped on her back. And Dusty and Cheyenne burned her with their cigarettes."

I wince, thinking of the dead girl on the autopsy slab in the morgue that day. "Darren . . . has size-eleven feet."

She nods. "He was wearing his work boots, the same brand as half the guys in town wore."

"Including Clay Pelley."

She nods. "It was so horrible. The group beat her so badly. I hit her once with my fist, and in the whole struggle, my locket got ripped off my neck, and it must have gotten tangled in Leena's hair." My daughter falls silent for a long while. Her eyes take on a haunted look. It's as though she's seeing back through a tunnel of time to that cold night under the bridge. I sense the clock ticking. It's growing lighter outside. Tension winds tighter in my chest.

"Go on, Maddy," I say quietly.

She inhales. "Beth tore Leena's backpack off her back and opened it, looking for her address book."

"But she didn't find it," I say. "Because it was in the side pocket of Leena's cargo pants."

"We didn't know that. Beth dumped everything out of the backpack, and stuff fell between the rocks. She found Leena's journal, opened it, and began reading with her headlamp, and Leena, who was bleeding, struggled to grab it away. And some of the pages ripped out." She takes another sip of water, coughs. "I said that was enough. I tried to stop them. They carried on hitting her, and I told them I was leaving. I marched away. I couldn't take it anymore. Darren tried to stop me, but I shrugged him off and kept going. I walked along the road, alone, to Ari's takeout. I threw up along the way. The others caught up with me—Cheyenne, Dusty, Seema. They told me that Darren and Beth were following behind them. I didn't know that Darren and Beth had gone back after Leena. When I heard her body had been found . . . I thought Leena must have stumbled back over the bridge and then died from the injuries we'd all inflicted, and that I was also partly responsible for her murder. Which is why I lied about my locket. Why we all lied about things. Then Mr. Pelley confessed that he'd killed her. I . . . I couldn't quite put it together, but assumed he must have found Leena on the north side of the bridge and drowned her there, and that's what he'd meant when he'd told me he was going to 'take care' of her after she'd spied on us in the bushes."

She lies silent, and for several moments I can't speak, either, as the enormity of what actually transpired sinks in.

Maddy then clears her throat and says, "After episode four of the podcast, Darren confessed to me. He said that he and Beth followed

Leena, who was staggering back over the bridge, severely injured. Dazed. And they took her down the path on the other side of the bridge and . . . he said they 'finished the job.'"

I stare at my child as images of Leena's naked body on the slab resurface so vividly in my mind that I can smell the morgue. I can feel Luke at my side. I can see Tucker's trembling hands as he aims the camera. I see Leena's damaged liver. Her cut-out heart on the scale. I hear Dr. Backmann's voice.

This is similar to what I'd expect to see in a crush convulsion injury. Which is something that often occurs with car-crash victims. This girl went through hell.

Very softly Maddy says, "Until Mr. Pelley confessed, I thought we'd killed Leena. I thought I'd helped do it."

"You did. You all did. You all helped."

She turns her head away again and just lies there. Like she's given up all will to live. I think of Lily and Daisy. I need to help my child. We all need to find a way through this.

"Why, Maddy? Why did Beth and Darren go back and do this?"

"Beth—she . . . she can be sadistic. Evil, even. She's got a mean streak. It's in her blood. And I think she took out her anger with me for having slept with Mr. Pelley on Leena. Perhaps she was taking out her frustration with him, too, because he liked Leena, and cared for her, and had admonished Beth before for bullying her." She inhales deeply. "Darren . . . he told me that he and Johnny planned to lose their virginity on the night of the Ullr sacrifice. They were both desperate to. And because Leena was so drunk, they sort of coerced her, and she agreed to do it with them, earlier that night, in the woods."

Nausea rises in my gut. Bile is bitter at the back of my throat. "So she was raped, prior to the bridge beating, by two of her classmates?" *My daughter's husband and my partner's son.*

"It was sort of consensual. She was always trying to do things in order to feel needed, or liked. She misread everything socially."

"That's not consensual and you know it, Maddy."

She closes her eyes. Tears leak from beneath her lashes.

"But why—why did Darren go back with Beth?"

She swallows. "He . . . he said he'd hoped that I would be his first lover. He said after being with Leena, he was so disgusted by what he and Johnny had done with her in the woods that he just wanted to bash her out of his existence. Make her go away. He was drunk, and probably high, and full of bloodlust from the beating."

I can barely breathe. My heart aches for Leena. For her parents, her family.

"What happened at your house last night, with the fire? What happened with Darren?"

She swallows. "He . . . said it was all over. It was going to come out in the podcast that he killed—drowned—Leena with Beth. And he couldn't have his girls growing up knowing. He'd basically downed a bottle of Scotch. He locked us up and set the house on fire. He said it was all finally over. He tried to kill us all. Like he was trying to burn the memory of the whole thing, including us."

I surge to my feet, walk to the window, and hug my arms tightly across my chest. I stare resolutely at the granite face of Chief Mountain. It glistens wet. Tattered curtains of mist blow across it in the gray dawn.

No wonder Johnny remained silent on the issue. And washed the jacket. He'd raped Leena, the dead girl. He loved Beth. He'd have done anything for that manipulative young woman. No wonder all the other kids lied. They knew what they'd done. They'd all had a hand in Leena Rai's demise.

No wonder they were happy to throw their teacher to the wolves, if he seemed prepared to take the rap.

"Maddy," I say, still facing the window. "The cops—RCMP—will be here soon. You need to tell them everything. All of it."

Silence.

I turn. "You must. This has to stop here. There can be no more collateral damage. You have to think of Lily and Daisy."

"Beth has kids, too."

"You need to do what's right. The truth is right."

She nods. "I know," she says softly. "I know that now."

I hear a strange noise and spin to face the door.

Eileen. She stands in the doorway, white as a ghost.

"Eileen? Did . . . How long have you been standing there? Did you hear everything?"

"She's gone," she whispers. "Beth. My baby's gone and she's taken the kids. There's an AMBER Alert out. Police everywhere are looking for them. Johnny said Beth also got a call from Darren. Just before the fire. By the time Johnny arrived home, she was gone. One of their neighbors said a guy with a big maroon truck came to pick them up. It had a spiderweb design on the side. I . . . Rex thinks it's Zane Rolly, one of the bikers who hangs out at the pub." She wobbles and reaches for the doorjamb to support herself. Her voice cracks. "Johnny thinks she might have been . . . seeing Zane on the side."

"Oh, Eileen. I'm so sorry." I go up to my friend and gather her into my arms. She rests her head in the crook of my neck, and she begins to sob. I stroke her hair as her body shudders and her tears wet my T-shirt. "You need to trust that the police will find them. You need to believe that they're going to find Beth and the kids, okay?"

"They're my grandbabies," she whispers into my shoulder. "They're my world."

"I know," I say gently. "I know."

But despite my words, I'm fearful. The odds of the kids being found safe, alive, sink with each minute they haven't been located. Especially if Zane Rolly is the Devil Riders' connection to Clay Pelley's murder on the inside.

"Mrs. Galloway?" We all turn. Two uniformed RCMP officers stand in the corridor outside the room, along with a Twin Falls officer. "Could we have a word, Mrs. Galloway?"

Eileen wipes her tearstained face and nods. The male RCMP officer leads her away. The female says to me, "Are you the mother—Maddison Jankowski's mother?"

"Yes. I'm Rachel Hart," I say.

"We'd like to speak to your daughter, Ms. Hart."

I nod and try to reenter the room with the cop, but the RCMP officer stops me. "Alone. We'd like to talk to her alone."

I glance at Maddy.

"It's okay, Mom. It's okay."

TRINITY

Gio has gone to the hospital cafeteria to find coffee. He and I arrived early this morning, after we heard on the news that some of the occupants of the house were brought here after the fire. No one is speaking to us about who was hurt or who is alive. Outside the main entrance doors to the hospital, photographers and journalists with mikes are clustering. Through the windows I see a couple of news vehicles farther down the road, one with a satellite dish atop. The AMBER Alert for the Forbes children—Doug, age six, and Chevvy, age four—is all over the news. Beth Forbes is on the lam with her children, and I believe I know why.

I returned the truck driver's call. I heard his description of the young woman with waist-length, white-blonde hair blowing in the wind. It was Beth. I'm sure of it. With an as-yet-unidentified male on Devil's Bridge that night, following Leena, right before she was killed.

Beth's mother, Eileen Galloway, works at this hospital as an equipment purchaser. Gio and I hope to ambush her if she comes in. We got inside before hospital security started barring journalists from entering the facility.

The reporters also want to talk to me. My cell has been ringing nonstop. A woman with Global TV broke the story this morning that I am the daughter of Clayton Jay Pelley, and that my father was murdered in prison. It's all going viral. My podcast and I have become the story. Reverb. It's the mark of the live narrative form—the unfolding, unraveling, and ripple effects occurring in real time. An old case, once thought to have been solved, has turned into a live and red-hot one.

Gio returns from the cafeteria with two coffees. Excitement crackles in his eyes.

"I think I just saw Maddy and Darren's girls in the cafeteria," he says, voice hushed as he takes his seat beside me so that no one can overhear. He hands me a coffee. "I followed at a distance as a nurse led the two little girls back down the corridor, and I heard someone say that their mother is okay, but that it's so sad about their dad."

Thank God. I look away. I want to cry. I no longer have any control over what I've unleashed. And as thrilling as it has become, I am now frightened, and it's overwhelming me. I think of Rachel's warning in the diner.

You can't air this. This . . . this is not the whole picture. You cannot let this go live until we've gotten to the whole truth. If you let this out, it . . . it'll do damage you don't understand.

Have I been reckless? Irresponsible? Should I have followed things further before just putting that last segment on the air?

"Rachel told me to hold off airing that last episode," I say quietly to Gio. I take a sip of coffee. "She said I didn't understand the full scope of the story yet, and people could get hurt. I . . . I just didn't think it would end up like this. People burned in a house fire. Little children almost dying. Other kids in danger and on the run with a mother who could be a killer. What have I done?"

"Hey," Gio says softly. He places his coffee on the table in front of us, and he wraps his arms around me, draws me close. I don't pull away. I just let myself be in his arms. I'm surprised at how comforting it feels. I am startled by the sense of warmth this contact sends through me, along with a feeling of solidarity. Connection. I need this man. I didn't realize just how much. I feel like I know Gio so well, and yet not nearly well enough.

"You couldn't have changed anything, Trin." He smooths hair away from my brow. "That clip—it was already scheduled to go live before you knew Clayton was dead. It was live before you even met with Rachel in the diner. You couldn't take it back from those who'd already tuned in. It was out there."

I rub my face. "Maybe I just should have held off in the first place, until I understood the context better. I'm worried about those children, Gio, Beth's kids." I hold his gaze and whisper, "Do you think Beth and that man who picked her and the kids up did it, organized to have my father silenced?"

"You're jumping to conclusions, Trin," Gio says.

"The AMBER Alert says to be on the lookout for a truck with a spiderweb graphic on the side."

He glances at the gaggle of reporters outside the windows. Wind is blowing their hair and flapping their coats. "Yes," he whispers. "Yes, I think it's possible. It adds up. If Beth was on that bridge, she could have done something really terrible she needs to keep quiet. Terrible enough to use a Devil Riders connection to silence your father, and then go on the run with her kids, leaving her husband and life behind."

"Poor Johnny."

"Yeah."

I see Rachel come out of the corridor and into the waiting area. She makes hurriedly for the hospital exit. I see the moment Rachel registers the media crowd through the windows. She stalls, as if slammed against a wall. Confusion chases across her face.

I jump to my feet and rush over to her. "Rachel—"

She spins. Her face tightens as she sees me. She looks trapped, drained, exhausted.

"Is Maddy all right?"

She regards me. Absorbing me. Her eyes laser on mine. The noises of the hospital seem to subside into the distance. And for a moment it's just her and me, locked in a capsule. I begin to fear the worst. That her daughter hasn't pulled through.

"I . . . Gio saw the girls—Lily and Daisy," I say. "I know they're okay. I—"

"Darren is dead."

I feel faint. Responsible. For all of it. Yet this is what I wanted, in some form, was it not? To poke and unravel the secrets of this town until the truth of that night came rattling out. "And . . . and Maddy?"

"She's going to be okay." Rachel wavers. Her gaze ticks to the gathering and growing throng outside the windows. She turns back to me. "I'm ready," she says quietly. "I will take you up on your offer. I will talk."

I open my mouth. "You mean—"

"I'll do it. Go on your show. The whole story. Maddy just gave the police her statement, and she told me she'll get advice from a lawyer, but she wants to talk to you, too."

Words escape me for an instant.

Softly, Rachel says, "I owe it to you, Trinity." She pauses, and her eyes mist suddenly. "Janie. We all owe it to you. We are part of this story. You are part of this story. And the time for secrets . . . it has to be over."

"Do you know who did it? Who Leena's killer was?"

"Yes."

Her direct response is a punch to my gut. A conflicting surge of adrenaline, excitement, edginess, anger, erupts in a hot cocktail in my chest.

"It was Beth, wasn't it?" I say. "And someone else. A guy."

She swallows.

I say, "I got a call from a long-haul truck driver. He was listening to the podcast. He remembers the rocket, and he remembers seeing Leena on the bridge that night. Two people were following her, farther back, in the shadows. One was a girl with waist-length blonde hair. The other a tall guy with a hat on."

"So there's a witness."

"It seems so."

She nods, and her gaze flicks again to the media phalanx outside. She looks broken suddenly, drags her hand over her tangle of hair. "That's good," she says quietly. "A witness is good."

"Rachel, who was the male?"

She meets my gaze. "Maddy's husband, Darren. It was the father of my grandchildren. My son-in-law. And I never knew. None of us knew. Not even Maddy. Not until just before he set their house, their lives, on fire. He wanted to take them all with him. He wanted to make it all go away."

Shock slams through me. "I . . . I'm so sorry, Rachel."

The ex-detective swipes a tear away.

"Maddy—she'll really be okay with this? To talk to me?"

Rachel nods. "Yes. And about . . . what your father did to her, if you want to hear it."

Emotion is a sudden blow to my stomach. So forceful it steals my breath. I do want to know. But part of me is suddenly unsure. Afraid to hear it all. But I must. I *need* to know. I've needed to know since I first saw that photo of my father. We are driven, all of us, to understand where we have come from. Who we are. This journey began when I was a child who started asking about her "dead" daddy. All roads have led me here, right here, into this Twin Falls hospital where I was born. In front of the old detective who changed my diaper and locked my dad away. I *have* to know.

Rachel wavers for a moment, as if debating whether to reveal more. Then she says, "There was something you said, Trinity, back in the first episode of the podcast series. You posed the question, 'If it takes a village to raise a child, does it also take a village to kill one?' You were right. It does. We all killed Leena Rai. We all turned away, looked away, one too many times. And if you ask me who started the fire last night . . . we all did."

Then she does something unexpected. She hugs me and whispers near my ear, "I'm sorry."

A photographer suddenly breaks past security and pushes in through the front doors of the hospital. He raises his camera, clicks. The flash goes off. I hear a yell. A security guy comes running and takes hold of the photographer's arm. As he's dragged out the entrance by the guard, the photographer calls out, "Rachel Hart, how is your daughter? How are your grandchildren? Do you have any comment?"

Gio comes rushing up to us. He keeps his voice low as fire burns in his green eyes. "I have news. I just saw it on Twitter. The RCMP have apprehended Beth Forbes and Zane Rolly. The children are fine." Emotion tightens his features, glitters in his eyes. "They were trying to get onto the Port Angeles ferry in Victoria. They were heading to the States, but the border patrol stopped them."

Beth's mother comes out of the corridor. She looks shell-shocked. She just stands there staring at us. Rachel rushes toward her. Eileen Galloway begins to cry. "I just got a call. They're safe. My grandbabies are safe."

RACHEL

NOW
Monday, November 22. Present day.

It's late afternoon, and I'm drinking tea and cuddling Scout by the fire when Granger enters the living room.

He stands in the doorway, studying me and Scout in silence. He looks like a wreck. Like he needs clean clothes and a shower. I don't know that I have the energy to even start this.

"Rachel, I—"

"You had a duty, Granger. As a therapist," I say quietly. "A duty to report a patient if you knew him to be an immediate danger to children. Your client was a teacher, for God's sakes. A guidance counselor. He worked with kids. Vulnerable human beings. He was sexually abusing my daughter, and he had a baby in his house, and he was seeking *help* from you. And if you knew he was in a position to do harm, that negates any idea of therapist-patient confidentiality."

He enters the living room and slumps into his leather chair. "I didn't know about Maddy, or about the porn, the pedophilia. Honest. Not until my last session with him did I learn about the child pornography, when I was trying to figure out whether there was any underlying trauma that caused him to drink. In retrospect, I believe now that he actually came to me for help with his paraphilia, but he was afraid to voice it. So he thought if I could cure him of the alcohol habit, he could apply the techniques to his deeper, more problematic addiction." He rubs the stubble on his jaw. "When his predilection for child porn was revealed to me while he was under hypnosis, I confess, I was shocked, and I . . . sort of lost my logic, lost my head . . . I seeded the details about Leena's murder into his unconscious, suggesting to him that he'd done it and was hiding from it. At that point I was worried about Johnny, and that jacket. I knew Leena was wearing a jacket like it, and I knew by then that Clay Pelley had been at the bonfire. And Merle had just been to see me, and I'd learned the details of the murder from her, and it just happened."

"Just *happened*? You just *happened* to insert holdback evidence into a client's brain?"

He rubs his face again, moistens his lips. "It put him away, Rachel. I figured if it got Clay locked up, it would be a good thing. He'd get help on the inside. It would get him into the system. The kids would be safe. He was not a well man."

"It allowed the real killers to go free. It allowed this damage to go on for years."

"You have two lovely grandchildren, Rache. If Darren had been taken away back th—"

"Are you *kidding* me?" I surge to my feet. "Are you actually trying to tell me that if Darren had been locked away as a teen that he and Maddy would not have gotten married, and I would not have Daisy and Lily in my life? I hardly *had* Daisy and Lily in my life. I barely had my own daughter in my life. They were estranged from me in part because Maddy could never live with her own guilt. She thought she'd killed Leena with her friends. When Clay confessed, it stopped anyone from coming clean. They all just shut up. Buried the trauma. And it made them ill."

"The coroner's report said she would've died from her injuries if she hadn't been drowned. Maddy was justified in believing she'd killed Leena."

"Damn you to hell, Granger. How *dare* you? I've gone through that report again several times, and Maddy told me exactly what was in her statement to the RCMP. The blows Leena sustained on the south side of the bridge were not fatal. It was the blows to her head—mostly from being run into the tree—and from a rock, and a head stomp, that caused the brain swelling that would have killed her had she not been drowned."

"What Maddy and the girls did was still wrong."

"Bullying and physically assaulting a fellow student is always wrong. But it wasn't murder. You know what? If you had not done this, Maddy might have told me what happened. Or Luke and I would have kept digging on the case. The bullies would have been brought in and punished. The two who 'finished her off' would have been dealt with by the law. And maybe, Granger, just maybe, Maddy and I would have had a relationship. Maybe she wouldn't have attacked me and everyone else. Maybe she wouldn't have continued throwing herself against that mountain as some kind of self-flagellation, a way of bashing away her own guilt and memories. Maybe"—I am shaking now, jabbing my finger in the air toward him—"maybe Johnny would have atoned for his rape of Leena, and he wouldn't have been deceived all his life by an evil little narcissist with sadistic and controlling tendencies, and married her. A sadistic little killer who was allowed to become the mother of his children. *Your* grandchildren. And now they have to deal for the rest of their lives with the fact their mother will be going to prison, responsible for the terrible killing of a classmate. And what about your son? He now has to live with the weight of likely having a wife behind bars. Because *you* helped us all blame the wrong man."

"He was still a sick man, Rachel."

"What you did is unconscionable."

"What about you? You sat on that photo of the girls with the locket around Maddy's neck. I saw it on the whiteboard in your office. If you'd acted—"

"I did ask Maddy about it back then. She claimed Leena took things, and that Leena had been in our house. And then Clay confessed. In. Great. Detail. Thanks to you. So I didn't follow it further."

"You are no better than I, Rachel."

Bile curdles up the back of my throat because I know he's right. But we cannot go on together. Not now. Not after he kept this from me. Our entire relationship is constructed on the back of this one devastating secret. And there may be more—how can I ever trust that he didn't seed things into my *own* unconscious when he treated me? I'm not even going to ask him, because I won't believe him. My job now is to go forward, to focus on saving what's left—my daughter and her girls. I need to atone for driving Maddy into Clay Pelley's office in the first place, in search of guidance about her home troubles. Jake and I—our lack of attention—rendered our child vulnerable to a cunning sexual predator.

I need to make sure my grandchildren will grow on a strong foundation in order to weather this narrative. Because their parents' history—their parents' past crimes—is scored into their present. It will come at them, in one way or another, for the rest of their lives. Like it has in Trinity's. Like it has in Ganesh's. And so many more lives. My grandchildren need to find a way to process this. I must be there for them all.

"Get out," I say, my voice strangling in my throat. "Get your things, and get off my farm."

"Rachel. Please—" He gets up, tries to touch me.

"Don't. Do not touch me."

"I told you not to listen to that podcast. I told you it would be bad news."

REVERB

THE RIPPLE EFFECT

NOW

EXCERPT FROM THE FINAL EPISODE
The Killing of Leena Rai—Beneath Devil's Bridge

MADDY: I don't even know when it started—the bullying of Leena Rai. Certainly long before that cold November night when the Russian satellite hit the earth's atmosphere. By the time it happened, there was nothing any of us could do to stop it. Like a train set on its rails miles away, it all just came trundling inexorably down the track. And . . . what's hard to stomach, what's really, really difficult to absorb, is how good people, people you love—friends, parents, children, lovers— do truly terrible things. And how small lies become so big, little snowballs growing into deadly avalanches. And how turning a blind eye over time to seemingly small things can contribute to something so terribly heinous.

TRINITY: And, Maddy, everything you've told us in this episode, it's all the truth?

MADDY: Yes. The same things I told my mother in the hospital when I realized I'd survived the fire, and that my daughters had survived. And it had to be for a purpose. To talk truth. About bullying. About integration. About buried sexual abuse. About how a community needs to step up. How kids at school need to understand what they're doing. And how their parents need to be aware that dangers often lie in wait in benign places.

TRINITY: It's an uphill battle.

MADDY: I've partnered with Jaswinder, Darsh, and Ganesh Rai. We had our first talk at Twin Falls Secondary. About Leena. Who she was as a person. All the things that were good about her, and what she could have become. And about how we got to that point under Devil's Bridge. I hope it helps the Rais toward a healing process, and that it also becomes a healing journey for the entire community linked to this tragedy. Maybe, just maybe, we can stop it happening again somewhere.

TRINITY: And if Leena's mother were still alive, what would you say to Pratima Rai?

MADDY: That I am so, so sorry. I participated in a bullying incident that got violent, and I deeply regret it. I will spend the rest of my life speaking out and trying to atone. I am sorry, too, Trinity, for the legacy that was left you. I was sexually abused by your father. I misguidedly thought it was an act of rebellion for me, but I was his victim. What we girls thought of as seduction was something else entirely. And that night of the bonfire . . . he unleashed something dark and awful in all of us. Beth especially.

TRINITY: The shadows that Leena wrote about?

MADDY: If you will. There's a beast that lives in each one of us.

TRINITY: And you've had legal counsel—

MADDY: I have. Yes. I will accept any consequences of my actions that day. As Beth must. And Granger, and Johnny, and everyone who lied must.

TRINITY: And your mother?

MADDY: And my mother.

Far away, across the country, Jocelyn Willoughby listens to the end of her granddaughter's podcast while knitting at her daughter's bedside. Lacey lies sedated. She's nearing the end. It's as if the final chapter of her life has now been written, the book closed, and now she can let go. The palliative doctor has just been to visit. Jocelyn looks at her child. And she whispers, "Look what our Trinity has done, Lacey. I'm so proud of her." She sets her knitting down and takes her daughter's cool, dry hand into her own. She strokes the veined surface. "Trinny has found justice for Leena." She pauses. "Although I don't know that justice makes anything better. But perhaps the truth does. Perhaps that is what really matters. And the truth will set you free, won't it, my love?"

Jocelyn isn't sure she believes that, either. Not entirely. Life is far more layered and complicated. Too many darn shades of gray. But she feels in her heart that Lacey's soul is now free to go. Clay is free, too. From the prison of his own deviances. Little Janie went back to Twin Falls and found out where she comes from. She owns who she is now. This podcast was her journey. She's prompted a national conversation about teenage bullying, and a discussion about racism, too. And about belonging.

"You'd be proud of her, too, Lacey. I know you would. You gave her a chance."

TRINITY

I stand near the barn on Green Acres farm. In the distance is the line of poplars where only months ago Gio and I watched the green tractor move. But today, those trees are full of bright-green leaves that flutter in the sunlight.

I walk down to the trees. There's no Granger to turn me away. He no longer lives here, and this time Rachel has invited me. She told me I would find her and her family along the riverbank on this glorious Sunday.

The strawberries are ready for picking, and some of the raspberries, too. I see the seasonal pickers moving along the lines of plants. The smell is of warm earth, herbs, and flowers. Rachel has planted rows of those, too. And a little farm stall has been built to sell her harvest. On the phone she told me that Maddy and the girls have moved out here and will live on the farm, or use it as a base, for the foreseeable future.

Last November, when I first approached Rachel for an interview, clouds had tumbled thick down the peaks. Today the mountains are exposed. Etched against a bluebird sky.

I hear the river as I near the row of poplars that grow along its banks. I hear squeals of kids' laughter and a dog yapping. As I near, I realize there are four children. A boy and three girls. A pool has formed off the river. It looks knee deep. They're splashing in there. Rachel is with them in the water, wearing shorts. Scout runs up and down along the bank. I see Maddy in a deck chair on the bank, watching them. Parked behind Maddy's chair is the quad that she now uses to get around the farm in order to supervise the pickers and other workers.

I observe them for a moment, but Rachel sees me. She shoots up a hand and waves.

"Just in time," she calls. "We're about to have lunch."

As I approach I see the picnic basket. The blanket. I see Johnny farther up the river with a fishing rod. He throws looping casts to drop his fly upon the surface.

"Hey, Maddy," I say, ruffling Scout's fur when he runs over to greet me. "How are you doing? . . . Are those Johnny's kids?"

"Yeah. Good to see you, Trin. He's spending a lot of time up here."

"I can see why. There's, like . . . I don't know, a healing quality to this place."

She laughs. "Wait until winter."

I sit on the blanket beside Maddy and think of something my gran said after my mother passed in early December last year. She said that while my podcast journey had burned a lot of people, sometimes a forest with too much dead growth tangled in the understory needed a fire. And from the scorched earth could come fresh shoots. New growth. A stronger forest that could withstand fierce storms. And that's what Green Acres feels like to me. From the black, wet earth that Rachel was plowing that day has come fruit. Beauty. Sustenance. Complicated, but growing and reaching for light.

Maddy holds up a bottle.

"We have bubbly in your honor. Congratulations. And where is he?"

I grin. I feel happy. As though I belong in some strange way to this disparate group of people, as if somehow, here in the Twin Falls area, where I come from, I have found some kind of family.

"Gio is working," I say. "He had to meet with one of the producers. It's coming together, the Netflix show. Thanks to you all. If all goes to plan, the streaming of *It's Criminal, the TV Show* goes live this coming fall, starting with the retelling of Leena's story—'Beneath Devil's Bridge.'"

"Did the Rais agree to be involved?" asks Maddy. She knows that Darsh, Ganesh, and Jaswinder were debating this.

"Yep." I smile. "Everyone's on board. And part of the proceeds will go to the new Leena Rai Scholarship Foundation that they've set up. Thanks for putting in a word."

Rachel calls the kids out of the water and whistles for Johnny downstream. He raises his hand and starts bringing in his line.

"Show us the ring," Rachel says as Maddy pours prosecco and orange juice for the adults and plain juice for the kids.

I hold out my hand. The tiny diamond winks as it catches a ray of sunlight. "It was Gio's grandmother's. We had it resized."

Rachel has tears in her eyes. "Have you set a day?"

"We're working on it. Want to see if we can wrap up the filming for the first season of *It's Criminal, the TV Show*." I say it with an exaggerated swagger.

They laugh.

"So has Gio always been, like, the one?" Maddy asks as we clink our plastic glasses and sip to the sound of the river and the clapping of leaves in the wind. An osprey circles and hovers up high, eyeing prey in the water.

"Maybe," I say. "I just never saw it, until . . . I managed to clear a mental block. I never understood until I went through those interviews with my father how much it meant to me to know who I was, who he was, what happened, where I came from." I sip. "I never realized in how many ways it was affecting me, and my interaction with others."

Maddy catches her mother's eyes. Johnny turns away and stares out over the river as the osprey dives. I wonder if he's thinking of Leena, and what he did to her, and what his wife did.

"I get it," Maddy says quietly. "I really do."

I see Johnny take Maddy's hand. He gives it a squeeze, then lets go, a little awkward. I glance at Rachel. She gives me a soft smile and a slight shake of her head, as if to say, *Don't mention it.* It's too fragile.

Later, as Rachel and I walk along the river, she regards me with her sharp, clear gray eyes. Those eyes I remember from the barn that day when I thought that Rachel was everything I had expected or anticipated her to be. Except she looks happier. More peace in her features. Maybe even younger because of it.

"So what's next in the lineup for *It's Criminal?*" she asks.

"They've asked me to dig into the Abbigail Chester murder that was never solved."

"Seems fitting."

We walk in comfortable silence for a few moments. The sun is warm on my back.

"What about Granger—can you ever forgive him?" I ask.

She inhales deeply and glances up at the peaks around us. "I can't really forgive myself, Trinity."

"I forgive you," I say.

Emotion floods into her eyes, and her mouth quivers slightly. She meets my gaze, and I know she is thinking about little baby Janie on that day she changed my diaper and Luke bounced me on his big knee. I know she is thinking that we can never bring Leena back. Or completely salve the pain of the Rai family.

"What is forgiveness, really?" Rachel asks quietly. "You can't make right this long-ago wrong. You can't fix what reverberated out of it. We can't go back and give you a good father and a decent home life. I can't take back what happened in my family. Eileen Galloway can't undo her daughter's crime." We walk in silence. "You know, you were

332

the last person I thought I needed in my life, that day you came to the farm." She pauses, looks at the river, then the mountains around her. Softly she says, "Sometimes we just don't know what's good for us, do we? Sometimes we think we are trying our best at the time to get things right, to raise our children, to nurture our families and our community, but we're really getting them so very, very wrong." She pauses again. Then gives a wry smile. "All we can do is acknowledge our past mistakes and use what we've learned in order to do our best going forward." Her smile deepens. "And right now, I need to be right here, on this farm, fully present, for my daughter and my grandchildren. I want to grow something for them here. A solid sense of home. Roots." She continues to hold my gaze. "Thank you for coming that day, to my farm. I believe we all have a lot to thank you for, Trinity."

EXCERPT FROM THE FINAL EPISODE
The Killing of Leena Rai—Beneath Devil's Bridge

TRINITY: I asked Leena's family how they feel now that they know the truth of what happened twenty-four years ago, on that night the Russian rocket hit the earth's atmosphere and exploded into comets through the cold November sky.

THEME MUSIC STARTS SOFTLY

JASWINDER: I am pleased to be able to talk in schools about bullying, but I am deeply relieved my wife, Pratima, has not had to endure this. It would be far too much for a mother's heart. Pratima, however, would be pleased about the new Leena Rai Scholarship Foundation. We are being overwhelmed by the donations coming in from across North America and even farther afield, from everyone who has been tuning in to the podcast and learning about Leena. Teens have been sharing their own stories with us . . . I like to think Leena would be happy about this. She always wanted to do some good in the world. To have a purpose. And to travel. Her voice in some ways has reached around the globe now.

TRINITY: Is there room in your hearts for forgiveness?

GANESH: Forgiveness is about freeing yourself from anger that can be crippling. I'm not sure I'm free. Not yet. I was shaped by the specter of what happened to my sister, and to my parents because of it. I grew up in a sad home because of it. But one thing I am grateful for now is that we have the answer to why. It was something my mother always wanted to know: Why Leena? Why did this happen? And I am thankful that the world has now also been reminded of all the good parts that were Leena. Her talent for writing. Her intellect. Her compassion. She always loved me dearly and was kind to me. She loved Darsh. She loved our parents in her teenage way.

A LONG PAUSE. GANESH CLEARS HIS THROAT.

GANESH: Leena had big dreams. I believe that if she'd managed to survive the challenges of her early teens, she'd have found her place in the world. She'd have come into her own. And thrived. If anything, the ripples from this old crime must show us how to listen, to care, and to give everyone a chance and a helping hand. Because that's community, after all, isn't it?

TRINITY: I believe it is. I cannot be free of who my father was, either, or what he did. He's part of me. Meeting you—Leena's family—hearing your stories, and the stories of everyone involved in the crime, and having you all hear mine, perhaps this is a form of justice that can be restorative.

GANESH: Perhaps. Yes. I think it can.

THEME MUSIC INCREASES IN VOLUME

TRINITY: Let us not forget, then, that we, as a community, are all responsible for watching our children. Let this podcast be our homage to Leena. A girl who shall not be forgotten.

FADE OUT

ABOUT THE AUTHOR

 Loreth Anne White is an Amazon Charts and *Washington Post* bestselling author of thrillers, mysteries, and suspense. With well over two million books sold around the world, she is a three-time RITA finalist, an overall Daphne du Maurier Award winner, an Arthur Ellis finalist, and a winner of multiple industry awards.

A recovering journalist who has worked in both South Africa and Canada, she now calls Canada home. She resides in the Pacific Northwest, dividing time between Victoria on Vancouver Island, the ski resort of Whistler in the Coast Mountains, and a rustic lakeside cabin in the Cariboo. When she's not writing or dreaming up plots, you will find her on the lakes, in the ocean, or on the trails with her dog, where she tries—unsuccessfully—to avoid bears. For more information on her books, please visit her website at www.lorethannewhite.com.

Connect with her on Facebook at www.facebook.com/Loreth. Anne.White, on Twitter at https://twitter.com/Loreth, or via Instagram at www.instagram.com/lorethannewhite/.